Rosemary and Crime

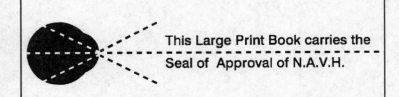

ROSEMARY AND CRIME

GAIL OUST

THORNDIKE PRESS
A part of Gale, Cengage Learning

GALE
CENGAGE Learning®

Farmington Hills, Mich • San Francisco • New York • Waterville, Maine
Meriden, Conn • Mason, Ohio • Chicago

GALE
CENGAGE Learning®

LIBRARY OF CONGRESS CATALOGING-IN-PUBLICATION DATA

Oust, Gail, 1943–
   Rosemary and crime / by Gail Oust.
     pages cm
   ISBN 978-1-4104-6688-4 (hardcover) — ISBN 1-4104-6688-4 (hardcover) 1.
Businesswomen—Fiction. 2. Cooks—Crimes against—Fiction. 3.
Georgia—Fiction. 4. Large type books. I. Title.
PS3620.U7645R67 2014
813'.6—dc23   2013045136

Published in 2014 by arrangement with St. Martin's Press, LLC

Printed in the United States of America
1 2 3 4 5 6 7 18 17 16 15 14

To my Michigan and South Carolina
BFFs.
Love you guys!

ACKNOWLEDGMENTS

For me the book isn't really finished until I've given special thanks to some people who have helped along the way. Leading the list is Mary Ann Beyer, amateur genealogist, golf buddy, and guardian of the books. What started out as a simple question from me ended up as a family tree. Thanks for Brigance and Zelda Zither. Friends Ann McNab and Fran McClain generously raided their cookbook shelves to come to my rescue. As for your cooking and entertaining, you set the bar high. Jessica Faust, BookEnds, LLC, superagent. What can I say, Jessica? You're a treasure. Last, but by no means least, thanks to Bob, husband and trusty sidekick. You make my life so much easier by valiantly tackling the lion's share of household chores — even grocery shopping, although I know you're often befuddled by all the brands and labels.

CHAPTER 1

Across the square, a Confederate soldier atop a concrete pedestal stared sightlessly at a couple enjoying ice cream on a wrought iron bench. Wrens warbled in the willow oaks. The sky was cerulean and cloudless; the breeze warm and gentle. But anyone who's ever been in the path of a hurricane wouldn't be lulled into complacency by ice cream, blue skies, or a balmy breeze. They'd recall another time, perhaps another place, and remember what it was like — this calm before the storm. Unfortunately, I had no such experience and thus went merrily about my business, unaware of the havoc barreling in my direction.

"I declare, Piper Prescott, you've gone and outdone yourself."

I gave Reba Mae Johnson, my very best friend in the whole wide world, a friendly jab in the ribs. "Unless my memory's failing, you told me I was out of my cotton pickin' mind the first time I mentioned a spice shop."

Reba Mae grinned, unabashed. "Guilty as charged. Wasn't just me who said that, either. Half the folks here thought you'd gone off the deep end, what with CJ dumpin' you and all. Talk was, you might be havin' a breakdown or somethin'."

I refused to take offense. Granted, owning a spice shop is a far cry from playing bridge at the country club, but like the sign over my brand-new antique cash register says, WHEN LIFE GIVES YOU LEMONS, MAKE LEMONADE. It just so happens that Spice It Up!, Brandywine Creek's newest enterprise, happens to be my own particular brand of "lemonade."

After my dear husband "dumped" me, as Reba Mae so inelegantly phrased it, in favor of chasing ambulances and a twenty-four-year-old in a short skirt, I squeezed my lemons dry. I'd taken the plunge and invested the entire sum of my divorce settlement in a dream I'd harbored for years. Even more than I loved to cook and bake, I loved to experiment with food, to improvise. And the best way to do this, I found, was by using spices. A pinch of this, a dash of that, and abracadabra, a good recipe became a great recipe.

After twenty-some years married to a control freak, being my own boss held enormous appeal. I'd been such a bundle of nerves after signing the documents that made me proprietor of a building dating back to Prohibition that I barely made it to the ladies' room before throwing up.

The original establishment, I'd been told, had burned to the ground when the still in the basement exploded and set fire to half the town. Two of the bootleggers had been killed outright, another injured. People still bemoan the fact that the event garnered little press since the fire coincided with the St. Valentine's Day massacre in Chicago. A small town in Georgia, even one that boasts a reenactment of a Civil War battle and is home to the Brandywine BBQ Festival, can't compete with names like Al Capone and Bugs Moran.

Unable to support the tanning salon–movie rental business of the previous tenants, the building had stood vacant for a couple years. The bank had been more than happy to unload it, and I counted myself fortunate it fit my limited budget. The upper floor provided living quarters — nothing fancy, like the home I'd once shared with CJ and my son and daughter, but adequate. I might be broke, but at least I wasn't homeless.

I drew in a deep breath and let it out in a contented sigh. The heady scents of cinnamon, cloves, and nutmeg permeated the air. "Don't you just *love* the smell of this place?"

Reba Mae sniffed. "Nope, can't smell a dang thing."

I aligned an already neat row of apothecary jars that contained sticks of cinnamon from such exotic locales as Sri Lanka, Sumatra, and China. "That's because you spend all day sniffing those nasty chemicals — perm solutions and the like."

"Maybe, but you won't catch me bellyachin'." Reba Mae fluffed her spiky magenta locks. Reba Mae loved nothing better than to experiment with hair color. She confessed she'd been aiming for auburn but wound up with magenta instead. "The Klassy Kut puts food on the table and a roof over the heads of me and my boys. Besides, there are certain perks that go along with runnin' the best beauty shop in the county." She gave me a wink. "You know I'm among the first to hear all the juicy gossip. Ask me, sugar, and I'll tell you, life is good."

"Yes, life is good," I agreed. "It'll be even better if tomorrow's grand opening goes off without a hitch."

"I think you're mighty brave askin' Mario

Barrone to give a cookin' demonstration. He's got quite the reputation with that temper of his."

I shrugged off Reba Mae's concern. "So, he's a little temperamental. That's the way with a lot of great chefs."

"A *little*? Honeybun, he's got the worst temper of anyone I know."

"He's a fabulous cook," I countered. I refused to admit, even to my BFF, that I had doubts of my own about Mario.

"Hmph! A fabulous cook with a fabulous ego. The man's not a happy camper unless one of his staff's in tears. Some nights you can hear him hollerin' and carryin' on clear out on the sidewalk."

At that precise moment, none other than the subject under discussion himself stormed into my shop. Mario is owner and chef at Trattoria Milano, Brandywine Creek's answer to fine dining. Most people simply refer to the little restaurant as the "Tratory," knowing it annoys him . . . but always with a quick glance over their shoulders first to make sure Mario isn't within earshot.

"This . . . ?" Mario stuck his opened palm under my nose. "This is what you give me when I ask for juniper berries?"

I stared down at the waxy purple-black

berries the size of small peas. I must admit they looked a little less round, and a lot more squishy, since I'd personally delivered them earlier that day to Mario's newest sous chef. What had the guy done to the poor things? Sat on them?

"What do you take me for? A fool? An imbecile?"

Angry at his tone, I felt my cheeks burn — the curse of being a redhead. I had half a mind to pull a Donald Trump and, with ringing finality, utter the words, "You're fired!" But I bit my tongue instead. My dream of a spectacular grand opening would go up in smoke. All the hard work and elbow grease. All the money spent purchasing only premium spices, choosing the best containers, designing the cleverest labels. Everything would be in vain without Mario Barrone, my superstar, to lure people through the front door. The man might be a prima donna, but no one, and I mean no one, questions his ability to prepare dishes that cause mouths to water. Temper or no temper, the man was a true genius in the kitchen.

Reba Mae shifted to peer over my shoulder. "Those . . . those . . . berries look okay to me. I don't see anythin' wrong with 'em."

"Bah! What would you know about such

things?" Mario glared at her briefly, his dark eyes glittering, then directed his ire back at me. "And furthermore, I distinctly requested juniper berries grown in Italy. Not ones grown in Albania."

That did it! Folding my arms across my chest, I looked him square in the eye. "Look here, Mario, stop treating me like *I'm* the idiot. You asked for juniper berries grown in the Mediterranean and that's exactly what I gave you. For your information, they are the only type I stock."

"Garbage! *Finito!*"

In a fit of rage, he hurled the juniper berries onto my newly polished heart pine floor and stomped out the front door.

Reba Mae wagged her head. "You've gone and done it this time, girlfriend."

"Dammit," I muttered as I trailed after him. "Mario, wait . . ."

We were now out on the sidewalk and passersby paused to watch the fireworks. But I ignored them. "The reporter from *The Statesman* is going to be here. He's bringing a photographer. Think of all the publicity for the trattoria." I'd nearly slipped and called it the Tratory but, thank goodness, caught myself in the nick of time.

He stopped and turned at hearing this. "Photographer, you say?"

I felt encouraged. "I was thinking of sending the photo along with a press release to *Southern Living.*" Necessity makes salesmen of us all.

"Hmm. *Southern Living,* eh?"

"And from time to time, Paula Deen features regional chefs in her magazine," I continued, ad-libbing at a furious pace. "Who knows, maybe . . . ?"

"Fine," Mario snapped, saving me from even bigger whoppers. "I will cook for you my roast lamb with juniper and rosemary. But this time, remember," he warned, shaking a thick finger in my face, "I want only the best. *Capisce?*"

"If that means 'understand,' then yes, I *capisce.*"

Mario turned on his heel and marched off.

The crowd parted in his wake. No one, it seemed, wanted to antagonize the man further. I found myself the center of attention and sensed sympathetic glances directed my way. I was about to return to my shop when I noticed a familiar figure lounging against the fender of a shiny silver Lexus. My heart sank. It was Chandler Jameson "CJ" Prescott III, my ex-husband. From the smirk on CJ's face, I knew he'd enjoyed seeing me grovel.

16

CHAPTER 2

CJ strutted into my shop as though he owned the place. "How ya doin', Scooter?"

I gritted my teeth at hearing the nickname I'd once thought endearing but now detested. "Fine and dandy, thank you very much."

"So this is what all the fuss is about." He made an expansive gesture, taking in the shop and all its accoutrements. "Rumor has it you invested every red cent I gave you into what's bound to be a losing proposition."

My tongue seemed glued to the roof of my mouth. Irritation does that to me sometimes.

Luckily, Reba Mae doesn't suffer the same affliction. "As I see it," she said with a smirk, "her only 'losin' proposition' was marryin' you."

With the aid of three-inch platform sandals, Reba Mae stood eye level with CJ. As

I watched, CJ's attention drifted downward like I knew it would. Drawn like a magnet to Reba Mae's impressive cleavage. The man always did have a weakness for large breasts. Still does if his twenty-four-year-old girlfriend is any indication. Pity I didn't have any of consequence.

"Hrmph!" Reba Mae cleared her throat.

Caught staring, CJ's gaze flew upward. He nodded. "Hullo, Reba Mae."

The chill in CJ's voice could have frozen pond water. But then he and Reba Mae never had hit it off. Once upon a time when CJ was starting his law practice and money was tight, we'd been next-door neighbors to the Johnsons. Our kids were just babies then. Reba Mae and I bonded over Pampers and *General Hospital.* Even though we'd long since moved to a bigger house in a neighborhood better suited to CJ's burgeoning success, Reba Mae and I had remained close. Some years back, Butch, Reba Mae's husband, drowned while bass fishing. A lot of folks claimed it was too much beer and too little bass that did him in. But no matter, dead is dead. When Reba Mae found herself up to her ears in credit-card debt and no means of support, I loaned her money for beauty school. CJ still believes I used the money for a tummy tuck. Goes to show the state of our marriage.

"What do you want, CJ?" I asked, finally finding my voice.

"Lindsey's gettin' her nails done," he drawled. "She'll be along in a minute or two. There's somethin' she wants to tell you."

It had been nearly a week since I'd seen my daughter, Lindsey Nicole — her doing, not mine. Even though CJ and I had joint custody, Lindsey seemed to spend so much time at her dad's sprawling new house that she might as well be living there. It had broken my heart to see her pack her bag. Deep down, I prayed she'd reconsider and start spending more time with me. Her room upstairs was kept ready and waiting.

Our daughter's always been a daddy's girl and had taken our divorce pretty hard. I really resented the fact that CJ could give her things I couldn't. Things like pricey iPhones, iPods, and an iPad with more apps than one could use in a lifetime. To seal the deal, he'd thrown in a sporty red Mustang convertible for her sixteenth birthday. How's that for alienating a daughter's affection? Any jury in the land would convict the bastard.

Our son, Chad, on the other hand, was too preoccupied getting into med school to care where he brought his dirty laundry. A junior at University of North Carolina in Chapel Hill over three hundred miles away, he didn't get home much these days.

"Haven't seen you around in a while, CJ," Reba Mae said, to fill the silence that stretched like Silly Putty. I noted a steely glint in her eyes that boded trouble. I didn't have long to wait. "Looks like you're gettin' a little thick around the middle. You been drinkin' too much of that Wild Turkey you're so fond of? Likker's loaded with calories, you know."

"None of your damn business, Reba Mae," CJ fired back.

"And what's with the hair?" When Reba was on a roll, there was no stopping her. Reaching out, she flicked a strand of CJ's perfect cut and blow dry. "If I didn't know better, I'd think you were usin' Clairol's Medium Golden Blond to hide that gray of yours."

"Don't you have a beauty parlor to run?" CJ snarled. "Mama's over there right now waitin' on you."

Reba Mae's eyes flew to her wristwatch. "Son of a gun! Nearly forgot Miss Melly's two o'clock. I'd best skedaddle before the old gal gets up a head of steam. Sorry, hon," she said, shooting me an apologetic look over her shoulder on her way out the door. "Gotta run, or I'll have hell to pay."

In her haste to exit, Reba Mae almost collided with Lindsey, who happened to be too preoccupied admiring her French manicure to pay much attention to where she was going. As I saw Lindsey's youthful figure backlit by the April sunshine, a realization nearly knocked me senseless. My sweet child, my sweet precious child, was teetering on the brink of womanhood. I desperately wanted to witness the transition from a ringside seat — not from afar. I vowed to try harder to mend fences, to build bridges between us.

Lindsey's gaze darted from her nails to Reba Mae's bright magenta hair. "Nice color, Miz Johnson. How do you suppose I'd look with my hair that shade?"

"Darlin', your mother would skin me alive if I dyed those pretty blond locks of yours this particular shade of auburn." With a sympathetic backward glance, Reba Mae hurried off.

"Hey, Mom," Lindsey mumbled.

"Hey, sweetie," I said, mustering a smile. I reached out and tucked a wayward curl behind her ear. She might be nearly grown, but she's still my baby.

Lindsey gave a jar of pink peppercorns imported from Madagascar her undivided attention. "Your place looks . . . nice."

Nice? Her faint praise filled me with disappointment. I wanted to hear it looked fabulous. Awesome. Amazing. Guess for now, though, I'd have to settle for a lukewarm "nice."

"Judgin' from the bare brick walls and old floorboards, you musta done yer own decoratin'."

CJ's snide tone set my teeth on edge. "I think the brick walls lend the shop a certain ambience. And those 'old floorboards,' for your information, happen to be heart pine."

"You always did have a fondness for old things. But time's awastin'." CJ nodded at Lindsey. "Baby, kindly explain to your mama why you won't be workin' in her little shop once school lets out."

Lindsey scuffed the toe of her ballet flat against the heart pine floor. Her blue-gray eyes, the same hue as her father's, looked rebellious. My daughter favored the Prescott side of the family, not mine. I'm petite, five foot two when I stand tall, with naturally curly red hair and eyes green as a tomcat's. Lindsey, on the other hand, has long, blond hair that falls to her shoulder blades. As for height, well, she's been gloating ever since she towered over me in middle school.

"I, ah, I'm failing math."

"You're what . . . ? Since when?" I shook my head in disbelief. Lindsey's never pulled the same kind of grades as her brother, but overall managed to maintain a B average. "Each time I asked about your classes, you told me things were fine."

"Everything was . . . except math."

I huffed out a breath. Counted to ten. Tapped my toes. "I don't remember receiving any progress reports to that effect."

Lindsey fiddled with her charm bracelet. "I asked the school to send them to Daddy."

She'd spoken so softly I had to strain to hear her. But when their full impact hit, I aimed an accusatory stare at CJ. "Why didn't you tell me she was failing math? And furthermore, why didn't you do something about it? Hire a tutor, check her homework, take away privileges, ground her? *Something.*"

"It's no big deal, Mom," Lindsey muttered. "I'm going to summer school."

"Summer school, eh?" Narrowing my eyes, I gave Lindsey my best mom-means-business look. "Well, young lady, I intend to make it my personal mission to see that you pass at the top of your class. You can do your homework right here in the shop between customers."

"Mom . . . ," she wailed.

23

"That was the other thing we wanted to talk to you about." CJ rocked back on his polished loafers. "Lindsey and I agreed that she needs to focus on her studies."

As I glanced from father to daughter, I had the unmistakable feeling I was being outmaneuvered. "Exactly what does that mean?"

CJ made use of the smarmy smile that showed off the caps on his teeth to perfection. "Surely, you can't expect to keep Lindsey busy twenty-four-seven. A girl needs to be able to relax, go out with her friends. Have a little fun now and then. After all, you're only young once."

Only young once? Unless, that is, you were CJ Prescott III. The man seemed to be going through his second childhood. Or was this phase called a midlife crisis? Amend that, I thought, to middle-age crazy.

What had I ever seen in the man? I asked myself, and not for the first time. Young and dumb, as the saying goes, I'd fallen head over heels for a handsome face and breezy Southern charm. We'd met one hot June afternoon when we were both counselors at a church camp in the wilds of Upper Michigan. Before summer ended, I was ready to follow CJ to the ends of the earth — in his case, law school at University of Georgia,

24

this Yankee's first time south of the Mason-Dixon Line. My folks were furious I'd dropped out of college. But I thought I had all the answers. If I knew then what I know now, I'd have hightailed it for the Canadian border.

I dragged my thoughts back to the problem at hand. "You'll have plenty of time to socialize, Lindsey, but once school lets out next month I expect you to help in the shop at least two afternoons a week and half a day on Saturday. I know Meemaw will back me up on this."

Meemaw, Southern-speak for Grandmother, was none other than CJ's mom. Not even CJ, a fully grown man, ever argued with his mama and won — at least not to my recollection. I knew for a fact Miss Melly blamed both of us for spoiling Lindsey rotten, and she'd gladly side with me in this instance.

"Whatever," Lindsey capitulated in her best bored-teen tone of voice.

She'd used that same tone with me plenty. It might not be very charitable on my part, but I was glad CJ was getting his share of Miss Teenage Attitude.

"Let's consider this matter settled, shall we," CJ said, assuming we'd exhausted the subjects of math and summer school. Little did he know that I planned to take this matter up with him next time we were alone. Right now, Lindsey didn't need to witness her parents arguing.

CJ pointed to the kitchen area I'd had installed at the rear of the shop. "Whatcha gonna do back there? Give cookin' lessons?"

"Chef Mario Barrone from the Trattoria Milano's agreed to demonstrate the use of juniper berries," I said stiffly.

"What the Sam Hill are juniper berries?"

"Juniper happens to be often overlooked when it comes to spices, but it's quite popular in northern European and particularly in Scandinavian cuisine."

"I thought Barrone was Italian."

"He is." I absently rubbed my hands on my faded jeans and noticed my nails were chipped and ragged. I mentally added a manicure to my to-do list. "Mario's making one of his specialties. A roast leg of lamb with juniper berries and rosemary, that's to die for."

"If you say so." CJ shrugged, straining the shoulder seams of his designer suit. "Give me a rare prime rib any day over some fancy shit concocted by a hotshot who claims to be a chef. I heard Barrone used to flip burgers at McDonald's."

"Whatever the rumor, Mario's a true

26

culinary artist."

"If the man's so all-fired good, what's he doin' in a place like Brandywine Creek? Why isn't he in Atlanta or Charlotte?"

I'd asked myself the same question numerous times. Mario's credentials might not be as top-notch as Le Cordon Bleu, but his ambitions were. He'd just finished creating a new menu, copies of which would be distributed at Spice It Up! I had a sneaky hunch, however, he wanted more than to merely attract new customers. Mario had higher aspirations. He wanted to be "discovered" and to hit the big time.

"Daddy . . . ," Lindsey whined. "I'm bored. Can we go now?"

"Sure thing, baby."

I watched, feeling resentful as CJ patted Lindsey's hand, and caught a glimpse of the gold Rolex on his wrist. A Rolex I'd given him for our twentieth anniversary. In return, I'd gotten a card from the dollar store. Should've been a clue the romance was over.

CJ gave me the patented grin identical to ones on billboards up and down the Interstate. "Got new clients comin'. Husband had a trip 'n fall in one of them big-box stores. Told 'em I could practically guarantee he and the missus a hundred thou for their pain and sufferin'."

I was trailing CJ and Lindsey toward the door when CJ halted so abruptly I nearly stepped on his heels.

"Sumbitch!" he swore under his breath.

"What's wrong, Daddy?" Lindsey asked.

"It's him. Wyatt McBride, in the flesh." CJ pointed to a Ford Crown Vic emblazoned with the Brandywine Creek Police Department emblem, which was slowly circling the town square. "Guess rumors were true after all. Behold, Wyatt McBride, Brandywine's new chief of police. Seems the mayor didn't take my advice to heart and hired the sumbitch anyways."

"I take it you don't care for the man."

CJ's eyes narrowed as he followed the cruiser's progress. "McBride was always too big for his britches, even back in high school. We hated each other's guts then, still do. I'd watch out for him, Scooter darlin'. He'd like nothin' better than to hassle anyone with the name of Prescott."

"But . . ."

He cut me off as if he read my mind. "Won't matter we're no longer married. He gives you any trouble, you hear, give me a call. You know my number."

Swell. Just peachy keen, I thought. Like I don't have enough to worry about. "Bye, sweetie," I said glumly, giving Lindsey a

28

quick hug.

I waited on the sidewalk as CJ climbed into his Lexus. Lindsey slid into the passenger seat and buckled up. She gave me a little wave as the car drew away from the curb.

I watched them go with mixed feelings.

CHAPTER 3

For dinner that evening, I didn't even
bother going upstairs to my apartment.
Instead, I nuked the last of the goulash
Reba Mae had sent over earlier that week in
the tiny microwave at the rear of my shop.
Closing my eyes for a moment, I savored
the lingering hint of sweet Hungarian-style
paprika she'd used for seasoning. Maybe
one day, I could convince Reba Mae to
share her recipe in front of an audience. It
might take a bit of arm twisting, though.
Some folks are funny about parting with
family secrets.

Bone-tired, I glanced around Spice It Up!
one last time before heading to my apartment. Tempting selections of spices from
around the world — tamarind from Madagascar, sumac from Sicily, galangal from
Indonesia, to name a few — were artfully
displayed on free-standing cabinets I'd com-
missioned from a local carpenter. I'd

stripped layers of paint off a Hoosier cabinet I'd found at a flea market down to the original oak. It now housed jars filled with the spices commonly used in baking: ginger, cinnamon, nutmeg, cloves, and, of course, vanilla beans.

Thanks to a flattering article in *Georgia Life,* Brandywine Creek was becoming quite the tourist destination. Folks were drawn to its antique shops and quaint town square. Now that the Opera House had undergone a complete renovation and was celebrating its hundredth anniversary, even more people were discovering the village's charms. I hoped to cash in by enticing tourists and locals alike to throw away old bottles of spices, and even older tins, in exchange for fresh and aromatic varieties from my store.

Heaving a weary sigh, I decided Spice It Up! was as ready as I could make it before flipping the sign in the window to OPEN tomorrow morning. Switching off lights as I went, I passed through the storage room at the back and was about to ascend the steps when I heard an eerie, bone-chilling sound that made the fine hairs at the back of my neck stand on end.

I froze. Listened.

I tried to convince myself that my ears were playing tricks on me. Then it came

31

again. A high-pitched keening that sent my heart knocking against my rib cage.

I stood there wallowing in indecision . . . and fear. It was late. The town had long since rolled up its streets. And I was alone. I no longer had an overweight husband or a brawny son to call upon to kill spiders or to check out things that went bump in the night. The only thing separating me from imminent danger was a flimsy wood door with an even flimsier lock. I gnawed my lower lip, debating my next move. What if someone was injured? Needed my help? And I ignored them. How would I be able to look at myself in the mirror?

Cracking open the door, I cautiously peeked out. With the moon tucked behind a cloud bank, the night was dark as pitch. I added "buy flashlight" to my lengthening to-do list right below "manicure."

I nearly jumped out of my skin when I heard the sound again. It was different this time — more whimper, less keening. More animal than human. Gradually my eyes grew accustomed to the dark.

Spice It Up! backs up to a vacant lot, which separates it from the street beyond. At first, I failed to see anything out of the ordinary. Then I spotted a slight movement in the weeds off to my right. My feet inched forward of their own volition. As I drew nearer, I made out what at first appeared to be a bundle of rags tossed haphazardly into long tufts of grass poking through the hard-packed earth. Then I saw a tail wave.

On closer inspection, the "rags" transformed into a small dog, a mutt of indeterminate breed, not much larger than a puppy. The animal looked at me with pleading in its liquid brown eyes. A look that melted my heart.

"What's the matter, girl?" I murmured, reaching out to stroke the matted fur. My fingers came away sticky with blood.

The little dog answered with another weak flop of its tail. It seemed to be having difficulty breathing. I knew I had to act.

And act quickly.

"Be right back, puppy dog." I raced back inside, ran upstairs, and grabbed a bath towel along with my purse. Outdoors again, I gently wrapped the dog in the towel and scooped it up. Minutes later I was headed away from town in my VW Beetle, with the injured animal next to me on the passenger seat.

Though I didn't own a pet — CJ claimed he had allergies — I knew where the animal clinic was located. I'd even met the vet a time or two, a nice gentleman by the name of Doug Winters. Cooking happens to be Dr. Doug's hobby. Curiosity had prompted the doc to check out Spice It Up! even before I finished stocking the shelves. He'd gone away pleased as punch with "coupe" grade Spanish saffron, the highest quality of saffron on the planet, for the paella he planned. Considering saffron is the costliest of all spices, I hoped paella would become a mainstay in his diet.

Several miles out of town, the VW's headlights illuminated a sign: PETS'R PEOPLE, DOUGLAS WINTERS, DVM. I hung a right into the long drive leading to a rambling ranch–style building with white siding and black shutters that served both as a home and an animal clinic. I saw the flicker from a TV screen in a window at the far end. A signpost with an arrow and OFFICE printed in block letters directed pet owners to an entrance reserved for clients.

"Hang in there, puppy dog," I crooned as I pulled to a stop. My words of encouragement were greeted by a tail wag even more pathetic than the previous one. Being careful not to jostle the poor little creature, I picked her up and hurried down the walk, hoping I wasn't too late.

I jabbed the doorbell repeatedly. "Hurry, hurry, hurry," I muttered under my breath like a mantra.

After what seemed like an hour, but in all likelihood was only a minute or two, a porch light came on and the clinic's door swung open. Kind brown eyes peered out of a boyishly attractive face. A pair of wire-rimmed glasses had been shoved atop a mop of prematurely gray hair. Dressed casually in jeans and a rugby shirt, the vet took in the situation at a glance.

"Follow me," he ordered. He led me down a short hallway, flicking on lights as he went. Turning into the second room on the left, he motioned toward an exam table.

"Piper, isn't it? From the spice shop?"

I nodded, carefully lowering the small bundle of canine onto the cold stainless steel.

"Your dog?" He jammed on his eyeglasses, then tugged on a pair of latex gloves.

"No." I swallowed hard. "Just tell me she's going to be all right?"

Doug gently unwrapped the bath towel I'd swaddled her in. Next he reached for his stethoscope and proceeded to press its bell against the blood-matted fur as the dog struggled to catch its breath. He scowled at me from across the table. "Care to explain what happened?"

"I heard sounds like someone or something moaning coming from the vacant lot behind my shop. When I went to investigate, I found this poor thing lying in the weeds. Why?" My worry ratcheted up a notch. Or three. "What's wrong with her?"

"Him," Doug corrected absently as he began assembling instruments and supplies. "The laceration in his side looks like a knife wound. Probably punctured a lung."

"Stabbed?" I recoiled in horror. "He's been stabbed . . . ?"

"You're not the squeamish sort, are you?"

Doug stared at me over his rimless eyeglasses and challenged me not to turn tail and run. I drew a shaky breath, then let it out. "What do you want me to do?"

While Doug cleansed the wound and inserted a slender tube into the dog's chest cavity, I did what I could to soothe the animal. I stroked, I petted, I prayed, all the while talking nonsense in the singsong voice I'd once used to calm fretful infants.

At long last, the pup's breathing less labored, Doug assured me there was nothing more to be done. I left him in the vet's very capable hands.

When I awoke the next morning, kettle drums beat an exuberant tattoo against my skull. My eyes felt gritty. Lack of sleep?

36

Stress? A combination of the two? Not exactly how I envisioned feeling at the kickoff of my new career. There was still a dozen things I needed to do before Spice It Up! officially opened for business at ten o'clock. But one thing took precedence. I had to find out how the dog had fared since I'd left him at the vet's in the wee hours of the morning. I reached for the phone and dialed.

Doug had promised to do what he could to locate the dog's owner, but warned me it was probably a stray. If the owner couldn't be found I'd promised to pay for the dog's care. A dog may be man's best friend, but time had come for man — or in this case, woman — to step up and be dog's best friend. Doug had taken pity on a penniless divorcee, however, and said he'd barter his services in exchange for saffron and other spices.

The phone at Pets 'R People went unanswered, but I realized it was early yet. Doug was probably either busy tending the injured mutt — or still fast asleep. I'd try again later. One thing for certain, I couldn't keep referring to the dog as "dog." He needed a proper name, even if it might only be temporary until someone claimed him. I'd ask Lindsey to put on her thinking cap and come up with something suitable for a scruffy, but adorable, pup.

After swallowing a couple Tylenol, I stood under the needle-sharp spray of the shower until I felt human again. I quickly dressed in a pair of slim black chinos, a crisp white cotton blouse with three-quarter sleeves, and my favorite citron green sling-back sandals. For good measure, I added a chunky necklace to my ensemble. Makeup was minimal since I no longer felt compelled to hide the smattering of freckles across the bridge of my nose. A little eye shadow, mascara, and a swipe of lip gloss, and I was good to go. A final glance in the mirror told me I looked okay for an impoverished woman in her mid-forties.

Breakfast consisted of a cup of tea and yogurt, to which I added my personal blend of trail mix — bits of crystallized ginger being my secret ingredient — then sprinkled on Ceylon cinnamon for extra oomph. When finished, I decided to make Mario Barrone my first order of business. I'd dropped off my entire stock of juniper berries at the trattoria last night. I figured this way Mario could pick and choose the ones he wanted, but I needed the remainder for any customers who might want to recreate his magic with a leg of lamb. Mario had already started prepping the lamb and had indicated that he planned to refrigerate it overnight. He'd also mentioned he was an early riser. Besides retrieving what was left of the juniper, we needed to review the timetable one more time. I didn't want any last-minute glitches in front of an audience and members of the press.

The Trattoria Milano was on a side street a block off the square. Knowing I'd find the front locked, I went down the alley leading to the rear of the restaurant. Trash cans flanked either side of the back entrance. Two steps with broken concrete led to the door. I was about to knock when I spotted the sun glinting off something metal in the weeds.

"What on earth?" I bent for a closer look, and was surprised to find a knife with a long, slender blade similar to those used for boning. Odd, I thought. Had rumors I'd heard about Mario been true? One tale that had spread like poison ivy through Reba Mae's salon concerned Mario actually *throwing* a steak knife at his hapless sous chef. Hoping no one had gotten hurt, I picked up the knife and went up the steps.

"Mario . . ."

The rear door swung open even though I barely touched it. I passed through a service area that ran the width of the building. A fully stocked pantry occupied one side, a commercial freezer the other.

"Mario," I called again. As I shoved aside the swinging door dividing the service area from the kitchen proper, I smelled alcohol. I sniffed. Then sniffed some more. The odor was distinctly woodsy, tangy, and unmistakably like juniper. Or . . . gin.

Dammit!

Gin? This early in the day? I vowed if Mario was in no condition to demonstrate how to roast a leg of lamb to a shop full of women, he'd rue the day. "If you're drunk . . ."

It was then I found Mario.

The man wasn't dead drunk. He was just plain dead.

CHAPTER 4

The knife I'd found dropped from my nerveless fingers and skittered across the floor.

Mario lay sprawled on his side. Blood darker than a habanero chili pepper pooled around his body. I stared, transfixed by the sight. Then, I dragged my gaze to his face. His eyes were shut. His usually swarthy complexion was a sickly gray-white. Bile, hot and bitter, rose in my throat. I swallowed it down.

Gradually, I became more aware of my surroundings. Juniper berries had rolled off the counter and onto the floor, where they'd been crushed underfoot. Juniper berries, I'd learned, are responsible for giving gin its distinctive flavor. No wonder I'd assumed the poor man was a drunk. Shame on me. That should teach me not to rush to judgment.

Somewhere in the nether region of my

brain, I knew I ought to do something. But what? Holler my fool head off? Throw up? Faint? Nothing in my relatively uncomplicated life had prepared me for discovering a dead body. Was there a certain protocol to follow?

Brrrrg!

The shrill sound of a phone ringing penetrated my shell shock. I pivoted slowly and spotted an old-fashioned wall phone hanging near the door I'd just entered. In a daze I moved to answer it, but the ringing ceased. The sudden silence seemed deafening.

I glanced over my shoulder at Mario — who I was rapidly coming to think of as the "corpse." Should I feel for a pulse like how they did on TV cop shows? I recoiled inwardly at the notion of tiptoeing close enough to press my fingers against his neck. Even to a novice such as myself, the man was obviously a goner. Why risk ruining my favorite sandals traipsing through blood and gore? Though it might seem heartless to some, there are times a woman has to be practical, especially when it comes to an expensive pair of shoes. Funny, the thoughts that cross your mind in a crisis.

As the hours crept by — in reality it was only minutes, but it seemed much longer — the neurons in my brain began firing. Sucking in a deep, steadying breath, I forced myself to think. I couldn't just stand here. I had to do something. Summon help. Report the crime. *Something.*

I groped through the pockets of my slacks before remembering I'd left my cell phone at home on the charger. Reaching for the grubby wall phone, I punched in 911 with a trembling hand. After listening to my stammering explanation, the dispatcher instructed me to remain on the line until help arrived. Stretching the spiral cord to its limits, I edged my way out of the kitchen and into the service area to await the arrival of Brandywine Creek's men in blue.

Seeing as how the police department was located on Lincoln Avenue, two blocks over, I didn't have long to wait before the wail of sirens and the flash of red and blue lights disturbed the quiet April morning.

Beau Tucker was first on the scene. The policeman happened to be one of CJ's poker buddies. Genial and good-natured, he shared my ex's fondness for Wild Turkey and fat, smelly cigars. But the man's usual jovial persona wasn't evident now. His round, moon-shaped face was more serious than I'd ever seen it.

"Hey, Piper," he greeted me. "What's goin' on? Dorinda said somethin' about you

43

findin' a dead body."

Clutching the phone so tightly my knuckles shone white, I pointed wordlessly toward the kitchen.

Beau unsnapped his holster and drew out an impressive-looking weapon. What threat could a dead body pose? I wondered. It seemed a bit overkill — sorry about the pun — but then our highly trained police officers didn't often get a chance to use all the skills they'd accumulated over the years at seminars and such.

Beau disappeared inside, but returned moments later. He pried my fingers from the phone and barked into the receiver, "Dorinda, find the chief. Tell him to get his butt over to the Tratory. Pronto!"

"Mind if I go outside and sit a spell, Beau?" I asked in a little-girl voice that didn't sound like my own. "My knees are feeling a bit rubbery."

"Sure thing, Piper," he agreed, eyeing me closely for the first time. "You're lookin' a mite peaked. Have a seat in the patrol car so as not to contaminate the crime scene. Don't want the new chief thinkin' we're a bunch of yokels."

I climbed down the crumbling concrete steps and crossed to the squad car, where I slid onto the seat Beau had vacated — the

44

driver's seat. I had no intention of sitting in the rear behind heavy wire mesh like a common criminal.

Tires squealed as more vehicles entered the alley and screeched to a halt. EMTs spilled out of a van. Not far behind were more local police as well as deputies from the county sheriff's department. I spotted Bob Sawyer, the reporter with *The Statesman,* among the new arrivals. Several men pointed or nodded in my direction. I might as well have been wearing a scarlet T-shirt emblazoned with I FOUND A DEAD BODY, WHAT HAVE YOU FOUND LATELY? Self-conscious under their scrutiny, I removed myself from the patrol car and took a position off to one side where I wouldn't be in the way.

Shock was gradually being replaced by cold hard logic. I took a quick look at my watch and grimaced. I had tons of things to do before Spice It Up! opened for the first time. I'd soon have people knocking on the door, peering in the windows, expecting to see a hotshot chef prepare his acclaimed roast lamb with juniper berries. But my grand opening wasn't going be very grand without Mario Barrone's showmanship. I brought myself up short. Shame on me. A man, still in his prime, had died and here I

45

was only thinking of myself. While Mario would never be a buddy, I respected the man's skill and ambition.

To keep myself from thinking of him practically floating in a crimson lake of blood, I reviewed possible options. Hanging an OUT OF BUSINESS sign in the front window wasn't one of them. And although it held great appeal, neither was going to bed and pulling the covers over my head.

I fought the urge to wring my hands. That wouldn't do. I *never* wring my hands. Far too melodramatic for my taste. Still . . .

My mind raced. What to do? What to do? I formed and discarded plan after plan. My mind kept circling back to the only possible solution to my conundrum. I'd have to perform the cooking demo myself. The recipe was fairly straightforward. Mario had explained it in detail when I delivered the juniper berries last night. Actually, he'd decided to do two separate legs of lamb. One he'd prep, refrigerate overnight, then pop it into the oven right before the demo was scheduled to start. The second one would be prepared before an audience. By the time he finished his tutorial, the first leg of lamb would be ready to come out of the oven — *voilà!* — and presented to the crowd with a flourish. Just like what the famous chefs do on the Food Network. Stand aside, Bobby Flay. Be warned, Tyler Florence. Mario Barrone was a man on a mission.

Another quick glance at my watch told me I had no time to lose if I wanted to put my plan into action. What was keeping Brandywine Creek's new police chief anyway? I couldn't stand around all morning; I had things to do. I consoled myself thinking it would only take a minute, two at the most, to tell him I had nothing to do with Mario's death. My sole involvement consisted of opening the back door, finding him on the kitchen floor, and dialing 911.

No sooner did these thoughts run through my mind when a spanking-clean Crown Vic turned down the alley and braked alongside the EMS van. As I watched, the dark-haired man I'd glimpsed the day before jumped out. He stood about six foot one or so and looked to be in his mid to late forties. From all the spine straightening and gut sucking taking place around me, I assumed the man must be the new head honcho. I grudgingly admitted that the newcomer would probably have quite an effect on the ladies as well. Broad shoulders, trim waist, narrow hips, Brandywine's new chief of police was the total package, all right. Tall, dark, and rugged, if you liked the type. He might cause Reba Mae's heart to flutter, but not mine. I'd sworn off men. Marriage to CJ had been enough to make me consider entering a convent. And I'm not even Catholic.

I tried in vain to recall the guy's name, but all I remembered was CJ's obvious dislike. And according to CJ, the feeling was mutual. A dislike so malevolent, it might even filter down to family members — or in my case, former family members. A shiver wormed its way down my spine in spite of the warm April sunshine.

As I looked on, Beau conferred with the chief, then pointed a stubby finger in my direction. The man nodded once, then without a single glance my way, disappeared inside the Tratory. Beau sauntered over, his face set in what I was coming to think of as his "official business" mode. "Chief McBride said you're to wait here."

"Will this take long?" People always seem to crave nicotine during times of stress. If I smoked — which I don't — I'd haul out a pack of Marlboro's about now and light up. I seemed to be suffering a severe case of opening-day jitters. Or of finding-a-dead-body jitters. Nervously, I checked my watch again. "I need to get to my shop."

"Don't worry none," Beau said.

"Shouldn't take but a minute or two. Just a few routine questions is all, then you can be on your way."

"Fine," I muttered as he walked over to greet a slightly stooped, balding man who'd just arrived at the scene. I recognized the newcomer as John Strickland, the local mortician who doubled as county coroner.

Gloves and paper booties seemed to be the uniform du jour. As I waited impatiently, a couple of Brandywine Creek policemen, along with a sheriff's deputy, entered the building. One toted a large stainless steel box that looked suitable for fishing tackle, but with one notable exception: the word FORENSICS was stenciled along the side in bold letters. An elaborate camera dangled from his neck. Another man unwound a spool of yellow crime scene tape around the perimeter of the Tratory's rear entrance.

At last the chief reappeared, but instead of acknowledging my presence, he stood with his back turned and spoke into his cell phone. I didn't even know the man and I was starting to dislike him already. He was not only rude, but also inconsiderate of a private citizen with a business to run.

Deciding to take matters into my own hands, I marched up and tapped him on the shoulder. "S'cuse me."

He whipped around, his hand automatically reaching for his weapon.

"Whoa there, big fella," I said, taking a quick step back.

"Never sneak up on a cop from behind," he growled.

"I didn't *sneak*. I *approached*," I corrected primly. "There's a difference."

He removed his hand from the butt of his gun. "Next time, give me fair warning before you *approach* from behind."

I dearly wanted to inform him in no uncertain terms that there wouldn't be a next time. I had no intention of approaching him again — front, back, or sideways. Ever. Instead, I got down to the matter at hand. "I have work to do. How soon will I be free to leave?"

He folded his arms across his chest and eyed me coolly. "Is a murder investigation disrupting your schedule?"

His eyes, I noted for the first time, were blue — a pale, icy blue — fringed with girly long lashes. A killer combination. I stifled a giggle at the inappropriate pun. "I'm sorry," I backpedaled. "I didn't mean that the way it must've sounded. I feel terrible about Mario, but other than discovering him on the floor of his kitchen, there's not much I can add."

He reached into the pocket of his crisp navy blue uniform and withdrew a notebook and pen. "Let's start at the top, shall we. I'm Wyatt McBride, chief of police, and you are . . . ?"

"Piper. Piper Prescott."

"Prescott, eh?" A lengthy pause ensued. "Any relation to Chandler Jameson Prescott . . . the Third?"

Dismay, thicker than day-old plum pudding, congealed in my chest as the cool blue eyes turned even frostier.

CHAPTER 5

"I'll repeat," he said. "Any relation to Chandler Jameson Prescott the Third?"

I recalled CJ's comment that the two had been archenemies once upon a high school. Forgive and forget, right? Both men were adults now. Both mature and moderately successful. Surely not the types to hold grudges? Staring up at McBride's implacable expression, however, it occurred to me that being grown — and moderately successful — didn't necessarily equate with mature.

Or forgiving.

I shifted my weight from one sandaled foot to the other and chose my next words with care. "CJ and I are what you might call . . . *formerly* related. All we share now are the children."

"I see," he replied.

I thought I detected a lingering trace of Georgia in his deep baritone as I cast another sidelong glance at my wristwatch. My heart rate bumped up a notch when I saw the time. "I'd like to hang around, but I really have to be going."

He ignored my sense of urgency. "Divorced or separated?"

"Divorced," I snapped. I really wanted to inform him that my marital status was none of his damn business. But what was the point? In a town not much larger than a postage stamp, he was bound to find out sooner or later that CJ had tossed me aside like an old pair of sneakers.

"What was your relationship to the vic?"

"The vic . . . ?" I inwardly cringed at hearing Mario — belligerent, larger-than-life Mario — being referred to with such a clinical term. "My relationship . . . ?" I echoed.

"Barrone your boyfriend? Lover?"

I nearly laughed aloud at the absurdity. "Surely, you're joking?"

"Do I look like I'm joking, lady?" he growled. "We're talking a murder investigation."

Murder?

Being dumped in a bucket of ice water would have had the same effect. Goose bumps reared on my arms like mounds of fire ants along the shoulder of the road. In spite of a day that promised to be warm and

53

sunny, I shivered. Until that moment, I hadn't allowed myself to contemplate *how* Mario had died, only that he was dead. For all I knew, he could have fallen on a meat cleaver. Or suffered a bleeding ulcer like my uncle Henry and hemorrhaged to death. Or slipped on spilled grease, striking his head against the counter. Head wounds, as most moms know, bleed profusely. Furthermore, head injuries are known to be fatal even without a lot of bloodshed.

How naïve of me not to think murder! Murder was something for books, newspapers, television. Not something that happened in peaceful, safe Brandywine Creek, Georgia. I shook my head to clear it, bringing my thoughts back to the present, only to find McBride watching me closely and waiting patiently for an answer.

I moistened lips suddenly gone dry with the tip of my tongue. "I, ah, Mario and I weren't even friends. To be perfectly honest, I didn't even like the guy very much."

"What brought you to Trattoria Milano so early in the morning?"

The man was relentless. "Call it dumb luck," I said with a shrug. "Or bad karma."

He scowled, obviously not pleased with my response. I knew I must've sounded flip and that my attitude wasn't winning any brownie points. Seems like finding a corpse in the kitchen was having an adverse effect on my usually upbeat disposition. I wasn't happy to start the day this way, and I guess it showed.

"Juniper berries," I answered sullenly.

He blinked. "Come again?"

"Mario happens — happened," I corrected, shifting to past tense, "to be a fantastic chef. He agreed to demonstrate how to roast a leg of lamb at the grand opening of my spice shop."

"What's the connection between a leg of lamb and juniper berries?"

"Juniper berries happen to pair well with lamb and rosemary." From his frown, I could see he wasn't the sort who liked to share cooking tips.

"Right," he growled. "Tell me again, but in greater detail, why you were at the murder scene."

"Fine," I said. "Like I already explained, it was because of the juniper berries. Yesterday, I gave Mario all those I had in stock with the understanding he'd return the rest this morning. I came by to collect them and review today's schedule."

He made a note of this in his little book. "Tell me about finding the body."

I looked toward the rear entrance of the

Tratory, which was now festooned in yellow plastic tape. "I knocked on the back door and when it opened — even though I barely touched it — I walked inside. That's when I spotted Mario sprawled on the kitchen floor in a pool of blood and dialed nine-one-one."

"That it?"

"That's it."

"Chief?"

McBride glanced over his shoulder. Curious, I looked, too, and saw John Strickland, the coroner, on the back step of the restaurant, beckoning to him.

"There's something here you ought to see," Strickland said, and I thought I detected an undercurrent of urgency in his tone.

McBride nodded. "Be right with you."

"Am I free to go now?"

"Fine." He tucked his notebook and pen into his shirt pocket. "You'll need to drop by the station later to make a formal statement."

I started to leave, but turned back. "Ah, McBride, I need to ask a favor."

He arched a dark brow. "Isn't this a little soon to be asking favors? Shouldn't that wait until we're at least on a first-name basis?"

I gaped at him, surprised. Did a sense of

56

humor lurk beneath the serious-as-a-heart-attack demeanor? But this was hardly the time to try to decipher the man's personality. Not when I needed a favor — and needed it fast. I cleared my throat and forged ahead. "If it isn't too much trouble, could I retrieve the leg of lamb from the Tratory's fridge?"

"Meat? You're asking me for meat?"

"It's not like Mario will have further use for it since he's — incapacitated." Incapacitated sounded ever so much nicer than "deader than a mackerel."

He shook his head as though he couldn't believe his ears. "Lady, are you for real?"

I huffed out a breath. "My name isn't lady, it's Piper, and I'm dead serious." Oops, poor choice of words, but I was sure he got my drift.

"You just can't waltz into a crime scene and abscond with what could be a vital piece of evidence."

"Evidence?" I snorted. "For crying out loud, I'm simply asking for a chunk of mutton. How could that possibly be construed as evidence?"

McBride gave me his cold-eyed stare. "Not an Alfred Hitchcock fan, are you?"

I glared back. "*Rear Window. To Catch a Thief. North by Northwest.* I happen to *love*

Alfred Hitchcock." Then the connection slowly became obvious to me. I'd recently watched a Hitchcock marathon on a cable channel. Apparently, McBride had viewed it as well. In one of the episodes, a classic, a woman used a leg of lamb to murder her husband, popped it into the oven, and later served it to the investigators. When the meal was nearly finished, one of the officers remarked that the murder weapon was probably right under their noses. Ah, sweet irony.

McBride read my dawning comprehension. "Then you realize why I can't hand over a hunk of possible evidence."

"Bludgeoned? Are you telling me Mario was bludgeoned to death with a leg of lamb?" I asked, aghast at the notion.

"I'm not implying Barrone was bludgeoned. Cause of death is up to the coroner to determine. And yes, you're free to go about your business. Just don't leave town in case you're wanted for further questioning."

I resisted the urge to roll my eyes. Where did he think I was going to take off to, anyway? The south of France? A tempting thought. But, I had a spice shop to launch. "Fine," I said, borrowing the same put-upon tone Lindsey often used. Too bad it was wasted on his broad back.

The show must go on. Mario might be dead, but Spice It Up! was still alive and set to open in less than two hours' time. I tried to tamp down the burst of panic. *Tried* being the verb of choice. People would arrive, expecting to learn Mario's secret for roasting lamb.

I *could* do the cooking demo, I reminded myself. I could bring home the bacon — in this instance the leg of lamb — and roast it up in a pan. I was woman, hear me roar. I'd do the darn demo myself. What I didn't know, I'd improvise.

Piece of cake, right? In a rare fit of generosity, and confident his recipe would soon be published in a popular cooking magazine, Mario had granted me permission to have copies made. The ingredients were easily obtainable — especially since I owned a spice shop. But lamb was key.

Turning on my heel, I headed toward Main Street.

Pete Barker looked up from behind the counter of Meat on Main and greeted me with a smile. "Hey, Piper. All set for your big day?"

"Hey, yourself." I'd known Pete since I arrived in Brandywine Creek years ago, pregnant with my son and optimistic about the future. I guessed Pete to be somewhere in his sixties. He'd lost most of his hair, gained some pounds, but remained as good-natured as ever. "Don't suppose you could come to the aid of a damsel in distress?"

"Not sure these old bones of mine are up to slaying any dragons, but if it's a prime cut of meat you want, I'm your guy."

"By any chance, do you happen to have a leg of lamb in that meat locker of yours?"

"Sure thing." He gave the tray of boneless pork chops he'd just placed in the meat case a final glance. "Got a couple extra in case that cooking demo of Barrone's sparked a run. Didn't want to pass up the opportunity."

"Great. Could you butterfly it for me, too?" I asked, shifting into Plan B.

"No problem." Pete lumbered into the back and returned with the prettiest piece of meat I'd ever laid eyes on. Squinting through a pair of bifocals, he announced, "Three pounds right on the nose. Will this do?"

"Perfect."

Pete produced a blade suitable for a samurai and proceeded to dissect the lamb with the precision of a neurosurgeon. "Lord knows I've had plenty of practice lately thanks to a certain hotheaded chef who will remain nameless. Listenin' to him, a person would think I've never butterflied a piece of meat in my entire life instead of bein' a third-generation butcher."

"Well, you'll never hear me complain," I said, salving his injured pride. "Everyone for miles around knows your meat's the best."

Even to my own ears, I sounded like an enabler, but Pete appeared mollified. A little praise can go a long way sometimes. Or as the eternal optimist, Mary Poppins, might say, "A spoonful of sugar . . ."

"Heard a bunch of sirens earlier," Pete commented as he neatly wrapped the lamb in heavy brown paper. "Next thing I knew, a bunch of police cars flew past, hell-bent for leather."

"Umm . . . they were headed for the Tra-tory."

"Barrone, eh? Always told folks the man's temper was going to land him in a heap of trouble. What's the guy gone and done this time?" He didn't wait for my reply, but continued. "Heard once he got so mad he threw a knife at his sous chef."

"Well, his temper won't be getting him into any more trouble."

Pete moved to the register to ring up my

61

purchase. "How's that?"

"Because he's dead," I muttered. It was then I realized I'd gone off this morning without my purse.

"Dead, eh?" Pete scratched his bald head. "Ain't that something."

"Sorry, Pete, it seems like I left my money at home. Okay if I pay you later?"

"Sure, I trust you."

Trust. That's one of the reasons I loved Brandywine Creek. People trusted each other to keep their word and, most of the time, they weren't disappointed. Safety was another thing I treasured in small towns. Then I remembered Mario lying in a pool of his own blood. As I exited Meat on Main, I crossed "safety" off the list.

CHAPTER 6

I heard the phone ringing off the hook as I unlocked the door of Spice It Up! I ran to answer, hoping it was the vet calling to tell me the condition of the poor little pup I'd rescued the night before. With all the commotion about finding Mario's body, then obsessing over my cooking debut, I'd nearly forgotten the pooch. Dropping the lamb next to the cash register, I picked up the cordless.

"Piper . . . ? That you? You sound out of breath."

I immediately recognized the voice on the other end of the line as belonging to Marcy Magruder, the young woman who'd agreed to assist in the shop from time to time. Waiting on customers, restocking shelves, assisting with inventory, that sort of thing. Marcy happened to be engaged to Danny Boyd, Mario's former sous chef. It wasn't until just recently that Danny had found employment at the Pizza Palace after leaving his job at the Tratory. To make matters worse, Marcy had been laid off from her job at the popcorn factory just outside the town limits, a small family-run enterprise that sold their product exclusively to specialty stores. Since the recent drought had affected the corn crop, she had no clue when she might be called back to her job as popcorn packer. I knew the two planned on getting married soon and were strapped for cash. I couldn't offer Marcy full-time employment, but a few hours here or there would benefit both of us.

And if I ever needed help, it was today.

"Hey, Marcy, what's up?"

"Umm, ah, I don't know how to tell you this. I feel just awful callin' this way after you've been so nice to me and Danny, but . . ."

I braced myself for the blow I sensed was coming. I didn't have long to wait.

"Mmm, Piper? I'm real sorry, but I won't be able to come in today."

"B-but Marcy," I sputtered, panic gripping me by the throat. "I'm depending on you. I have to do the cooking demo myself, and there's no one else I can call at the last minute to help with customers."

"I've been heavin' my guts out all

mornin'.""

I sighed when I really wanted to cry. "Don't worry, Marcy. I'll manage . . . somehow. After all, I wouldn't want you spreading germs all over town. If you're sick, stay home, and take it easy. Go back to bed."

"Sorry to let you down, but . . . gotta run." The call ended abruptly.

I gave myself a pep talk as I retrieved the lamb and headed for the rear of the shop. Think of the money I'd be saving by not having to pay a clerk, I told myself. Clerk? Salesperson sounded better. Or was sales associate more politically correct? I was obsessing again. Everything would be fine, just fine. I kept repeating the words like a mantra.

I didn't know why I was making this into such a big deal. I happened to be a darn good cook, if I did say so myself. CJ certainly never lodged any complaints — at least not in the food department. He managed to find plenty other things to criticize, though. My hair was too red, too curly. I was too short. And my backhand was why we always lost at doubles.

The most difficult part of the demo would be addressing a store full of people. The thought of everyone staring back at me was enough to make me want to book a flight to Fiji. Public speaking had never been my forte. The mere thought of it made my palms damp. While I'm perfectly okay meeting people one on one, or even one on four, speaking in front of a large audience was just not my cup of tea.

But this was not the time to bemoan my inadequacies. It was time to get to work. After spreading a linen cloth over a long folding table, I set out the ingredients and equipment I'd need. To my immense relief, I'd discovered a lone jar of juniper berries hiding among the baking spices. When finished, I stood back to admire my handiwork, but had the nagging suspicion I was forgetting something. A pounding on the front door startled me out of my reverie. Hurrying over, I twisted open the lock and found Reba Mae grinning at me.

"I'm between perms," she announced. "Thought I'd drop by and see how you're holdin' up."

"If being a nervous wreck is holding up, then I'm holding up great."

Reba Mae pulled a tortoise shell case out of her teal blue smock. "Here, hon, let me fix you up. You're looking a mite washed out." She proceeded to dab blush on my cheeks, then stepped back to inspect the results. "There, that's better. The Klassy Kut's been buzzin' worse than a hornet's nest about Mario Barrone. I told the girls I'd run over and get the skinny firsthand."

"There's not much to tell." I took a feather duster from beneath the counter and started dusting shelves that didn't need dusting. "I went over to the Tratory to get the rest of the juniper berries and found Mario on the floor. Called nine-one-one. That's about it. Now you know as much as I do."

Reba Mae shook her head in frustration. "Must be more to it than that, girlfriend. What was it like, findin' a dead body? Anythin' like the movies?"

"I didn't stick around long enough to take in the details."

"Lotta blood and guts?"

"No guts, lots of blood," I retorted.

"Who do you think did him in?"

"I've no idea. Your guess is as good as mine."

Reba Mae folded her arms across her chest and cocked her head to one side. "Outside the fact folks liked his cookin', no one has much good to say about him. Pinky Alexander thinks Mario most likely was shot by a jealous husband. Claims she got it from a reliable source that Mario's had affairs with more 'n a half dozen women who frequent the Tratory."

"Pinky likes to exaggerate."

Satisfied the free-standing shelves were spick-and-span, I turned my attention to the Hoosier cabinet. Reba Mae trailed after me. "So was he . . . you know . . . shot?"

"I didn't examine the body for bullet holes," I replied tartly.

"More 'n likely he was shot. Did I ever mention most of my customers brag about havin' concealed-weapons permits? You oughta hear 'em. They talk about handguns like brides talk about silver patterns. Glocks, Berettas, Rugers. One even admitted ownin' an Uzi."

"The cause of death is up to the coroner to determine," I told her, mimicking Wyatt McBride. "And that's a direct quote from our brand-new chief of police."

"What's McBride like?" Reba Mae asked with a sly smile. "Vicki Lamont claims he's a hottie."

"More like a 'coldie,' if you want my opinion." I returned the duster to its proper place and studied a clipboard with today's agenda. A quick look told me Ned Feeney, The Eternal Rest's number one gofer, was due to arrive momentarily with the chairs that I was borrowing from the funeral home.

"Don't think McBride would crack a smile if he won the Powerball in the Georgia lottery."

"Ruby Phillips heard he was a hotshot detective down in Miami. Got his name in the papers a lot. Swears she saw his picture in *People* once or twice with some celebrity at a premiere in South Beach."

"Doubt he'll last long," I said, shrugging off Ruby's idle talk. "McBride's manner strikes me as too heavy-handed. Abrasive, even arrogant. It's only a matter of time before he has a run-in with the town council. Folks are used to our former chief's laid-back ways."

"Yeah, Uncle Joe's a good guy, all right. He went easy on my boys a couple times when they pulled a few pranks back in high school."

"Didn't hurt any that Joe Johnson was Butch's uncle."

"You know how it is in these small Southern towns." Reba Mae shrugged. "The Johnsons are kin to half the folks in Brandywine County, the Abernathys the other half."

I nodded my agreement. When compared with the Abernathy family, who arrived with the Mayflower, the Johnsons were the new kids on the block. "Well, McBride's a total opposite of Joe — a real hard-ass. Mark my words, he'll antagonize people in droves. Before long, the mayor will be clamoring for his resignation."

"Mmm, I take it you don't like the guy."

"Subject closed, okay?"

Reba Mae smiled, but thankfully let the matter drop. "So," she said, waving a hand toward the table at the rear, "who's gonna give the cookin' demo with Mario dead?"

"You're looking at her." My stomach lurched at the thought. I wondered for a second whether I might be coming down with the same flu bug that had laid Marcy low.

"Wait and see. I bet this place will be standin' room only now that news is out about you findin' Barrone in a puddle of blood."

"I think I'm going to hyperventilate." I held my hand to my chest.

"Just breathe into a paper bag, and you'll be fine. Gotta check on my perm, hon, but I'll drop by first chance I get." A quick hug and she was gone.

Ned Feeney arrived next with a hearse-load of folding chairs. "Where do you want me to put 'em, Miz Piper?"

I gave Ned instructions, then moved out of his way.

"Brought extra just in case," he huffed as

70

he deposited another load. "S'pect you might have quite a crowd seein' as how you found a dead man and all. Must've been quite a sight. Is it true blood was splattered from kingdom come and back?"

Though I tried not to stereotype people, Ned Feeney always put me in mind of Gomer Pyle, ably played by Jim Nabors on the old *Andy Griffith Show*. Maybe it was the perpetual ball cap and scuffed sneakers. Or the prominent Adam's apple. But more likely it was Ned's goofy smile that struck a chord. Don't remember if Gomer cared for gossip or not, but Ned Feeney loved it even more than he loved fried catfish.

"Mr. Strickland said seein' Barrone layin' in all that blood was quite a sight. And Mr. Strickland's used to seein' dead bodies, as he's the coroner an' all."

I refrained from comment, and instead donned a sunny yellow bib apron with SPICE IT UP! written in black letters and a bright red chili pepper embroidered underneath. I returned to the table I'd set up for the demo at the rear of the shop and nervously reviewed the recipe.

Ned didn't seem to notice my silence. "Mr. Strickland told me soon as I'm done deliverin' chairs, I was s'posed to drive the corpse down to Decatur."

71

"Mmm." I chopped a sprig of rosemary and dropped it into a prep dish.

"That's GBI headquarters, you know," he added importantly. "That's the Georgia Bureau of Investigation."

I paused in separating cloves of garlic. "What else did Mr. Strickland tell you?" Apparently curiosity tended to be contagious.

Gomer — I mean Ned — wiped his brow. "Tried my best but Mr. S was pretty tight-lipped about the case. One thing for sure though," he said, heading for the hearse parked at the curb. "He said it was a homicide. Chief McBride swears he'll find the killer."

No sooner had Ned departed when my former mother-in-law, resplendent in her signature pearls, a peach cashmere twin set, and a tailored skirt, arrived with Lindsey in tow. I often envied Melly Prescott. She was the rare sort whose clothes resisted wrinkles, her perfectly coiffed hair could weather a hurricane, and her nails were never in dire need of a manicure. I'd seen her address the Brandywine Creek Garden Club with the finesse of a skilled orator. And her tomato aspic was the odds-on favorite at every funeral. Funerals, along with weddings and christenings, happened to be major social gatherings here in the South. Some folks regard getting out the fine china and polishing the silver to be grief therapy. Melly was a fine woman, bless her heart — to quote a Southernism — but she could be intimidating.

"Good morning, Melly."

"Mornin', Piper." Melly gave me a dry peck on the cheek in case others might be around to speculate on how well the two of us were getting along since the divorce.

"Hey, Lindsey." I turned to my daughter and gave her a hug, which she returned in her typical lukewarm fashion.

"Meemaw worried people might talk if we didn't come today," Lindsey said as she pulled away.

The fact that Lindsey was here at all attested to Melly's power of persuasion. I knew from experience how hard it was to rouse a teenage girl from bed before noon on a Saturday. "Well," I said brightly, "whatever the reason I'm glad you're here to show your support."

"So, this is what all the fuss is about," Melly said, parroting her son's comment of the previous day. She pivoted slowly, taking in the shelves of carefully selected spices from the far corners of the globe. "Anise . . . ?" she said, wrinkling her aristocratic nose. "Who uses anise?"

I bridled at her tone. "Anise happens to be used in baking cakes, breads, and cookies. Next time I make Italian biscotti, I'll be sure to bring you some. You'll love the sweet licorice taste."

"Hmph," she sniffed, moving on to another display. "And what is this? Surely, dear, you can't expect anyone in their right mind to spend so much money for such a teensy amount?"

"Saffron happens to be the most expensive spice there is." I gently took the jar from her hand and replaced it on the shelf. "Fortunately a little goes a long way."

"Interesting. . . . What does one do with saffron?"

"It's wonderful in paella."

"Paella? Another of those fancy, foreign dishes you seem to favor. What's wrong with plain-old meat and potatoes? That was good enough for my husband. Good enough for my son. Plenty good enough for the rest of us, too."

"Why don't you and Lindsey find yourselves a seat?" I suggested.

CHAPTER 7

Standing room only.

Reba Mae's prediction proved true. A steady stream of people poured into Spice It Up!, filling chairs and jamming the aisles. Among the crowd, I spotted Gina and Tony Deltorro, owners of the Pizza Palace. Behind them were Diane Cloune, wife of the local councilman Dwayne Cloune, and Dottie Hemmings, the mayor's wife. Dottie waggled her fingers at me. Diane gave me a brittle smile. I wished it was my newly opened spice shop that captured their interest, but I knew better. It was the prospect of pure, unadulterated gossip that drew them like honeybees to buttercups. A dead chef trumps a grand opening any day.

I took my place behind the demo table and looked out over an expectant audience. They stared back. I felt like an exhibit in a freak show. My gaze chanced on Melly, who pointedly tapped her watch with a fingernail, signaling it was time for me to get this show on the road. Bored already, Lindsey stifled a yawn behind a French-manicured hand.

"Good morning!" I cleared my throat. "Welcome to Spice It Up!"

The shop was so still you could have heard the proverbial pin drop. From the fluttering in my stomach, it felt like I swallowed a hummingbird along with my morning's yogurt. People had come to gawk, to ask questions. I crossed my fingers they wouldn't leave without purchasing bags and bottles of my precious spices. I desperately wanted — needed — to hear my cash register jingle.

"All righty then," I said with false heartiness. "Let's get started, shall we? Today I'm going to demonstrate how to prepare one of Trattoria Milano's specialties, Roast Lamb with Rosemary and Juniper. Naturally the first thing you'll need is lamb." I surreptitiously wiped damp palms on the sides of my apron. "After all, you can't expect to serve roast lamb with rosemary and juniper without the lamb, right?"

No one laughed at my feeble attempt at humor. No one even cracked a smile.

I soldiered on. "Ask the butcher for a leg of lamb that weighs approximately three pounds. Like this lovely choice cut." I held up the meat for a little show-and-tell. "Then ask him to butterfly it for you."

"Must take a pretty sharp knife to slice through a piece of meat that size," a woman in the second row commented loudly.

Ignoring the outburst, I continued with my presentation. "Pete at Meat on Main will be happy to accommodate you, but I'm sure the manager of the meat department at the Piggly Wiggly will be equally agreeable." I had no idea if this was true or not, but at this point in my fledgling career I didn't want to risk alienating the chamber of commerce. Best to give them equal billing.

"Next, add four cloves of chopped garlic, a sprig of finely chopped rosemary, and Chef Barrone's secret ingredient — juniper berries. Six ought to do it." I dumped the contents of three small prep dishes into a marble mortar. "For those of you unfamiliar with this particular spice, juniper berries are the ripe, dried cones from the juniper evergreen shrub that grows throughout the northern hemisphere. If any of you are married to hunters, juniper helps tame the gamey character of venison."

"Told Harvey, my husband, the mayor, next time he brings home a deer, I'm going to Mother's. He can cook the dang thing himself," Dottie Hemmings declared.

The audience tittered at hearing this. To the best of my recollection, Dottie rarely mentioned her husband's name without reminding everyone within earshot that he was the mayor of our fair town. I waited until quiet prevailed, then continued. "Juniper berries have a pleasant woody odor and when crushed smell unmistakably like . . ."

". . . gin," a member of the audience offered.

"Is it true the Tratory reeked of booze when you found Mario?"

"Heard Barrone was in a pool of blood the size of Lake Lanier," another volunteered.

Pretending deafness, I grabbed the pestle. "Pound the garlic, rosemary, and juniper berries into a smooth paste."

"Someone said he was shot," a man in the back piped up.

"I heard he was stabbed to death."

Stabbed? Did the woman on the far end of the first row say *stabbed*? I'd conveniently — too conveniently — forgotten about finding a knife in the weeds outside the Tratory's back door. I must've dropped it when I spied Mario on the floor. To make matters worse, Dr. Doug, the vet, said the mutt I'd found the night before had sustained a *knife* wound.

Coincidence? I felt the blood drain from my face. Personally, I've never been a great believer in coincidence.

"Hey, Piper, you okay?" Gina Deltorro asked, frowning.

I mustered a smile. "Fine, thanks."

My mind on guns and knives and blood, I pounded the garlic, rosemary, and juniper into mush. I realized I was being overzealous when bits of the concoction flew out of the mortar. As casually as I could, I wiped a gob of goo from my cheek and whisked flecks off my apron to a chorus of snickers.

Darting a glance in Lindsey's direction, I tried to catch her eye, but her attention was fixed on a nonexistent spot on the heart pine floor.

"Yes, well," I said, regrouping. "Season the lamb with salt and pepper. I carry a great Kosher salt. If you only purchase one type of salt, you might consider making that your mainstay." I sprinkled on a generous amount, then reached for the pepper mill and ground away. "There's nothing to compare with fresh ground pepper. It's a spice that adds great flavor to almost every dish. Spice It Up! sells not only black Tellicherry peppercorns from India, but sophisticated white peppercorns from Borneo, and pink peppercorns from the French island of Reunion."

Just then a door opened and a latecomer slipped inside. None other than Chief Wyatt McBride in the flesh. I groaned inwardly at the sight. I doubted he'd come hoping to find a new recipe for lamb. His presence made me even more nervous.

"Hey, Piper," Dottie prompted. "What're we supposed to do next?"

I took a calming breath, which did little good, then searched my work area for a utensil of some sort. It occurred to me then that I'd forgotten spoons or spatulas. They were nowhere to be found, which left me little choice but to improvise. "Hands were made before spoons and forks, as Granddad once told me. Take about half the paste," I instructed. Using my fingers, I scooped up a portion and flung it on the meat. "Smear it around."

I heard my former mother-in-law gasp at my technique.

"Now roll the lamb into a compact roast." Juniper paste oozed out of each end as I worked. In the dim recesses of my mind, I wondered if Mario had encountered this problem as well. I daintily ran my index finger down one edge and flicked the excess paste toward the mortar. It missed by a country mile, landing instead on the large bosom of Bertha Fox in the front row. This time the snickers turned into outright laughter.

"S-sorry," I apologized, my cheeks flaming. I plastered on a smile so wide it made my face ache.

Melly, tight-lipped with disapproval, leaned over and handed Bertha a handkerchief with which to wipe her blouse. Lindsey, I noted, slouched further down in her seat.

"Almost finished," I announced cheerily, picking up a ball of string I'd scrounged from my junk drawer. "Now tie the damn . . . I meant *dang* . . . lamb with string or twine to hold it together while it cooks."

To be honest, I'd never been especially creative when it comes to wrapping packages. This time proved no exception. It was like wrestling a greased pig at the county fair. Slick with juniper paste and the meat's inherent fat, the leg of lamb shot out of my hands, skidded off the worktable, and landed on the floor with a *plop*.

I was so mortified, I'd like to have died right then and there. Knowing my face matched the color of my hair, I picked the roast off the floor and brushed it off as best

81

I could and proceeded to hog-tie the blasted thing. "That ought to do it," I muttered, and was surprised to hear a smattering of applause.

"Piper, dear, what about the rest of the juniper paste?" Melly prompted.

I stared at her blankly for a moment. *The rest of the juniper paste? What "rest"?*

"What do you do with the other half, dear?" Melly persisted. "Surely it shouldn't go to waste."

"Right," I muttered, absently shoving back a rebellious curl. This had to be the worst cooking demonstration in the history of cooking. Bad enough to find a dead body, now I had to pretend to know what I was doing. "Okay," I said, reaching for a paring knife. "Make a series of slits."

I vented my frustration on the miserable hunk of mutton with more vigor than probably necessary. After forcing what was left of the juniper paste inside the slits, I sprinkled on enough salt to make a cardiologist cringe, and dropped the sorry mess into a roasting pan. Praise the Lord. I was in the homestretch.

"Pop this baby into a four-hundred-fifty-degree oven. Roast for thirty minutes, then add a cup of dry red wine."

Blame it on a combination of nerves and

oratory, but my throat suddenly felt parched. Reaching for the wine I'd poured earlier for this part of the demo, I took a big glug of Cabernet Sauvignon. Straight from the measuring cup.

"Now," I continued, "scrape the browned bits from the bottom of the pan with a wooden spoon and cook for another ten minutes for medium rare. *Bon appétit!*"

Sweeping my gaze over the audience, I had the distinct satisfaction of knowing I'd wiped the boredom from Lindsey's pretty face. Amid all the mashing, splashing, slashing, and plopping, it had disappeared, leaving her staring at me wide-eyed.

Then, to my dismay, I looked toward the front of the shop and saw McBride approach. Not caring who watched, I took another swallow of wine.

I attempted to avoid him by doing an end run toward the register near the front of the store, but Melly intercepted me. "You need to work on your presentation, dear. I suggest you consider a course in public speaking."

Out of the corner of my eye, I noticed McBride elbowing his way toward me. The crowd parted in his wake like he was Moses and they were the Red Sea. "We need to talk," he said without preamble.

"Now?" I squeaked.

Melly's eyes slid from me to the sheriff. "You go ahead, dear. Lindsey and I will man the register. I expect sales to be quite brisk."

Why, now of all times, did my ex-mother-in-law pick this moment to be helpful? Conscious of dozens of pairs of eyes boring into my back, I trailed after McBride out the store.

"You need to come down to the station to make a formal statement," he said the minute we hit the sidewalk.

I gestured behind me. "Can it wait? I have a shop full of customers."

"Looks like we found the murder weapon."

My heart about came to a screeching halt at hearing this. "Oh," I said, trying to sound noncommittal.

"My men found a knife. We think someone tried to hide it under the refrigerator."

Why couldn't Mario simply have hit his head and died of a fractured skull? Then I brought myself up short. I was a terrible person. Here I was blaming Mario for his own untimely death.

"Are you sure you told me everything that happened this morning?"

"Everything . . . ?"

"The coroner gives cause of death as a

stabbing. You'll need to be fingerprinted."

"Fingerprinted . . . ?" I seemed incapable of sentences consisting of more than one word.

"Just routine." McBride drilled me with laser-blue eyes. "We need to rule you out as a possible suspect."

He paused to let this sink in. At what point was I was supposed to ask for a lawyer? Were we there yet?

"Mom?" Lindsey stuck her head out the door. "Meemaw said some lady wants to know the difference between cinnamon from Vietnam and cinnamon from Ceylon."

"Be right there, sweetie." I gave her a weak smile. When she disappeared back inside, I turned to McBride. "Listen, every cent I own has gone into making Spice It Up! a success. I can't just walk off and leave it in the hands of someone who doesn't know diddly squat about spices. I promise, I'll come to the station as soon as the shop closes at five."

His gaze shifted from me to the store crowded with people. "All right," he agreed, albeit reluctantly.

I was too relieved to wonder whether he responded to the desperation in my voice or merely decided I wasn't a flight risk. Either way, I was itching to ring up sales.

"Not so fast," he ordered as I turned to go.

I watched wordlessly as he reached out to me with his index finger.

"Missed a spot," he said, dabbing my cheek. "Thought it might be a speck of that juniper concoction, but, nope, it's a freckle." He started toward the patrol car parked at the curb. "Five o'clock. Don't be late. I don't take murder investigations lightly."

I doubted the man ever took anything lightly, I thought as I watched him drive away.

CHAPTER 8

The day passed in a flurry of activity punctuated by the sweet chime of the cash register. At closing time, I decided to forego tallying the day's receipts till later and trudged the short distance to the police station.

"Hey, hon."

A dark-skinned woman, her elaborate braids tied back with a red ribbon, looked up from a computer screen and greeted me with a friendly smile. Her black polo shirt bearing the Brandywine Police Department logo had either been purchased a size too small or laundered in the wrong wash cycle to house her ample frame.

"You must be Miz Prescott. Chief said you'd be by. I'm Precious Blessing."

"Nice to meet you, Precious. Just call me Piper."

"Heard all about your cookin' show.

Dorinda said it was a hoot. Sorry I missed it."

Great. I suppose I should be happy if it didn't go viral on YouTube. "Chief McBride wanted me to come down to make a formal statement about . . . you know."

"Yeah, the whole town's talkin' about how that stuck-up cook who called hisself a chef died all at once."

"Right," I said.

"Who would've thought the chief would land a murder case right off? Best of my recollection, Brandywine Creek ain't had a killin' in years. Not since that country singer down at High Cotton got hisself shot by a jealous husband."

"Guess that was before my time."

"I'll let the chief know you're here."

While Precious called to inform her boss of my arrival, I took a quick look around, more depressed than impressed by the décor. Worn wooden benches huddled against scuffed beige walls. A giant wall calendar courtesy of the local lumberyard comprised the lone artwork. Functional and drab has never been a favorite of mine, not even in the early days of my marriage to CJ when functional and drab were all we could afford.

"Best not to keep the chief waiting,"

Precious said, rising from her chair. "C'mon. I'll show you the way."

Precious waddled down a short hallway, with me lagging behind. She paused outside a door, which still bore the faint imprint of the former chief's name, and stepped aside. "Don't let 'im scare you none. Some folks growl worse 'n they bite."

I managed a sickly smile. "Thanks."

Feeling a bit like Little Red Riding Hood, I mentally braced myself to meet the Big Bad Wolf or, in this case, the Big Bad Policeman. I gave myself a pep talk. There was no need to be nervous. After all, I had nothing to hide. Why, then, was I a wreck about this whole statement thing? Only the thought of meeting Reba Mae afterward for nachos and a margarita kept me from bolting. When Reba Mae heard about my command performance to appear before McBride, she made me promise to stop by — no matter the hour. Taking a deep breath to steady my nerves, I shoved open the door.

McBride glanced up from a sheaf of papers on his desk. "It's about time."

"Chief . . . ?" Precious poked her head in the door. "Can I get you and your guest something to drink? Coffee, sweet tea? A soda?"

"Mrs. Prescott *isn't* a guest, Miss Blessing. She's here for questioning. Please see that we're not disturbed."

"Yes, boss." Precious gave me an impudent wink as she quietly closed the door, leaving me alone with Big Bad McBride.

"Have a seat," McBride ordered, pulling a yellow legal pad from a drawer. "How did your first day go — after the cooking demonstration, that is?"

I lowered myself into the chair opposite a battered desk that didn't look like it would fetch twenty bucks at a garage sale and eyed him suspiciously. Was he genuinely interested in my day? Or was this some sort of ruse designed to put a "suspect" at ease? "I haven't totaled up the receipts yet," I returned cautiously, "but Melly seemed pleased."

He fixed me with his cool blues. "Melly? She the woman who offered to help out behind the counter?"

"Yes," I replied. "Melly Prescott, CJ's mother."

"Ah," he said in a this-explained-it tone of voice. "Thought she looked familiar, but I couldn't quite place her. The two of you still close after the divorce?"

"We've never been what you might call 'close.' "

"Not even while you and CJ were married?"

"Melly . . . tolerated me. I always had the impression she thought CJ could do better than marrying a girl whose daddy worked on the line in an automotive plant in Detroit."

What I didn't understand, though, was Melly's unexpected willingness to help at Spice It Up! today. That had come as a shocker. Pleasant, but a shock nonetheless. Granted, the woman knew next to nothing about spices, but what she lacked in knowledge she made up for with enthusiasm. Time and again, I'd heard her convince customers they ought to try this or try that. Who would have thought the heart of a saleswoman beat beneath the twin sets and pearls?

And best of all, she'd gotten Lindsey involved.

McBride picked up a ballpoint and clicked it, a signal the chitchat over. "How long have you known Barrone?"

I shifted my weight, cleared my throat, and wished I were somewhere else. Turks and Caicos or Grand Cayman would be nice. I always wanted to learn how to scuba dive.

McBride waited for my answer, infinitely

patient, infinitely watchful.

"I've known Mario ever since he first opened Trattoria Milano," I finally said. "Even though CJ prefers prime rib, we occasionally dined at the Tratory when he entertained clients. Mario happened to be quite particular about the ingredients that went into his signature dishes. When he learned I was opening a spice shop, he made it a point to check it out long before I was scheduled to open. On a whim, I approached him about doing a cooking demo, and he agreed. Claimed this particular recipe would soon be published in a well-known food magazine so he didn't see the harm in revealing his secrets to the folks in an obscure little town in Georgia."

"Can you name anyone who might harbor a grudge against Barrone? Might want to harm him?"

"I don't know much about Mario's personal life," I confessed, "but he did have a temper and antagonized a lot of people. According to rumors Reba Mae overheard in the Klassy Kut, he also had a reputation as a ladies' man."

"Reba Mae have a last name?"

"Johnson. She's the widow of Butch Johnson, who died some years back."

The cop mask slipped a little. "Butch is dead?"

"Drowned while bass fishing."

"Sorry to hear that," he said, and for a moment looked almost human. "I remember him from junior varsity. Nice guy."

"Yes, he was," I agreed. "Everyone liked Butch." I exhaled a slow breath. So far, so good. At this rate, I'd be out of here in no time flat.

"Let's back up a ways, shall we?" he drawled, bursting my little bubble of optimism. "Think back to when you arrived at the Tratory. Notice any suspicious cars on the street?"

I frowned. To me, cars are cars — four tires and a steering wheel. "I'm not sure exactly what a 'suspicous' car would look like."

Judging from the scowl on his face, I don't think he appreciated my inquiring mind. "See anyone loitering in the alley when you approached?" he asked.

This question just didn't seem to make sense. "Why would a killer 'loiter' at the scene of the crime? Wouldn't he want to get away as fast as possible instead of sticking around?"

"What about after you entered the restaurant," he said, trying a different approach.

"See anything unusual? Hear anything?"

"N-no," I stammered as the ramifications of his questions hit me. *The killer might have still been there!* What if I'd surprised him? Caught him in the act? I could very well have been his next "vic."

While McBride made a production of scribbling everything I'd said on his legal pad, I tried to distract myself by letting my gaze wander. His office, like the waiting area, was done in minimalist institution-on-a-budget style. No plants, no photos, no personal touches. Brown linoleum floor, beige walls pockmarked with holes where pictures used to hang. I noticed a cardboard box next to the desk piled high with what appeared to be framed diplomas and certificates, a reminder the guy was new in town and still settling in. Maybe I should cut him some slack. Or maybe he should cut me some. I was new to the murder business.

For the first time since meeting McBride, I wondered about his personal life. Things like, did he have a wife and kids tucked away? I sneaked a peek at his left hand, but didn't spy a wedding band. But then again, not all married men wore rings. I've been wrong before, but he just didn't strike me as the paternal type. Try as I might, I couldn't imagine this tough, no-nonsense

94

cop coaching Little League. Or proudly photographing little girls in pink tutus.

On the other hand, I could imagine him escorting a starlet to a Miami premiere.

McBride looked up and found me assessing him. Caught in the act, I felt my cheeks pinken. Sitting up straighter, I folded my hands primly in my lap. "What else do you want to know?"

"Anything else that might prove helpful," he clarified.

His expression didn't betray his thoughts, but I had a sneaky feeling he knew more than he was letting on. I waged an inner debate. Should I mention finding a knife near the Tratory's rear door? My conscience said yes, just do it, but I knew the admission would implicate me in a way I didn't want to be implicated. I could guess how things would look — and how easily they could be misinterpreted.

"Do you know anything about the knife found at the scene?" McBride fired, exhibiting an uncanny ability to read my mind.

You have the right to remain silent. I watched TV. I read mysteries. I'd heard that phrase dozens of times, maybe thousands. I had nothing to hide, done nothing wrong. But why then did I feel guilty? "The knife . . . ?"

Reaching into a desk drawer, he pulled out a plastic evidence bag. "The coroner believes this knife will correspond with the weapon used to murder Mario Barrone. As soon as we're finished here, I'm sending it to the Georgia Bureau of Investigation, Latent Print Section, for testing. Will your prints be a match?"

Anything you say can be used against you in a court of law. Wasn't that how it went? But it didn't really matter what I said or didn't say. The prints would be a match. It was time to come clean. Confess my innocence, proclaim I had nothing to hide. Surely, McBride couldn't seriously think I had anything to do with Mario's death. The very idea was just too . . . too . . . outrageous!

"That looks like the knife I found near the back door of the Tratory," I admitted reluctantly.

"And . . . ?"

"And I picked it up. It seemed the logical thing to do," I said, knowing I sounded defensive. "I picked it up and brought it inside. It must have fallen from my hand when I saw Mario."

McBride repeatedly clicked his confounded ballpoint, the modern-day equivalent of Chinese water torture. "Let me get this straight," he said with exaggerated patience, "you just happened to find the murder weapon, pick it up, drop it — and forget to mention it."

"That's exactly what happened. I was just about to tell you," I replied, relieved all the facts were finally out in the open.

"Where were you between the hours of ten o'clock and midnight?" he asked, dropping another bomb from his arsenal.

You have the right to have an attorney present. I belatedly wondered if I should've phoned CJ and asked him to meet me here. Knowing my fingerprints were on the knife — and I needed an alibi — was starting to freak me out. And it probably showed. I swallowed what felt like a whole nutmeg lodged in my throat. "I was at the vet's. Dr. Winters can verify my whereabouts."

"Isn't that a strange time to be taking your pet in for a checkup?"

I recrossed my legs, trying to get comfortable. "I don't have a pet."

His Nordic blue eyes bored a hole straight through me. "If you don't have a pet, what were you doing there? You and the vet have a thing?"

"That is absolutely none of your business!" I felt my face burn. With anger, not embarrassment. "No, we don't have a *thing.*

Doug's practically a stranger. For your information, I discovered a small dog, hardly more than a pup, in the bushes behind my shop. It had been injured and was in dire need of medical attention. I did what any animal lover would do. I took it to the vet's."

"And this Dr. Winters will verify this?"

"Of course."

He jotted a few more notes on his blasted pad. "By the way, what was wrong with the dog?"

I squirmed. I actually squirmed. "He'd been stabbed."

Surprise on McBride's face quickly changed into skepticism. I could tell from his expression that he didn't believe in co-incidence any more than I did. Pressing a button on his intercom, he said, "Precious, would you have Sergeant Tucker fingerprint Mrs. Prescott?"

Innocent until proven guilty. Wasn't that one of the principles this country was founded on? Wasn't it written somewhere? Bill of Rights? The Constitution? The Declaration of Independence? I wished back in the day I'd paid more attention in civics class. You can't lock a person up and throw away the key because they were first on the scene. Or because they might've "accidentally" picked up what might turn out to be the murder weapon.

Or can you?

CHAPTER 9

"Fingerprinted? Is the guy loony tunes?"

Reba Mae's outrage was music to my ears. Balm to my wounded spirit. "I guess it's standard operating procedure in a murder investigation."

"Hmph!" Reba Mae snorted.

"McBride said something about eliminating me as a suspect." We were relaxing in Reba Mae's sunroom. A partially eaten platter of nachos and half-empty glasses of margaritas rested on the coffee table in front of us. "He sounded pretty positive the knife I found at the scene will turn out to be the murder weapon."

"He can't seriously think you killed Barrone?"

I wiggled my toes, happy to have kicked off my shoes and to be curled up in a comfy chair. "It's impossible to figure out what's going on behind that cop face of his. And there's more," I said, helping myself to another nacho gooey with cheese and chili.

Reba Mae took that as a cue to top off our glasses. "Shoot, girlfriend. I'm all ears."

I proceeded to tell her about me finding a wounded mutt and rushing him to the vet's, ending the account with Dr. Winters's opinion that the dog had been stabbed.

Reba Mae shook her head. "What're the odds? I'd bet a month of Sundays that whoever stabbed Mario stabbed the dog, too."

"The same thought occurred to me." I crossed my ankles on the flowered ottoman and sipped my drink. "Dogs are darn good judges of character. The poor thing was probably barking his head off when the murderer came out of the Tratory."

". . . and whoever it was tried to silence him — permanently."

"Exactly."

"Who could do that to a little pup?"

"Who could do it to a human being, albeit a surly, temperamental one?" I countered. I watched Reba Mae scoop salsa onto a nacho chip. Personally, I thought the salsa could have used another dash of cumin with its wonderful earthy flavor.

"Barrone would never be voted Mr. Congeniality, but who'd think someone would actually off the guy. Nothing like this ever happens in Brandywine Creek."

"But it did."

My words dropped like a boulder, squashing further conversation for all of three minutes.

"Soooo . . . ," Reba Mae said, breaking the silence. "Who do you suppose killed Mario?"

"I haven't a clue." I found the idea of a murderer walking the streets of Brandywine Creek a scary one.

"If I had to venture a guess, I'd say it was a botched robbery attempt."

I considered the possibility. The more I thought about it, the more I warmed to the notion. "You might be on to something, Reba Mae. Picture this: it's late at night, Mario's alone. Most likely he still hasn't deposited the day's receipts. The . . . perp . . . cut through the alley, saw a light on in the Tratory, forced his way in. And the rest, as they say, is history."

"Yeah, that might explain it," Reba Mae agreed. "Probably someone zoned out on drugs."

"Could have been a drifter passing through town."

"Someone needing quick cash."

"Or looking to score," I said, borrowing a

phrase I'd heard on numerous TV cop shows.

"Makes sense."

Then doubts started corroding my perfect scenario. "Wouldn't a robber likely carry a weapon of some sort?"

Reba Mae nodded sagely. "A .44. Maybe a .357."

I stared at Reba Mae incredulously. "Since when did you become an expert on guns?"

She shrugged, but made no effort to hide her smirk. "Sheesh, Piper, I grew up in the South. Butch taught the twins to shoot soon as they were big enough to hold a gun. Took 'em huntin' once they were old enough to get licenses. Both Clay and Caleb own pistols. Like to talk weapons. I'm thinking of gettin' one myself and applyin' for a concealed weapons permit. Some manufacturers even make ladies' guns with pretty pink grips."

"Well, I'll be." I shook my head in wonderment. Who was this stranger with the magenta hair and her talk of guns? You think you know someone well, then bam! Suddenly you see a whole different side of them.

"I'm dead serious, Piper. You oughta think about it, too."

"No way am I ever going to own a gun.

I'd probably end up shooting myself in the foot."

"Never say never," Reba Mae counseled. "If Mario had had a gun handy he might not be layin' on a slab at the coroner's this very minute."

"But if the robber had a gun, why didn't he shoot Mario instead of stab him?" There went those pesky doubts again.

"Good point. Unless —"

"He didn't have a gun after all," I said, cutting her off mid-sentence. "What if . . . Mario interrupted some creep trying to steal him blind. He grabbed a knife to defend himself, and . . ."

". . . the thief turned it on him instead."

Proud of our powers of deduction, we high-fived. "We'd make a fine pair of detectives."

"We could call ourselves Spice and Klassy, sort like that old TV show *Starsky and Hutch*. Or am I thinking of *Cagney and Lacey*?"

"More like Lucy and Ethel," I said, stifling a yawn.

"Well," Reba Mae said, undeterred, "if the culprit's obvious to us, he ought to be obvious to McBride, too."

Easing myself out of the chair, I shoved my feet into sandals. "I hope you're right. I've had all the drama this girl can stand for a day. I'm exhausted."

Reba Mae picked up the nacho platter and headed toward the kitchen, with me close at her heels carrying the glasses. "Glad tomorrow's Sunday, and we both have a day off."

As I put the glasses in the dishwasher, I noticed a smudge of black fingerprint ink around the nail bed of my index finger. "I still haven't checked today's receipts or restocked supplies."

"It'll keep, sugar." Reba Mae walked me to the door and gave me a hug. "Wait 'n see. Things'll look brighter after a good night's sleep. McBride will find whoever offed Mario, and all your problems will be solved."

In spite of being bone weary, I tossed and turned, finally falling into a deep sleep in the wee hours before dawn. Next time I looked at the alarm clock on my bedside stand, it was after ten. Drat! I not only missed church services, but would be subjected to Melly's tight-lipped disapproval — again. Times like this, I wondered if CJ was ever on the receiving end of his mother's censure. I knew for a fact that Melly was unhappy with his recent behavior. Bad enough he'd created a scandal by divorcing his faithful and loving wife — that would be *moi* — but he'd taken up with Miss Amber Leigh Ames, former beauty pageant winner, a woman nearly half his age. No, Melly Prescott wasn't happy with her only child.

After a quick shower, I dressed for comfort in black yoga leggings, a lavender cami under an oversized shirt with dolman sleeves, and a pair of flats. For breakfast, I ground French vanilla coffee beans I'd been hoarding for a special treat and enjoyed a cup along with a blueberry muffin seasoned with citrusy Ceylon cinnamon.

Before going down to my shop, I dialed Pets 'R People for news of the pup I'd rescued. The phone rang and rang, then went to voice mail. I left a message for Doug — I felt assisting in emergency surgery qualified us to be on a first name basis — and asked him to call me. I squelched my vague unease at not being able to reach him, telling myself it was silly to expect to find him sitting by the phone on this lovely April Sunday. I'd try again later.

Filling a mug of fresh brew, I went downstairs and looked around. Instead of the upheaval I half-expected, I found Spice It Up! neat as a pin. The yellow bib aprons were folded on a shelf under the counter. The jars of spices were perfectly aligned. Credit card receipts, I noted, had been arranged alphabetically. Master Charge in one pile, Visa in another. I caught myself smiling. I should have known. Leave it to Melly, my borderline OCD ex-mother-in-law, to take command. My smile widened when I read the message she'd left taped next to the cash register, explaining she'd taken it upon herself to rearrange the stock in the Hoosier cabinet. Her way was much more efficient — or so she claimed.

Against my better judgment — I didn't want to be a pest — I called the vet's office one more time. Still no answer. Disappointed, I hung up and set to work.

A handful of this, a cupful of that. Spicy sweet cinnamon, tangy cloves, licoricelike star anise, Szechwan peppercorns: I poured all of the ingredients into a coffee mill, which I reserved exclusively for grinding spices. When finished, I'd have my very own blend of spices, which worked great as a rub on baby back ribs and also with chicken and pork dishes. Between the disco music blaring through the earbuds of a hand-me-down MP3 player — CJ had replaced Lindsey's with a fancier iPod version — and the *whirr* of the coffee mill, I almost didn't hear someone bang on the front door. I hurried to answer and found Wyatt McBride standing there.

Not even the make-you-want-to-dance Bee Gees music was an antidote against the lawman I'd quickly come to regard as toxic. "You . . . again?"

"Going to invite me in, or not?"

I stared up at him, not answering. Did that mean I had a choice? He was the last person on earth I wanted to see. That might be a cliché, but it best described how I felt.

Reaching out, he removed the earbuds from my ears. "I asked if you were going to invite me in," he repeated, apparently not attuned to my inner debate. Or chosing to ignore it.

I stepped aside. "What do you want, McBride? I told you everything yesterday."

"Thought I'd let you know your prints have been sent to the GBI. We should have the results soon."

"You came here to tell me that?" I stalked back to the counter where I'd been working. "Of course, you'll have a match. I already told you I found the darn knife."

He picked up a jar of cloves, took a whiff, and set it down. "You also mentioned you found a dog. Took her to the vet."

"Took *him* to the vet," I corrected. "The dog was a he, not a she."

"Sure you don't want to change your story?"

I started to fill one of the small Ziploc bags with my concoction, but noticed my hands were shaking, so I stopped before spilling everything all over the floor. "Change my story . . . ? Why would I want to do that?"

Folding his arms across his chest, he stared down at me, his gaze cool and assessing. "I drove out to the place you told me about — Pets 'R People on Old County Road."

He let the statement hang, let it dangle, wanted to see me sweat. And I didn't disappoint. The direction in which this conversation was heading made me a trifle nervous. But I didn't want to give him the satisfaction of knowing that.

"Stop playing games, McBride." Hands on hips, I assumed a belligerent stance. My shirt slipped down one shoulder, and I resisted the urge to tug it back in place. "Say what you came here to say and let me get back to work."

"Pets 'R People was locked tighter than a drum. And the vet was nowhere in sight."

I gestured wildly. "It's Sunday. Dr. Winters might have gone for a drive. Or maybe he was invited out for dinner."

"That was my first thought too, until . . ."

"Until . . . ?"

"I found a note on the office door. Apparently, Winters left town and took your alibi with him."

I gasped in disbelief. "That can't be."

"It not only can be, but is."

This scrap of information knocked me for a loop. I felt the same out-of-breath sensation I'd experienced when CJ and I took the kids to Six Flags over Georgia, and I'd let my son dare me into going on a thrill ride that featured a twenty-story free fall.

"If there's something you're holding back, now might be a good time to come clean."

"What about the puppy I told you about?"

"Gone, just like the vet. Vanished without a trace."

"I *told* you the truth about what happened. Are you insinuating I'm a liar? How dare you?" I asked, not caring if I sounded like an outraged virgin in some paperback novel.

He shrugged but didn't reply.

"You're wasting valuable time checking out my perfectly good alibi when you should be hunting down Mario's killer." I turned and poured a generous portion of peppercorns into a second spice mill. "If it's obvious to Reba Mae and me what happened, surely a big-city cop like you shouldn't have a problem figuring it out."

110

He moved close enough for me to smell the piney tang of his aftershave. "I'd like to hear this theory you and your girlfriend cooked up."

I huffed out a breath, and added a few whole cloves to the mix I was preparing. "Reba Mae and I think Mario Barrone was killed during a botched robbery. That the killer was some druggie. A stranger passing through town who needed money for a quick score. Mario grabbed a knife to defend himself, and, well, you know the rest."

"Mmm, interesting," he murmured. "Except for two things."

My head jerked around. He had my full attention. "What two things?"

"No money was missing. The night's cash was still there, ready to be deposited at the bank."

"Maybe the thief got scared and ran off without it," I offered. "What's the second reason?"

"There were no defensive wounds found on the body. From everything I learned about the man, Barrone wasn't the type to give up without a struggle."

Hmm. So much for the botched-robbery theory — and back to square one, which left me top billing on McBride's parade of suspects. I decided to try a different tack. "I was depending on Barrone's cooking demo to attract a slew of potential customers. Why would I kill the guy?"

"That's what I intend to find out," he said, giving me a hard look. Then he turned and left the shop.

Without thinking, I added more black peppercorns to the spice concoction and switched on the grinder. As it began to hum, I told myself that McBride had been bluffing. Trying to get me to confess to a crime I didn't commit. It would behoove him as the brand-new chief of police to solve this case ASAP and get on with the business of writing out parking tickets.

I pondered my dilemma. Purely because of circumstance, I was the prime suspect in a murder case. Now my life, my reputation, as well as my livelihood were at stake. Knowing this frightened me, but as I thought about the unfairness of the situation, fright gradually turned into outrage. I didn't kill Mario, but whoever did was walking around footloose and fancy-free while I squirmed like a bug under a microscope. Flicking off the grinder, I placed both hands on my hips and scowled. Seems I had a choice to make. I could either sit meek as a mouse — or I could take matters into my own hands and do a little investigating on my own.

The little Ziploc bags piled in front of me would have to wait until later to be filled with jerk rub. Right now a more urgent matter needed my attention.

Jumping into my car, I headed out of town. Before I knew it, I was on Old County Road and turning down the drive leading to Pets 'R People. I braked in front of the clinic. The place had a deserted air about it. On my last visit here, in spite of my panic, I'd noticed an SUV parked to one side of the drive. There was no sign of it now. I got out of my VW and approached the office warily. Doug had a thriving veterinary practice. He couldn't simply "vanish without a trace" like McBride had intimated.

But according to the note taped to the door — "Out of town. Family emergency" — that's exactly what he'd done. And along with him, my alibi had vanished as well.

CHAPTER 10

Nothing like a good funeral to bring out the Who's Who of Brandywine Creek society, I mused the following Wednesday. The last notes of "Amazing Grace" had scarcely faded at First Baptist Church before folks hopped into their cars and headed for the VFW Hall. The Thursday night Bingo ladies had volunteered to oversee the event. Even before the last folding chair had been unfolded, the finest in Southern cuisine had begun arriving in covered dishes. The crowd represented an eclectic blend that included the butcher, the baker, and the undertaker. Die and they will come, to paraphrase a movie tag line. No one, it seemed, wanted to pass up a free lunch.

"The joint's jumping," Dottie Hemmings commented to no one in particular as she made a beeline for the buffet table.

"The VFW hasn't seen this much activity since the Brandywine Creek Twirlers placed third in the state semifinals," Reba Mae commented as, smiling and nodding, we wended our way through the crowd.

"People still talk about how Shelly Anne Bixby dropped her flaming baton and caught the high school gym on fire."

"Lucky her dad's a volunteer firefighter and was standing by with the hook and ladder," Reba Mae said as we skirted a trio hell-bent on beating a path to the dessert table. "Any word yet when the vet's going to return?"

"Not a peep."

"What do you s'pose 'family emergency' means?"

I shrugged, hoping to convey the impression that my lack of an alibi wasn't a cause for concern. Truth was, it was keeping me awake at night. "Your guess is as good as mine."

"What do you think happened to that dog you found?"

"I don't know what to think." I sighed. "I've been driving out to the clinic every day after closing in the hope of finding Doug home — not to mention filling up his answering machine with messages."

Reba Mae shot me a look of sympathy, then tugged the sleeve of my black wraparound dress. "C'mon, there's Uncle Joe.

Wouldn't seem right if I didn't say hey."

"Hullo, darlin'." Joe gave Reba Mae the best squeeze his pot belly would allow, then turned to me. "Hullo, Piper."

"Chief." His greeting seemed less effusive than usual, but maybe all this finding a dead body stuff was making me paranoid.

"Not chief of police anymore. Handed in the title when I handed in my badge," he said, smoothing his wildly patterned tie. "There's a new kid on the block now."

"Uncle Joe, your replacement has got me worried." Reba Mae rested her hand on his arm and all but batted her eyelashes. "Surely the man can't think for a second that Piper had anythin' to do with Mario Barrone dyin'?"

"Sorry, Reba Mae. The man's gotta go where the evidence leads. That's how big-city detectives like McBride are trained these days. And speak of the devil, there he is now."

Reba Mae and I turned in unison. There he was, all right. Wyatt McBride in the flesh, standing alone just inside the entrance. He'd traded in his uniform for a navy blazer, khaki pants, pale blue dress shirt, and tie. And looked better than a man had a right to look to a divorced woman who'd sworn off men for life.

"Ooowee!" Reba Mae fanned herself with her free hand. "Think I'm having a hot flash."

"Too much information for an old codger like me," Joe chuckled. "Now if you two ladies will kindly excuse me, I'm going to avail myself of some of these fine vittles. Maybe a nice thick slice of that honey-glazed ham to go along with some of Miss Melly's tomato aspic. Might even sample one or two of Cousin Bitsy's deviled eggs."

As he strolled off, I saw McBride step in my direction. "Reba Mae, I need to visit the little girls' room," I improvised. "Catch up with you later."

I darted off in the general direction of the restroom, leaving my friend to fend for herself. No better than she deserved for having a hot flash — or lust flash — over my sworn nemesis.

Preoccupied with making my getaway, I narrowly avoided crashing into Diane Cloune, the councilman's wife, and her pal Vicki Lamont. Thankfully the pair was too immersed in their discussion to notice. Diane patted Vicki's shoulder in a consoling manner. Next I saw her hand Vicki a fistful of tissues. Sniffing back tears, Vicki dabbed her eyes, careful not to smudge her mascara. At least one person was genuinely upset at

Mario's passing, I thought to myself as I continued my retreat.

I didn't get far before being waylaid by Dottie Hemmings, who stood talking with Ned Feeney. "Hey there, Piper," Dottie said, beaming. "Nice service, wasn't it?"

"The Eternal Rest gives the best." Ned was quoting his employer's motto. Funeral or not, he wore his signature ball cap.

"However" — Dottie wagged her head sorrowfully — "as I said to my husband, the mayor, it's hard to get teary-eyed an' all staring at an urn. I may be old-fashioned, but I'll take a casket any day. What about you, Piper? Cremation or casket?"

"Er . . ." The question stopped me cold. "I confess, I really haven't given the matter much thought."

"You shouldn't put these things off, dear, regardless how unpleasant. Just think, Mario could have ended six feet under instead of sitting on a pedestal."

"Barrone's was the fanciest urn we stock at Eternal Rest. Cost a pretty penny." Ned tugged his hairy earlobe. "Yes sirree bob, a pretty penny."

Dottie nodded knowingly. "Mario must have kept his insurance premiums up to date. I hope you have life insurance, Piper. One minute you're fixing meat loaf, the

118

next" — she snapped her fingers — "someone sticks a knife in your gullet."

A surreptitious glance over my shoulder showed McBride making progress in my direction. I heaved a sigh of relief when I saw Dottie's husband, Harvey, corner him. Harvey Hemmings could filibuster with the best of them. Some believe that's why he runs unopposed year after year. It's easier to vote for him than to listen to him rattle on about why you should.

"If you'll both excuse me, I want to have a word with the Deltorros," I said, slipping away from Dottie and Ned. I didn't especially wish to speak with the owners of the Pizza Palace, but the couple was strategically the farthest away from where Hizzoner had corralled McBride.

"Hey, you two," I said by way of greeting.

"Hey, yourself," Gina, the more outgoing of the pair, said with a smile. In spite of the fact that Gina Deltorro's once voluptuous figure had fallen prey to a diet of pizza, pasta, and Italian subs, she remained strikingly pretty with her dark eyes and jet-black hair.

Tony merely grunted, his attention elsewhere. His eyes kept sweeping the crowd as if searching for someone. Though dark and slick and Italian, Tony Deltorro didn't pos-

119

sess Mario Barrone's matinee-idol looks. Still, the pizza man cooked up a mean marinara with just the right blend of herbs and spices. His calzones weren't too shabby, either. I made a mental note to drop off a sample of freshly ground cumin seeds.

"Must've been awful," Gina continued, "what with finding Mario's body and all." She scooped a forkful of chocolate chess pie, a classic Southern sweet, into her mouth. "If it'd been me, I would've screamed bloody murder."

Mention of the deceased snagged Tony's wandering attention. "Bloody murder is precisely what Piper stumbled upon," he replied with thinly veiled sarcasm. "I doubt Barrone will be missed."

I sneaked another look in McBride's direction, and he caught me peeking. I quickly turned back to Tony. "Why do you say that?" I asked, feigning interest.

"Barrone suffered delusions of grandeur. The fool thought his food was better than everybody else's. It was just a matter of time before he fell flat on his face."

"Hush, honey," Gina murmured, "it's bad luck to speak ill of the dead."

Tony brushed aside his wife's admonishment with a wave of his hand. "The man was a pompous ass. All he ever did was crow about opening a four-star restaurant in Atlanta or Charlotte. The competition there would eat him alive. He'd have been bankrupt within a month."

Tell me how you really feel? I wanted to say, but didn't. Instead, I asked, "If you didn't like him, why come to his funeral?"

"Tony and Mario go way back," Gina explained. "They had big plans once . . ."

"Gina, did I ever tell you that you talk too much?" Taking his wife by the arm, Tony steered her away.

Hmm.

"Piper Prescott," Reba Mae scolded. "Shame on you for abandonin' me." She handed me a cup of fruit punch. "Take a gander over there, will you?"

Turning, I observed Dwayne Cloune, local entrepreneur and city councilman, approach an elderly gentleman ensconced in the only chair in the room that didn't fold like a pretzel. A much-used walker was parked at his side. With his high forehead, sharp nose, and narrow face, Dwayne always put me in mind of a fox, clever and cunning.

"Is that old coot who I think it is?" Reba Mae whispered.

"Yep." I nodded. "Brig Abernathy making one of his rare appearances."

The man's age could have been anywhere between eighty and a hundred. He was thin to the point of emaciation, with sharp cheekbones and a bold nose. Snowy wisps of hair protruded from a shiny scalp speckled with liver spots.

"Haven't seen Brig in years. Thought he must've died, and I missed the party."

I took a sip of punch. "He's become something of a recluse of late. Poor health, rarely ventures out. CJ used to do some legal work for him; still might for all I know."

"Rumor's flyin' around that Dwayne intends to make a run for the state legislature. He's startin' to accumulate funds. I'm not sure, but I think the pair are distant relatives. Brig's related to more folks in town than Uncle Joe. The Abernathys can trace their roots back to the beginning of time. Do you think Dwayne is hittin' him up for a campaign contribution?"

"Fat chance of that happening," I said with a laugh. "From CJ's comments, the old guy is loaded, but a real Scrooge when it comes to parting with his money."

"Well, whatever Dwayne is sellin', it doesn't look like Brig is buyin'. Good thing he has better luck peddlin' used cars."

"Pre-owned," I corrected absently, referring to Dwayne's primary business, although I knew he also dabbled in real estate.

"Diane ought to enjoy life in Atlanta. The woman spends half her time there anyway. Gives me a headache, listenin' to her go on about the shoppin' in Buckhead, the plays at the Fox, all the trendy restaurants." Reba Mae pointed to a young couple seated at a nearby table. "Well now, isn't that just the sweetest thing," she cooed.

I shifted to see Marcy Magruder and Danny Boyd huddled together. Danny had fixed a plate of food and was coaxing Marcy to take a bite.

"They make the cutest couple. See how he waits on her hand and foot."

"Well, I'm happy Marcy's finally over the stomach flu."

"Stomach flu? Sugar, where have you been?" Reba Mae stared at me in amazement. "The girl wasn't down with no flu bug. She's preggers. Two or three months along."

I felt like a fool. I'd been so focused on my own problems it simply hadn't occurred to me that the girl might be pregnant. My biggest problem being a handsome lawman who didn't believe my alibi. Glancing McBride's way, I saw that he finally succeeded in disengaging himself from the loquacious mayor.

"I'm famished," I said, grabbing Reba Mae's arm. "Let's hit the buffet table while there's any food left."

"Fine by me, but I'll have to eat quick. I have to get back to the shop in time to do highlights."

"That works for me. I left a note on the door saying Spice It Up! would reopen at two."

We headed for the buffet. Luckily there was no line since most of the people had already consumed their fill of casseroles and side dishes. Reba Mae and I piled Styrofoam plates with the best Southern kitchens had to offer. Glazed ham, mac and cheese, mashed sweet potatoes, green bean casserole, cornbread, the works. Our plates loaded, we found ourselves a quiet spot in a corner half hidden behind an artificial ficus.

"With all the healthy choices, such as my tomato aspic, I simply don't understand why folks gobble up Becca Dapkins's green bean casserole. Everyone knows Becca's heavy on the cream soup — and not a fat-free version, either."

Hearing my ex-mother-in-law's voice, I looked up and found her standing in front of us, perfectly groomed, wearing timeless black Chanel and her ever-present pearls. "Hello, Melly," I said. "Care to join us?" I secretly hoped she'd refuse. But my luck was in its usual state — absent.

"Well, maybe just for a minute or two, dear," she said, easing herself into the chair next to Reba Mae. "Hope you didn't mind me rearranging some of your spices the other day."

I forced a smile. "Of course not."

"You get your best food at funerals, don't you think?" Reba Mae commented, sensing tension. "This your tomato pie, Piper? It's delish."

"I added a teaspoon of curry along with the mayonnaise."

"Curry?" Melly frowned. "Those spicy dishes don't agree with my digestion."

Speaking of digestion, make mine indigestion, I thought as Wyatt McBride appeared seemingly out of nowhere, holding a plate with a slab of coconut cake the size of Kansas.

"Mind if I join you ladies?" Not giving us time to refuse, he plunked himself down next to me. "Good cake," he said, spearing a chunk.

Melly smiled and nodded. "Lottie Smith's Can't-Die-Without-It Coconut Cake is always a big hit at funerals. Piper," she said, turning her attention back to me, "you need to convince Lottie to use the vanilla from that little store of yours instead of the awful imitation stuff she buys by the gallon at one of those wholesale warehouses."

I fiddled with my butter beans. "Yes, ma'am."

"Quite a turnout," McBride remarked.

"You've been in the big city too long, young man. You've forgotten folks in small towns come out for their own."

"Who knew Mario was *this* popular?" Reba Mae said, in a valiant attempt to relieve the awkward silence that followed Melly's comment.

"Who knew," I echoed.

"Well, I, for one, think it's mighty gracious of Piper to not only attend Mario's funeral, but to bring her tomato pie. Especially in light of the huge argument they had the very day he got himself killed."

McBride stopped eating cake. "Argument . . . ?"

"It was nothing, really." I wished I could disappear in a puff of smoke.

"Oh, you're wrong, dear. It happened right out on Main Street," Melly elaborated. "I must've heard about the ruckus from at least three different people."

"This is the first I've heard. Care to tell me what it was about?" McBride's cool blues cut through me like Luke Skywalker's laser.

I shrugged, busy making furrows through my sweet potato casserole. "Mario threatened to cancel his cooking demo at the last minute. I persuaded him to change his mind. Like I said, it was nothing."

"I'm certain everyone will tell you that Mario had quite a temper," Melly persisted, then gave me a sweet smile. "And Piper does, too — when provoked. It comes with being a redhead."

The indigestion gnawed yet another hole in my stomach. And I couldn't blame it on Becca Dapkins's green bean casserole.

CHAPTER 11

"Mo-om," Lindsey wailed. "All my friends are going."

"All your friends aren't failing math. You are," I reminded her. "If that's not bad enough, your language arts teacher stopped by today and mentioned you haven't even started a report that's due on Monday."

Teenage daughters, I've observed, often tend to make their mothers out to be more wicked than the Wicked Witch of the West. Especially when they can't get their own way. Lindsey, unfortunately, was no exception.

"I hate Mrs. Walker."

"I thought you liked her."

"I used to, but she's always picking on me."

I glanced up from the spice catalog I was thumbing through. Grilling season was getting underway, and the chamber of commerce had set the date for the Brandywine

Creek annual BBQ cook-off. I planned to do an eye-catching display featuring grilling spices: Cajun, Jerk, as well as one of my own special blends, which was heavy on coriander and paprika for a mildly spicy but intensely aromatic rub that's terrific on both ribs and chicken. "Perhaps Mrs. Walker wouldn't 'pick' on you if you completed your assignments on time."

"But Mom . . ."

I held up my hand to forestall the storm I saw brewing. "Just food for thought."

"The Wipeouts are only going to be in town one night. Taylor's father has a friend who works at Bell Auditorium and can get us tickets close to the stage."

I'd never heard of The Wipeouts until now, but judging from Lindsey and her friends' taste in music, my guess would be that they were an alternative rock group. "Unless it moved, last I heard Bell Auditorium is in Augusta. That's a good hour's drive late at night."

"Taylor's a great driver. She's never put a single dent in the bumper," Lindsey said, rushing to defend her BFF. "Besides, Taylor said I could spend the night at her place."

I sighed wearily. Lindsey and I had been going around and around on the subject ever since she came here after school. Since

CJ had been in Charlotte all week attending a litigation seminar, Lindsey was camping out at my place. Not that CJ needed any help in the litigation department. When it came to slip and falls, he was smooth as the ice his clients claimed they fell on. He was due back soon. He'd called to say he'd take Lindsey out for dinner. The time with my daughter had been . . . less than stellar. Lindsey was either talking on her cell phone, at the computer, or listening to music. So much for the mother-daughter bonding I'd hoped for. It didn't help matters any that I was preoccupied with Doug Winters's whereabouts. It made me nervous knowing my fingerprints were on the murder weapon.

And I still didn't have an alibi.

Well, technically I did have an alibi, but it did me little good since it couldn't be confirmed. Where could Doug have disappeared? Did he take the pup with him? Or . . . ? I didn't want to think of the other possibility.

Lindsey flicked a feather duster lackadaisically over various types of salt and peppercorns. "Jason Wainwright asked me to prom."

"That's great, honey!" I exclaimed. CJ and Jason's father, Matt, were law partners. We often socialized with his parents. Jason was basically a good kid, but going through a "phase." Blame my lack of enthusiasm on my not being a big fan of tattoos and piercings. A sign of old age? I reminded myself to be more open-minded about these things and to simply remember that Jason was a decent young man from a fine family.

"Yeah, well, now I need to shop for a dress."

Happier than I'd been since discovering Mario's body, I grinned at the prospect of shopping with my daughter for the perfect prom dress. "We'll make a day of it. We can drive to a mall in either Augusta or Atlanta, shop, have lunch, maybe take in a movie. I'll ask Marcy to mind the shop. She needs the money now that she's expecting and planning a wedding and all."

Lindsey stopped dusting and looked at me. "Um, Mom, that's what I wanted to talk to you about."

"About Marcy?" I closed the spice catalog. "This sounds serious."

"No . . . about shopping for prom. Amber offered to take me."

My heart sank. I swear I could actually feel it drop to my knees. "Amber . . . ?"

"Amber's taste in clothes is absolutely amazing," Lindsey rushed on. "And since

131

we're closer in age, she actually remembers what it's like to be sixteen."

It's hard to speak after you've had the wind knocked out of you. Amber Leigh Ames was a thorn in my side. Not only had she usurped my place in CJ's affections, now she was trying to insinuate her way into my daughter's as well.

"Amber knows all the managers in all the coolest shops from her pageant days. She said they'd probably give me a discount."

"And Amber can walk on water," I muttered under my breath. It so happens, Amber Leigh Ames, the bane of my existence, was Brandywine County's former Miss Peach Blossom and first runner-up in the Miss Georgia Pageant. Privately, I referred to her as Miss Peach Pit. Amber was a role model for many local teen girls, my daughter among them. Could the week get any worse? I asked myself. But I didn't have to wait long for the answer.

The front door swung open and in walked Wyatt McBride, accompanied by Beau Tucker and a third policeman I'd seen before, but didn't know by name. Beau and Officer Unibrow both avoided meeting my eyes.

"If you boys are looking to buy spices, make it quick. It's nearly closing time."

McBride held out an official-looking document. "Search warrant."

If my heart dropped to my knees before, it now landed on the floor. "A search warrant?" I repeated, though it was hard to form words when my lips felt numb. "Surely, you can't be serious."

"Do I look like I'm joking?"

That had to be the finest example of understatement I'd ever heard. I've seen people less solemn at a funeral.

Lindsey watched our exchange wide-eyed. "M-mom, you okay?"

"Fine, honey," I murmured. I grabbed the warrant from McBride's hand and pretended to read it but, in my befuddled state, the legalese failed to register.

"Tucker, take the downstairs," McBride ordered crisply. "Moyer," he said, turning to Officer Unibrow, "you and I will search upstairs."

"Sorry, Piper." Beau Tucker sent me a sheepish look, then set about searching through cupboards and drawers, looking for what, I had no idea.

I felt sick to my stomach knowing the same was going on upstairs. A shudder of revulsion rippled through me at the thought of McBride pawing through my underwear drawers — an invasion of privacy of the worst kind.

"Mom . . . are you going to let them get away with this?" Lindsey cried. "Call Daddy. He'll know what to do."

I shook my head, stubborn to a fault. "I *didn't* do anything wrong. I *don't* need a lawyer."

No sooner had the words left my mouth when CJ steamed through the door.

"Hey, baby," he beamed, addressing Lindsey, ignoring me. "Got the text message you sent. Of course, you can go to the concert. Wouldn't want you to miss out on havin' yourself a good time."

I caught the look on Lindsey's face, part guilt, part triumph. The child was growing quite adept at pitting one parent against the other. That nasty little habit needed to be nipped in the bud.

Folding my arms across my chest, I glared at CJ. "There, you're doing it again. Undermining my authority with our daughter. Whenever I say no, Lindsey goes straight to you. What about her report for language arts? Its due Monday and counts for nearly half her grade. She hasn't even started it yet."

"Don't be so uptight, Scooter darlin'. The girl's got all day Sunday to work on that damn paper. Amber can help her if she needs it."

"Amber Leigh Ames barely squeaked through finishing school," I reminded him angrily.

CJ conveniently forgot concerts, failing grades, and Miss Peach Pit when he spied his poker-playing buddy emerge from the storeroom. "Hey there, Beau. Saw a couple police cruisers at the curb. Some cook need cinnamon and decide to rob the place?" He laughed heartily at his own joke, and seemed surprised when no one joined in.

Beau cleared his throat. "Chief got Judge Herman to issue a search warrant."

"Why'd he go do a crazy thing like that?"

"Have to ask the chief."

CJ turned to me, his face flushed. "I warned you, Scooter! The man has it in for me. Has ever since high school. Can't say I'm surprised he's hasslin' you — you're a Prescott."

"Hate to disappoint you, CJ," McBride said as he came down the stairs, "but this has nothing to do with you — and everything to do with your wife."

"Ex," I corrected. "Make that ex-wife."

The two men stood almost toe to toe, sizing each other up, gauging the changes the years had wrought. As much as I disliked McBride, he won the competition hands down. He was trim, fit, and still possessed good looks in abundance. To be fair, however, I had to give CJ points for trying. His teeth were a dazzling white that God never intended. His hair was styled, not merely cut, and restored to its original gold brilliance. His suit screamed designer and so did his pricey cologne. A girlfriend practically half his age added to his cache in the good ol' boys club.

"Why, Judge Herman's known my family for years. Dated my mother way back when. What trumped-up excuse did you use to strong-arm him to issue a warrant?"

"Gentlemen." I cleared my throat. "Need I remind you, you're no longer in high school." Turning to McBride, I said, "If you and your men are finished, I'd like you to leave so I can put my home back in order."

He held up a bag marked EVIDENCE. "I'm afraid it's not going to work that way."

Lindsey edged closer to my side. "Mom, what did the police find? What's in the bag?"

I tried to think what they might have discovered, then groaned aloud when the answer came to me with knock-the-breath-out-of-you clarity.

"Care to explain the bloodstained shirt and bath towel we found in the trash?"

My mouth was suddenly as dry as burnt

toast. "I know this looks bad, but it's not what you think."

"Then enlighten me."

CJ's head swiveled back and forth between us in a fair imitation of a spectator at Wimbledon. "What's the guy talkin' about, Scooter?"

I moistened my lips with the tip of my tongue, then directed my next words at McBride. Beau Tucker and his cohort listened with undisguised curiosity. "We've been over this before, McBride. I told you. I found a small dog, hurt and bleeding, outside my shop the night of the murder. I did what any person would do. I wrapped him in a towel and raced him to the vet's."

McBride widened his stance, his expression set. "That explains the blood on the towel, but not the shirt."

"Are you dense?" I asked, exasperated that I had to spell it out for him when it should be crystal clear. "Apparently, I got blood on my shirt when I assisted Dr. Winters putting a chest tube in the dog."

"A dog?" Lindsey asked. Forget about the bloodstains, I thought, "dog" was the only word that had lodged in Lindsey's consciousness. "Mom, why didn't you tell me you had a dog?"

"I don't *have* a dog. I *found* a dog. There's

a difference," I pointed out.

She tugged on my sleeve. "Is he all right? Are you going to keep it?"

"Honey, right now, I have no intention of owning a pet," I explained as gently as I could, knowing how much my daughter loved animals and hating to disappoint her. CJ and I had argued endlessly on the merits of owning a pet, always with the same results. CJ wanted nothing to do with cats or dogs. He claimed he had allergies to both. And that, as they say, was that.

Placing my hand on Lindsey's back, I made small circles like I used to do when she and Chad were my babies. "The dog was scarcely more than a pup, a mutt actually. I'm afraid he was seriously injured. At this point, honey, I have no idea whether he survived or not."

"Hmph!" Officer Moyer snorted. "A likely story."

"Quiet," McBride growled, and the policeman lapsed into a sullen silence.

"It seems the vet was called away on a family emergency so I have no way of knowing the outcome," I said, in an attempt to clarify the situation.

"No alibi, eh?" CJ shoved his hands into pants pockets. "Not looking good, Scooter."

"Dammit, CJ," I flared. "Tell me something I don't know."

"Ma'am," McBride interrupted the potential feud. "You need to come down to the station with me for further questioning."

"Am I under arrest?" I was embarrassed to hear the quiver in my voice.

"Depends on how the questioning goes."

"Daddy," Lindsey squealed. "Don't just stand there! Do something."

"Sure thing, baby." CJ drew on his meager theatrical talent to appear concerned. "Scooter darlin', don't say a word without an attorney present."

"You her attorney, Prescott?" McBride wanted to know.

"Sorry, that rules me out." CJ shed McBride's question as easily as water off a duck's back. "I'd be more than happy to offer representation, but considerin' our history together, it's probably not a wise decision. Unfortunately, what my ex-wife needs is a criminal lawyer. Not my area of expertise."

"Thanks," I muttered as McBride led me away.

CHAPTER 12

McBride propelled me past Precious Blessing, who seemed engrossed in the nail art on her index finger, and down a short hallway. "Why are you doing this to me?" I asked.

"Doing what?"

"Treating me as though I'm a murder suspect."

"Don't make this personal."

I thought I detected a flicker of regret in McBride's icy blues, but it vanished so quickly I thought maybe I'd imagined it.

"I'm only doing the job the good citizens of Brandywine Creek hired me to do." He opened the door of a small windowless room and motioned me inside. "Have a seat. I'll be right back."

The room was bare except for a narrow table and two uncomfortable-looking chairs. Dingy beige walls and speckled brown tile comprised the décor du jour.

Too restless to sit, I made laps around the table. Part of me rebelled at the notion that anyone might even remotely think me capable of killing a man. The other part was too frightened to think clearly. I wanted to turn tail and dodge out the back door. I wished I'd never heard of Mario Barrone, much less cajoled him into performing a cooking demo. Now, all because of him and some stupid juniper berries, I was about to be thrown into the slammer.

Tired of pacing, I slumped down in one of the chairs. McBride let me stew for a good fifteen minutes, then returned carrying a tape recorder and a file folder in one hand, a brown bag in the other. If his ploy was to make me nervous, it worked like a charm. If I knew the notes, I'd sing like a canary.

I eyed the recorder warily. "Do I need a lawyer?" I swallowed. "Of the criminal variety?"

"That's up to you," he replied, his tone noncommittal. "You're not under arrest. Just here for questioning."

I crossed my arms over my chest, knowing the gesture was defensive, but didn't care. "I didn't *do* anything. I have nothing to hide."

"Good. Let's get started then, shall we?"

141

"Fine." I sat up straight.

McBride took the chair opposite me and clicked on the recorder, stating our names for the record along with the date and time. This was as official as it gets. Reba Mae was going to get an earful once this was behind me. The two of us would probably share a good laugh comparing reality against TV shows and movies. But this wasn't TV. Wasn't a movie. And I was scared spitless. At what point would McBride read me the Miranda rights? Oh yeah, I remember, when they slap on handcuffs and announce I'm under arrest . . .

. . . for murder.

Unbelievable.

Then fear left me, replaced by red-hot anger. "Why are you wasting your time questioning me when you should be hunting down the real killer?" I demanded.

"Allow me to give you a brief tutorial on the way things work in law enforcement," McBride said, his expression as inscrutable as ever. "At the moment, you happen to be the prime suspect in the death of Mario Barrone. The three fundamentals of a homicide investigation are motive, means, and opportunity. You score high on all three counts."

Generally speaking — with the exception

142

of golf — I like being a high scorer. In this instance, however, I didn't want to be an overachiever. I wanted to retaliate with some smart-aleck remark, but thought it wise to remain silent. Instead, I fixed an unblinking gaze on McBride. For the first time, I was aware of the thin scar bisecting his brow near the corner of his left eye. I shifted uneasily. Too much information. I didn't want to know about his scars. Or wonder if he got them in the line of duty or on the football field.

"First off," he said, unaware of my unruly thoughts, "your prints are a positive match to those on the murder weapon. That provides 'means.' "

"Haven't you been listening?" I snapped. "How many times do I have to tell you I found the knife outside the Tratory? Of course the prints match. Why wouldn't they?"

He leaned back, his eyes never leaving my face. I'd like to think my counterattack caught him off guard, but it was impossible to tell what was going on behind that cop mask of his. "Why in the world would I kill Mario?" I'd discovered asking questions held more appeal than answering them. "I needed Barrone's help to get my shop off to a running start. I was depending on his cooking demonstration to bring in a slew of customers."

"You seemed to handle the demo without his help — more or less."

Narrowing my eyes, I regarded him with suspicion. *Was he poking fun at me?* I wondered, recalling how the juniper paste splattered Bertha Fox minutes before the leg of lamb took flight.

"A number of people witnessed your argument with Barrone just hours before he was killed. Melly Prescott, your former mother-in-law, attests to the fact you have a temper."

"Of course I have a temper," I flared. "I was married to her son, who happened to be cheating on me with Miss Peach Pit. That would be enough to rile Mother Teresa."

"Here's a possible scenario. There was bad blood between you and Barrone as demonstrated by your disagreement. You went to confront him after his restaurant closed for the night. One thing led to another. Things got heated, and the situation got out of control. He ended up dead and you fled the scene."

"Ridiculous!" I scoffed. "Have you ever considered writing fiction?"

He ignored my jibe. "All that goes to supply motive. And last, but by no means least, the third member of the triad — opportunity."

The air in the small room suddenly seemed heavier, harder to breathe. I watched him carefully, dreading what he'd say next. Meanwhile, the tape recorder quietly whirred away. Recording every angry syllable. Every nervous swallow.

McBride opened the file folder and flipped through the pages. "The medical examiner gives the time of death as between ten o'clock and midnight. Need I remind you that you have no alibi for that period of time?"

Bingo! There it was — the elephant in the room.

"You're wrong," I said, with all the bravado I could muster. "I do have an alibi."

"Right." He gave an exaggerated sigh. "Some wild fabrication about finding and taking an injured dog to a vet. Too bad it can't be verified. All we have is your word for it. Thing is, Piper" — he leaned forward, his look intent — "the vet disappeared. No telling when he left — or when he might return. For all I know, he might've been called away on a 'family emergency' days before Mario was killed. To make matters worse, there's no trace of a dog — injured or otherwise."

He paused to let this sink in.

"You need to give it more time. Be more patient. Dr. Winters has a booming practice. He wouldn't just abandon it." I was grasping at straws, and we both knew it.

Reaching down, McBride opened a paper sack and produced the sealed evidence bag I'd first seen in Spice It Up! "As you already know, our search of your apartment uncovered this hidden in the trash."

I huffed out an indignant breath. "It wasn't 'hidden,' it was stuffed. If I'd 'hidden' it, you'd never have found it. But I stuffed it, so you did."

I could see from the pained expression on his face that this interrogation wasn't going exactly according to his game plan. But I wouldn't allow myself to feel sorry for the man, so I resumed attack mode. "You're going to have egg on your face when the lab results prove the blood is canine and not human."

McBride pinched the bridge of his nose between thumb and forefinger and re-grouped. "Piper, are you sure you aren't holding something back? It'll go much easier on you if you just come out with it and admit you killed Barrone. The prosecutor will likely call it a crime of passion and reduce the charge to second degree. After all, you never went to Trattoria Milano intending to kill Barrone. You simply lost your temper and . . ." He shrugged. "These things happen."

I jumped to my feet so suddenly the chair toppled backward. "Are you freaking nuts? I want a lawyer, and I want one now!"

With the racket caused by my shouting and the noise from the chair clattering to the floor, neither of us heard the quiet knock until it was repeated.

"Chief . . . ?" Precious Blessing's muffled voice came through the closed door. "Someone here to see you."

"Tell them to take a number," McBride growled. "I'm busy."

"Er, Chief, I really think you're going to want to talk to 'im."

McBride shot me a look and, rising to his feet, strode toward the door. The instant it opened, a tan ball of fur charged through, trailing a leash. Amid tail wagging and excited barks, the small dog spotted me and vaulted into my arms, covering my face in wet kisses from its raspy pink tongue. I laughed out loud at the exuberant greeting, my mood lighter than it had been in days.

"Easy, boy," I said, stroking the pup's shiny coat. "Easy."

Glancing over the pup's head, I became

147

aware of both Precious Blessing and Doug Winters watching the reunion with varying degrees of amusement. McBride hid his reaction beneath his usual bland expression. Probably displeased to discover his "prime suspect" was no long quite as prime.

"Sorry for any confusion my absence might've caused," Doug Winters said, with an apologetic smile, one I found quite endearing. "I drove here as soon I found the chief's card stuck in the door and listened to Piper's messages. Thought it might be better if I clear this matter up in person rather than with a phone call."

"Since I didn't think you'd mind me interruptin', Chief," Precious said, "I brought along another chair." She uprighted the toppled chair, which I sank onto gratefully, and she placed the other next to it.

After she left, the two men shook hands and introduced themselves while the pup lay curled in my lap and wagged his stubby tail. Running my hand along his side, I felt the newly healed scar and a stiff row of sutures. Thankfully the pup seemed no worse for wear after his close brush with death.

McBride gestured for Doug to take a seat. "For the record, Dr. Winters, can you tell me where you've been for the last week?"

Doug raked his fingers through his silvery mop. "My mother called with news that my father had suffered a massive heart attack. I dropped everything and drove through the night to get to his side."

McBride picked up a pen and made a note of this. "Exactly when was this?"

I breathed a sigh of relief when the date corresponded with what I'd told the chief.

"Do you recall the approximate time of Mrs. Prescott's visit?"

"She must've gotten to the clinic shortly after ten. I remember because the news was still on. It was nearly one in the morning when she left. I tried to convince her that I'd done everything I could, but she insisted on staying until the pup was breathing easier."

I gave McBride my best I-told-you-so smirk, which he studiously ignored. "Since Dr. Winters has corroborated my so-called 'fabrication,' am I free to leave?"

Rotating the pen in his hand end for end, McBride gave me a long, hard look, then turned to Doug. "One more question, Dr. Winters, if you will. Do you happen to recall what Mrs. Prescott was wearing the night in question?"

Doug's brow furrowed, then smoothed. "I

149

believe she had on a green T-shirt and jeans."

I tensed and stopped petting the pup's shaggy fur. Green T-shirt? No doubt the very same one I'd last seen in a bag marked EVIDENCE.

"Do you remember what type of shoes she wore?"

Puzzled, I glanced from one man to the other. What on earth did my shoes have to do with anything?

"Sneakers," Doug replied, sounding confident. "The flat-soled kind women wear for aerobics. I know because my sister's into aerobics big-time."

Setting the pup on the floor, I rose, antsy to get out of the confining room and to draw a breath of fresh air. "Unless you're charging me, I'm out of here."

McBride closed the folder and gave me the evil eye. "You're free to go, but don't leave town without checking with me first."

I couldn't get out of there fast enough. Doug trailed close behind.

"Cute dog," Precious commented as we passed her desk. "My auntie had a schnauzer once. He a schnauzer?"

Doug shook his head. "Nope. This little guy's from a long line of mutts."

"Well, he's a cute little mutt," Precious

said, then looked up at me. "He yours?"

I glanced down into the pup's big brown eyes and felt my heart turn into goo. The little dog gazed back at me with undisguised love and adoration. I wasn't made of stone. I felt my resistance melt like a snow cone at the state fair. "He's mine if no one claims him."

"Congratulations." Grinning, Doug stuck out his hand. "Consider yourself a pet owner."

CHAPTER 13

Attempting to relax after my close encounter of the worst kind, I wriggled deeper into the soft, worn cushions of Reba Mae's sofa while my newly adopted mutt snoozed alongside. A half-finished bottle of wine and an almost empty pizza box rested on the coffee table.

Reba Mae topped off my wine. "Then what happened?"

"Dr. Winters — Doug — asked me out."

Reba Mae's jaw dropped. "No way."

"Way," I answered smugly.

"You go, girl."

"Call it temporary amnesia that made me forget I'd sworn off men. Doug caught me off guard, but I thought to myself, heck, why not." Kicking off my shoes, I propped my feet on a hassock and wiggled my toes. "We're just going for Mexican at North of the Border, not the prom. It's no biggie."

"It *is* a big deal, sugar. How long has it

been since you were on a bona fide date?"

I pulled a face. "Twenty-some years, but who's counting? After the grilling McBride put me through tonight, Doug's offer was balm to my wounded spirit. Imagine McBride thinking me capable of murder."

"That's his job, hon. He's paid to be suspicious."

"Well, his suspicions are wasted on me. He ought to spend his time tracking down the real killer and not harassing innocent citizens. And all because my fingerprints were on the murder weapon."

"Don't forget half the town knows about your argument with Barrone." Reba Mae studied nails painted with a color she called Cat House Carmine. "Like McBride or not, you've got to admit he's got it all over Uncle Joe in the looks department. I bet he could pose for *GQ* if he had half a mind to."

I sipped my wine. "You're welcome to him. I'll take sweet, mild-mannered Dr. Doug, premature gray hair and wire-rimmed glasses, over tall, dark, and dangerous any day of the week."

"You want the last slice of pizza?"

Reaching down, I scratched the pup behind his ear. "Go ahead, you take it."

"Better yet, I'll let the boys fight over it."

"How's Clay's computer class coming

along?" I knew Reba Mae's twins were her pride and joy. I had to hand it to her: she's done a great job raising them since Butch died. Caleb and Clay were the same age as my Chad. The three had been inseparable before Chad, bent on becoming a doctor, headed off to college in Chapel Hill.

"Okay, I guess, but unlike Chad, Clay has no idea what he wants to be when he grows up. For now he's content to work construction, take an occasional night class at the technical college, and leave the more serious stuff to others."

"What about Caleb? He still happy with his job?"

"Dwayne pays him a decent wage as a mechanic at that garage and used-car lot of his."

"Pre-owned," I corrected, more from habit than political correctness.

"Whatever. Long as it doesn't interfere with his bowlin' league, Caleb's not gonna complain."

"You've got great boys, Reba Mae. Except for a couple shenanigans, they've never given you a moment's grief."

"Yeah, you're right. Once in a blue moon they even take out the garbage without being told. If I could only teach 'em to put the toilet seat down, I'd die a happy woman."

"Lindsey's failing language arts," I blurted.

"I thought she was failin' math."

"That, too. According to her language arts teacher, she hasn't even started a report that counts for nearly half her grade."

"CJ know about this?"

"No sooner had I told Lindsey she couldn't go to a concert this weekend when he went right over my head. Said she could write the report on Sunday. That Amber would help her."

Reba Mae gave an unladylike snort. "Amber Leigh? The only writin' that girl does is to sign her name to a credit-card receipt."

That was it in a nutshell. With nothing more to be said about Amber Leigh's writing skills, we lapsed into a companionable silence. My newly acquired pet lazily opened one eye, then promptly closed it again after making sure I hadn't gone off and abandoned him.

Reba Mae aimed a thumb at the pup. "Looks like a dog Butch's cousin had. A wheaten terrier, but it's kinda small for a Wheaton. So what are you goin' to do with your new BFF?"

"Unless someone comes forward to claim him, which is unlikely, he's all mine. Besides, he'll be good company, what with Lindsey spending the majority of her time at CJ's." I reminded myself to speak to CJ regarding the disproportionate amount of time our daughter spent with him. Let him know in no uncertain terms I was unhappy with the present arrangement. That it needed to change. And while I was at it, we needed to establish that when one parent said no, it meant end of discussion.

"A watchdog's not a bad idea with a killer on the loose."

Reba Mae's words struck home and brought me back to the present. With McBride focusing all his attention on me, the real murderer was free to prowl the streets of our peaceful little town. Would there be other victims? I wondered. Or had Mario's death been an isolated "crime of passion"?

I made a mental note to invest in a security system as soon as my finances were in better shape. For the time being, however, a stouter lock on my rear door would have to suffice. A watchdog would also act as a deterrent. I smiled to myself. The little animal napping peacefully at my feet didn't look capable of defending itself against fleas, much less a hardened criminal.

"Well, he's a cute little bugger," Reba Mae

continued, unaware of my worries. "At least you don't have to worry about him leavin' the toilet seat up."

I stared into my half-empty wineglass. "You know, in spite of Doug coming to my rescue in the nick of time, I still don't feel like I'm off the hook."

Reba Mae took oversized gold hoops out of her ears and placed them on the coffee table. "What do you mean?"

"McBride told me the medical examiner puts the time of death between ten and midnight. Technically speaking, I could still have killed Mario, then rushed the dog to the vet's."

Reba Mae stretched her long legs. "Okay," she drawled, "but why would you stab a helpless little animal in the first place?"

Leave it to Reba Mae to find the hole in my logic.

"I wouldn't, of course. Being a 'person of interest' is making me crazy." Frustrated, I ran a hand through my hair, mussing my already messy red curls. "I haven't a clue what goes on inside McBride's head. Maybe he thinks I stabbed the dog to keep him quiet, then in a fit of remorse rushed him to the vet's to save his life. The man's so intent on me being the guilty party, he's not even looking for any other suspects."

Reba Mae gave me a hard stare. "What are you gettin' at?"

I blew out a breath. "I'm worried that since McBride is a stranger in Brandywine Creek, he might not ask the right people the right questions. As the newly appointed chief of police, he must feel compelled to wrap this case up quick. He needs to look good in front of Mayor Hemmings and the town council."

"I'm not sure where you're headin' with this, honeybun. Care to enlighten me?"

An idea, although vague, was starting to form in the recesses of my brain. "I think he needs help is all," I confessed.

"Help?" she asked. "What kind of help?"

I looked her in the eye. "Our kind."

"Girl, what on earth are you talkin' about?"

Reba Mae's voice had crept up loud enough to wake the pup. He raised his head and cocked one ear. Reaching down, I patted him and he immediately settled down again.

"Between the two of us, we know most everyone there is to know in these parts. You hear all sorts of gossip at the Klassy Kut. Maybe we need to keep our ears open. Check out a few folks."

"Like who?"

I could tell from her expression she was skeptical — skeptical but curious — so I forged ahead. "We could start with Tony Deltorro. Gina said he and Mario went way back. Said they had 'big plans' once upon a time. At Mario's funeral, Tony didn't make any bones to hide his dislike."

"In case you haven't figured this out, sugar, watchin' cop shows on TV doesn't make us detectives."

"You're right, but . . . ," I said, warming to the idea, "McBride gave me a tutorial on how to catch a killer. All we have to do is find someone with motive, means, and opportunity. Other than me, that is."

"You're serious, aren't you?"

I nodded grimly. "How hard can it be for two reasonably intelligent women to find the solution to a real-life whodunit?"

Reba Mae appeared to give the matter some thought, then broke into a wide grin. "What are friends for?"

We high-fived.

CHAPTER 14

Most small towns in the South are homes to either a Mexican or a Chinese restaurant. At least that's the way it seems to me. Brandywine Creek is fortunate enough to have one of each. CJ, being strictly a meat-and-potatoes kind of guy, didn't care for either. He was more a prime rib at the country club sort. When he was out of town, however, I'd take the kids to either North of the Border or Ming Wah. Somehow I felt it was my duty to educate their palates as well as their minds. As a result, Lindsey developed a fondness for Moo Goo Gai Pan while Chad loved nothing better than to chow down on a beef and bean burrito. CJ complained his children had been unduly influenced by a Yankee.

I glanced at my watch, then made a final entry into the computer. Sadly, none of my stock needed to be reordered. Business had slowed to a trickle and, if it didn't pick up soon, I didn't know what I'd do. To borrow from CJ's poker glossary, I was "all in" — every red cent. If I didn't win this hand, I'd go bust. Mostly though, I didn't want to give CJ the satisfaction of saying, "I told you so." I couldn't keep from believing that being a suspect in a murder investigation was having a negative effect on business. Seemed like folks I'd known all my married life had started avoiding me. This gave me even more incentive to do a little snooping around. But that would have to wait. Tonight I had other plans.

Doug said he'd be by a little after six o'clock to pick me up. With North of the Border just around the corner, we agreed he'd leave his car here and, since the weather was so nice, we'd walk the short distance. I had to admit I was more than just a tad nervous. Dating was for youngsters Lindsey's age, kids in high school, not women who'd been married twenty-plus years. I tried to convince myself this wasn't really a "date." Just two people getting better acquainted over dinner. No different than Reba Mae and I sharing a pizza. Yeah, right! I'd picked up the phone at least a half dozen times to cancel our *un*date, then changed my mind. I'd never been a coward. Didn't intend to start now.

161

I powered down the computer and pulled my compact out of my purse. Flipping it open, I checked my reflection and reapplied lipstick. Ever since he'd invited me for Mexican, I'd debated what to wear. In the end, I'd settled on black chinos with tapered legs and a tailored yellow blouse. A chunky necklace I'd purchased years ago on a trip to Cancún completed my attempt at casual chic. I was as ready as I was going to get.

Doug tapped on the front window and, with butterflies flitting in my stomach, I hurried to let him in. "My, don't you look pretty," he said, giving me a once-over, his voice warm with approval.

"Thanks," I replied, feeling a telltale blush creep into my cheeks. I'd nearly forgotten how good it felt to be on the receiving end of a man's full attention. "It'll only take a minute to lock up."

"Brought you something," he said, holding out a heavy paper sack.

I peeked inside and smiled. Doggy chews and a book titled *How to Train a Puppy.* "No one can ever say you're not a smooth operator."

Now it was Doug's turn to look all shy and boyish. And charming and cute as all get-out. "I thought about flowers, or candy, but didn't want to scare you off so I brought

162

these instead."

Minutes later, we strolled down Main Street. A soft breeze wafted through the willow oaks in the town square. Boys on bikes whizzed past as we turned onto Washington Avenue. I felt self-conscious, jittery, knowing people would report seeing us together and speculate on our relationship, but Doug seemed oblivious to the fact we'd be fodder for gossip. He kept the conversation light, and by the time we reached the restaurant, I'd begun to relax.

Nacho, one of the owners of North of the Border, seemed happy to see us. "A booth or table, señor?"

"Table."

"Booth."

We answered simultaneously.

Confused, Nacho looked from one to the other.

"The lady would prefer a booth, so a booth it is." Doug placed a protective hand at the small of my back as we followed Nacho.

Maybe it was silly, but the tables were near the front. I didn't want to be conspicuous to everyone passing by. Thus far, I found the evening more stressful than fun. I hoped things would improve with time.

Nacho deposited a basket of warm tortilla

chips and thick salsa in front of us. As soon as he'd left with our drink orders — margaritas, frozen, no salt — Doug leaned over and lowered his voice, "Isn't 'Nacho' an odd name for the proprietor of a Mexican restaurant?"

I matched my tone to his. "I used to think so, too, until I learned it was a nickname for his real name — Ignacio."

"Well then, that makes perfect sense." Behind wire-rimmed glasses, his brown eyes twinkled with humor.

Our drinks arrived along with menus. Doug studied the extensive list of specials and combinations with single-minded concentration. I didn't bother. I invariably ordered the same thing. While Doug was trying to decide, I let my gaze roam.

Colorful sombreros hung on the brightly painted walls along with photos of various locales in Mexico. Mariachi music seeped out of speakers. What North of the Border lacked in sophistication, it made up for in service and tasty but inexpensive food. Judging from the lack of customers, however, most folk weren't in the mood for Mexican on this particular night. Except for us and another couple in a booth at the rear, the place was virtually deserted.

I recognized the pair as Vicki Lamont and

Kenny, her estranged husband. As though sensing me watching, Vicki glanced up, then quickly turned away. Vicki and I had never been what you might call pals, but we'd traveled in the same social circles during my marriage to CJ. Now she didn't even acknowledge me. Fine, I thought, I can take a hint. I know when I'm not wanted.

"Have you decided on a name for your dog yet?"

Doug's question jerked me back to the present. "Um, no. Not yet."

Just then Becca Dapkins and Buzz Oliver entered the restaurant. Becca, the brazen hussy, was the reason Buzz jilted his long-suffering fiancée, Maybelle Humphries. Maybelle was Brandywine Creek's undisputed queen of Southern cuisine. Becca, to put it mildly, was not. *Had the woman exhausted her repertoire of mushroom soup recipes?* I wondered as Nacho led them past us. Or had Buzz, tired of food swimming in a gluey gray sea, pleaded amnesty?

"Hey Becca," I said.

Buzz was about to stop and gab, but Becca clutched his arm and hurried him along, making me feel even more like a pariah. Doug scowled at their rudeness and was about to comment, but I dipped a chip into

165

the salsa and pretended I didn't notice the slight.

"Umm, good salsa," I murmured around a mouthful. "Could have used a bit more heat, though. Poblano or jalapeño peppers would have been a nice addition."

Doug gallantly pretended he didn't notice the snub, either, and we retreated to the neutral territory of my pet's current state of health. I was happy to report it seemed excellent, and that the pup suffered no ill effects from the recent trauma.

When Nacho arrived with our dinners — a chicken chimichanga for me, beef fajitas for Doug — I happened to glance again at the corner booth. I was surprised to see Vicki and Kenny holding hands and acting all lovey-dovey. Reba Mae had mentioned Vicki had filed for divorce. She'd heard Vicki had been having an affair, but not the name of her lover. Mario Barrone had been mentioned as a possibility. From the looks on their faces, I surmised the couple were reconciling.

"Everything all right, señora?" Nacho asked anxiously when I failed to attack my meal.

I assured him that it was, and he retreated to the kitchen. I added a dollop of sour cream to my chimi, then turned my attention back to my . . . date. "How is your father doing after his heart attack?"

"Great. He's ready to start cardiac rehab soon. Mom's bought a half-dozen heart healthy cookbooks. They're determined to eat better and exercise more."

"By the way, what did you do with my dog while you were away? Did you take him with you?"

Doug speared strips of steak and peppers and heaped them on a warm tortilla. He had nice hands, I noticed. The fingers were long, square-tipped, competent yet gentle. "I left the pup with a friend from veterinary school. He has a practice about fifty miles from here. The dog needed to be closely monitored. I knew I couldn't do it so I asked Josh to keep an eye on him for me as a favor."

As the evening progressed, we chatted about any number of things. My mood gradually changed from nervous to relaxed to simple pleasure. Doug loved his work and was interested in mine. As I'd suspected, he was a fledgling gourmet cook who enjoyed experimenting with various cuisines and trying new spices. He readily fit the profile of my ideal customer.

The subject gradually shifted from the mundane to the personal. Doug confessed

167

that he, too, was divorced and knew what it felt like to be dumped. His wife had left him for a former high school sweetheart she'd reconnected with at a reunion. "She hoped to find a pilot's life more exciting than a veterinarian's," he confided. "After the divorce, I decided a change of scenery was in order. I quit a busy animal clinic in a Chicago suburb and moved south."

"Children?" I asked.

My question was met with a long pause. "One — a daughter. She attends Northwestern and lives with her mother."

Reaching across the table, I gave his hand a sympathetic squeeze. I knew how much that must hurt, but he seemed reluctant to say more so I didn't pursue the subject. We were debating whether to share an order of sopapillas when the front door opened and in sauntered Wyatt McBride.

"There goes my appetite." I sighed. *And my good mood.*

Doug glanced over his shoulder and nodded at the lawman. "He seems a decent sort, but I can understand why you might have a different opinion."

"Brandywine Creek's a small town. People know I've been hauled down to the police station for questioning. That I'm the prime suspect in a murder case." I toyed with the stem of my empty margarita glass. "If McBride is the hotshot, big-city detective he's purported to be, he should be tracking down the real perpetrator before my reputation — and business — are a shambles."

I slid a glance sideways and was dismayed to find McBride, still in uniform, heading our way. Suddenly, the spicy salsa started giving me heartburn. Or maybe McBride had the same effect on me.

McBride hooked his thumbs in his belt, canted his head, and stared down at us without smiling. "Somehow I was under the impression you two didn't know each other before Mrs. Prescott found a wounded dog on her doorstep."

"That's an apple from another tree. He *wasn't* on my doorstep," I explained in a tight voice. "He was in the vacant lot behind my shop."

"I stand corrected. Again," he added.

I gave him a resentful look, hoping he'd take the hint and leave, but he didn't budge. "Actually, Doug came into my shop before it officially opened, looking for saffron."

"I was making paella," Doug explained. "You can imagine how thrilled I was to discover she carried Spanish coupe saffron. Piper doesn't disappoint."

I felt heat rush to my cheeks. "What Doug

meant to say was that my *shop* doesn't disappoint."

I disliked the speculative gleam in Mc-Bride's cool blues as his gaze traveled back and forth between the two of us. "So, Winters," McBride said, widening his stance slightly, "I take it you're something of a cook?"

"I like to experiment with various dishes, though I'm far from being a gourmet."

"Take me, for instance." McBride shrugged one shoulder. "I'm just the opposite. If it weren't for takeout and frozen dinners, I'd probably starve. Maybe it's time I learn to experiment. Broaden my horizons."

Nacho approached our booth and handed McBride a see-through bag loaded with Styrofoam carry-out boxes. "Here you go, Chief. Nice and spicy, just like you ordered."

McBride thanked him and favored us with his trademark humorless smile. "See you around."

I watched him leave with a queasy feeling in the pit of my stomach that had nothing to do with the chimichanga I'd just consumed and everything to do with Wyatt McBride. I didn't trust the way his mind worked. I could easily imagine him wondering whether Doug Winters had furnished me with an alibi because it was the truth — or for personal reasons. Had opportunity, one of the unholy three, just returned for an encore?

CHAPTER 15

"Yoo-hoo!" Dottie Hemmings glided into Spice It Up! with all the majesty of the QE2 gliding into New York Harbor.

I glanced up from the supply catalog I'd been thumbing through. If — I mean when — business perked up I wanted to carry a variety of cooking accessories. Nothing grand, just things like pepper mills, salt cellars, recipe cards, and such.

"Afternoon, Dottie," I said, closing the catalog. "What can I help you with?"

"I have some time to kill before bridge at Patti's so thought I'd stop by and say hello."

"Well," I said brightly, "as long you're here, take a look around. You might find something you'd like to try or replace."

"Replace? Oh, I don't think so, dear. I've had some spices in my cupboard for ten, fifteen, maybe twenty years. They last forever."

I shuddered at the notion of dried, tasteless powders masquerading as spice. "Experts recommend buying a year's supply of ground spice, and a one- to two-year supply of whole spices."

"Oh, pooh, what do the experts know?" Dottie brushed aside my advice with a wave of her pudgy hand. "My husband, the mayor, likes my cooking fine the way it is."

I could see the suggestion fell on deaf ears, so I gave up.

Dottie picked up a jar of crystallized Australian ginger, then, uninterested, set it back down. "Pinky Alexander was telling everyone at the Klassy Kut how Jolene Tucker had a nasty trip and fall last night."

"I'm sorry to hear that," I replied. Jolene was the wife of police sergeant Beau Tucker. We'd served together on various PTA committees in the past. "I hope she's all right."

"Poor thing." Dottie wagged her helmet of blond curls, but it was so stiff nary a strand moved. "Doctor told her she needs pins and plates to put her ankle back together."

"How awful!" I exclaimed, imagining painful surgery and months on crutches.

"It happened coming out of Bunco at Shirley Randolph's. If you want my opinion, too much drinking goes on during those wild dice games." Dottie nodded knowingly.

"Ned Feeney told me their trash bins are filled with empty wine bottles the next day."

"I'll call Jolene and take a meal over."

"Becca's already sending over a pan of her famous tuna noodle casserole. She's the clever one when it comes to soup. You have to admire a woman who knows that many ways to use cream of mushroom."

"As you said, Becca's a clever one."

Failing to recognize my sarcasm, Dottie rattled on. "As I was saying to my husband, the mayor, just the other day, you're a clever girl, too. I don't care what anyone says."

"Why, thank you," I said, for lack of a better response.

"Don't let life get you down, dear." She reached out and patted my hand. "CJ's just sowing his wild oats with Amber Leigh. Men are always attracted to younger, prettier women. It's a problem many face as they grow older and can't compete anymore."

Was I suddenly old, ugly, and out of the race?

I couldn't help but wonder how Dottie would react if Harvey Hemmings, "her husband, the mayor," suddenly developed the hots for someone younger and prettier in a short skirt. I doubted she'd be quite so philosophical.

Dottie's gaze swept around Spice It Up! "This shop of yours is such a cute little place — and always smells so good. Sorry to hear it's on the verge of bankruptcy."

I bit back an angry retort. Leave it to Dottie Hemmings to spread her own particular brand of doom-and-gloom. I forced a smile when I really wanted to scream.

"Granted, business has been slow, but I'm hoping things will improve once the annual Brandywine Creek Barbecue Festival gets nearer. I'm planning a special display of spices that ought to attract cooks."

"I hope so, dear, for your sake." Dottie absently rearranged a selection of baking spices on a shelf. "Other than Jolene's unfortunate accident, the only topic of interest is Mario getting himself stabbed to death. Things like that just don't happen in Brandywine Creek. Folks are bundles of nerves what with a killer on the loose. Some are locking their doors for the first time ever. Lot of talk about buying guns."

I shuddered at the notion of a local militia. Someone was bound to shoot themselves.

"Everyone will sleep better once Chief McBride makes an arrest. My husband, the mayor, said the man had a top-notch reputation as a detective in Miami."

"So I heard," I added drily.

"The sooner the guilty party's caught, the better it will look for him. Some members of the city council are starting to have second thoughts about hiring him." Dottie ran her finger along a shelf and inspected it for dust. "By the way, I almost forgot one other little tidbit of gossip. The Deltorros are taking over Trattoria Milano. And not wasting any time doing it, either."

"Do they intend to close the Pizza Palace?"

"Well, I suppose." Dottie checked her watch for the time. "It doesn't make sense to operate two restaurants. Talk is, they plan on turning the Tratory into, as Gina described it, a more user-friendly Italian eatery. Not serve the hoity-toity kind of food Mario favored."

The front door opened, and I welcomed a reprieve from Dottie Hemmings. I felt even better when I saw the new arrival was none other than my daughter. She carried a plastic garment bag draped over one arm.

"Hey, sweetie." I quickly went and gave her a hug. "What brings you here this afternoon?"

Stepping back from my embrace, Lindsey gave her long blond hair a toss. "Meemaw said I should come by and show you the dress I bought for prom."

"That was quick," I said, trying to hide my dismay. I'd secretly hoped she'd abandon her plan to shop with Amber and pick me instead.

"Ohh," Dottie cooed, clapping her chubby hands together. "A prom dress. Let me see."

"Hey, Miz Hemmings," Lindsey replied politely, making me proud of her good manners.

"What an exciting time for a pretty youngster like yourself. Who's your date for the big night?"

"Jason Wainwright."

"Jason?" Dottie frowned. "Mary Beth and Matt's youngest? The one with an earring in one eyebrow?"

"The boy's going through a phase," I explained, saving Lindsey from having to defend her date. "Jason's the star pitcher on Brandywine Creek High's baseball team."

Dottie gave me a saccharine sweet smile. "Well, I guess an earring wouldn't interfere with a boy's pitching arm, would it?"

Lindsey unzipped the garment bag. "I can only stay a minute. Taylor's picking me up, and we're going to the movies."

"Then let's see this dress of yours."

And see it, I did. At any rate, what there was of it, all strapless and slinky.

Lindsey correctly interpreted my tight-lipped silence as disapproval. "You don't like it, do you, Mom? Is it because you don't like Amber?"

"Amber has nothing to do with it," I said, though that wasn't entirely true. "To be honest, Linds, the style is much too sophisticated for someone your age. Call me naïve, but I'd been hoping for more frills, more fabric. More sweet. Less sexy."

"For your information," Lindsey retorted angrily, "all the girls in my class are wearing short and strapless. You act as if I'm still ten and you want to put ribbons in my hair."

I sighed, recognizing mutiny when I spotted it. "Look, I've got an idea. What if you and I drive down to the mall in Augusta one night and see if we can find another dress you like just as much? Something a little bit . . . more youthful." At the last minute I substituted "youthful" for "less revealing."

"Whatever," she huffed.

Dottie reached out and fingered the fabric. "So this is what girls are wearing these days? Back in my day —"

"So, honey," I ruthlessly cut off Dottie's reminiscences, "what movie are you and Taylor going to see?"

Before she could answer, the pup, barking and wagging its tail, came bounding down the stairs and scooted around the barrier I'd erected between my shop and the storeroom. I'd left him snoozing in my apartment, but apparently he nudged the door open and found his way here.

"A puppy!" Lindsey squealed, her irritation of moments ago apparently forgotten.

Thrusting the prom dress, garment bag and all, into my arms, she made a beeline for the little dog, which was now regarding her curiously, one ear up, one ear down.

"I was saving him for a surprise."

"Cute dog," Dottie commented. "Labradoodle?"

"According to the vet, he's a purebred mutt," I replied, watching Lindsey bend down and scoop the dog into her arms.

Instantly, the pup bathed her face in wet, sloppy kisses as she laughed in delight. My new little pet might never turn into much of a guard dog, I mused, but he could win an award for congeniality.

"I'd best be on my way. Don't want to be late for bridge. Bye, Piper." Dottie waggled her fingers at us as she made for the door, then stopped and turned. "Nice seeing you, Lindsey. Sure hope it doesn't rain the night of the prom. It'd be a pity for that nice blue dress to get water-stained."

As soon as the door clicked shut behind

179

her, Lindsey glowered at me. "You didn't tell me you had a dog."

"I've only had him for a few days. I'm still getting used to the idea of being a pet owner." I absently scratched the dog's right ear.

"What's his name?"

"He doesn't have one yet. Any suggestions?"

Lindsey lowered herself to the floor, and sat cross-legged. "You'll really let me name him?"

"Of course." I carefully rezipped the garment bag, placed it on the counter, and sank down next to her, grateful for the yoga classes I'd taken over the years. "I can't keep calling him 'dog' or 'puppy.' "

Lindsey's brow furrowed in thought. "What about . . . Buffy? No," she quickly discarded the idea. "Buffy's the name of Taylor's cousin's Yorkie. I've got it!" Her face lit up. "Let's call him Casey after the hamster Chad gave me for my birthday when I was ten."

Ah, yes, I thought, how could I ever forget Casey-the-Hamster. In a rush to get to a sleepover one night, Lindsey had neglected to latch Casey's cage. Well, needless to say, the wily rodent had decided to go exploring. CJ and I had finally cornered him in the dining room. The sight of my usually dignified husband down on all fours in his boxer shorts, lettuce leaf in hand, trying to cajole the critter out from behind the china cabinet, started me laughing uncontrollably. The evening had ended with us grateful both kids were away for the night.

"Casey's a fine name," I said, smiling to myself at the memory. "It suits him." I tended to forget there were plenty of good times during the course of my marriage. That was something I needed to work on if I wanted to move forward with my life.

The little mutt barked his approval, making us both laugh.

Lindsey left a short time later, but promised to return the next day. A puppy, she'd informed me, needed plenty of exercise. She planned to take the newly christened pup to the park with her and let him romp.

I returned to my seat behind the counter where the catalog lay forgotten. My mind kept replaying Dottie's conversation regarding the Deltorros purchasing Trattoria Milano. As Dottie was quick to point out, the couple certainly weren't wasting any time. Mario's ashes had hardly cooled before Tony put his plan into play.

I tried to recall exactly what Gina had said at Mario's funeral before Tony had whisked her off. Tony hadn't tried to hide the fact he didn't care for Mario. He'd even gone as far as calling Mario a pompous ass. Gina hinted the two men had a history. That they once shared big plans.

Hmm, interesting, I thought, as I reached for the phone. The situation called for some amateur sleuthing, and I knew just the pair. I dialed my BFF.

Chapter 16

"I brought snacks."

"Me, too."

Reba Mae settled her cooler on the VW's rear seat next to mine and wedged a bulging tote bag alongside the one I'd brought. No one could claim we didn't have our priorities straight.

"Always be prepared, as they say."

A quick glance told me Reba Mae and I were on the same page, too, when it came to How to Dress for a Stakeout. Black was the prevailing color scheme: pants, sweatshirts, and ball caps. Only thing spoiling Reba Mae's ensemble was a giant elongated red "G" emblazoned across the front of her hoodie. It might look great at a University of Georgia football rally, but I wasn't sure it was appropriate attire when one wanted to go unnoticed. She might as well have had a bull's-eye painted across her 38DDs.

She snapped the seatbelt. "So what's the plan?"

"I'll drive. You ride shotgun."

"Okay. Hungry yet?"

I gave her a look. "Let's at least wait till we reach our destination."

"Fine, but I'm ready to try those pretzel chips Ruby Phillips was ravin' about. Brought some honey mustard to dip 'em in."

I turned into the alley behind the Pizza Palace, proud of myself for remembering to switch off my headlights like I'd seen in movies. We rolled to a stop a safe distance from, but with a good view of, the back door. "This ought to work," I announced.

"Now what?"

"We wait. We watch. That's why it's called a stakeout."

"I knew that," Reba Mae grumbled.

I cut the engine. "I thought we'd follow Tony. See what he does after hours."

"Maybe catch 'im in the act?"

I rolled my eyes. "In the act of what? Stealing pepperoni from Meat on Main?"

"You know what I mean. Maybe we'll spot him tryin' to kill someone else."

"Perish the thought!" Even as I scolded, I double-checked my cell phone to make sure 911 was preprogrammed. Satisfied it was, I adjusted my seat to a more comfortable position and prepared to wait and see.

Reba Mae unfastened her seatbelt and, twisting around, dug through the cooler she'd brought. "How about a Diet Coke?"

"All right," I agreed. "How about some of those pretzel chips?"

"Sure thing." We popped the tabs on our sodas and started in on the snacks. "You sure Tony's workin' tonight?" Reba Mae asked.

"Yeah," I told her. "He's here all right. Just before we left, I called the Pizza Palace and asked for him. Claimed I was from the consumer affairs branch of the health department and wanted to talk to him about his marinara sauce. I hung up when he came to the phone."

"Wow," Reba Mae said. "I'm impressed. Does the health department even have a consumer affairs branch?"

I dunked a pretzel in honey mustard. "Don't have a clue, but it sounded nice and official."

"Aren't you afraid he might've recognized your voice?"

"No way." The salty pretzels were making me thirsty so I drained my diet soda. "I disguised my voice by putting a washcloth over the receiver like I saw on TV once."

Tired of pretzels, Reba brought out a bag of nacho chips and a jar of con queso. "I think washcloths have been replaced by one of those electronic gizmos."

I shook my head in wonder. "You never cease to amaze me."

Reba Mae shrugged off my praise. "There's a lot of cop shows on TV these days. I find them educational."

Clicking open the glove box, I hauled out my digital camera along with a pair of binoculars I'd purchased years ago for bird-watching.

Reba Mae let out a low whistle. "Now you're the one who's amazin'. You're a real pro at your very first stakeout."

"Like I said before, always be prepared."

So far the team of Lucy and Ethel — make that Piper and Reba Mae — was doing a respectable job at surveillance. Maybe if my shop failed to thrive, I could hire out as a private investigator. If tonight's adventure was any predictor, I'd weigh three hundred pounds in no time flat.

"You honestly think Tony might've killed Mario?" Reba Mae asked at length.

"The only thing I know for sure, it wasn't me." I kept my gaze fixed on the Pizza Palace's rear door in case Tony made an appearance. "I want to check out anyone who might have a motive to kill Mario, and Tony is a good place to start. We already know there's bad blood between the two."

Reba Mae nodded knowingly. "And I smell somethin' fishy in Tony's rush to buy the Tratory."

"Mm," I agreed as I watched Reba Mae drown a nacho chip in con queso. "I brought along a couple tuna sandwiches. Protein to cancel out the junk food."

"We have chocolate chip cookies for dessert. Let me tell you, it was no mean feat hidin' 'em from the twins."

"They'll taste great with the thermos of coffee I brought along. Cops on stakeout always drink lots of coffee. I'm experimenting with an Ethiopian blend."

"Maybe we oughta be eatin' donuts instead of cookies. You know all the jokes about cops and donut shops."

"We'll do donuts next time," I promised.

We were contentedly sipping diet sodas when I saw Tony's head poke out the pizzeria's rear door. "Get down," I hissed.

Slouching lower in our seats, we watched Tony Deltorro dump a load of trash into a bin, then disappear back inside.

"Gee, that was excitin' as watchin' paint dry," Reba Mae complained, wiping spilled soda off her sweatshirt with the palm of her hand.

"Be patient," I counseled. "Tony shouldn't be much longer, then we'll follow to see whether he goes straight home or not."

Time crawled by with no further Tony sighting. I slunk lower in my seat, bored to tears. So far the evening had been a complete bust. "How do you suppose cops stay awake?"

Reba Mae yawned. "They must read a book or somethin' to keep them from goin' bonkers."

"You can't very well read a book in the dark."

"Maybe they have one of those book-light thingies."

"Well, let's at least listen to the radio." Seconds later, my favorite female DJ was taking requests from callers and dispensing advice to the lovelorn.

Reba Mae cut me a sly smile. "Maybe I should phone in a request, ask her to play somethin' for you and your new boyfriend."

I sighed. "We've already been over this, Reba Mae. I've told you all there is to tell." Truth was, I liked Doug Winters. Liked him a lot. But I wasn't sure I was ready to enter into a relationship. My life was complicated enough as it was. Yet . . . it had been rather nice to be the object of an attractive man's attention.

We lapsed into desultory conversation ranging from Jolene Tucker's broken ankle to the new hair color Reba Mae was considering once she tired of magenta. We'd finished half a thermos of Ethiopia's finest and wolfed down a half-dozen cookies, but no further appearances of Tony Deltorro. Finally I shoved back the cuff of my sweatshirt to see the time. "It's nearly eleven o'clock. What can be taking the man so long to close?"

Reba Mae squirmed restlessly. "Well, if he doesn't come out soon, I'm goin' to knock on his door and ask to use the ladies' room. All that Diet Coke and coffee makes me have to pee."

I shot her a look. "How do you propose to explain you being in the alley this time of night?"

"I can't help it," Reba Mae whined. "You know I've got a weak bladder. You try pushin' out two future football players, and you might be a tad more understandin'."

Another ten minutes elapsed. I was ready to throw in the towel and admit defeat. Our very first stakeout had been a flop. "Okay," I said. "Let's call it a night. We'll try again another time."

"Suits me." Yawning hugely, Reba Mae sat straighter and buckled her seatbelt. "I've got a busy schedule tomorrow. Perms and touch-ups all day long."

"Wish I could complain about being busy." I twisted the key in the ignition. The engine grunted, but didn't catch. Reba Mae and I exchanged worried glances. Wordlessly, I tried again. With the same dismal results.

I voiced the obvious. "Battery's dead."

"Deader 'n roadkill," Reba Mae agreed.

"I'll call AAA." I'd reached for my purse, but Reba Mae stopped me.

"Don't bother," she said. "I'll have one of the twins come over and jump-start it."

She was riffling through her purse for her cell phone when a car turned into the alley behind us, the beams set on high. Light shone directly into the VW's rearview mirror, nearly blinding us.

"Uh-oh," Reba Mae moaned. "Do you suppose Tony caught us spyin'? What'll we tell 'im if he asks what we're doin' here?"

I bit my lower lip. "I don't know, but I'll think of something."

"What if it's not Tony?" Reba Mae asked anxiously. "Are the car doors locked?"

I nodded, my mouth too dry to speak. Squinting, I managed to make out a figure approaching the driver's side. With the other car's brights trained on us, it was nigh unto impossible to identify who its driver might be.

Reba Mae clutched my hand. "Next time, I'm gonna be packin'."

"Packing what?" I whispered hoarsely.

"That means comin' armed and dangerous. I'm bringin' a gun."

"You don't own a gun," I reminded her tersely.

"Then I'll get me one. You should, too," she added as an afterthought.

My heart practically leaped out of my chest at a sharp knock on my window.

"Problem, ladies?" a rich baritone inquired.

I slowly released a pent-up breath, knowing the voice didn't belong to Tony Deltorro but to Wyatt McBride. Part of me was grateful, the other part annoyed. "No problem, officer." I forced a smile so wide it hurt my face. "We're fine. You can move on."

McBride didn't budge. Instead he shined a Maglite around the interior of my Beetle. "Wondered what y'all were doing sitting in an alley with the lights off, but now I know. You girls were having yourself a nice little picnic."

Reba Mae leaned over. "We were just out

191

for a little drive, and all of a sudden, the car stopped. Just like that." She snapped her fingers to demonstrate. "No tellin' about cars, is there?"

"No, ma'am, there sure isn't."

McBride gave her a slow — and sexy — smile. It occurred to me this was the first genuine smile of his I'd seen. And damn, wouldn't you know, the man had the cutest dimple in his right cheek. Don't know why that irritated the heck out of me, but it did. I'd always harbored a secret fondness for dimples.

"You must be Reba Mae Johnson. We weren't properly introduced the last time we met," McBride said, turning on charm like a faucet. "Heard you and Piper were good friends. Sorry to learn about your husband. Butch was a couple years behind me in high school. I didn't know him well, but remembered he played junior varsity back then."

"Both our boys made varsity, followed in their daddy's footsteps."

"You must be proud."

"You're darn right I am. Neither of 'em ever gave me a lick of trouble. They're good kids, both of 'em," Reba Mae informed him. "Just before you drove up, I was about to call one of 'em and ask for help, but maybe you have a set of jumper cables in that big ol' police cruiser of yours."

"Yes, ma'am, I do." Another killer smile. "Be right back."

"Now look what you've gone and done," I fumed as soon as McBride was out of earshot. "You're consorting with the enemy. Next thing, the two of you will be comparing high school yearbooks."

"Tsk, tsk," she clucked her tongue, unfazed. "No need to get your panties in a twist. I was just bein' sociable is all. Besides, he's a real looker. Not bad body-wise, either, near as I can tell."

"Shame on you, Reba Mae, flirting with a man who'd like nothing better than to lock me up and throw away the key."

I had to give the man credit, though, I admitted grudgingly. McBride knew his way around a set of jumper cables. Within minutes, my VW coughed a time or two, then purred like a kitten with a bowl of cream.

"I'll follow to make sure you ladies get home safely," he announced after he replaced the cables in his trunk.

"Thanks, but don't bother," I said hastily. "I need to drop Reba Mae off first."

"No bother," he assured us. "Don't forget there's a killer on the loose."

"Just peachy keen," I muttered under my breath. I drove off with a police cruiser practically on my rear bumper.

A sidelong glance in Reba Mae's direction found her grinning ear to ear. "Hello, tall, dark, and handsome," she drawled, channeling Mae West with a distinct Southern accent.

Chapter 17

"A new battery?" I wailed.

"Sorry, Miz Prescott." Caleb Johnson stuffed a greasy rag into the pocket of his jeans.

"But I don't understand *why* I need a new battery. My car's only two years old." The whine in my voice refused to give up the ghost. The only time I liked wine was when it was served up with cheese and crackers. Or a steaming bowl of pasta. "Dwayne swore on a stack of Bibles when I traded in my BMW that the Beetle was in mint condition."

Caleb shrugged linebacker-sized shoulders. "These things happen, Miz Prescott. Rest of the Beetle seems to be in good shape, though."

Caleb was employed as a mechanic by Dwayne Cloune, owner of Cloune Motors. After his mom had told him about my car troubles the night before, Caleb had offered to come by and check out my car before starting work that morning. Like Reba Mae always said, she had good kids.

I did some mental calculations. A battery would make a serious dent in my checking account. My budget didn't allow for unexpected auto repairs. Before my divorce, I'd never had to contend with anything under the hood of a car, that was CJ's department. He'd either whip out his trusty American Express card or have the bill forwarded to his office. Unfortunately, I didn't own an AmEx card, or for that matter, have an office. I was simply the proprietor of a struggling spice shop, a shop largely ignored by the general population.

"I have to get over to the garage. Tell you what, Miz Prescott. What if I bring over a new battery at lunchtime? I'll do the labor for you free of charge. You can come down later and pay Mr. Cloune for the battery."

"Thanks, Caleb. I'd really appreciate that," I told him. I didn't know whether to be grateful or embarrassed that he sensed my financial dilemma. "I'll have lunch ready for you."

"Gee, Miz Prescott, don't go to any trouble on my account."

"No trouble at all," I assured him.

Soon as Caleb left, I raced upstairs to my

apartment. Reba Mae's pride in her sons was justified. They had grown into considerate and generous young men. Caleb and his twin, Clay, were big, strapping boys with Reba Mae's dark brown hair — minus her current magenta shade — and Butch's hazel eyes. Caleb's hair always looked in need of a trim, while Clay favored a shorter, almost military, style. That's how I told them apart. If Caleb ever got a decent haircut, I didn't know what I'd do.

I decided right then and there that one good deed deserved another. Recalling how much the twins loved my chili, I set about making some. While ground beef sizzled in a pan, I tossed the remaining ingredients into a Crock-Pot — tomatoes, chopped onion and green pepper, minced garlic, and, of course, plenty of spices. I liked my chili best with a little heat. Not scalding, mind you, but hot enough to take notice. To achieve this effect, I was often a little heavy-handed with the ancho chili pepper, cayenne, and cumin.

I drained the meat when it finished browning, added it to the Crock-Pot along with some kidney beans, and lugged it all downstairs. Soon my entire shop was filled with the mouthwatering aroma of simmering chili. I tasted a sample, then added a dash of cinnamon. Mmm. Perfect.

True to his word, Caleb returned shortly after noon, toting a spanking new battery. A wide grin split his face when he caught a whiff of my chili. "Boy, that sure smells good. I'm hungry as a bear."

In no time flat, he'd installed the battery and wolfed down two large bowls of chili along with three hunks of cornbread I'd whipped up.

No sooner had he left Spice It Up! when several potential customers wandered in. I recognized one of the pair as Maybelle Humphries, former fiancée of Buzz Oliver's and sworn enemy of Becca Dapkins. Maybelle introduced the other woman as Charlotte Gibbons, her houseguest from Florida. After browsing for a few minutes among the shelves, the women asked what smelled so good. I gladly gave them each a sample. That launched a lively discussion of spices used in various chili recipes. We agreed nothing added better flavor to a meal like well-chosen spices. Needless to say, I was pleased as punch when both ladies left with purchases.

I had just given my chili another stir when in strolled Wyatt McBride. I barely stifled a groan. Groans always seemed to be my first reaction whenever I saw the man. Setting down the spoon, I placed my hands on my hips and glared at him, my head cocked to one side. "Come to arrest me?"

"Are you always this feisty?"

Feisty? I decided not to pursue the subject. "What can I do for you, McBride? You in the market for some cinnamon?"

"You've got the wrong guy," he said.

He shot me an impudent grin. Much to my chagrin, that darn dimple in his cheek made a brief appearance. My stomach did a strange little flutter. I blamed it on the chili peppers.

"I can't fry an egg without breaking the yolk," he confessed, looking anything but helpless in his starched and pressed navy blues and shiny gold badge.

"I'd be happy to recommend a good cookbook," I said, my smile saccharine sweet. "I believe there's one titled *How to Boil Water.*"

Instead of being insulted, he sniffed the air appreciatively. "Is that chili I smell? Don't suppose you provide takeout orders to underpaid lawmen?"

"What do you want, McBride?" I folded my arms over my chest. "If you're here to hassle me, get it over and done with."

"Are you always this prickly?"

"No," I snapped. "My 'prickly' is very

selective. I reserve it for folks who think I'm capable of murder. Everyone else confuses me with Rebecca of Sunnybrook Farm."

Another smile. Another hint of dimple, which caused the same tummy flutter. I promised myself next time I made chili I'd cut down on the cayenne.

"I was in the neighborhood, so I thought I'd drop by and see if you had someone take a look at that car of yours. It isn't safe for a single woman to be driving around with a finicky battery." He paused a beat before adding, "Especially in alleys late at night."

"How thoughtful, but you can rest easy." I leaned against the counter, refusing to fall prey to this display of friendly concern. "It just so happens I bought a new battery from Cloune Motors so I don't expect any more problems in the foreseeable future."

"Good to hear."

He'd turned to leave, but I saw him cast a final look in the direction of the Crock-Pot. In spite of myself, I felt my irritation soften. "Wait up, McBride."

Before I gave myself a chance to reconsider, I dug a plastic container from underneath the counter and ladled in a generous portion of chili. For good measure, I slipped a wedge of cornbread into a plastic sandwich bag. "Hope you like spicy. I always add green chilies to the cornbread batter for a little extra kick."

"I learned to get along with spicy while in the army. I was stationed at Fort Huachuca in Arizona, fifteen miles from the Mexican border. I developed a fondness for Tex-Mex down there."

I had to admit I was taken aback by McBride sharing personal history. What had come over him? I wondered. I had no clue what went on in that head of his. Was he trying out a "good cop" persona rather than "bad cop"?

"In no way will this be construed as a bribe, right?" I asked, handing him a paper sack with the food.

"Just don't let it get around town I'm easily swayed." He started to leave, but turned back. "By the way, whatever happened to the pooch?"

"Doug couldn't locate his owner, so I decided to keep him."

"Doug, being Dr. Winters the vet?"

"One and the same," I replied, trailing after him as he headed for the door.

"How's he doing?" He paused a beat before adding, "The pooch, not the vet."

"Great. At the moment he's upstairs napping — the pooch, that is, not the vet. And these days, the mutt goes by Casey."

201

"A watchdog's handy to have around — especially with a killer on the loose."

As if I needed another reminder, I thought glumly.

"Piper . . . ?" As he reached for the doorknob, McBride turned back one last time. "Don't be tempted to try anything foolish."

Frowning, I watched him disappear out the door and down Main Street. What the devil did that mean? Did he think I was going to flee the country on an expired passport? Or did he suspect me of spying on Tony Deltorro? Maybe he, too, had overheard rumors of the enmity between Tony and Mario. Or worse yet. In spite of my alibi, did McBride still think deep down that I killed Mario?

I didn't have time to ponder the matter further because just then Marcy Magruder came into my shop. Marcy was a small girl with dishwater blond hair, pale gray eyes, and a perpetually timid expression. I couldn't help but notice the girl was developing a sizeable "baby bump."

"Hey, Piper," Marcy greeted me with an uncertain smile. "Hope you're not mad at me."

"Of course not." I returned the smile. "Why would I be mad?"

"Well, 'cause I called in the day of your grand opening. Sorry about leaving you high and dry, but I was too sick to get out of bed. I'm pregnant and having morning sickness something fierce."

"Congratulations," I told her.

"Doc says mornin' sickness is normal the first couple months." She rested a hand on the expanding mound beneath her knit top. "I'm havin' an ultrasound next week. We're hopin' for a boy."

"This must be an exciting time for you." Marcy, however, didn't look the least bit pleased by the prospect.

"It would be a heap more exciting if Danny and I weren't strapped for cash. That's the real reason I stopped by. Wanted to ask if you need any help around here. I'm available any time you have stuff to do — or just want to take a day off."

I couldn't really afford help, but the poor girl looked so dejected, I didn't have the heart to tell her no. In an odd way, she reminded me of Casey the night I'd found the little pup, frightened and injured. I couldn't ignore the plea in Marcy's eyes any more than I could've ignored Casey's. "Well, actually," I heard myself say, "I do have a couple errands to run. Think you could mind the shop for an hour or so?"

"Sure thing." She beamed me a smile that transformed her narrow face from plain to almost pretty. "Does that mean I get to wear one of those cute little aprons?"

"Here," I said, "wear mine." I quickly slipped my apron off and gave it to her. "I don't expect there will be many customers but, if so, do you remember how to work the register and operate the credit-card charge machine liked I showed you?"

"Don't you worry none. I've got a good memory for that sort of stuff. I'm real good with computers, too."

I stored this information away for later. If my business ever took off, I might need help with the software I'd bought to track inventory and sales. "If there's a problem, you can always call my cell. The number's next to the register."

"I'll be fine. And, Piper, thanks. Danny says things will be looking up for us real soon. Once the Deltorros get the Tratory up and running, he'll have a steady job again."

I pawed through the contents of my purse, searching for my car keys. "I don't believe you ever mentioned why Danny no longer worked for Mario."

Marcy tucked a limp lock of shoulder-length hair behind one ear. "The two men never did get along. Mr. Barrone got so mad at Danny once he even threw a meat cleaver at him. Didn't hit him, of course, but Danny claimed it was the last straw. He quit right then and there, but Mr. Barrone said he couldn't quit 'cause he was already fired. Never did pay Danny what he was owed. Try explaining that to your landlord."

"Right," I muttered. Apparently, Danny Boyd numbered among those persons Mario had managed to antagonize. As I left the shop, I wondered how many others there were walking the streets of Brandywine Creek.

CHAPTER 18

Stepping out of Spice It Up!, I paused to draw a deep breath. The air smelled as fresh as newly laundered clothes left in the sunshine to dry. The sky overhead was a robin's egg blue, and in the square across the way, wrens warbled in the willow oaks. Instead of driving, I decided to enjoy the lovely April afternoon by walking the short distance to Cloune Motors.

As I passed Second Hand Prose, Brandywine Creek's used-book store, I collided with Shirley Randolph carrying an armload of books. I bent to help retrieve several she'd dropped. The hero on the cover of *Passion's Surrender* reminded me of Wyatt McBride so I hastily shoved the book back at her.

"Sorry I haven't been into your store since it opened," Shirley apologized, but avoided eye contact. "I've been meaning to try the lamb recipe you demonstrated."

"I've still got plenty of juniper berries in stock. Any time you want to experiment . . ."

"I'm kinda busy right now, what with getting ready for the Friends of the Library's annual fund-raiser. Maybe when it's over. . . ."

"Sure," I replied as I watched her scurry off with her treasure.

Next, I spotted Judge Malcolm R. Herman, briefcase in hand, trotting down the front steps of the stately courthouse that occupied one end of the square. Maybe I should rush over and personally thank him for signing the search warrant that allowed McBride and his crew to ransack my place. Yeah, right. Over my dead body. We studiously ignored each other.

I continued on my merry way, determined to enjoy playing hooky from the role of shopkeeper. The bay door of the garage was open as I approached Cloune Motors, and I saw Caleb bent over the engine of a late-model Ford. He responded to my greeting with a quick grin, then went back to work.

I entered the front office and found Dwayne Cloune behind his desk, talking on the phone. He acknowledged my presence with a nod, and motioned me to have a seat while he finished his conversation.

This gave me an opportunity to study

him. Dwayne — of I-Don't-Clown-Around fame, an annoying slogan seen on print ads and repeated ad nauseam in radio spots — was an entrepreneur, dabbling in everything from repairs and sales of autos to real estate to city politics. Judging from his dapper, button-down appearance, one would never guess he owned a grimy repair shop. Dwayne struck me as the persnickety sort, not the type to dirty his hands. He made a practice of hiring young, top-notch mechanics such as Caleb to do the work for him. The grease-under-the-fingernails look was unbefitting a city councilman with aspirations of becoming state senator.

"Afternoon, Piper." He ran a hand over dark hair liberally salted with silver, slicked back from a high forehead. "You here to settle up on that battery?"

I fished my checkbook from my purse. "Nice of you to let Caleb install it during his break."

"If you're short of cash, all you needed to do was say so. I'da cut you some slack. CJ and I been friends for years." He flashed his best vote-for-me grin.

"That's kind of you, Dwayne, but I'm doing just fine," I lied. I'd repent later.

He rattled off a figure, and I scribbled a check. I waited while he made an entry into the computer and printed out a receipt. Glancing around, my gaze rested on a stack of glossy posters against the far wall. Dwayne the candidate posed in front of the courthouse with the American flag prominently displayed in the background.

"I see the rumor's true," I commented, gesturing at the posters.

"Yes, indeedy." His head bobbed with emphasis. "It'll be a tough fight, but I aim to give the incumbent a run for his money."

I rose to my feet and tucked the receipt into my purse. "Well, good luck."

"Here's a little somethin' for you to take along." Reaching into a drawer, he handed me a ballpoint pen bearing the image of a clown scary enough to give toddlers nightmares and I DON'T CLOWN AROUND printed in large red letters.

"Gee, thanks," I muttered, consigning it to the nether regions of my purse.

"By the way," he said, treating me to another patented preelection smile, "expect an invite to a reception I'm hosting for local businesspeople. I hope to see you there."

The thought of a party boosted my flagging ego. I felt pleased to be numbered among Brandywine Creek's professionals. Once my shop was on more solid ground, I planned to join the chamber of commerce.

Maybe the Rotary Club, too. "Great," I said. "I'll be watching for it."

"Wonderful." He lounged back in his swivel chair. "I'll tell Diane you plan to attend. She thinks it's the perfect venue to welcome our new chief of police to town."

"Sounds like fun," I managed, after finding my voice.

About as much fun as a root canal.

I decided to take the Scarlett O'Hara approach and obsess over McBride's welcome reception another day. As long as Marcy was minding the store, I'd make the most of the afternoon. This was a good time to put my ideas for the upcoming BBQ Festival into action. For this I needed to visit Pete Barker, my friendly neighborhood butcher at Meat on Main.

Except for my ex-mother-in-law, I found the market void of customers.

"Piper," she said, giving me a perfunctory peck on the cheek. "Shouldn't you be minding your shop instead of out gallivanting? That's no way to run a business."

I tensed at the censure in Melly's voice. My former mother-in-law has a God-given talent for getting my back up. "Marcy Magruder's 'minding the shop' while I run a few errands."

"Marcy, eh?" Melly's lips pursed. "Heard

210

the girl is . . . in the family way."

"Pregnant?" The heck with propriety. I wasn't afraid to come right out and say the word. "Yes, Marcy told me she and Danny are expecting."

"Oh, my," Melly gasped. "I do hope they plan to marry before the baby's born."

"That's not for me to say. I'm afraid you'll have to ask Marcy or Danny what their plans are."

Before Melly could voice a reply, Pete Barker emerged through the double set of swinging doors behind the meat counter. "Will that be all, Miz Melly?"

Frowning, Melly examined the chuck roast he held out for her inspection. "That'll do nicely, Pete. Much better now that you trimmed off all that nasty fat."

"Have this ready for you in a jiff."

While Pete busied himself weighing and wrapping, Melly turned to me with a smile. "CJ and Lindsey are coming for dinner tonight. You know how CJ loves red meat. The town's certainly fortunate to have a butcher like Pete. The man can carve a side of beef with the best of them. He certainly has a way with knives, doesn't he?"

Her purchase completed, she waved and sailed out the door.

A way with knives . . .

"Piper . . . ?"

Startled, I swung back to Pete.

"Caught you wool gatherin'," he said with a grin. "I asked what can I get you this afternoon."

"S-sorry," I replied, collecting my scattered wits. "I need some baby back ribs, nice and lean."

"You don't want 'em too lean," he cautioned. "Ribs need a little fat to give 'em a decent flavor, that's what makes 'em good and juicy."

"Whatever you say, Pete. You're the expert."

"Have some choice ribs in the back if you don't mind waitin' a minute or two while I fetch 'em."

"No hurry," I assured him.

Pete hustled into the back in a quest for the perfect baby backs. I stared into the display case at the various cuts of pork and beef without really seeing them.

A way with knives . . . ? Funny thing was, Pete *did* have a way with knives. I'd seen him slice tenderloin with the precision of a surgeon.

And Mario had been stabbed.

Pity, I hadn't stayed at the murder scene long enough take in details. Had Mario been stabbed repeatedly? Or had a single, well-placed knife wound been responsible for his death? McBride would surely know. Too bad I wasn't on better terms with the man, or I'd ask him.

Pete returned, triumphantly hoisting a giant slab of meat. "This here's just the ticket."

"Perfect," I murmured.

Pete wiped gloved hands on the heavy cotton twill apron that swathed his ample girth, leaving bloody streaks against bleached white. I observed this with a sinking feeling in the pit of my stomach.

"Just bought a couple hogs off a farmer over in Lincoln County. This is as fresh a slab of ribs you'll ever set eyes on. So fresh it's practically oinkin'."

Who was more skilled with a knife than someone who dissected dead animals for a livelihood? The notion caused my stomach to clench.

Pete peered at me over the scale, his usually cheerful countenance serious. "You're looking a bit green around the gills, Piper. You okay?"

"Fine," I fibbed. "Could you cut the slab into sections of about four ribs apiece?"

Selecting a wicked-looking blade, Pete finessed his way through meat, fat, and connective tissue. "You fixin' to have a party?"

"I, um, I'm thinking ahead to the Barbecue Festival. I'm going to experiment with various spices, find out which ones work best for a rub, which work best for sauce."

"Heard this year's festival is gonna be bigger and better 'n ever. Always brings in quite a crowd."

"I certainly hope you're right. I could use the business." No time like the present, to do a little amateur sleuthing. Pretending to admire a neat row of pork chops in the meat case, I cast about for a clever way to slip Mario's name into the conversation. Not feeling particularly creative, I cleared my throat and dove in head-first. "Rumor going around town that the Deltorros are taking over Trattoria Milano."

"More than rumor, it's a fact." Pete plopped the ribs — now cut into riblets — onto a sheet of white butcher paper. "Met with Tony this morning. Says he wants me to be his main meat supplier. He's bound to be a damn sight easier to deal with than Barrone. Compared to him, Deltorro oughta be a walk in the park."

I smiled inwardly. Sleuthing was proving easier than I imagined. I seemed to have a natural flair for detective work. "I heard Mario could be temperamental."

"Temperamental?" Pete huffed out a

breath. "Insane is more like it. And a crook to boot."

"A crook?"

"The man owed me five hundred bucks for some Kobe-style beef he had me special-order for an event. I tried to tell him the dang stuff was way overpriced, but would he listen? No sirree. Said he wouldn't settle for second best. Claimed he was catering a private dinner, and everything had to be top-notch."

"What happened?"

"Oh, I got it for him, all right. Cost me an arm and a leg, too. When the time came, Barrone weaseled out of paying me. Claimed the meat was tough. Accused me of trying to pass off an inferior grade as Kobe. I threatened to take him to small claims court."

"Why didn't you?"

"You got any idea how much lawyers charge?" I started to speak, but he cut me off with a humorless chuckle. "Of course you do. You were married to a shyster. Next thing, I'd have to take a day off work. Who's gonna look after this place if I'm not here? Besides" — Pete shrugged his pudgy shoulders — "Barrone said he'd take his chances with the judge. Went as far as boasting he had 'connections.' "

As I walked slowly back to Spice It Up!, my mind gnawed like a puppy with a milk bone on everything I'd just learned. Motive, means, and opportunity, McBride had said. The "means" in this case were a cinch to name. Knives were tools of the trade to butchers the world over. And knives were readily available in the kitchen of a restaurant. Large and small — paring knives, butcher knives, boning knives, to name just a few.

Motive in this case was easy — money. Mario owed Pete money, which he refused to pay. A sum great enough for Pete to consider taking Mario to court. It wasn't a stretch to think the two might have argued and things got out of hand. Men have been killed over lesser things.

That left opportunity. Did Pete have an alibi for the night Mario was killed? My first instinct had been to come right out and ask. But I had stopped myself in the nick of time. That was a question for the police, not me. There must be a way to ferret out this information. Maybe if Reba Mae and I put our heads together. . . .

CHAPTER 19

Needing time to think, I leisurely strolled down Main Street toward Spice It Up! I'd just added Pete, my favorite butcher, to my list of possible murder suspects. A short but growing list. By their own admission, Mario owed both Pete Barker and Danny Boyd money.

Follow the money.

Was that advice I'd read in a detective novel? Or heard in a movie? If I'd known I'd be involved in a real-life murder mystery, I would've paid closer attention. Taken notes.

With doom and gloom uppermost in my mind, I nearly bumped into Ned Feeney coming out of Gray's Hardware. "Hey, Miz Piper," he greeted me with his familiar loopy grin and tipped the bill of his ever-present ball cap.

"Hey there, Ned." I tried to skirt around him, but he blocked my path.

"Heard you got a new man in your life. Whole town's talkin'."

Shoving a stray curl behind one ear, I mentally counted to ten. "What 'new' man?" I hoped my voice sounded calmer than I felt.

"Why, that nice Dr. Winters, the vet out on Old County Road."

"We had dinner is all. We both happen to like Mexican food."

"Becca Dapkins told Bitsy Johnson-Jones she saw you two canoodling at North of the Border the other night." He shifted the brown paper sack he carried from one hand to the other. "Bitsy told Jolene when she brought her a tray of deviled eggs. You know, don't you, Jolene had a nasty fall?"

I only had time for a nod before Ned's mouth started running again. "Everyone knows Jolene, bless her heart, is such a klutz. She'll be laid up for months. Anyways, Jolene told Lottie Smith about your new beau when Lottie dropped off a coconut cake. Lottie told Pinky Alexander, and well, I don't need to tell you the rest."

I hitched the strap of my purse higher. "Dr. Winters offered advice on raising a puppy."

"Becca said you two make a right cute couple."

I felt compelled to make a last-ditch effort to keep my private life private. "We aren't a 'couple,' and we weren't 'canoodling.' "

I supposed I should be grateful my love life — or lack thereof — was a topic of conversation rather than my being a murder suspect. Call me crazy, but I preferred my life *not* be the hot topic of anyone's conversation but my own.

"Right," Ned said, giving me a broad wink. "Well, I'd best skedaddle. Mr. Strickland will be worryin' what's keepin' me."

I shook my head as I watched his retreating back. As long as Ned Feeney resided in Brandywine County, *The Statesman* would never need a gossip columnist. With him efficiently sowing rumors and spreading tales, any news would be old hat long before the ink dried.

Minutes later, I shoved open the door of Spice It Up! and discovered Marcy wasn't alone. Unfortunately, her visitor wasn't a customer, but her fiancé, Danny Boyd, who occupied the space near the counter. Not that I have anything against fiancés, but a cash-paying customer would have been nice.

"Hey, Miz Prescott," Danny hailed me. "Hope you don't mind me hanging around to keep Marcy company. She gets bored with no one to talk to."

"Of course not." For a split second, I envied Marcy. I wished I had a Danny to call whenever the hours dragged past.

"Here, that looks heavy. Let me help you." Danny rushed over to take the plastic grocery bag containing the baby back ribs I'd purchased.

"Thanks," I said.

"Where do you want this?"

"You can set it on the counter in the rear." Reluctantly, I conceded that beneath the scruffy goatee and John Lennon eyeglasses Danny Boyd held a certain appeal. Not my type — not that I have a type — but he seemed thoughtful, considerate, and when it came to Marcy, utterly devoted.

"Looks like you've been to Meat on Main. This stuff weighs a ton. You planning a party?"

"If you are," Marcy interjected eagerly, "Danny does catering. In spite of Mr. Barrone firin' him, he's a fantastic cook."

"I wasn't fired," Danny corrected. "I quit."

"That's what I meant." Marcy reached for her purse, then straightened. "I almost forgot, this came while you were out."

I took a heavy cream-colored envelope from her. My name, along with the name of my shop, were written across it in elegant calligraphy.

"Mrs. Cloune delivered it personally. She said I was to give it to you the minute you returned. Said to tell you 'no excuses.' "

I ran my thumbnail under the flap, pulled out the enclosed invitation, and scanned the contents. Diane and Dwayne Cloune requested the pleasure of my company at a reception welcoming Wyatt McBride to Brandywine Creek. All business owners and prominent citizens were cordially invited.

"Anything wrong, Piper?" Marcy's small face pinched with worry.

I glanced up to find both Danny and Marcy watching me, concerned. I never had what CJ called a "poker" face. When I was happy, it showed. And vice versa. This happened to be one of those vice versa times.

"I'm invited to a party the Clounes are hosting for the new chief of police."

Marcy beamed. "Danny's been asked to do the catering. Isn't that great?"

"Great," I echoed. What were the odds against contracting hoof-and-mouth disease before the fateful day? I wondered.

"Mr. Cloune asked Mr. Deltorro to cater, but Tony told him he was too busy what with getting his new restaurant ready to open." Marcy gave Danny's arm an affectionate squeeze. "Mr. Deltorro recommended Danny."

"No biggie. Just heavy hors d'oeuvres." Danny smiled as if to say "Shucks, ma'am, 't weren't nuthin'."

I tapped the invitation thoughtfully against the palm of my hand. "Since it's in the afternoon, Marcy, I could use your help in the shop for an hour or two that day."

"Sure thing, Piper. Danny and I can use some extra money. Danny lost not only his job at the Tratory but also his medical benefits."

One look at Danny's face told me all I needed to know.

"That . . ." Danny's cheeks flushed as struggled for control. "Barrone had a mean streak a mile wide. Ask me, he was a sorry excuse for a human being. Good riddance, I say."

For long minutes after Danny left the shop, his arm protectively wrapped around Marcy's waist, I stared at the closed door. Finally, a tail-wagging and wiggly Casey woke from his nap and let me know in doggy terms he needed to go outside. Snapping on his leash, I waited while he did his business in the vacant lot where I'd once found him. My thoughts weren't on the pup, however, but remained on Danny Boyd. It was obvious to me that Danny was furious with Mario. The poor guy lost not only his livelihood but his medical benefits about the same time Marcy found out she was expecting. Talk about lost and found. I could hardly blame the young man for feeling resentful. But was his resentment strong enough to build into a killing rage?

"Sure I can't coax you into a few highlights?" Reba Mae wheedled. "A couple streaks of lavender would look great against your red."

"No thanks," I said. "When it comes to hair color, I'm a monochromatic kind of gal."

The last of the Klassy Kut's patrons, cut, curled, and sprayed, had departed for the day, leaving just the two of us alone. I snuggled deeper into one of Reba Mae's cushy styling chairs. She sat in the other, studying her reflection in the mirror.

"I'm ready for a change," she said, tugging at a lock of spiky magenta. "Somethin' edgier, more hip."

"If you looked any edgier, you'd frighten small children in the Piggly Wiggly."

"I'm thinkin' blue. What about azure?"

"We talking sky or hair color?"

Reba Mae's adventures in Crayola Land never ceased to alarm and amaze me. My BFF was a brave and fearless traveler in hues I'd never dare venture. I preferred my God-given head of curly red. No artfully applied highlights of lavender, magenta, or azure would make me look or feel "hip." Foolish, yes; hip, no. However, Reba Mae, bless her heart, could carry off the look with aplomb.

Fumbling through a drawer, she pulled out a swatch of synthetic hair the same blue as cotton candy hawked at the county fair. "What do you think?"

I tipped my head to one side, then the other, and finally shook my head. "Not unless you're trying for carnival punk."

" 'Fraid you'd say that." She tossed the color sample back in the drawer. "Lindsey brought a couple of her friends by the other day. Some girls think it would be cool to have streaks in their hair match the color of their prom dresses."

I held my hand against my heart. "Please don't tell me Lindsey wants colored streaks in her hair. If so, just take me out and shoot me."

"No," Reba Mae laughed. "Actually Lindsey seems content her hair is natural blond. She said Amber told her that pageants frown on wild variations. They think it shows lack of character."

"Well, for once, I'm grateful for Amber's

influence, but" — I aimed a finger at her — "if you breathe a word of that to anyone, I'll have to kill you."

Reba Mae made a twisty motion in front of her mouth with thumb and forefinger. "My lips are sealed." She pantomimed throwing away a key. "By the way, how did your mother-daughter shopping trip go?"

"Great. We happened across an adorable pale pink dress in a bridal boutique that's suitable for prom. Lindsey looks like an angel in it and," I added, "it's much more age-appropriate."

"Can't wait to see her in it."

Glancing down, I spied a square cream-colored envelope peeking out from beneath a month-old issue of *People*. "Looks like you got an invite, too. You going?"

"Of course." Reba Mae's eyes met mine in the mirror. "And you are, too."

"But —"

"No ifs, ands, buts, or maybes. You're goin'."

I'd looked forward to Mario's funeral with greater anticipation than a party welcoming McBride.

As close friends sometimes do, Reba Mae read my mind. "If you don't show, sugar, people will talk. You're not only goin' to show up, but you'll act like you're havin' yourself a gay ol' time."

"Fine." I made a face at my own reflection. "And if I manage to pull that off, I'll audition for a role in the next production at the Opera House."

"Wear somethin' hot that makes a statement. Like that sassy red number of yours."

"Great," I grumbled. "I can masquerade as the scarlet woman."

She ignored me. "Be sure to wear those killer heels you bought at Neiman Marcus before CJ shredded your charge card. They make your legs look a mile long."

"If McBride doesn't zero in on the real killer soon, I could be wearing one of those awful prison jumpsuits. You know orange clashes with my hair."

"Don't be so down in the dumps, hon. He'll find the guy."

I fiddled with a teasing comb left lying next to a curling iron. "Easy for you to say. You're not number one on McBride's personal hit parade."

"Call me a romantic, but my gut feelin' is your bein' number one on his hit parade has nothin' to do with Mario gettin' hisself killed. I saw the way Mr. Wyatt McBride, chief of police, looked at you when he didn't think you were lookin' back."

"Yeah, right," I said. "You're not a romantic, girlfriend, you're delusional. Certifiably stark, raving bonkers. McBride'd like nothing better than to slap on the handcuffs."

Reba Mae smiled a sly, knowing smile. "Now that's what I call bein' on the same page."

"Enough about McBride." Suddenly restless, I got up from the chair and started prowling the confines of the beauty salon. "I stumbled across another name to add to the list of suspects this afternoon."

"Who?" Reba Mae spun around. "Bet it's a woman. Mario had quite a reputation as a ladies' man. First Diane Cloune, then Vicki Lamont . . . and it didn't bother him none they were married."

I stopped pacing to give Reba Mae a long, hard look. "You don't really think a woman stabbed Mario?"

"I'm not sayin' it was a woman. Just that it *could've* been a woman." Reba Mae replaced the cap on a can of hairspray. "Rumors in the salon were thicker 'n molasses for a while. I knew Diane and Mario had had a fling, but assumed it ended ages ago. Vicki, however, was another matter."

I nodded thoughtfully. "I gather their affair was hot and heavy."

"Yeah." Reba Mae nodded knowingly. "One of my clients heard her describe

Mario as her 'soul mate.' "

"Makes her sound like a teenager."

"Makes her sound like a woman in love."

"And women in love do crazy things when it comes to keeping their man."

Reba Mae nodded in agreement. "Stabbin's too messy for most women. Besides, it's a surefire way to ruin perfectly good clothes. Last I heard, Mario had a new woman in his life."

I was curious. "By any chance, did this 'new' woman in Mario's life have a name?"

"Nope." Reba Mae toed off her shoes and wiggled her feet. "He kept whoever it was under wraps. Probably the best-kept secret in Brandywine Creek since Buzz Oliver started seein' Becca Dapkins behind Maybelle Humphries's back."

That brought a smile. "Didn't take Maybelle long to figure out Buzz developed a fondness for recipes featuring cream of mushroom soup." I remembered the incident well. Maybelle had made the connection at the Methodist church supper. She'd picked up a coconut cream pie and hit Buzz smack-dab in the face with it. The woman had quite an arm on her.

"So who is this possible suspect you're referrin' to? Anyone I know?"

"Pete."

228

"Pete who?"

I threw up my hands, exasperated. It wasn't as if Brandywine Creek was filled to overflowing with men named Pete. "Pete Barker. The butcher at Meat on Main."

"Why would Pete want to murder Mario?"

"Because Mario special-ordered some pricey beef, then refused to pay. Each time Pete tried to collect, Mario'd stonewall him. Claimed Pete sold him an inferior cut and tried to pass it off as Kobe-style."

"Why didn't he just sue him? Ever see Judge Judy in action? She would have made mincemeat out of Mario."

I shrugged. "Maybe Judge Judy makes Pete nervous."

Reba Mae nodded knowingly. "She has that effect on people."

"Who is more skilled with a knife than a butcher?" I challenged.

Reba Mae scrunched a brow. "A surgeon?"

"Stop being obtuse." I plunked myself back in the styling chair and gave it a spin. "I've seen Pete filet tenderloin quicker than you can say Jack Robinson." That got Reba Mae's undivided attention, so I continued, "According to McBride's theory, Pete has motive and means. All he lacks is op-portunity."

"So what are you gettin' at?"

"We need to find out whether Pete has an alibi for the night Mario was killed."

"Duh!" Reba Mae bopped herself in the head with the heel of her hand. "Of course, that's what we *need* to do. Only question, how do you propose we do it?"

"I was hoping you'd help think of a way."

Reba Mae was silent for a long moment, then a slow smile spread across her face. "Leave it to me, sugar. I have an idea."

CHAPTER 20

I considered, discarded, then reconsidered the notion of trailing Pete. From my vantage point across the square, I'd watched him lock up Meat on Main and drive off. Curious to see if he did anything shady after hours, I followed him home. I parked a discreet distance down the block and waited. Fifteen minutes later, Pete emerged from the attached garage wearing baggy jeans and a John Deere T-shirt, and pushing an ancient lawnmower. The only time he came close to anything "shady" was when he mowed the grass under a Japanese maple, so I finally gave up. Later that evening, Reba Mae and I did a drive-by past Pete's place. We watched as his buddies, armed with six-packs of Budweiser, started to congregate.

"Baseball game," Reba Mae informed me succinctly. "Atlanta Braves versus Arizona Diamondbacks."

"Plan B, here we come."

The two of us decided on an encore performance of "Lucy and Ethel on Stakeout." We followed Tony Deltorro at a safe distance to avoid detection in my trusty VW bug, as he deposited the night's receipts from the Pizza Palace. Instead of driving home as expected, he'd headed for a section of town known as the historic district. Stately antebellum homes, some meticulously restored to their former glory, some patiently waiting for a fresh coat of paint, lined the streets. Tony had turned into a circular drive of one of the former, a drive that once had been used by carriages and gentlemen on horseback. I'd parked the Beetle a couple houses down, partially concealed from the house in question by towering oaks, and we settled down to wait.

"What do you s'pose Tony's doin' here of all places?" Reba Mae took another noisy slurp of her Diet Coke.

"Beats me."

"Whose house is this anyway?"

I reached for a handful of Doritos. "Beats me."

"Some place," Reba Mae commented, peering through the window for a better look at the two-story plantation-style structure complete with Doric columns and a wraparound porch.

"You don't suppose this belongs to Tony, do you?"

"Uh-uh," Reba Made disagreed. "No way. This end of town's reserved for those with real money, old money. It's too rich for my blood. Most of these homes have been in the same family for generations."

"Maybe the owner's so wealthy that Tony personally delivers the pizza. Maybe the guy's a big tipper."

"Whatever." Twisting around, Reba Mae rummaged through a sack of food on the backseat. "All this surveillance works up an appetite. I brought subs, but told 'em to hold the onions . . . just in case."

"In case of what?" I asked, peeling the wrapper from the one she handed me. Turkey, lettuce, tomato, pickle, banana peppers, and a sprinkling of oregano. Just the way I liked them.

"In case of whatever," she replied, nonplussed. "Diet soda?"

I shook my head. Reba Mae's thirst apparently matched her appetite because she popped the tab of her second Diet Coke and took a swallow before attacking her sandwich.

"Don't suppose you've concocted a brilliant scheme to discover whether Pete has an alibi for the night Mario was murdered?"

I asked, after polishing off my sub.

Reba Mae brushed crumbs from her black hoodie. "Consider it a done deal, sugar."

I glanced at her sharply. "What's that supposed to mean?"

"Just so happens . . ." She let me stew, giving me a broad grin, followed by another swig of Coke. "Pete's wife, Gerilee, came into Klassy Kut this afternoon to be treated for a severe case of hair trauma. Her niece is goin' to beauty school and needed some practice so Gerilee, bein' a nice auntie, volunteered. Gerilee told the girl she wanted it layered. Well, it was layered all right. Took me almost an hour to *un*layer it."

"Nothing worse than a bad haircut," I agreed, my impatience barometer steadily rising. "But what did she say about the night Mario was killed?"

At times, Reba Mae couldn't be rushed and this was one of them. If anything, she seemed to relish my mounting frustration. "Well," she drawled, once she was satisfied I was chomping on the bit, "I decided to have a little fun with it. We played ourselves a game called Where Were You When . . . ? Started off with something simple like where were you when Dale Earnhardt crashed during the last lap of the Daytona 500."

234

"That's not simple," I protested. "Why not ask where were you on nine-eleven?"

"That's too depressin', darlin'. Besides, every Southern gal worth her salt knows where she was the day Dale Earnhardt, one of NASCAR's all-time greats, bought the farm. February 18, 2001. Know it like my own birthday. Anyway, from there, I led into some other questions. When I asked, how do you and your sweetie spend your Friday nights — takin' into account it was a Friday night when Mario ended up deader 'n a skunk — I thought Gerilee would burst into tears."

I tapped my fingers on the steering wheel. "Why was that?"

"Seems Fridays, Gerilee sits home alone. She said Pete's been on a Friday night bowlin' league for the last couple months. He's always home no later than ten o'clock, but by then it's too late to go out to for Chinese like they used to do."

"Terrific," I muttered. "Since McBride said the coroner placed the time of death between ten o'clock and midnight, might as well cross Pete off the list of possible suspects."

"Sorry." Reba Mae placed a hand over her mouth to stifle a burp. "But don't let that get you down-in-the-mouth. That still leaves

Tony. And didn't you mention Mario not only owed Danny money, but had weaseled out of payin' him medical benefits?"

"Yeah, you're right."

"Course, I am, now stop your broodin'. How about a brownie? Chocolate's always good for what ails you."

Truer words were never spoken, so I helped myself to not one but two of the brownies Reba Mae had brought in a take-and-go container. No sooner had we licked the last traces of chocolate from our fingers when Reba Mae announced, "I shouldn't have had that last can of soda. Now I have to pee."

"Fine time to think about it," I grumbled. "Guess we'll have to call it a night?"

"Shucks, no," Reba Mae said, already reaching for the door handle. "A client of mine owns the bed-and-breakfast down the block. She's a night owl. I'm sure she wouldn't mind if I popped in and begged to use the facilities."

"How do you intend to explain why you're in her neighborhood this time of night?"

"I'll think of somethin'." Reba Mae stood on the curb, practically doing the Texas two-step. "I'll tell her that a friend and I were out walkin' her dog when the urge hit. After five kids, she'll relate to a weak bladder."

"Fine, but make it snappy," I said, but Reba Mae was halfway down the block before I finished my sentence.

Without Reba Mae's company, the minutes crawled by. Stakeouts certainly weren't as glamorous as they looked on TV or in the movies. How did real detectives survive the long, lonely hours? Read? Listen to music? And what did they do for emergencies of a personal nature? My mind didn't want to go there.

I thought of switching on the radio but was afraid of running the battery low. Even with a new one, I didn't want to take the risk. If I had my MP3 player with me, I could listen to music and not have to worry. Once business perked up maybe I'd buy myself a fancier version like Lindsey's.

Leaning forward, I squinted through the windshield at the house we were watching. Tall trees — magnolias probably — shrouded it in shadow. Even so, I could see lights on in a room to the left of the entrance. An old-fashioned parlor? I caught an occasional glimpse of Tony as he moved about, but didn't see anyone else. To whom did the house belong? I wondered. And why was Tony visiting at such an odd hour? Was there another woman in his life? If so, it wouldn't be wise if Gina Deltorro got wind of the affair. Gina was more than a wife; she was his business partner. Wasn't there a saying about hell hath no fury like a woman scorned?

I peeked at my watch. What was keeping Reba Mae? It wouldn't be the first time she started talking and lost track of time. Suddenly, headlights loomed in the rearview mirror. I slunk down in the seat, pulled my knit ski cap lower, and tried to act invisible. No such luck. The car drew to a stop directly behind me.

I tensed.

The sharp sound of knuckles rapping against the driver's side window signaled my vanishing act was a total flop. With a sigh, I slowly, reluctantly, straightened and turned my head.

"Damn," I muttered when I found Wyatt McBride staring back at me. "What are you, some kind of stalker?"

Not even the tiniest hint of a dimple was evident on McBride's face. Dirty Harry and Dick Tracy all rolled into one. His expression stern, he motioned me to roll down my window. I smiled and faked incomprehension.

"Now," he growled, clearly not buying into my theatrics.

Much aggrieved — and more than a little

nervous — I did as he asked. "This is a public street. It isn't a crime to park here."

"True," he agreed, "but it's my job to investigate when the captain of the neighborhood watch calls the station about a suspicious vehicle parked on her street. She demanded we send someone out to check."

"Well, consider it checked. Job done." I made to roll up the window.

"Not that simple." Curiously, my bad temper didn't faze him. "You're making some of the residents nervous. They need to be reassured that they're in no imminent danger of robbery."

"R-robbery . . . ?" I sputtered.

"You heard me."

"Give me a break, McBride. Do I look like a robber?" The minute the words popped out of my mouth, I wanted them back.

McBride raised his Maglite and let the beam play over me. His shrewd icy blues didn't miss a trick. "Judging from your attire, I'd say you could be the poster child for the well-dressed cat burglar, right down to the knit cap and black turtleneck." He paused a beat, then asked, "Don't suppose you have a ski mask tucked away somewhere?"

"Of course not!" I returned indignantly.

Resting his free hand on the roof of the Beetle, he swung the flashlight beam around the interior of the car, the light picking up discarded sub wrappers, empty Diet Coke cans, and a half-empty bag of Doritos. "You having another of your impromptu picnics?"

"Look, McBride, we're not doing anything illegal."

His eyes narrowed, sharpened. "We . . . ?"

"Hey there, Chief." As if on cue, Reba Mae cheerily announced her return. "Fancy meetin' you again."

"Might've known," he said, shaking his head. "Care to explain what you two are up to?"

I clamped my mouth shut. Unfortunately, Reba Mae didn't share my reticence. "We're on a stakeout."

"A stakeout?" His lips twitched, and I could swear he was trying to hide a smile. "Ladies, take a piece of advice from a pro on the matter of stakeouts. Next time — heaven forbid, there is a next time — choose a vehicle less conspicuous than a gecko-green Volkswagen Beetle."

"We're checking out Tony Deltorro," Reba Mae volunteered.

I gave her a dirty look for spilling the beans, which she, in turn, ignored. If hauled into an interrogation room at police headquarters, she'd fold like a cheap suit. Five minutes tops.

"Our theory is that Tony might've offed Mario."

"That's some theory." McBride shook his head. "As far-fetched as it might sound, my guess is you two are watching way too many cop shows on TV. Might be a good time to switch to the Lifetime Channel."

Folding her forearms on the roof of the VW, Reba Mae leaned forward and expounded on our theory. "Doesn't Tony Deltorro buyin' the Tratory so soon after Mario's death strike you as a little . . . suspicious? He could've been plannin' all this from the get-go."

"It isn't against the law to expand your business."

Reba Mae snorted in disbelief. "Before Mario's ashes even cooled?"

"Did you know Tony and Mario had a long-standing feud?" I asked, part question, part challenge. "Everyone in town knows they both had hot tempers. If you weren't so *fixated* on pinning the blame on me, you'd be trying to find out who had a motive for wanting Mario dead. Checking to see who had alibis — and who didn't."

Sensing tension in the air, Reba Mae drew away from the car and looked uneasily from me to McBride. "Um, Piper," she said, clearing her throat and breaking the strained silence, "guess we should call it a night." She got back into the car.

McBride stepped back, but kept his gaze fastened on me. "Leave the investigation to the professionals. Word gets out to the wrong person, the killer for instance, and you could find yourself up to your cute little butt in alligators."

I cranked the engine and drove off.

"What do you s'pose he meant by that?" Reba Mae asked.

"I guess he's worried we might stumble across the truth." I tried to convince myself his warning hadn't scared me. But, truth was, it had.

"That, too," Reba Mae said. "I liked the part best about your 'cute little butt.' Shows he's payin' attention to detail."

Lucky me, I thought with a sigh.

CHAPTER 21

By the time I arrived, the welcome reception was in full swing. I'd taken Reba Mae's advice and donned my snappy red dress and the four-inch stilettos that cost nearly as much money as my shop had made since it opened. Silver drop earrings were my only accessory. I'd bought them as a consolation prize a couple years back after CJ canceled our trip to Hawaii in favor of a bar association seminar in Minneapolis. Instead, he magnanimously offered to take me to Oktoberfest held every year in Helen, Georgia. Nothing against a Bavarian village, Georgia style, but it can't compete with Maui. Not even if you throw in tubing down the Chattahoochee River as a bonus. I did get suspicious, however, when CJ returned from Minnesota with a tan. Especially since the Weather Channel reported torrential downpours during his stay there.

I staged my arrival to avoid the receiving

line. Or more succinctly to avoid having to "make nice" to a man who regarded me with blatant suspicion, skepticism, and curiosity. Like a heat-seeking missile, I zeroed in on McBride off to one side, out of uniform and looking spiffy in a navy three-button blazer and tan chinos, and cut a wide swath.

"Piper, good to see you." Diane Cloune, dressed in matte black jersey, smiled the gracious hostess smile. "I was afraid you might not show, considering your recent . . . trouble."

My lips stretched into a tight smile. "I wouldn't have missed your little party for the world."

"Hmm." Her shrewd dark eyes gave me the once-over. Probably inspecting me for signs of jailhouse pallor or police brutality. "Nice earrings. A craft bazaar?"

"No," I replied, not caring if I sounded smug. "Tiffany's." Diane tended to be a name-dropper, but two could play this game. In the not-too-distant past, I could navigate my way through the upscale malls on Atlanta's Peachtree Road — namely Phipps Plaza and Lenox Square — like a veteran. Nowadays, my shopping trips to Atlanta are restricted to the farmers market in the pursuit of fresh and exotic spices.

"Tiffany's is overrated," Diane sniffed. "Bar's over there." She pointed toward the far wall, then breezed off leaving a cloud of designer fragrance in her wake.

I threaded my way through knots of guests happily imbibing and noisily chattering. I'd been surprised to discover that McBride's reception was being held at the Clounes' two-story Tudor home rather than the country club. But maybe the venue wasn't strange after all, given Diane's newly remodeled kitchen. Not that Diane cooks, mind you, but a realtor friend had insisted kitchens and baths can make or break a sale. Thus, gleaming granite countertops, top-of-the-line stainless steel appliances, hardwood floors, and custom cabinets. Nothing but the best for a city councilman with political aspirations and his social-climbing wife.

"Hey, Piper," I heard someone call my name.

"Ned?" I did a double take at the man behind the bar. "I hardly recognized you without your ball cap."

"Miz Cloune ordered me to leave it in my pickup. Said it wasn't fittin' for this sort of shindig."

"I didn't know you moonlighted as a bartender."

"Overheard Danny mention he was fixin'

to hire one, so I offered my services." He treated me to a lopsided grin. "Can I pour you a nice glass of wine? We have either red or white, but if you want, I could mix 'em. Makes a real pretty pink that way."

"White will be fine, thanks."

Scratching his head, Ned pondered his choice of wineglasses, then selected the narrower one. "Beats me why the shape of a glass makes a difference, but Miz Cloune gave me specific directions. Fat glass for red wine, she said; skinny for white. You'd think wine would taste the same even in a jelly jar, but what do I know. Be sure 'n help yourself to the food," Ned advised, handing me my drink. "Danny coaxed Maybelle Humphries into givin' him her recipe for pimento cheese spread. Maybelle sure is the bomb when it comes to cookin'."

Dottie Hemmings bustled up to the makeshift bar and offered her empty glass for a refill. "Heard you mention Maybelle's pimento cheese spread. Once, for bridge club, she made teensy sandwiches shaped into hearts, clubs, and spades."

"What happened to diamonds?" I couldn't help but ask.

Dottie wagged her heard sorrowfully. "Ever since Buzz Oliver broke off their engagement and asked for the ring back,

Maybelle can't stand to look at a diamond."

"Poor Maybelle." Ned clucked his tongue. "She had her heart broken."

Dottie patted her bleached blond helmet. "Can't blame her none. Her and Buzz been dating for eight years."

"And engaged another five," Ned added.

It didn't seem to occur to either of them that I wasn't participating in the conversation. Had I wanted to join in, I might've volunteered that Maybelle was fast becoming Spice It Up!'s one and only best customer. The woman was determined to become the best cook in Brandywine County and make Buzz rue the day he dumped her for Becca Dapkins.

"Did you hear about Sue O'Connor?" Dottie asked, changing the subject. "Poor thing's been havin' a terrible, terrible time with psoriasis. The last medication Doc gave her caused a rash to break out all over her body. She was itchin' something fierce."

"Excuse me," I murmured. "I just saw someone I need to talk to."

I eased away from the pair. Knowing Dottie's love of the morbid, a discussion was bound to follow of the side effects of various medications, ranging from changes in behavior to risk of suicide, and concluding with warnings not to drive a car or operate a blender.

Out of the corner of my eye, I spotted McBride literally cornered by Harvey Hemmings, Dwayne Cloune, and the former chief, Joe Johnson. No one was smiling. From their expressions, I guessed some serious dialogue was taking place.

I'd been too preoccupied with Wyatt McBride to notice I was about to be ambushed until it was too late.

"Well, well, well," CJ boomed. "How ya doin', Scooter?"

"CJ," I returned, hoping my voice sounded cool, calm, and collected. "Shouldn't you be rubbing elbows with the movers and shakers instead of wasting time with little ol' me?"

"Business must be picking up if you can afford to take the afternoon off." His signet ring flashed as he ran a hand over his hair.

I had to admit Reba Mae might be on to something when she insisted he was coloring it. I remembered it being more sandy, less brassy. I forced a smile. "I couldn't pass up the opportunity to congratulate our new chief of police on the stellar job he's doing here in Brandywine Creek."

Smirking, CJ shot a look in McBride's direction. "Stellar isn't exactly the word I'da picked, darlin'. Heard the mayor and city council aren't too happy about the lack of progress in the Barrone killin'. Told me they planned to give him a good talkin' to."

I followed the direction of CJ's glance. McBride wore the impassive expression he seemed to don with ease. The other three made no effort to hide their agitation. I almost — *almost* — felt sorry for McBride.

"His lack of success isn't for lack of trying. He did his darndest to blame Mario's murder on me. Too bad, he didn't succeed. The mayor would be pinning a medal on his chest this very minute."

"You're no more a killer than I am," CJ scoffed. "McBride gives you any more grief, you know how to reach me."

"Thanks for the vote of confidence." And I meant it. It was nice to know CJ believed in my innocence — in spite of the rumors and innuendos bandied around town.

"Hell, darlin', you were even squeamish about squashin' bugs. McBride's case against you doesn't stand a snowball's chance in hell. If gettin' you riled is all it took to be a dead man, well, shoot, I'd be six feet under instead of standin' here talkin'."

I felt some of my resentment toward him soften. CJ wasn't such a bad guy after all. True, he could be an insensitive clod at times, but he had his moments.

"There you are, Pooh Bear."

Even before I turned, I recognized the sweet-as-honeysuckle-on-the-vine voice as belonging to Miss Peach Pit, otherwise known as Amber Leigh Ames.

"You naughty boy, I've been lookin' for you high 'n low," she scolded, tucking her hand in the crook of CJ's elbow.

"Hello, Amber," I said, mustering a smile for the former beauty queen.

In spite of my antipathy, I had to admit she was striking, with flowing mahogany locks that would have made a shampoo manufacturer weep with envy and limpid gray-green eyes framed with spiky lashes. Her slender, but curvy, figure had won the swimsuit competition hands down. If I had to find a flaw — and with her being the "other woman," I felt obligated to do so — it would be her smile. She had big teeth. Not only big, but unnaturally bright. The glow-in-the-dark kind. I often wondered if she and CJ used the same dentist.

And to make matters worse, she wore a snappy red dress, one very similar to the one I wore.

Amber treated me to a toothy smile. "I do hope, Piper, that you won't make a scene."

Even if it killed me, I was determined not

to let my dislike show. "Why would I make a scene, Amber?" I answered sweetly. "The fact we're wearing practically the same dress only goes to show we both have exquisite taste in clothes."

"I wasn't talkin' 'bout the dress, hon." She extracted her hand from the crook of CJ's elbow and held it up for me to see. A huge diamond — at least two, maybe three, carats — twinkled on her ring finger.

I was rendered speechless. Why so stunned, I couldn't comprehend. I'd listened while CJ talked ad nauseam about needing more freedom. Needing "space." And, God help me, I'd believed him. I'd swallowed his pathetic ramblings, hook, line, and sinker. Silly, foolish me!

"Congratulations." I squeezed the word through partially paralyzed vocal cords.

"We haven't set a date yet," CJ hastened to add.

As I stared at the couple, Amber slipped her arm through CJ's once more and looked up at him adoringly. For a second, I swore she actually batted her lashes at him, but in my dazed condition I could have been mistaken. Only heroines in Victorian novels batted their lashes, right?

"We're thinkin' a destination weddin' would be nice. Somewhere tropical. Maybe

251

the Dominican Republic. Or Costa Rica. I'm plannin' to ask Lindsey to be my maid of honor. Surely you don't mind?"

"Not at all. Why would I?" I couldn't shake the feeling that this entire conversation was surreal. "I'm sure Lindsey will be flattered."

Amber gave CJ's arm a squeeze. "Imagine me, a stepmother." She giggled. "I'm not much older than Lindsey."

"Imagine," I echoed. "I wish the two of you a happy ever after."

"Look, Sweetums, there's Matt and Mary Beth," CJ said, addressing Amber, then he turned to me. "If you'll excuse us, Piper, I need to speak to Matt about a new client we just signed. We're representing him in a suit against a concrete manufacturer and a contractor. Our client claims they made a curb too high, resulting in a sprained ankle. We think we've got a strong case. With the right judge, we could win a bundle."

I watched Pooh Bear and Sweetums walk away. News of their engagement had caught me off guard. Part of me felt hurt, a little sad. We'd been blissfully happy once, and I thought our love would last forever. I'd imagined CJ and me sitting in matching rockers on the front porch, growing old together. Another part of me felt a sense of closure. As in most marriages, CJ and I had had some good times together, some bad. During the "good," we'd produced two beautiful children whom I adored. But nothing stays the same. Time had come to put the past where it belonged and look to the future. I took another sip of wine and went to find Reba Mae.

I slipped out the French doors and found her on the patio. "There you are." I gave her a quick hug, then stepped back. "Don't you look pretty. You look like a gypsy . . . or a butterfly."

"Like it?" She twirled around, showing off a bright, wildly patterned skirt.

"On you, it's perfect."

There must have been something in my voice because she looked at me strangely. "Anythin' wrong, sugar? McBride givin' you a hard time?"

"I've been avoiding the guest of honor," I confessed. "The problem's CJ."

She placed her hands on her hips. "What now?" she demanded. "He promisin' Lindsey a trip to Cancún if she cleans her room?"

"The Dominican Republic or Costa Rica would be more like it."

"Come again?"

"He and Miss Peach Pit are engaged," I informed her glumly.

Reba Mae let out a low whistle. "Didn't see that one comin'. I thought he wanted to be footloose and fancy-free."

"Amber's wearing a rock nearly the size of a golf ball. The happy couple are planning a destination wedding with Lindsey as maid of honor."

"Sorry, sugar." This time it was Reba Mae who initiated the hug.

"Me, too." I sniffed, caught in a wave of nostalgia.

"Is this a private party, or can we make it a group hug?"

We broke apart to find Doug Winters, glass in hand, smiling at us from five feet away. "Just a little girl talk," I said, happy at finding him there.

Reba Mae held out her hand. "I don't think we've had the honor. I'm Reba Mae Johnson, Piper's BFF."

"BFF . . . ?" A smile played around his mouth. "I'm afraid I'm not up on the latest jargon."

Judging from Doug's slightly dazed expression, he clearly didn't know quite what to make of a woman with spiky magenta hair who looked like a refugee from a gypsy camp. Color rose slowly in his cheeks as his gaze settled on her awesome cleavage. I

chuckled silently. Men could be so predict-
able.

"Best friend forever," Reba Mae supplied,
with a laugh that made the gold hoops in
her ears sway.

"Ah," he said, releasing her hand. "Pleased
to meet you Ms. Johnson. That must make
me Piper's BVF."

"BVF . . . ?"

He winked at me, a twinkle in his eyes.
"Best vet forever."

Smiling, I glanced away as McBride, head
down, a scowl on his face, strolled onto the
patio. He looked up with a frown, apparently surprised to see he wasn't alone.
"Sorry, didn't mean to interrupt."

"No need to apologize, Chief." Doug
extended his hand. "We're happy to have
the guest of honor join us."

"You don't seem very perky for someone
havin' a big splash welcomin' 'im to town,"
Reba Mae commented.

"I'm not one for politics. I hoped I'd left
all that behind in Miami."

"Small-town politics can be just as vi-
cious," Doug observed wryly.

I took a sip of wine. "I don't suppose
'politics' had anything to do with finding
Mario's killer?"

"Seems my job depends on it."

"Well, McBride, if you don't find the killer, I will," I announced with quiet conviction. "My *life* depends on it."

McBride gave me a long, searching look, but I didn't back down, didn't flinch. Later, back in my shop again, I wondered if I'd only imagined it, but had Reba Mae and Doug shifted closer in a flanking move as if to signal, "We've got your back"?

Was I being paranoid? Melodramatic? Maybe I should just take a chill pill. After all, Doug had provided me with a much-needed alibi. Still, having McBride and his men search my shop and living quarters had unnerved me. And worse yet, it made me heartsick to have folks I'd known all my married life avoid me as if I were Typhoid Mary. I missed their smiles, their friendliness, their acceptance. I'd heave a huge sigh of relief when the lab confirmed the bloodstains found on my T-shirt were canine — not human.

CHAPTER 22

At first, it sounded like distant thunder. A summer storm that had yet to materialize. Then, suddenly, what I'd mistakenly labeled "thunder" exploded into a frenzy of barking. Startled from a sound sleep, I sat bolt upright in bed. My heart hammered against my ribs as though trying to escape.

Instead of being in his usual spot curled at the foot of the bed, Casey stood by the door leading from the apartment to the shop downstairs, barking for all he was worth.

"Hush!" I scolded, my mind still sluggish with sleep.

The dog responded with another series of barks. Even in the dark, I could see that his entire body was so tense it fairly vibrated. My instinct was to burrow deeper into the covers, block out the racket, pretend this wasn't happening.

"Stop," I pleaded. "Lay down!"

Rather than cease and desist, Casey pawed and scratched at the door. "Okay, okay," I muttered. I darted a look at the bedside clock. The luminous dial read 2:15 A.M. Was this the pup's way of telling his owner he needed to relieve himself? Maybe Reba Mae wasn't the only one afflicted with a weak bladder.

As I started to fling aside the covers, I heard a loud crash from downstairs, followed by what sounded like footsteps beating a hasty retreat.

Then silence. Absolute, utter silence.

The quiet was short-lived, broken by another spate of barking. Then in the distance, I heard a car start and drive away.

A shiver raced through me. Someone had just broken into my shop.

I needed to call 911. Frantic, I looked around the bedroom. Where was my stupid phone? I groped along the nightstand and dresser, in the process sending a paperback novel thudding to the floor, nearly knocking over a lamp. It wasn't there. *Penny-wise and dollar foolish,* my grandmother whispered from her grave. To save money, my only landline was in the shop below. I used my cell phone for all personal calls. Problem was, I was forever forgetting where I'd put it. Pushing back my unruly mop of curls, I

258

tried to think. Tried to concentrate. To form a plan.

Phone, phone, phone. Where did I leave the dang thing?

Then it dawned on me. I'd used the cell phone the night before to call Chad at UNC and managed to snag him on his way to the library. I'd probably left it sitting next to the register. Unless I wanted to cower in my bedroom until dawn, I had little choice but to retrieve it. The sounds of running feet and a car driving off had signaled that my unauthorized guest had fled. That and the fact Casey's frenzied barks had subsided into a steady, low growl.

"All right, boy," I told him. "Let's get some help."

I padded downstairs, the worn wood steps cool under my bare feet. Casey scampered ahead, alternately barking and growling. If I didn't know better, I'd say the small dog sounded ferocious. As I neared the landing, a chilly draft of air caused my arms to pebble with goose bumps. Careful to avoid the creaky fourth step from the bottom, I crept down the remaining stairs.

The rear door stood ajar. I pushed it shut, but the latch refused to catch. I felt for the switch plate on the wall, and instantly the shop was flooded with light. A box of glass containers had been overturned, the small bottles scattered across the storeroom floor. Casey rubbed against my leg and gave a tail wag as if to let me know he was on the job.

"Brave boy," I praised. "My protector."

Spying my phone, I snatched it off the counter. My fingers trembled as I dialed 911. "This is Piper Prescott," I blurted the instant my call was answered. "Someone just broke into my shop, Spice It Up!, and tried to rob me."

"Be right there," a gruff male voice replied.

My legs felt rubbery so I perched on a stool and waited, Casey at my feet. I rubbed my arms to fend off a chill. A chill that had little to do with the cold air seeping through a door that refused to close. After what seemed like hours, but in reality was less than ten minutes, I saw red and blue lights strobe as a patrol car screeched to a stop in front of my shop.

Hurrying over, I threw open the door. Wyatt McBride stood there, his holster unsnapped, his right hand on the butt of his gun. Even in my flummoxed condition, I noted he hadn't taken the time to don his uniform. Instead, he wore his shiny gold badge clipped to the waistband of faded jeans that fit like a glove and a navy T-shirt under an aged hoodie bearing the MIAMI-DADE PD logo. With his dark hair all tousled and a five o'clock shadow, he looked sexy as hell. I quickly banished any prurient thoughts.

"You okay?"

I nodded.

"Step aside while I look around."

I stood as still as a cigar-store Indian and let him do his thing. I was not one to argue with a man and his gun.

He spent a good deal of time in the storeroom — peering into closets, checking out cupboards, inspecting first the back door, then the alley itself — before returning. "No sign of the intruder," he stated. "Care to describe what happened?"

"Why do you always show up?" I asked irritably. "Aren't there others on the force?" I slowly walked toward him, Casey close at my side. I kept my arms wrapped around myself, conscious I wore only a thin oversized sleep shirt. I'd been too rattled to run upstairs for a robe. And too afraid the robber might return if I didn't keep watch.

"We're short staffed at the moment," he explained with marked patience. "Beau's at a seminar in Charlotte. Gary's in the ER while the doc tries to decide if it's appendicitis or a kidney stone. I offered to take call on the night shift. Now" — he produced a small notebook — "it's your turn to do the explaining."

"Fine." I drew a breath to steady myself. "I . . . ah . . . Casey . . . my dog, woke me up with his barking. At first I thought he needed to go out and . . . you know . . . relieve himself, but then I heard a loud crash. A minute later, I heard what sounded like footsteps. Next, I heard a car start and drive off."

"And then what did you do?"

"I ran downstairs. The rear door was ajar. I tried to shut it, but it wouldn't close. When I turned on the lights, I could tell someone had been here. That's when I phoned nine-one-one."

"What took you so long to call for assistance? Most people reach for the phone the second they hear a strange noise."

"Oh, that." I made a small shrug, embarrassed at my stupidity. "I couldn't remember where I left my cell phone. Finally, I realized I must've left it in the shop after calling my son last night."

"How many kids do you have?" McBride asked, his pen poised over his pad.

"Two." I rubbed my arms. Strange to be talking about my children at a time like this, but thoughts of them helped calm me.

Maybe someone with McBride's training could see I was in dire need of calming. "Lindsey's in high school. My son, Chad, attends the University of North Carolina in Chapel Hill. He's in premed."

"Sounds like you're proud of them."

"Aren't most parents proud of their offspring?"

"No, not always."

I hoped he'd elaborate, but he didn't. Instead he shrugged out of his hoodie and draped it over my shoulders. "Here," he said. "You're shivering."

"Thanks." I drew it closer. It felt deliciously warm and smelled vaguely of pine.

"I'll have one of my men dust for prints first thing in the morning. Looks like someone jimmied the lock. You'll need to call a locksmith and have it replaced."

"Fine." Great, another expense. Just what I didn't need.

"I want to show you something." McBride disappeared into the storeroom only to reappear a moment later holding an item in his gloved hand. A hand that wasn't gloved previously. "This yours?"

I stared at the wrinkled piece of fabric he held up for my inspection. "No, I never saw it before."

"You sure?"

"Positive," I replied, with a vigorous nod. "I never wear purple. Ask anyone. It's not my color."

He frowned, obviously puzzled. "What does whether it's your 'color' or not have to do with anything?"

"Purple makes my complexion look sallow," I explained. "It's not a good choice for redheads."

"Of course," he muttered. "I'm fresh out of evidence bags. Don't suppose you have a Ziploc I can put this in?"

"Evidence?" I peered at the cloth he held. It was not only wrinkled, but stained and stiff. "What sort of evidence?"

"A bag, please."

I rooted through a drawer and came up with the requested Ziploc, then watched McBride carefully lower it inside and seal it shut. Now that I'd had a closer look at the article of interest, it appeared to be a T-shirt. A nondescript purple T-shirt. But the sixty-four-thousand-dollar question was, what was it doing in my shop?

"I'm going to send this to the GBI crime lab for analysis," he stated in a matter-of-fact tone. "If my hunch is right, the blood-stains will match those of Mario Barrone."

Suddenly, I felt nauseous. "Certainly, you don't think . . . ?"

"That, in spite of the shirt not being your 'color,' it really belongs to you?" The corners of his mouth curved upward in a hint of a smile. "No, I believe you."

"Why?" The word hung between us as if suspended by an invisible cord. I simply couldn't comprehend why this hardheaded cop would take my word for even the time of day. I didn't understand the man at all.

"Remember Judge Herman signing a search warrant for your place?"

"How could I forget?" I retorted, making no effort to hide my resentment. "I hated it. My home, my place of business, were violated. The thought of strangers pawing through my personal possessions still makes me cringe."

"Well, after Sergeant Tucker finished, I took a second look myself. Trust me, if you'd hidden it there — or anywhere else, for that matter — we'd have found it. I'd bet my last dollar this evidence" — he held up the bag for emphasis — "has been planted. Best be on your guard, Piper; someone's trying to frame you for Barrone's murder. Whoever the killer is, he'll go to any length to draw suspicion away from himself. Even if it means pointing the finger at an innocent person."

Casey, whom I'd nearly forgotten, whined

and huddled closer to me. Bending down, I picked him up and cuddled him. "Seems like my detective work is starting to show results."

"This isn't a game you're playing."

He stepped closer, successfully breaching my personal space. My instinct was to step back, but I held my ground. His lake blue eyes glittered with anger and an emotion I couldn't decipher. He looked dangerous. Dangerous and . . . attractive? A wicked combination. I felt nerves flutter in the pit of my stomach.

"Promise," he said, his voice low, his face grim, "that you'll keep your phone close at hand. Next time — God forbid there is a next time — call nine-one-one if you even *think* someone might be downstairs."

I swallowed audibly. "Promise."

"As long as you're being agreeable, one other thing," he said, peeling off his latex gloves and executing a perfect hook shot into a nearby wastebasket. "Never confront a would-be burglar dressed in a flimsy nightshirt. It's asking for trouble. A simple robbery could turn into a far more serious offense. I wouldn't want to see you hurt."

I hugged Casey tighter. "I didn't think . . ."

"Enough said." He jerked his thumb in the direction of the stairs. "Just to be on the

266

safe side, it might be wise to spend what's left of the night at your friend Reba Mae's. I'll call and let her know what's going on while you pack a few things, then I'll follow you over."

I wanted to argue with him. Assert my independence. Tell him, in no uncertain terms, he had no right to boss me around. But a quick glance at his unyielding expression, and I held my tongue. In this instance, silence, not discretion, was the better part of valor.

CHAPTER 23

All day long, the spicy-sweet tang of slow roasting baby back ribs drew people into Spice It Up! like ants to a Fourth of July picnic. I was experiencing the best sales since my grand opening. The hours I'd spent experimenting with various spices had paid off. I'd concocted the perfect combination of paprika, nutmeg, peppercorns, and my secret ingredient, a hint of ginger, for a fantastic rub. Now, I knew some folks preferred their ribs with a dry rub Memphis style. Others insisted the best way to go is heavy on the sauce à la St. Louis or Kansas City. Some started dry and ended with 'em dripping. I intended to appeal to both camps. For my next project, I was going to put together a sauce that — to borrow a Southernism — would make your tongue slap your brains out.

Just as I was mentally giving myself a pat on the back, Diane Cloune entered the shop accompanied by Vicki Lamont. "Oh, yum, ribs."

Vicki greeted me with a smile. "Hey, Piper."

"Hey, you two," I greeted back. The pair could have been mistaken for sisters. Pretty, pampered, look-alikes with perfect features and long, dark hair. They were dressed for a day on the links in coordinating skorts and shirts.

"Diane and I played nine, then had lunch at the club," Vicki volunteered. "She chipped in on number six. It was awesome."

Diane smiled, but it was more of a smirk. "You remember number six, don't you, Piper? Isn't that where CJ once shot a hole in one?"

I feigned amnesia. "I can't recall, sorry."

Diane yawned and changed the subject. "Dwayne loves barbecue, but eating it can be such a mess. Our housekeeper has a terrible time getting sauce stains out of his custom-made shirts."

"Wish I had a husband to complain about," Vicki said. "Kenny's still staying at his friend's cabin."

Information overload. I had too many problems of my own to sympathize with a wife caught cheating. No wonder Kenny hightailed it to the woods to lick his wounds.

As a matter of fact, problems or no problems, I couldn't scrounge up one iota of sympathy for a philandering spouse. Chandler Jameson Prescott III, in particular.

Clearing my throat, I inquired, "Is there something in particular I can help you ladies with this afternoon?"

Diane waved her hand in a dismissive gesture. "Thanks, but we're only killing time. We'll let you know if we need anything."

With those words, I was summarily dismissed. I'd been relegated to the role of shopkeeper, the ex-wife who no longer belonged to a country club. I went back to entering the day's receipts into the computer. I tried not to eavesdrop, I really did, but found it impossible not to and soon gave it up as a lost cause.

"Don't lose sleep over Kenny, sweetie," Diane advised her friend. "You'll have him eating out of the palm of your hand in no time."

"I don't know what I was thinking in the first place. Mario just caught me in a weak moment. Kenny was taking me for granted, not paying a lick of attention to me and, I guess, it was nice to meet a man who did. For a time, I foolishly thought I'd found my soul mate."

"Leave it to Mario." Diane chuckled. "The man could turn charm on and off like a light switch. If you recall, I tried to warn you about falling head over heels for the swine. Now that he's dead, hon, you can tell me, your very best friend, who called it off. You? Or did he?"

"Let's just say, the bastard broke my heart, then stomped on it."

Diane let out an unladylike snort. "Say no more, girlfriend."

Out of the corner of my eye, I saw Vicki pick up a jar of cinnamon and take a sniff. "What about you, Diane? You're a fine one to talk."

"Mmm, perhaps." Diane examined a display of peppercorns. "When I got involved with Mario, I knew exactly what I was letting myself in for. Neither of us wanted, or were looking for, a serious relationship. Our paths happened to cross in Atlanta. I was bored; he was horny. You know the rest."

Vicki swung toward me, a container of juniper berries in one hand. "Piper, are these the things you used in your cooking demonstration the day your shop opened?"

I glanced up from my computer. "Yes," I replied. "Juniper berries."

"I don't suppose you still have a copy of that lamb recipe laying around?"

"I'm sure it's here somewhere. Let me take a look while you browse."

Diane frowned at her friend. "I thought you hated cooking."

"I do," Vicki admitted, laughing. "But isn't there an old saying about the way to a man's heart is through his stomach?"

"Aren't you the sly one for trying to seduce poor Kenny."

"A home-cooked dinner, candlelight, soft music, an expensive bottle of wine. And for dessert, I thought I'd serve him Victoria's Secret. By the time I'm finished, he won't know what hit him."

"*If* I was in the market for seduction," Diane drawled, "I'd set my sights on the new chief of police. He's hot."

Hell hath no fury like a woman scorned. My mind churned with possibilities. Vicki had sounded furious when talking about Mario. He wouldn't be the first man killed by an angry ex-lover. I went through the motions of sorting through a folder, but my attention remained focused on the conversation of the two potential customers. And perhaps one potential murderer?

"Pinky Alexander swears she saw his picture in *People* with some Hollywood starlet in South Beach."

"Well, any seduction of Wyatt McBride better take place before it's too late."

"Why's that?" Vicki smoothed her already smooth ponytail as she continued to prowl the aisle.

"Shirley Randolph and I were having our nails done the other day. You know, don't you, that Shirley works part-time at Creekside Realty?" Diane picked up a bottle of Spanish paprika, scanned the label, set it down again. "Well, anyhow, she told me McBride is interested in making an offer on the old Walker place he's currently renting out on Route 78. But according to Dwayne, if the man doesn't make an arrest soon, he might as well kiss his shiny new badge goodbye. All those commendations from Miami won't be enough if he can't deliver the goods. How hard can it be to find a murderer in a town the size of Brandywine Creek?"

Vicki cast a sly look in my direction. "Just think, the killer could be under our noses right this very minute."

I couldn't keep my mouth shut at hearing this. How dare they? I fumed at the notion of being tried and found guilty in the court of public opinion. "I'm sure finding a killer, ladies, is harder than you make it out to be.

I'm no expert on the subject, but my guess is Chief McBride is more concerned about finding the real killer than harassing innocent citizens just so he looks good in front of the mayor and the city council. And if McBride doesn't discover who killed Mario, I swear I'll do it myself. I'm sick and tired of everyone looking at me as if I'm some deranged ax murderer."

My declaration was met with stunned silence.

"I suppose you'd view things differently if you weren't the only suspect," Diane said, regaining her equilibrium.

"Really, Piper," Vicki chimed, "it's no secret Judge Herman signed a search warrant for your place. The whole town's talking about it."

"And," Diane was quick to add, "I heard from a reliable source that the police confiscated several items simply covered in blood."

Instantly, I leaped to my own defense. "I found a dog behind my shop the night Mario was killed. He was hurt, so I wrapped him in a towel and took him to the vet."

Diane made an exaggerated show of searching under shelves and peering around corners until I wanted to shake her. "A likely story. I don't see any dog. So . . . ," she drawled. "Where is this mystery animal of yours?"

I marched over to the stairs. "Casey," I yelled. "Here, boy."

At hearing his name called, the pup bounded down the steps and slid to a stop when he encountered the baby gate I'd installed across the bottom. "Not all my customers appreciate a puppy underfoot," I explained, unlatching the gate.

Casey scampered into the shop, a furry, wriggling mass of excitement and enthusiasm. He tap-danced at my feet until I rubbed behind his ears, then he raced over to welcome the visitors with a flurry of yips and tail wags. Unfortunately his enthusiasm got the better of him, and he peed on the floor, the spray narrowly missing Diane's sandaled foot.

She leaped back. "Well, I never!"

"Casey loves meeting people. If anything, he's overly friendly." I tried to keep the smile off my face, but wasn't sure if I'd succeeded keeping it out of my voice.

"These sandals are Ferragamo," Diane huffed. "Do you have any idea how much they cost?"

"Tsk, tsk," I scolded the little dog who now cowered at my feet. "Bad puppy. Go show the nice lady you're sorry."

"No, no, that's all right." Diane leaped back as though she'd just stepped into a mound of fire ants.

Vicki skirted the puddle. "Diane, didn't you mention stopping by the antique shop? Let me pay for these berries and then we'll go."

I rang up the sale, happy it was time for the Vicki and Diane Show to hit the road. Feeling generous, I stuffed the recipe for roast lamb into the bag as a goodwill gesture. "Y'all come back now," I said as the door swung shut behind them.

I'd no sooner finished cleaning up Casey's accident when Doug Winters strolled in. Canting my head to one side, I studied him as he approached. After meeting him at the welcome reception for McBride, Reba Mae had nudged me and exclaimed over and over how "cute" he was. And I had to agree with my friend. Prematurely silver hair. An engaging, boyish charm. Eyes the color of melted chocolate. Yes, definitely a cutie. Why had it taken me this long to pay closer attention?

"I brought some new doggy snacks one of my vendors dropped off." He set a bag on the counter. "I saw a couple women leave a few minutes ago. Business picking up?"

"Hardly." I peeked inside the bag and

discovered treats resembling Tootsie Rolls. "If I had to depend on those two, I might as well declare bankruptcy."

Doug chuckled. "Not much on cooking, are they?"

I chuckled, too. "Their favorite recipes are box dinners and the pop-in-the-microwave variety. Vicki, however, plans to woo Kenny, her estranged husband, with a home-cooked meal. Roast lamb with rosemary and juniper, to be precise."

Doug stooped to pet Casey, who was prancing at his feet in a bid for attention. In exchange, the vet's face was lathered in wet puppy kisses. "Do you like Indian food?" Doug asked me as he straightened.

"I've only tried it once, but I'm game. What do you have in mind?"

"I came across a recipe for tandoori chicken. Thought I'd try it out, provided I could find a suitable victim . . . er, volunteer . . . for my experiment. Are you free tomorrow night?"

I couldn't think of a single reason to refuse, then realized I didn't want to. I genuinely enjoyed the man's company. Besides, it's just dinner — not sex. "Gee, let me check." I thumbed through an imaginary datebook. "Seems I have an opening. Pencil me in."

"Great." He grinned and pulled a slip of paper from his pants pocket. "I brought along a list of the spices I'll need for garam masala: cumin seeds, Tellicherry black peppercorns, coriander seed, cardamom seed, whole cloves, and mace."

As I wandered along the shelves of spices, picking up items as I went, I felt proud I had done my homework. Garam masala, I'd learned, was an aromatic blend of spices often used in Indian cuisine. "I'll even grind them if you like," I offered.

"Deal." Doug trailed after me.

After consulting a reference book on the exact amounts, I carefully measured the ingredients into a coffee grinder reserved exclusively for spices. I finished my grinding and was surprised to find Wyatt McBride patiently watching from just inside the doorway. I found his presence unsettling. Maybe it was the gun-and-badge thing. Maybe the don't-mess-with-me expression. Or, even more unsettling, maybe it was the man himself.

"Sorry," I mumbled. "I didn't hear you come in over the sound of the grinder."

"We need to talk."

Frown lines appeared between Doug's brows as his eyes darted back and forth between the two of us.

"You in the market for garam masala, McBride?" I asked. "It's the spice du jour." He'd once called me prickly, and I had to admit that whenever he was around I was. Best defense is a good offense, as CJ used to say. Or was it, a first offense deserves a good defense? Words to that effect, at any rate.

"Consider this an official visit," he said, ignoring my offer.

I nervously wiped my hands on my apron. "Can it wait until I finish with my customer?"

At his curt nod, I gave the grinder an extra go-round, more for effect than necessity. I smiled at Doug as I transferred the mixture from the grinder into a lidded container and added a label. "If memory serves, translated garam masala literally means 'sweet mix.'"

"Nice," Doug said, sniffing the concoction I'd just whipped up. "What makes garam different from curry powder?"

I didn't know if Doug was a culinary whiz kid masquerading as a bespeckled veterinarian or was merely attempting to keep the conversational balloon afloat. Whichever the case, I was grateful. "Garam lacks the heat of chili peppers and turmeric as a base."

"Interesting." Doug's gaze slid to McBride's impassive face. "Um, how much do

I owe you?"

I was in no frame of mind for high finance. "Let's call it an even trade, shall we? Doggy treats for garam."

"Thanks, Piper," Doug said, accepting the container I held out. "Want me to stick around?"

I wiped sweaty palms on my apron. Touched by Doug's protectiveness, I managed a brave smile. "Thanks, but I'll be fine."

Doug's nod conveyed reassurance. "See you tomorrow night then. Six o'clock okay?"

"Six is perfect." I watched him leave, then, with a sinking sensation, I turned to McBride. "Well," I said, "are you here to arrest me?"

CHAPTER 24

"Arrest you?"

I crossed my arms over my chest knowing, but not caring, that McBride might interpret the gesture as defensive. His analysis would be spot on. I admit I felt anxious about the possible reason for McBride's visit. Could it be because of the damned purple T-shirt someone had hidden in plain sight? The man tended to make me jittery — even in the rare times he was being nice. "I'm not in the mood for games," I snapped. "You said you were here on official business."

"The forensics report came back on the bloodstains on the bath towel and T-shirt that we found when we executed the search warrant of your place."

I knew the bloodstains belonged to Casey, not Mario, but what if the lab had made a mistake? Mistakes were made all the time. Innocent people went to jail. Some even were condemned to death row. Reaching down, I scooped Casey up and held him like a shield against bad news.

McBride eyed me cautiously. "Are you going to sic your dog on me?"

"I might." I stroked the little animal's silky head, but kept my gaze fastened on McBride. "Don't underestimate him. He's a trained attack dog."

McBride raised a brow as he studied the pup that was starting to doze off in my arms. "Consider me warned."

"Looks can be deceiving," I said, reading his skepticism of Casey's hidden talent. "What did the lab say about the blood-stains?"

"Forensics identified them as canine, not human." He paused a beat before adding, "I wanted to tell you in person."

I walked across the shop and sank down on the stool behind the counter. "I hope the news didn't come as a shock," I told him peevishly. "I told you that from the beginning."

"I know you did." He sauntered closer, thumbs hooked in his belt. "Until now, however, we — meaning law enforcement — had only your word for it. Now with the GBI report to back it up, all doubts are gone. You can rest easy."

"Aren't you forgetting about the purple T-shirt? You said yourself that you thought the results would come back positive for Mario's DNA."

"I still think that, but I'm also convinced the shirt was planted to throw suspicion your way."

"But will anyone believe you?"

"I'm ready to swear in a court of law if need be that the shirt wasn't present at the time of the search. Why would I perjure myself?"

Hearing that should have made me feel better, but it didn't. Even though McBride believed the evidence was planted, once forensics unequivocally identified the blood-stains as Mario's, it could still be an uphill battle to convince everyone else. I was still in a boatload of trouble — and my boat kept springing leaks. "Did your men find any prints on the lock?"

" 'Fraid not. Whoever planted the evidence must've worn gloves."

"Great," I muttered as I continued to pet Casey. Icy water kept spurting into my imaginary leaky craft. "Surely your men could see the lock had been tampered with?"

"Good point." McBride ran a hand over his thick dark hair. "Any prosecutor worth his salt might claim you did it yourself."

"But why would I jimmy a lock on my own door, plant a bloodstained item that was certain to incriminate me, then call the police to report a burglary? That doesn't make any sense."

"An even better point," he agreed. "You're right. It doesn't make sense. My theory is that the killer planted the bloody garment in your shop. If you hadn't dialed nine-one-one when you did, I'm equally certain an anonymous caller would have phoned in a 'tip.' Told us right where to look. You're being set up, Piper."

I let out a shaky breath. "Find the killer, McBride," I said. "Find the danged killer and let me get on with my life."

The hour was late — and except for Reba Mae and me — not a creature was stirring, not even a mouse. Conditions were perfect for the plan I was about to set in motion.

Reba Me darted a nervous look over her shoulder, then followed me down the dark alley. "Tell me again what we're doin' here?"

"We've discussed this a gazillion times," I reminded her. "We're going to check out the scene of the crime. See what we can find."

"Why?"

"Why?" I repeated, trying to keep the frustration from my voice. "Because someone is making me the fall guy, and I'm really, really pissed. McBride doesn't seem to be making any headway solving Mario's murder — and neither do we. All we've done so far is put together a list of possible suspects. It's time to start eliminating a few. Besides, aren't you more than a little curious who really killed Mario?"

"Course I am," she replied heatedly. "Just wish we could do it without all the cloak-and-dagger stuff."

Since technically Trattoria Milano was still an official crime scene, we agreed it best to keep our mission on the down low. I'd finagled a key from Shirley Randolph at Creekside Realty on the pretext of having a rich friend who might counter Tony's offer for the place. Dollar signs had replaced any misgivings the realtor might've had. She handed over the key along with a warning not to get caught. With that in mind, we'd decided to walk rather than advertise our presence with a VW that resembled a scoop of lime sherbet. We'd also dressed for the occasion in all black.

Reba Mae clutched my sleeve. "I think I saw somethin' move."

We paused, our senses on high alert. A

crescent moon played hide-and-seek behind a cloud bank, swathing the alley in shadows. Trash cans hunkered down behind various business establishments like a bevy of Jacob Marley's ghosts. Bottles, cans, and Styrofoam containers littered the cracked pavement. Just then a trash can toppled over, its lid clattering noisily to the ground, and we nearly jumped out of our skin. With a blood-curdling howl, a cat leaped from behind one of the cans, streaked down the alley, and disappeared between two buildings.

"See," I said in a shaky voice. "Nothing to be afraid of."

"Speak for yourself, sugar." Reba Mae reluctantly released her death grip on my arm. "Meemaw used to say a black cat crossin' your path at night was bad luck."

"That's just superstition," I said, refusing to acknowledge my own fright. "Anyway, the cat wasn't black. It was a tabby."

"Looked black to me."

I knew nothing would convince her otherwise so I hastened my step, anxious to take a quick look around and return home. Several yards down, I spotted the rear entrance to Trattoria Milano.

"Careful," I cautioned as I climbed the crumbling concrete steps and inserted the key. The lock snicked open. Ducking under the yellow crime scene tape, I stepped inside, with Reba Mae stuck to me like bubblegum. "Reba Mae Johnson," I scolded. "What's gotten into you tonight? I never figured you for a wuss."

She shrugged. "Midnight, dark alley, black cat . . . dead people. Take your pick."

I dug a slender flashlight out of the black patent tote bag I'd brought along and turned it on. The service area was just as I remembered. Pantry shelves stocked with industrial-size cans on one side, a jumbo freezer on the other.

"Why go all CSI?" Reba Mae whined. "Turn on the damn lights."

"I don't want to get caught snooping. Even with the key, it would be tricky to explain what we're doing here in the dead of night. It wouldn't take a genius long to find out there's no rich friend interested in this place."

"Do you honestly think we might stumble across somethin' the police overlooked?"

"Won't know until we try." I swept the beam side to side as we passed through the swinging door that separated the service area from the kitchen proper. I wasn't sure I'd know a clue unless it had a flashing neon sign with a red arrow pointing to it. But I wasn't about to let inexperience stand in the way of progress.

"Umm, ah . . ." Reba Mae hemmed and hawed ". . . where exactly did you find Mario?"

I traced a path with the flashlight to an area near a counter. "Over there."

Transfixed, Reba Mae stared at the darkened floorboards. "Is that a . . . ?"

"Bloodstain." I suppressed a shiver. Mario's name might not have been on my Christmas card list, but the poor guy deserved better than to die like a stuck pig. He deserved . . . justice.

Reba Mae rubbed her arms as though chilled. "This place gives me the willies. Let's do what we came here for and blow this pop stand."

"Gotcha." I stooped for a closer look, hoping to see something I might've missed. I recalled seeing Mario sprawled on his side. And a puddle of blood. I hadn't stayed around long enough to take in any details.

"This kitchen feels haunted." Reba Mae took up a post near the door, ready to bolt at a moment's notice. "You believe in ghosts, Piper?"

I heaved a sigh. "No."

"I didn't used to," Reba Mae confessed, "until Butch took me to Savannah. Went on one of those ghost tours. I came away a believer. Did you know Savannah's considered America's most haunted city?"

"If I did, the fact slipped my mind," I muttered. Just then, my heart started to pound. "Look, Reba Mae." I pointed to a series of dark splotches leading away from where I found the body.

She edged closer and peered over my shoulder. "I'm lookin', I'm lookin'."

"Do you see what I see?"

"All I see is a floor that needs a good scrubbin'."

"That's not dirt. Those are footprints."

I scrounged through my tote bag for supplies. Pulling out a digital camera, I snapped pictures from various angles like I'd seen done countless times on TV. Later, I'd download them into my computer and zoom in for a closer look. Next, I took out a small tape measure, a holdover from my knitting days, and measured from toe to heel and jotted the figures in a spiral notebook. That was when I noticed a second set of prints, smaller ones, probably mine.

"I heard a noise," Reba Mae said in a hushed tone.

"Don't be such a worrywart. Old buildings are full of creaks and groans." I stowed my stuff back into my tote. "Give me another minute to look around, then we'll go."

I knelt down and shone my light under the cabinets. When that failed to turn up anything more significant than dust, I ran my hand as far as it would go under the refrigerator. As every housewife knows, the floor beneath the fridge is a target-rich environment for everything from lost hair barrettes to Matchbox cars.

"Piper," Reba Mae whispered. "I swear I heard a footstep."

"Well then, that rules out a ghost," I replied absently as my fingers closed around a small round object. A pebble? A pea? A juniper berry?

Then I heard it, too. A muffled footstep. Like someone trying hard to be quiet — but not quite succeeding.

Scarcely daring to breathe, I straightened, clicked off the flashlight, and listened intently. Had the killer returned to the scene of the crime? Wasn't that their modus operandi? Or was that an urban myth? Maybe owning a handgun wasn't so crazy after all. I frantically searched for a weapon of some sort. Half-turning, I felt along the countertops. Almost of their own volition, my fingers curled around the rim of a pan. I snatched it up. With both hands around the handle, I assumed a softball stance, feet spread, bat at the ready.

Suddenly, the overhead fluorescent lights flashed on.

"Freeze!"

Squinting against the harsh glare, I saw a gun barrel pointed at my midsection. A lump of fear lodged in my throat. My gaze slowly traveled from the gun to the man who held it.

Wyatt McBride, his expression grim, stood in the doorway separating the kitchen from the service area. "Might've known," he muttered. "Drop your weapon."

I did as he said and a sauté pan fell to the floor, the noise like a gunshot.

McBride slid his pistol into a leather holster at the small of his back. "You alone, or did you bring your sidekick?"

Reba Mae, hands in the air, rose from a crouched position behind a prep table. "We under arrest?"

"Don't tempt me," he growled.

Reba Mae and I exchanged uneasy glances, but wisely remained silent.

"S'pose I could charge you with interfering with an investigation," he said, rubbing his jaw thoughtfully. "Or maybe breaking and entering?"

I wasn't about to let him intimidate me

291

further. "Nice try, McBride, but you can't make a case for breaking and entering when I have a key." Bending down, I retrieved the sauté pan, and placed it on the nearby gas range. I used the opportunity to slip the small object I'd found into my pocket, and then pulled out the key and dangled it in front of him. From his frown, I could see he didn't appreciate my showmanship.

"The real estate people were under strict orders not to allow anyone access without my expressed permission. Did you ladies fail to see the crime scene tape stretched across the back door? What part of 'do not cross' don't you understand?"

"It must have been the 'not.' "

Reba Mae shot me a warning glance that clearly said *do not poke a bear with a stick.* "Since you're not going to arrest us," she said, "guess we'll be on our way."

I wasn't as eager as she to leave, however. "Have you discovered who those shoeprints belong to?" I asked McBride.

"I'm not at liberty to discuss an active investigation."

"Ah, c'mon, McBride, you can tell me," I wheedled. "It's not as though you're selling government secrets to a foreign spy."

He ignored my question in favor of one of

his own. "Exactly what did you expect to find?"

"Piper thought she mighta dropped an earring when she found Mario. We wanted to take a look around. See if we could find it."

Quick thinking, girlfriend. I made a mental note to compliment her later.

"Ah," he drawled. "So a lost earring's an occasion for you two to get all dolled up in your cat-burglar finery?"

I felt my cheeks burn with irritation. "Maybe we're making a fashion statement. It isn't a crime to dress in black."

He raised a brow, but stepped aside. "Luckily for you, Trattoria Milano is no longer off-limits. A fax just came through that GBI is done here. I thought I'd take down the crime scene tape before heading home. That's when I noticed the door ajar and caught a glimpse of light."

I breathed a quiet sigh of relief. "Since this is no longer off-limits and I have a key, you have no reason to detain us. Say good night to the nice policeman, Reba Mae."

Reba Mae gave him a cheeky grin. "G'night, Wyatt."

A corner of his mouth twitched upward. "G'night, Reba Mae."

Once outside, it was all I could do not to

pinch her. "Since when are you and that man on a first-name basis?"

Reba Mae shrugged. "He dropped by the shop the other day with an old picture he found of Butch in his football uniform. He thought the boys might like it."

"Hmph." McBride disguised as Mr. Nice Guy? It was hard to wrap my mind around the notion.

We'd already reached Spice It Up! before I remembered the small object I'd found beneath the fridge. I fished it out of my pocket and studied it under a nearby street light. It wasn't a pebble after all. Neither was it a black-eyed pea or a juniper berry.

Reba Mae hovered alongside and together we examined the item I held in the palm of my hand. "What is it?" she asked. "A piece of glass?"

"There's one surefire way to tell." I swiped the object in question along the edge of the window and a faint scratch was instantly visible. "It's not glass, Reba Mae. It's a diamond."

"Some rock," she breathed. "Has to be at least a carat. Who do you suppose lost it?"

My eyes locked with hers. "Good question."

CHAPTER 25

It started to drizzle as I was about to leave for dinner with Doug. I grabbed my trench coat from a hook near the back door and sprinted across the vacant lot toward my VW on the street behind my shop. A little inconvenient, but I didn't want to break a city ordinance banning overnight parking on Main Street. The last thing I needed was parking tickets to tax my already overtaxed budget.

My wipers slapped to and fro at the moisture on the windshield. Tuning in to a country-western station, I sang along with a song about tequila making some woman's clothes fall off. It brought to mind Reba Mae's comments about my love life — or the lack thereof — so I switched stations. The only time my clothes fell off these days was before taking a shower. Sad, but true. The drizzle had turned into a light rain by the time I turned down the drive leading to

Pets 'R People. Doug must have been watching for me because he stood in the opened doorway. I threw my trench over my head and made a mad dash for the house.

"I should have met you with an umbrella," Doug said, taking my coat. "Never seem to have one handy."

"Something else we have in common," I laughed. "I doubt my umbrella knows what a raindrop feels like."

While Doug stowed my coat in the guest closet, I indulged my curiosity. I'd been in the clinic portion of his home, of course, but never the living quarters. The foyer opened into a spacious living room decorated in I'm-a-bachelor style. Neutral beige walls and Berber carpet. Black leather sectional. Pricey stereo equipment. Flat-screened TV that took up most of one wall. Little artwork and no live plants completed the décor.

"How about a glass of wine?" he asked.

"Sounds great."

I followed him into a dining nook complete with candles, an opened bottle of wine, and soft music — jazz, not country-western. Doug might have shared notes on how to stage a seduction with Vicki Lamont. With the exception of Victoria's Secret for dessert. Maybe the thoughts I'd had postdivorce of becoming a nun were a bit premature. I had to admit, it felt good spending time with a man who found you attractive. One who seemed sincerely interested in what you had to say. Not to mention a man who cooked you dinner. "You've gone to a lot of trouble."

"No trouble at all. I like to cook, but it's more fun to cook for two. An appreciative audience is a crucial ingredient, especially when trying a new recipe. That's where you come in."

I sniffed the air. "Dinner smells wonderful."

"Finding the right combination of fresh spices is key." He opened the oven and poked the chicken with a fork.

"If it tastes even half as good as it smells, I want the recipe. I've learned cooking attracts customers. Aromas waft out, customers drift in."

"Sounds like a solid business practice. I chilled a nice pinot grigio. Why don't you pour us a glass while I plate the salad."

I did as requested and, when he was finished with the salad, handed him a glass, then took a sip of my own. "Mmm." I smiled my approval. "Cold and crisp, light and fruity. The perfect pairing."

He shot me a boyish grin. "Hoped you'd like it."

"What else can I do to help?"

"Nothing. Let's enjoy the salad while the rice steams."

Like the wine, the salad was perfect. Thinly sliced cucumber and red onion in a refreshing, tangy dressing perfectly seasoned with dill. "You missed your calling, Doug. You should be the one opening a new restaurant, not Tony Deltorro."

"Thanks, but no thanks." Doug laughed, obviously pleased at the compliment. "Cooking should be fun," he said as he collected the empty salad plates. "I think I'd find it more stressful than enjoyable if I had to do it for a living."

"Mario Barrone didn't seem to be find cooking fun," I commented, watching Doug arrange the tandoori chicken on a bed of long-grain basmati rice.

He garnished a platter with slices of tomato and lemon. "I didn't know Mario well, but I got the impression he was an intense sort of guy."

"I guess you'd say his was an artistic temperament. Difficult to please, impatient, volatile. Ambitious."

"I gather Barrone didn't endear himself to a lot of people."

"In addition to his personality flaws, Mario owed some people money and refused to pay. Who knows" — I shrugged — "there could be more I don't know about."

"Any truth to the rumors that he was quite the ladies' man?"

"I have to admit I never understood Mario's appeal." I helped myself to a dinner roll. "Granted, the man was attractive enough — if you favor the Rudolph Valentino or Latin-lover type. I don't. Mario was much too arrogant, too into himself."

Doug set the platter in the center of the table and motioned for me to help myself. I selected a piece of chicken and a healthy portion of rice. Doug watched anxiously as I cut off a small bite and tasted it. Instantly, my taste buds were assaulted with the rich infusion of spices. Ginger, mace, and cardamom among others. "Umm," I said, sighing with pleasure. "Delicious. Incredible."

Happy his experiment was deemed a success, Doug relaxed. Over a plate filled with chicken and rice, he resumed the conversation where we'd left off. "I overheard the two women who came out of your shop yesterday mention Mario. I got the impression they'd both known him rather intimately at one time or another."

"One of the pair, Diane Cloune, Councilman Cloune's wife, ended the affair with Mario some time ago."

Doug sipped his wine. "What about the other woman?"

"Vicki Lamont." I speared another bite-size piece of chicken. Just as I'd anticipated, Doug proved an excellent cook. A culinary wizard. A vague idea began to crystallize. If — and that's a pretty big if — I managed to keep Spice It Up! afloat, maybe I could persuade Doug to do a cooking demo. The tandoori chicken and pungent garam masala were a great example of Indian cuisine.

"How does Vicki figure into all this?" Doug asked, pulling me back to the present.

"Ah, yes, Vicki," I said. For Doug's benefit, I rehashed info I'd recently discussed with Reba Mae. "Vicki's affair with Mario was fairly recent. She was serious enough about him to leave her husband. Their relationship nearly destroyed her marriage. From what I can gather, she was quite upset when Mario broke it off. Now she's trying to worm her way back into her estranged husband's good graces."

"You don't suppose . . ." Doug stared at me over the rim of his wineglass.

I stared back. ". . . that the killer could be a woman?"

Doug shook his head, his brown eyes serious. "I'm thinking more along the lines of a jealous — or estranged — husband."

A jealous husband? Duh! Why hadn't that occurred to me before? Goes to show I was a rookie in the private detective department. This meant I needed to add Dwayne Cloune and Kenny Lamont — as well as a good share of the husbands in Brandywine Creek — to my growing list of subjects. And this could possibly explain the man-size shoe print found at the scene. I set my fork down, no longer hungry.

Over coffee and dessert, we lapsed into small talk. I discovered Doug and I shared a lot of the same likes and dislikes. What's more, Doug was a good listener, a trait many women find sexy, me included. He seemed genuinely interested in hearing about my children, was sympathetic to my divorce woes, and understanding when I expressed concerns about my fledgling business. Since he owned a small business of his own, he could identify with the demands and uncertainties.

At the end of a pleasant evening, after helping me on with my coat, Doug gave me a chaste kiss on the cheek. I must admit that deep down, I felt a trifle disappointed, then gave myself a mental shake. No need to rush things, Piper. You have plenty of time to get to know each other.

The rain beat harder on the roof of the VW as I turned onto the county road and aimed for home. The wipers kicked up a notch to match the rain's pounding tempo. My thoughts roamed as I tuned out the voice of a late-night DJ offering advice and playing song requests. By the time I got home, Casey would be practically dancing a jig, ready to be let out for his nighttime ablutions. I made a mental note to grab an umbrella before snapping on his leash.

I cruised to a stop in my usual spot behind Spice It Up! Except for a darkened car halfway down the block, the street was deserted. No surprise there. Frowning, I peered across the bleak, rainy expanse that separated me from my shop and upstairs apartment. As usual, I'd forgotten to leave the back light on. Did I dare, just this once, defy the ban on overnight parking along Main Street? After weighing the matter, I decided against it. To borrow a word from Lindsey's lexicon, Lady Luck had "unfriended" me. With my spate of bad karma, the VW would be towed to an impound yard.

Put on your big-girl panties, I berated myself, and deal with it. You won't melt.

The worst that can happen is that you'll get a little wet. Pulling the hood of my trench over my head, I stepped into the rain. I was about to make a mad dash across the vacant lot when I spotted the plastic container of leftovers Doug had insisted I take.

Bright lights flared behind me, blinding me in their glare. Not again, I thought irritably. I don't care if Wyatt McBride is the chief of police, I'm going to charge him with harassment. But before I do, he's going to get a piece of my mind. He'll have a first-hand demonstration of redheads and their legendary tempers. I slammed the Beetle's door shut and waited, my purse in one hand, tandoori chicken in the other.

With a throaty growl, the car's engine sprang to life and leaped forward. I stood my ground, an angry diatribe forming in my head. I'd let McBride know in no uncertain terms that I didn't appreciate him following me. But instead of the vehicle slowing as it approached, it accelerated.

And pointed straight at me.

Instinct took over. Fueled by sheer terror, I dove across the hood of my car in a move that would have made a Hollywood stunt double turn green with jealousy. I heard a whoosh of air as the car passed mere inches away. Smelled the exhaust. Twisting my head around, I saw it disappear around a corner, tires squealing.

I slowly picked myself off the ground, biting back a groan. My shoulder pained where it had hit the hood of the VW; my knee stung from landing on the hard-packed soil. What the heck had just happened? Had someone tried to kill me? I couldn't seem to wrap my mind around the possibility. Dazed, I glanced around. My acrobatics had catapulted me into the vacant lot. The container of tandoori chicken had vanished. After retrieving my purse from where it had landed in a clump of weeds, I hobbled through a lot littered with soda cans and beer bottles.

I locked the door behind me even before flicking on the lights. Casey greeted me with a frenzy of excited barks. "Hey, boy," I said in a voice that didn't sound quite like my own. I absently brushed at grass and mud stains. My favorite coat looked as if it had been through a war. My slacks, I noted, were beyond repair, ripped at the knee and bloody from my tumble.

Someone had deliberately tried to run me down.

This finally seeped through the murky haze of denial. Although running on three cylinders instead of the usual four, my brain started to function again. I knew one thing with absolute certainty. I was making someone nervous. Very nervous. I had Mario's killer worried. Who was it? Pete? Tony? Danny? An ex-lover? A jealous husband? The possibilities made my head spin.

Sensing something was wrong, Casey whined and pranced at my feet. Picking him up, I nuzzled the furry little body, seeking comfort from an armload of puppy love. In return, Casey lathered my face with moist, raspy kisses.

Now that my initial shock was wearing off, I set Casey on the floor, located my cell phone in the jumble in my purse, dialed 911, and sat down to wait.

I nervously chewed a fingernail as the minutes ticked past. "Get a manicure" was another item I'd yet to cross off my to-do list. I wasn't eager for still another confrontation with McBride. Confrontations seemed to be what our meetings always turned into. Would I be subjected to another lecture? Regarded with skepticism? Viewed as a hysterical woman?

Red and blue lights flashing, a police cruiser braked to a stop outside my front door. When its dome light clicked on, I saw my fears were unfounded. As I hurried to unlock the door, I could see it wasn't

McBride who'd responded to my call, but Beau Tucker. Relief warred with disappointment.

Disappointment won.

CHAPTER 26

"Oh my God!" With a dramatic gesture, Reba Mae pressed her hand to heart. "Sugar, that's simply awful! Are you okay?"

I gave her an award-worthy imitation of a brave smile. "I'm fine except for a few bumps and bruises, but I had to pull the plug on a perfectly good pair of slacks. My favorite coat is a disaster. I bundled it up and dropped it at the dry cleaners. The clerk said it needed CPR."

"A damn shame." Reba Mae wagged her head sympathetically. She'd stopped by Spice It Up! following a long day of teasing and lacquering. "I always loved that coat. I still remember the day you brought it home."

"Me, too. Not every day Dillard's has a sale like that one."

Together, we contemplated the sad fate of my designer trench coat. Finally I tried to shake myself free of the funk I'd fallen into.

"We need to shift into happy mode. This is Lindsey's big night. Prom night."

"So, what did the police do after you called 'em?" Reba Mae asked, obviously not ready to abandon my near-death experience. "Are they lookin' for the driver?"

"Beau asked a lot of questions. Made out a report."

"What did you tell 'im?"

"Not much to tell," I confessed. "It was pitch-black outside, raining cats and dogs. I'd just missed meeting my Maker by mere inches. If I'd known some psycho was going to mow me down, I would've had my camera phone primed and ready."

"What did Beau put in his report then?"

I grimaced. "It was pretty much a blank page. I didn't see the driver. Didn't get a license plate number."

Reba Mae cocked her head to one side. "What kind of car was it?"

"Big."

"Uh-huh." She nodded. "That's good. Color?"

I winced. "Dark."

"Big and dark narrows it down some."

"Right," I muttered. "I've just eliminated all the light-colored small cars in town."

"Don't beat yourself up, hon. You gotta start somewhere."

I suppose she had a point, though it didn't make me feel any better. Reba Mae, bless her heart, was only following the BFF code of ethics and supporting a friend who was down and out.

"Do you really think the driver meant to kill you?"

I picked a stapler off the counter and played with it. "No doubt about it. Whoever it was knew exactly where I park each night and was waiting for me."

"That's some scary stuff." Reba Mae shook her head, sending earrings the size of tangerines dancing. "Any idea who the diamond you found belongs to?"

"Hmm." I pretended to poinder the question. "Who sports diamonds *and* who might've had a reason to visit the kitchen of a certain deceased chef?"

Reba Mae's eyes widened at the implication. "Diane Cloune is never without diamond studs in her ears."

"And I noticed Vicki Lamont wasn't wearing her wedding or engagement ring when I rang up her sale the other day."

"Coincidence?"

"Maybe," I murmured, glancing at my watch. "Wonder what's keeping Lindsey? She should've been here by now."

Reba Mae straightened and snapped her

fingers. "Duh! Lindsey is due here any minute. Where's my head? I ran off this mornin' without my camera."

I set the stapler down and dug through my apron pocket for my cell and handed it to her. "See if one of your boys is home and can run it over."

Reba Mae did just that, then returned the phone. "Work finished early at the construction site where Clay's working. He said he'd bring it over."

I motioned toward the Nikon half-hidden behind a stack of catalogs. "Mine's ready to point and shoot. I promised Mom and Dad that I'd e-mail them photos."

"Life in Florida agreein' with 'em?"

"What's not to love in a mobile home park for 'fun-loving seniors'?" I untied my apron and slipped it over my head. "I call often, but it's hard to catch them home. If they're not out line dancing, Mom's at Zumba or Dad's learning to fly-fish. They spend their spare time picking oranges and lemons off trees in their backyard."

I glanced up as a long white limo slinked to a stop curbside.

"Woo-hoo," Reba Mae chortled, catching sight of it. "Girlfriend, that's what I call arrivin' in style."

I hurried to the door in time to see Lindsey step out, looking every bit the modern-day fairy-tale princess in her short and flirty dress of sapphire blue. Short, flirty, and sapphire blue? I expected pretty in pink. Shock, anger, and dismay played tug-of-war with my emotions. Instead of the blush-colored floaty tulle dress I thought we'd both fallen in love with at a boutique, Lindsey had opted for the strapless number Amber selected. I felt mad as a hornet, yet knew I had a choice to make. Either I could make a scene and ruin Lindsey's big night, or I could postpone our heart-to-heart until another time. My decision made, I put on my game face.

"Like how I did her hair?" Reba Mae asked, matching her stride to mine. "By the way, I voted for loose ringlets, but was over-ruled. Amber Leigh insisted on a more sophisticated updo. Said it would give the girl a pageant look."

"You done good, Reba Mae," I told her as I threw open the door.

Lindsey flashed an apologetic smile, but avoided making eye contact with me. "Sorry we're late. Meemaw was at Daddy's so picture taking took longer than I planned."

Jason Wainwright, Lindsey's date and current boyfriend, climbed out the opposite side of the limo. Jason, a tall, gangly youth, his sandy brown hair gelled and artfully mussed, looked uncomfortable in a black tux and a cummerbund that matched the blue of Lindsey's dress. A sparkly stud gleamed in an earlobe, but he'd removed the earring from his brow for the occasion. "Hey, Miz Prescott," he said. "Hey, Miz Johnson."

Lindsey pirouetted in front of me. "How do I look, Mom?"

Sixteen going on twenty-five. I blinked back moisture. "You look beautiful, sweetie. Like a princess."

She grinned. "Daddy said the exact same thing."

In spite of our differences, I guess CJ and I still shared a few things in common.

"Amber did my makeup," Lindsey continued. "She said this was how she wore it when she won her crown."

Amber, eh? That explained the smoky eyes, the glossy lips. Explained why my baby girl looked ready to go clubbing and not have to show ID. "Nice." I tried to keep the sarcasm under control. I didn't want to let my animosity toward Miss Peach Pit dampen Lindsey's pleasure.

"You said you wanted to take pictures. Do you have your camera ready? We still have to swing by and pick up Taylor and Brad.

Mr. Wainwright made reservations for us to have dinner first at the country club."

"Well, let's get this party started," Reba Mae said, taking charge.

Using my Nikon, Reba Mae no sooner finished taking a variety of shots — me and Lindsey, then Lindsey and Jason — when Clay arrived with the camera she'd forgotten in her rush that morning.

Reba Mae snatched the camera from her son. "Call that timin' or what?"

"Hey, y'all," Clay said, encompassing us all with a grin that never failed to remind me of his mother's. His faded jeans and equally faded red UGA T-shirt were a sharp contrast to Jason and Lindsey's formal attire. His hair, damp from a recent shower, was mussed but, unlike Jason's, was gel free. "Sorry it took so long but that big ol' limo out front is hoggin' all the best parking spaces."

Reba Mae gave his arm a playful swat. "Hush, now."

I knew that beneath all the teasing, Clay harbored a soft spot for his best friend's baby sister. He'd been her champion since grade school when Joey Tucker, Beau and Jolene's youngest, had swiped her favorite Barbie. Clay had gotten it back for her and given Joey a bloody nose in the process.

We went through the picture-taking routine all over again. I thought we were finished when Reba Mae said, "One more shot. I want a picture of Lindsey and Clay together."

"No problem." Clay agreeably took his place next to Lindsey while the rest of us moved out of camera range.

"Closer, you two," Reba Mae instructed, peering into the viewfinder.

Clay did as requested, his hand resting lightly at my daughter's waist. "You clean up well, Linds," he teased. They stood smiling at each other as Reba Mae captured the moment.

Maybe it was only my imagination, but I thought my baby girl looked a tad flushed beneath the layer of expertly applied makeup.

Jason cleared his throat. "Ah, Lindsey, it's getting late."

"I made Daddy promise to call the club and let them know we might be running behind schedule. Even so, we'd better scoot." Lindsey bestowed a bright smile on us, then grabbed Jason's hand and dragged him toward the door. "Bye, y'all."

They left amid a flurry of "good-byes" and "have funs." Clay, Reba Mae, and I stood in the doorway as the limo drew away from the curb as smoothly as a cruise ship leaving port. My little shop grew strangely silent in its wake.

"Well, I guess that's that," Reba Mae summed it up.

"They sure grow up fast, don't they?" I sniffled. "I swear I don't know where the time's gone. One day you're putting Band-Aids on scraped knees, the next you're waving them off to the prom."

Reba Mae draped her arm over my shoulder and squeezed.

"How long has Linds been seein' Jason Wainwright?" Clay asked, snapping me out of my pity party.

I frowned, trying to recall how long they'd been dating. With Lindsey spending so much time at CJ's, it was hard to stay on top of things like I knew I should. "Oh," I said at last, "about six months I'd guess, more or less. Why do you ask?"

He shrugged. "Nothing . . . just wondering."

Reba Mae narrowed her eyes as she looked at her son. "Doesn't sound like you care for Jason much."

Clay shrugged again. "Don't know the guy well enough to form an opinion, but . . ."

"But . . . ?" I prompted. Little alarm bells started clanging inside my head. Surely in a town the size of Brandywine Creek, I'd have heard if Jason Wainwright had ever been in trouble. Besides, Jason's daddy was CJ's law partner. Back in the day, his mother, Mary Beth, and I had cochaired a number of charity auctions. Many an evening had been spent in the company of his parents.

"Out with it, son," Reba Mae ordered. "Can't start somethin', then leave us hangin'."

Clay glanced uneasily at his mother, then back to me. "It's just that I've seen him hot-rodding around town in his daddy's Porsche. A time or two, I spotted it parked around the corner from the liquor store. Got me wonderin' is all."

"That all?" Reba Mae made a dismissing motion. "Probably his daddy stockin' up on Jim Beam."

"Yeah, probably."

But from Clay's tone, I could tell he wasn't convinced. Surely CJ would've put his foot down if he thought there was even a hint that his darling daughter was moving with the wrong crowd. Or would he? Was CJ too involved with his own love life to monitor a teenage girl's activities? I vowed to make it a priority to find out.

"What are your plans for this evenin'?" Reba Mae asked Clay, unaware of my inner

316

turmoil. "You and Caleb goin' bowlin'?"

"Yes, ma'am. Our team's tied for first place. Only one makeup game stands between us and a trophy."

"I don't recall you missin' any games."

"Couple weeks back, the boiler at the Super Bowl busted and flooded the place."

I had started to collect my camera and cell phone, but for some odd reason, this snagged my attention. "Do you remember exactly what night the boiler broke?"

Clay scratched his head. "Yeah, I remember. It was the night all the ruckus started."

"Ruckus? What ruckus?" Reba Mae asked, her voice unusually sharp.

"Gee, Ma, no need to get riled. That's just how I refer to the night Mr. Barrone got killed. All of the bowling leagues were canceled that Friday until they got the place back up and running."

A chill raced up my spine. A quick glance at Reba Mae's face told me the same thoughts ran pell-mell through her head. Hadn't Gerilee, Pete's wife, claimed Pete bowled every single Friday? Every Friday, including the night Mario was killed? But how could he when the Super Bowl had been closed because of flooding? If Pete wasn't there, where was he on the night in question? I was no hotshot detective, but it seemed to me that Pete Barker's alibi was gone with the wind.

CHAPTER 27

Why had Pete lied about his whereabouts the night Mario was killed? Who had tried to run me down one dark and stormy night? What if Clay was right about Lindsey's choice of a boyfriend? These worries spun around in my mind like a kaleidoscope. I glanced at the bedside clock for the umpteenth time. It was late. By now the prom was over, and Lindsey was snuggled into her bed at CJ's. Tomorrow — today, I corrected — we'd have our long overdue mother-daughter chat. I'd been entirely too lax with her since the divorce. And that had to stop. In Lindsey's eyes, CJ could do no wrong while I'd been cast as the villainess. In order not to alienate her further, I'd bent over backward not to be overly critical or too strict. But if her failing grades and inappropriate choice of clothing were any indication, my approach didn't seem to be working. I needed to stop being such a pushover.

I finally gave up trying to sleep. Slipping on a robe, I wandered over to the small desk in a corner of the bedroom and opened my laptop. Now was as good a time as any to download the prom pictures into the computer. I cringed, thinking about my parents' reaction to Lindsey's prom dress. My dad would have a cow seeing his granddaughter's skimpy attire. I quickly scanned through the photos, then sat up straighter. Along with the prom pics were those of the shoe prints I'd taken at the Tratory.

Why hadn't I done this sooner? Oh, yes, I recalled. Having narrowly missed being turned into road kill had temporarily affected my memory. I clicked on zoom and studied the zigzag pattern on the sole of the shoe. I was no shoe expert, but there were probably hundreds, thousands even, of shoes bearing this same design. Nevertheless, I hit the print button. There was also a second set of shoe prints leading away from the body. A woman's? Mine? I printed a copy of them, too.

How did one go about matching a pair of shoes with its owner? I wondered. Curious, I clicked on a popular shopping Web site, selected men's shoes, and chose a pair at random. Presto! A size chart appeared, which converted the measurements I'd taken at the Tratory into shoe sizes.

The murderer wore a perfect size ten.

I glanced up as headlight beams cut a swath across the wall. I heard an engine stop, followed by the sound of a car door opening and closing and the low rumble of voices. Instantly alert, Casey popped his head up, ears cocked. He barked even before the knocking sounded on the door to my shop below.

I jumped to my feet and raced downstairs. Casey brought up the rear. My heart hammered in my chest. I could hardly breathe. It has been my observation that good news rarely arrives after midnight. A parent's worst fear flashed through my brain. What if there'd been an accident? What if, right this very minute, Lindsey was injured, lying on a gurney in the emergency room? The knocking changed to pounding. Even in my current state of heightened anxiety, I made note of the subtle but distinct difference. "All right, already. I'm coming, I'm coming." I flipped on light switches as I went.

My jaw dropped when I recognized the two figures standing on my doorstep — none other than Wyatt McBride and my daughter, Lindsey Nicole. A Lindsey who, to borrow my father's phrase, looked rode hard and put away wet.

I flung open the door. "What happened? Is she hurt?"

McBride brushed past me while keeping a firm grip on Lindsey. "Your daughter needed a ride home."

"Sorry, Mom," Lindsey mumbled, her blue-gray eyes bleary and unfocused. "I'm sorta sick."

The flu? Food poisoning? She'd been perfectly fine earlier.

Lindsey pressed her hand against her mouth. "I'm gonna puke."

I darted for the wastebasket and made it back just in the nick of time. Lindsey sank to her knees on my heart pine floor and embraced the trash basket like a long-lost friend. I held long tendrils of hair away from her face as she vomited; I sent up a prayer of thanksgiving for plastic liners.

"Sorry." Lindsey climbed unsteadily to her feet.

I quickly shoved a handful of tissues at her. My girl still looked green around the gills. "What about Jason and the other kids? Are they sick, too?" When Lindsey failed to answer, I turned to McBride for an explanation.

"You could say there's been an outbreak of epidemic proportions among certain prom-goers." McBride gestured at Lindsey.

"Best get her to bed. She'll have one hell of a hangover come morning."

"She's *drunk*?"

I stared at my daughter in disbelief. Of course she was. I'd been an idiot not to see she was inebriated when it was as plain as the nose on my face. Her dress was rumpled, her makeup smudged, and her fancy updo had turned into a down-do. And she was barefoot! God only knew what happened to her shoes.

"Lindsey Nicole Prescott, what were you thinking?" I wanted to shake her silly. Here she was, only sixteen, and drunker than a skunk. Lord, where did I go wrong?

"Mo-om, don't yell. You're making me dizzy." As if to prove her point, she swayed on her feet. She might've fallen if I hadn't caught her around the middle.

"Time for bed, young lady. We'll talk in the morning." I put my arm more securely around her waist and headed for the stairs.

We must have looked an odd couple with Lindsey towering over me and me valiantly trying to support her weight. Tight-lipped with disapproval, McBride watched our slow progress.

"Where's her bedroom?" he asked. Before I could muster a protest, he picked Lindsey up and carried her toward the stairs. Lindsey's body went limp, her head lolled against his shoulder.

"Second room on the left," I said as I trailed after them. "What happened?"

"Get her settled first, then I'll explain. I'll wait in the kitchen."

Getting her settled proved somewhat of a challenge with Lindsey in her present state. It took a great deal of prodding and pushing, tugging and wrestling to get her out of her slinky blue dress. I found a baggy sleep shirt in the bottom drawer of the dresser she's had since childhood and wrangled her into it.

"Mom . . . I puked all over the cop's truck," she confessed as I tucked the quilt under her chin.

"You what . . . ?" I stared down at her. "Please tell me I heard wrong. That you didn't really toss your cookies in Chief McBride's personal vehicle."

Lindsey's eyelids slid to half-mast. "Tell 'im I'm sorry."

I sighed. "Don't worry about it now. We'll deal with everything in the morning." I brushed a kiss across her brow, but she was already sound asleep.

As I turned to leave, I noticed Casey perched on the threshold. Judging from his bright eyes, I gathered the little dog had followed the goings-on with interest. As though reassured all was under control, the pup hopped onto Lindsey's bed and snuggled down. Knowing my daughter was in capable hands — make that paws — I quietly closed the door behind me.

I'd nearly forgotten about McBride, or more likely I'd hoped he'd get tired of waiting and leave. No such luck. I found him sitting at my kitchen table.

"She all right?" he asked, his expression unreadable in the dim light.

I shoved an unruly mop of curls away from my face. "As well as can be expected — considering the circumstances."

I peered at him more closely as I approached. He looked tired, somehow more vulnerable, less intimidating. Approachable. Maybe it was the hour. Maybe the shadows. Whatever the reason, I heard myself ask if he'd like coffee.

"Coffee sounds great, but can you make it decaf?"

I measured decaf into a filter, added water, and clicked on the pot. "Care to fill me in on the gory details?"

He leaned back, causing the ladder-back chair to squeak in protest. For the first time that evening — make that morning — I noticed he was dressed casually in jeans with a windbreaker pulled over a T-shirt instead of his usual uniform. "A complaint was logged in about a disturbance. Caller said there was loud music and a wild party going on next door. Since all my men were out assisting the sheriff's department to reroute traffic around an overturned semi on the Interstate, I took it upon myself to check things out."

While the coffeemaker gurgled, I got mugs down from the cupboard and put some of Miss Melly's gingersnaps on a plate. The coffee done, I filled our mugs and sat opposite him at the kitchen table. "What did you find when you answered the call?"

"A lot of underage drinking." He took a sip of coffee, then helped himself to a cookie. "I broke up the party and called the parents to come get the kids who hadn't already fled the premises."

"I see." I cradled my hands around the coffee mug, savoring its warmth. "Precisely where did this so-called wild party take place?"

McBride locked eyes with me over the rim of his coffee mug. "At the home of your ex-husband."

"CJ's . . . ?" This bit of information caught me off guard. "Where was CJ when all this underage drinking was going on?"

"Nearest I can tell after talking to your daughter, CJ and his . . . friend . . . planned to take in a Braves game in Atlanta, then spend the night."

I sipped my coffee, needing a moment to digest this. Lindsey must have been aware of their plans from the beginning — and schemed accordingly. Between CJ and the Wainwrights' fully stocked bars, a generous liquor supply shouldn't have posed a problem.

McBride studied me guardedly. "I couldn't very well leave your daughter alone in her condition so I brought her here."

"Thank you. I appreciate it," I told him, my voice husky with emotion.

"You're welcome."

I cleared my throat. "Will there be any legal ramifications?"

"No." He shook his head. "Since it's a first-time offense, I didn't cite the kids. I let them off with a stern warning instead."

"Thanks again." Though I didn't like being beholden to McBride, he *was* being unexpectedly nice. He could just as easily have called me like he did the other parents and had me fetch Lindsey. But he didn't. He'd brought my daughter to me instead. *Don't look a gift horse in the mouth,* another of my father's sayings, sprang to mind. To hide my confusion, I refilled our coffee mugs. "Lindsey said she threw up in your truck. Is that true?"

He grimaced. " 'Fraid so. Normally, I'd have taken one of the police cruisers, but they were all in use tonight. It's not as bad as it sounds. I managed to pull to the shoulder so the roadside got the worst of it."

There, he was doing it again — being unexpectedly nice — and again it unnerved me.

"I'll bring Lindsey to your place tomorrow, and she'll clean your truck from top to bottom. No," I said when he opened his mouth to protest, "she needs to be held accountable."

"Can't argue with that." Reaching into his shirt pocket for pen and paper, he scribbled an address and shoved it across the table. "I've got tomorrow off so I'll be home all day."

"Good. We'll be there." I nudged the plate of cookies closer to him. "Melly's gingersnaps have won blue ribbons at the county fair."

He took the hint and scarfed down his third — but who's counting — cookie. "That would be Melly Prescott, CJ's mother?" At my nod, a tiny smile teased the corners of his mouth. "I've always wondered, does she even wear her pearls when she bakes cookies?"

"I think she sleeps with them," I replied, straight-faced.

My response prompted an honest-to-goodness smile. The sort that showed off the cute little dimple in his cheek. It was easy to see how a Hollywood starlet would fall prey to its devastating effect, much less a humble li'l shopkeeper like *moi.* I jumped up to refill cups that didn't need refilling. "Ah . . . more coffee?"

When I glanced over my shoulder, I saw his attention wasn't on the coffeepot but on the expanse of thigh visible below my robe. "I thought you told me purple wasn't your color," he said.

I carefully replaced the carafe on the warmer. "It isn't."

He pointed to my scraped knee and the bruises visible below the hem of my short robe. Amethyst and grape, lilac and plum, a palette of purple. "Oh, those," I said. "Souvenirs from my flying leap over the hood of my Beetle. If I'm going to pursue a career as circus acrobat, I need to work on my landings."

"I read Tucker's report." There was not even a ghost of a smile now; he was sober as a judge. "You need to back off, Piper. You're playing with fire and you're bound to get burned. Leave the investigation to the professionals. Now," he continued, his tone less stern, "why don't you give me a first-person account of what happened the other night?"

I slowly lowered myself into a chair. "There's not much to tell. I didn't see the driver. Couldn't tell make or model of the vehicle. Big and dark is the best I can do."

"Memory's a funny thing," he mused. "Sometimes details come back later when you least expect them."

CHAPTER 28

McBride's prediction of a hangover had been right on the nose. Lindsey woke late the next morning with a walloping headache. I quickly smothered a tiny pang of sympathy as she stumbled into the kitchen. It was the time for tough love not "poor baby" pats on the head.

"Mornin', Lindsey," I said perkily. I held out a tumbler. "Hair of the dog that bit you?"

She eyed the concoction in the glass with barely disguised horror. "Mo-om, what are you tryin' to do? Poison me?"

I smiled sweetly. "Did you know that in Poland the cure for a hangover is pickle juice?"

Lindsey paled at the notion, but I continued, heartless mother that I was. "In Ireland, the poor sod might be buried up to their neck in moist river sand." I slammed the tall glass on the table, and Lindsey winced at the sound..

"Booze . . . ?" Her shocked gaze darted from the glass, then back to me.

"It's a Virgin Mary — a Bloody Mary minus the vodka," I explained. "Tomato juice and celery are rich in vitamins."

"Are you trying to kill me or cure me?"

"Drink," I ordered. "And when you're finished, I want you to take a shower and brush your teeth while I fix lunch."

"Food . . . ? I don't think . . ."

I turned to the stove and picked up a spoon. "I made a pot of vegetable soup while you were sleeping. It's chock-full of more of those vitamins you lost after 'puking,' as you so eloquently phrased it."

Lindsey whimpered but drained the juice. Minutes later, I heard the shower running. When she returned to the kitchen, she looked more like my child than the glammed-up version of the night before.

I set soup and crackers on the table and dug in. Lindsey, a martyred expression on her pretty face, took a cautious spoonful. Then another and another until she'd finished most of the bowl.

"I thought we'd bring Chief McBride some homemade vegetable soup as a thank-you," I commented as I loaded the dirty dishes into the dishwasher. "Now that you're done eating, we're going to take a ride over to his place. I put together a bucket of rags and cleaning supplies."

Her eyes widened. "You're going to make me clean his house?"

"Not his house, sweetie. His truck," I corrected. "In case your memory's a little hazy, you threw up in it while he was driving you home."

"Mo-om," she wailed. "What'll the kids at school say if they find out you made me clean the ick out of his truck?"

"The more intelligent ones will say you got what you deserved. We're not going to waste brain cells worrying about the rest."

"That it?"

"No, but it's a start. After you're done making his truck sparkle like new, you're going to thank the nice man for not throwing you in the clink for underage drinking, disturbing the peace, and a handful of other charges. Whether you want to admit it or not, you and your friends got off easy, but don't expect lightning to strike twice."

Lindsey had the good sense to drop her eyes. "Are you going to snitch to Daddy?"

I deposited a dishwashing pellet into the dispenser and punched the wash cycle. "I'm sure your daddy will figure things out for himself once he steps foot inside his home and sees the chaos you created. Not to mention seeing his liquor cabinet depleted."

She hung her head. "Are you finished?"

"Not quite."

Lindsey rolled her eyes. "All right, go ahead. Yell at me."

"As tempting as that sounds, I'm not even going to raise my voice." Yelling, I realized, would go in one ear, out the other, and in the end wouldn't make a lick of difference. Instead, I decided on a calm, rational approach to hammer the truth home. Lindsey watched me with blatant suspicion, but I knew she was in listening mode for our come-to-Jesus meeting.

"Don't think for one minute, young lady, that I wasn't on to your underhanded tactics of switching one dress for another. You purposely arrived here late and counted on the fact I wouldn't insist on you changing dresses and making a scene."

Lindsey's lower lip jutted out. "Pink is for babies . . ."

I held up my hand to forestall her paltry excuses. "Nevertheless, your actions were deceitful and unworthy of you. The underage drinking you engaged in later that evening, however, far overshadows your poor choice in evening wear. Not only is it illegal, but did you stop to consider what might've happened if one of your friends insisted on driving home drunk? Not only could they have been killed or seriously injured, but an innocent person as well."

"Are you done yet?" Lindsey traced a pattern on the tabletop with a fingertip, her eyes downcast.

"Not by a long shot," I fired back. Chopping vegetables for soup had given me plenty of time to reflect on my relationship with my daughter — and decide on a course of action. "There is no justification for your failing grades. I intend to closely monitor your work in summer school and make sure you complete the course with flying colors. In the future, if I say no, that answer is final. No running to your father for a second opinion. And if I *ever* hear about you drinking again, I'll see to it that you're grounded until you're twenty-one. You have to learn that actions have consequences. I love you more than life itself, but I'm disappointed in your recent behavior."

"Disappointed in me . . . ?" Lindsey sprung to her feet, balled up the paper napkin, and tossed it down. "Well, I'm disappointed in you! It's your fault Daddy wanted a divorce."

Stunned by her outburst, I sank onto a chair.

Lindsey gestured wildly. "If you'd made more of an effort, tried a little harder to be more glamorous like Amber, Daddy wouldn't have left us."

How do I find words to make a young, impressionable girl understand the complexities of marriage? To explain that over decades people change? That goals and interests diverge with time, often in opposite directions? "Honey, think about it," I said quietly. "If beauty and glitz were all that were needed to hold a marriage together, there would be no divorces in Hollywood. In the case of your father and me, I did try, but it wasn't enough. It might have been a case of too little, too late, but I was no longer what your father needed — or wanted." My gaze strayed to the ring finger of my left hand, now barren of jewelry. "I've been doing some soul-searching," I confessed. "Maybe, just maybe, our divorce wasn't such a bad thing after all. It's giving me the chance to discover a whole new side of myself that I didn't know existed. For years, I've wanted my own business, to be independent. Always standing in your father's shadow, I never had the chance to grow, much less bloom — and now I do."

A single tear trickled down Lindsey's cheek, and she brushed it away. I took this as encouragement so I continued. "Our lives — your daddy's and mine — sadly veered off-course. I'm sorry our divorce hurt you, sweetie. But the one thing that's remained constant, and always will, is that we both love you as much as ever."

"Sorry, Mom. I love you, too," she said, sniffling.

I rose and gave her a hug. We stood like that for a long moment, mother and daughter, woman and child-woman. Lindsey finally stepped back. "Can Casey come with us to Chief McBride's?"

As it turned out, Casey was overjoyed at the prospect. The little dog was an enthusiastic traveler, wagging his tail and leaping into the backseat the second the car door opened.

To Lindsey's unbridled relief, McBride had already cleaned the worst of the mess. Attuned to the fact that this was an object lesson, he informed Lindsey the exterior of his Ford F-150 pickup could stand a good wash.

While Lindsey set to work with a bucket of soapy water and a chamois, McBride and I watched from the porch steps of his rented cottage. Casey romped about and wrestled with the garden hose until Lindsey sprayed him with water. The pup loved it and kept coming back for more, sending Lindsey into a fit of giggles.

"Great little mutt you found," McBride commented.

"Great attack dog you mean," I corrected, enjoying the playfulness of Lindsey and Casey.

"Sorry," he grunted. "My mistake."

"Casey has a ferocious bark, but right now his bark is worse than his bite. He'll be your best friend forever, and you can bribe him with a doggy treat."

McBride shot me a sideways glance. "By the way, thanks for the soup. I hope you don't think I'm as easily bribed as that mutt of yours."

"My, oh my, what a suspicious mind you have," I said flippantly, then grew serious. "You mentioned you lived on takeout, and I wanted to thank you for last night. You could've thrown the book at Lindsey and her friends."

He shrugged off my gratitude. "No big deal."

We continued to watch Lindsey and the dog's antics for a while in companionable silence. It was early May, one of my favorite months, sunny and bright, but without the humidity that plagues June, July, and August. The trees were a verdant green. Carolina wrens flitted among the branches of a huge old magnolia tree.

"I like your place. It suits you." And it did, I thought. The style could best be described as country Southern with a dash of New England Colonial and a hint of Greek Revival thrown in for good measure. Simple and unassuming, the wide porch cried out for rockers and sweet tea.

I tilted my face up to the sun, enjoying its warmth and ignoring its freckle factor. "Rumor has it that you're thinking of buying it."

He lounged back, one arm braced on the step above. "After standing vacant for some time, the house needs work but shows potential. Provided the owner accepts my offer, I'll start with the kitchen. Maybe then, I'll be tempted to try my hand at cooking."

I idly tracked the path of a bright yellow butterfly as it hovered over an overgrown hydrangea bush. "Is it true that if you don't find Mario's killer soon, the mayor and city council might fire you?"

"Where'd you hear that?" he asked, his voice sharp.

"I overheard some women talking the other day. True or false?"

He kept his gaze fastened on the progress Lindsey was making on his Ford F-150.

"There's a ninety-day probationary clause in my contract. It reads that if the town is dissatisfied with my performance for any reason whatsoever they have the right to rescind the contract."

"That's a lot of pressure."

"Pressure comes with the territory."

"You'd make a lot of people happy if you arrested me. Life in Brandywine Creek could return to normal."

He merely grunted.

A grunt, I realized, was difficult to interpret. Did that mean he agreed? Disagreed? "Well, then," I challenged, "why haven't you arrested me?"

He turned to face me and, once again, I was intrigued by the small scar at his left eyebrow. "I'm not about to make an arrest," he said, "until I can build a case strong enough to hold up in a court of law."

Gathering my courage, I voiced the question uppermost in my mind. "Any word from the lab on the bloodstained T-shirt you found at my shop?"

He returned his attention to the truck. "Not yet, but expect I will soon."

My mouth suddenly felt like sawdust. "What if the DNA matches Mario's?"

"There are other things that have to be

taken into consideration beside a DNA match."

"Such as?"

"A skilled lawyer would make mincemeat of the notion that you planted incriminating evidence in a place where it would be easily spotted, then called the police to come find it."

"Maybe I'm diabolically clever," I offered.

"Maybe you're innocent," he countered.

"Almost done, Mom," Lindsey called out, garden hose in one hand, dripping sponge in the other.

I was grateful for the interruption. McBride's assertion had left me momentarily speechless.

"I just want to go over the tailgate one more time." Lindsey turned her attention back to the truck. Casey, tired of play, snoozed in the grass alongside the drive.

"Have at it," I told her when I regained my voice. I decided right then and there to take a leap of faith. I turned to McBride. "Reba Mae and I have been conducting an investigation of our own and came up with a list of suspects. She suggested we lay our cards, so to speak, on the table since you're more experienced in these matters." He rolled his eyes, the gesture reminiscent of Lindsey's, but I forged ahead undaunted.

"Tony and Mario go way back. According to Tony's wife, Gina, Mario weaseled out of a deal and left Tony in the lurch."

"Go on," he prompted. "Who else is on your list?"

"Mario owed money and refused to pay both Pete Barker at Meat on Main and Danny Boyd, who used to be Mario's sous chef. Neither of them have alibis. Being new in town you might not be aware of Mario's reputation as a ladies' man. He's had affairs with both Diane Cloune and her friend, Vicki Lamont. The killer could be a woman."

"Or a jealous husband."

"Exactly," I said with satisfaction. "Reba Mae and I are on the job." I briefly considered telling him about the diamond, but changed my mind. No telling if it was even connected to the murder at this point.

He frowned at hearing this. "Didn't I warn you just last night about interfering with police business? I meant what I said. It's dangerous, and I want you to keep your nose out of it."

Wanting to head off another lecture, I deliberately changed the subject. "You're somewhat of an enigma around town, McBride. Tell me a little about yourself."

"Not much to tell."

"Oh, I doubt that. You seem the strong, silent type."

"Is that how you see me?" The corners of his mouth quirked in a wry grin. "What is it you want to know?"

I pondered the matter for all of half a second. "Well, for starters, are you married, single, or divorced?"

"Widowed."

"Widowed . . . ," I echoed. That option hadn't occurred to me.

"Got married while I was in the army. My wife, Tracey, died in a car crash less than a year later after a night of heavy partying."

"I'm sorry," I said quietly. "I shouldn't have pried."

He stared into the near distance. "It was a long time ago. Shit happens."

Case closed. I could tell from his shuttered expression my interrogation was over. I sat quietly contemplating what he'd just told me. Judging from the fact he hadn't remarried, my guess was that Tracey had been the love of his life. Her death undoubtedly hit him hard.

"Truck's spick-and-span," Lindsey announced, coming out from behind the vehicle and depositing the cleaning equipment by the front steps. "Can we go now, Mom?"

"Aren't you forgetting something, Lindsey?"

She stared at me blankly before comprehension dawned. "Oh, yeah." She shifted her weight from one foot to the other. "I apologize, Chief, for causing so much trouble. I promise I won't do it again."

"Apology accepted, Lindsey," he replied gravely.

"Jump in the car, sweetie, and I'll be right with you."

I slowly rose to my feet. McBride did likewise and walked with me toward the Beetle. "Have you given any more thought to your near miss the other night?" he asked.

"Uh-uh." I shook my head. "Like I told you last night, it all happened so fast I didn't get a good look at the car or driver."

"Remember," he said as I cranked the engine. "Something might still trigger a memory. When it does, call me."

CHAPTER 29

CJ's place was trashed. At a glance, it could easily be mistaken for the town dump. Beer cans and half-empty liquor bottles littered the entire lower level. Crystal bowls and china saucers had been used in lieu of ashtrays. The house reeked of stale tobacco and spilled beer.

"Open the window and let in some fresh air," I instructed Lindsey. "Meanwhile, I'll see if I can find some trash bags." Call me a pushover if you will, but I felt sorry for my girl after seeing how much elbow grease was required to make this place fit for human habitation.

We worked for over an hour and gradually CJ's grandiose two-story began to resemble a home and not a frat house. I had just finished hauling the last of the debris out to the bins when CJ pulled into the garage. I was happy to see he was alone and not accompanied by Amber. What I had to say was for parents only. Not parents *and* home-wrecker.

"Hey, Scooter," he hailed me as he climbed out of his Lexus. "What brings you here?"

"I took mercy on our daughter and helped her with some chores."

He popped the trunk, removed a garment bag, and slung it over one shoulder. "I don't make Lindsey do 'chores.' Chores are why I pay a housekeeper."

"How do you propose Lindsey learn responsibility if nothing is expected of her?"

He brushed aside my concerns with a wave of his free hand. "She's got plenty of time to be responsible. You need to lighten up, darlin.' Let the girl have some fun."

I trailed after him into the kitchen where Lindsey was putting the last of the dirty glasses in the dishwasher. "Hey, baby." CJ put a pudgy arm around her shoulders and gave her a hug. "How was prom?"

Lindsey, her face pinched with worry, shot me a nervous glance. "Um, fine."

I cleared my throat to get CJ's attention. "We need to talk."

"Uh-oh." CJ winked at Lindsey. "Never a good sign, baby, when a woman says those words."

"Lindsey," I said, turning to my daughter,

"would you give me some time alone with your father?"

She dried her hands on her jeans. "Er, sure. I've got some homework to do."

As she ran off, I wondered if homework translated meant calling or texting friends to compare notes. Cynical me. Shame, shame, shame.

CJ flung the garment bag over the back of a chair and headed for the living room, where he lowered himself onto an imported Italian leather sectional the size of Milan. Late-afternoon sunlight streamed through windows that overlooked the golf course. "Okay, Scooter, what's all the fuss about? Our newly appointed chief of police hasslin' you? Threatenin' to throw you in the pokey?"

"No, of course not," I snapped. "How can you even say such a thing?"

CJ merely grinned, the caps on his teeth gleaming pearly white. "I can see it now. Think of the headlines." He extended both arms, wrists cocked, thumbs angled at ninety degrees to form an invisible picture frame. "PROMINENT ATTORNEY DEFENDS EX-WIFE ON HOMICIDE CHARGE."

"I thought, citing our 'history' together, you refused to be my lawyer. That I needed a criminal lawyer."

"Let's just say I reconsidered after thinking of all the free publicity your case would bring. I'm talking appearances on the *Today* show, interviews in *People.* Can't put a price tag on that kind of exposure."

He wanted to see me lose my temper, but I refused to be drawn into his mean-spirited little game. "I'm here because I wanted to inform you that your house was turned into party central last night. The police had to be called."

"Damn . . ." He bit off a more colorful expletive. "Listen here, Piper, when I informed Lindsey that Amber and I had box seats for a Braves game and intended to spend the night in Atlanta, she said not to worry. She'd stay at a friend's house."

"Which friend?"

"Sorry." CJ scratched his head and did his best to appear perplexed. "Don't recall the girl's name just now."

Too restless to sit still, I prowled the width of the room. "Seems as though Lindsey invited the whole gang here for the afterglow. You might want to check your liquor supply. Your inventory might be running low."

It amused me to watch CJ leap from the sofa, his indolent pose abandoned, and stride over to the bar. He rummaged through the liquor cabinet to check what was left of his stock, then let out a loud sigh of relief. He straightened, triumphantly brandishing a bottle of Wild Turkey. "Lucky for me, those kids missed the full bottle I hid at the back."

"Is that all you have to say?" I snapped. While I looked on, hands on hips, foot tapping impatiently, he poured a double bourbon into what must have been the only clean glass on the premises. He didn't offer to pour one for me.

"Lindsey doesn't realize how fortunate she is that McBride didn't arrest the lot of them for underage drinking along with a slew of other charges. Think how those headlines would look," I added for good measure.

CJ tipped his head back and took a deep swallow. "Sumbitch would like nothin' better 'n to embarrass me."

"This isn't about you, CJ," I reminded him. "It's about Lindsey."

He ran his fingers through dyed hair. "It's not easy raising a daughter," he said, slumping back down on the sofa.

"Tell me about it." I sank onto the opposite end of the huge sectional, only to be nearly swallowed whole in its cushy softness. "That's not all I wanted to talk about," I said, struggling to regain my balance —

and a modicum of dignity. "Lindsey needs more supervision. Her grades are failing, not only in math but in language arts, which used to be her favorite subject."

He frowned into his bourbon. "So, what are you gettin' at?"

"School will soon be out for the year. I'd like you to insist that she spend more time at my place and less time at yours."

"Fine," he agreed. "Much as it pains me, darlin', I have to admit you're right when it comes to our daughter. Between dealin' with new clients and keepin' up with Amber, doesn't leave much time for supervisin'. Would hate to see her turn down the wrong path 'cause her daddy paid her no nevermind. Consider your request a done deal."

I stared at him in disbelief. His answer came much too quickly for my suspicious mind to accept. "A done deal . . . ? Just like that?"

He snapped his fingers. "Just like that."

The leather cushion wheezed as I shifted my weight to better see his expression. "You usually fight me tooth and nail whenever I broach the subject of Lindsey spending more time with me. What's up? Why the change of heart?"

He took another sip of bourbon, then gave me a sheepish grin. "I finally convinced

Amber to move in with me. We could use some privacy. Havin' a teenager hangin' around sorta cramps my style . . . if you get my drift."

"Oh, I got your drift all right, but will Lindsey?" I pushed myself out of the sectional's cloying embrace. "Our daughter's not going to be happy being displaced in favor of Miss Peach Pit."

"Wh-what . . . ?" CJ sputtered, his face flushed.

"Did I say Miss Peach Pit?" I retrieved my purse from where I'd left it. "I meant to say *fiancée.* How quickly I forgot that teensy detail. I'll let you explain the situation to Lindsey. And," I added, "you might want to give our son a heads up on the current state of the union."

After saying good-bye to Lindsey, I returned to my car, knowing I'd erased the self-satisfied smirk from CJ's face. Casey woke from his doggy nap on the front seat and greeted me with a series of excited yips. His small body fairly hummed with joy at my return. I rubbed his head, pleased at the unabashed response. As I drove away from CJ's palatial home, I prayed my daughter's fondness for the pup would help lessen the sting of her father's defection in favor of a blond bimbo in a short skirt.

■ ■ ■ ■

The following afternoon I was leafing through a food magazine when Melly entered Spice It Up!, accompanied by her friend Dottie Hemmings. "Hello, Piper," Melly smiled. "Quilting club ended early so Dottie and I thought we'd stop by to say hello."

"Lottie Smith spilled sweet tea all over the bunny quilt she's making for her niece's new baby." Dottie wagged her head sorrowfully, but her helmet of teased blond hair didn't move one iota.

"Poor dear was inconsolable," Melly explained. "We voted to end our meeting early."

"Did you hear about Buzz Oliver?" Dottie asked eagerly. Before I could answer, she launched into a tale of woe. "Buzz had gall bladder surgery. In and out of the hospital the same day. Imagine! When I had mine removed years ago, I stayed in the hospital a whole week. Had one of those little tubes that drained awful yellow-green bile. My husband, the mayor, stayed by my side night and day."

"Poor Buzz," I murmured. "How's he doing?"

"Oh, he's doin' fine. Becca Dapkins buzzes over him like a bee around honey."

Melly straightened a stack of mail I had yet to sort. "Becca's probably got a guilty conscience from feeding the poor man a steady diet of casseroles featuring creamed soup."

Dottie nodded. "Maybelle Humphries heard the menu that set off Buzz's attack was turkey à la king. But Becca swears it wasn't the cream of mushroom soup. She's blaming it on the chopped turkey she found in the freezer."

"Unfortunately," Melly said, pursing her lips, "Becca doesn't remember if the turkey was from last Thanksgiving . . . or the year before."

Dottie patted her hair. "Rumor's flying around about a wild party after the prom. Don't suppose by any chance Lindsey mentioned the details."

"Dottie Hemmings!" Melly looked shocked by the suggestion her precious granddaughter would be privy to such information. "Lindsey has far too much sense to be even remotely involved in such goings-on."

"Simmer down, Melly," Dottie was quick to protest. "Don't get all high-and-mighty on me. I was curious, is all."

Melly fingered her ever-present string of pearls. "Lindsey happens to be dating Jason Wainwright. From everything I've heard, Jason is an upstanding young man destined to follow in his father's footsteps."

I bit my tongue at the "upstanding young man" comment. In my opinion, Jason was nothing more than a spoiled boy with a lot of growing up to do. But in all fairness, Lindsey had a lot of growing up to do as well. She hadn't demonstrated much maturity of late.

Dottie gave me a sly smile. "Jolene Tucker told Gerilee Barker that after Beau got back from helping the sheriff reroute traffic early Sunday morning, he spotted Chief McBride's truck parked outside your shop. Anything cooking between the two of you?"

Indignant, Melly turned to me. "Piper, tell Dottie that Beau was mistaken."

"Tsk, tsk," Dottie scolded. "Shame on you, Melly. You didn't always used to be such a stick-in-the-mud. I remember a time or two, you liked to kick up your heels. Besides," she continued, "Wyatt McBride's a right-handsome tall drink of water. If I was younger — and single . . ." She giggled.

The idea of Melly Prescott kicking up her heels was giving me a headache. "Actually, ladies, Chief McBride *was* here," I admitted, boldly deciding on a white lie — if there really is such a thing — rather than trash my daughter's reputation in front of her grandmother. "The chief was kind enough to inform me personally that the security system at CJ's home had been breached."

Melly's blue-veined hand flew to her pearls. "Oh, dear. Was everything all right?"

"A malfunction of some sort. The chief quickly managed to get the situation under control." What I'd just told her hadn't been a total lie. I failed to mention the security system in question wasn't a fancy electronic method, but rather CJ's next-door neighbor. "Since I was listed as a contact person," I continued, "McBride thought I should be notified."

Melly frowned. "Where was CJ when all this was going on? He never breathed a word to me he was leaving town."

"Goodness gracious, Mel," Dottie chimed. "CJ's a grown man. You can't expect him to run everything by his mama for approval."

Dottie had a good point, I mused. Given a chance, Melly would have nipped his affair with Amber Leigh Ames in the bud. Wait till she discovered he planned to have Amber move in as a permanent houseguest. Sparks would fly. "I'm sure he meant to tell you, Melly," I said, adopting a placating tone. "With all those new cases his billboards have brought in, it probably slipped his mind."

"Yes, dear, but I *am* his mother," she said. "CJ tells me everything."

"CJ had box seats for a Braves game. Rather than drive home late, he decided to stay overnight."

My explanation brought a smile to Melly's lined face. "CJ's been a Braves fan since he was a boy."

Not long afterward, Dottie made her excuses and left. The headache that had started small but was steadily worsening made me long for some fresh air. On impulse, I turned to Melly and asked, "Would you do me a favor and mind the shop while I run a couple errands. I promise, I won't be gone long."

"No trouble at all, dear." Melly beamed. "Take your time."

I grabbed my purse and was out of the shop in a wink. The sky had changed from sunny to silver with a hint of rain in the air. The gloom mirrored my present state of mind. Head down, I nearly collided with Ned Feeney, who emerged from Gray's Hardware, with a can of paint in one hand and spackle in the other. A putty knife protruded from the pocket of his jeans.

"Hey, Miz Piper." He gave me his slightly lopsided grin.

"Hey yourself, Ned," I said, but kept walking. Ned was as big a gossip as Dottie, and I wasn't up for more questions about wild parties or why McBride's truck was parked outside my shop in the wee hours of the morning.

I paused to examine a display of estate jewelry in the window of Yesteryear Antiques when Diane Cloune barreled out. She either didn't see me standing there or chose to ignore me. Whichever, I thought her attitude off-putting for the wife of a man running for public office. You'd think she'd want to curry favor from one of his constituents. Diane apparently had more important things on her mind than being polite to little ol' me. I watched her slide into a car, which was parked at the curb.

A big, black Lincoln.

Frozen in place, I stood on the sidewalk as the car accelerated down Main Street and disappeared around the corner. It was then I noticed the dealer logo on the rear bumper. A grinning circus clown with the slogan: DON'T CLOWN AROUND, VISIT CLOUNE MOTORS.

The exact same logo I'd seen on the car that had nearly ground me into mincemeat.

A tingling sensation started at the base of my spine and crept its way up my scalp as my brain processed this information.

Memory's a funny thing. McBride's words came back to haunt me.

CHAPTER 30

So what if Diane Cloune drove a big, black Lincoln. Diane had no reason to want me dead. Or at the very least, seriously injured. Unless, that is, *she* was Mario's killer. I quickly dismissed the notion as ridiculous. I'd heard Diane tell Vicki Lamont that her affair with Mario ended amicably some time ago. Diane's driving a car similar to the one that tried to run me down was coincidence.

Coincidence. Pure and simple.

Besides, how would that explain the larger of the shoe prints?

As I continued on my merry way, I waved to Pete Barker, who stood in the doorway of Meat on Main. He waved back. Guilt nipped at my conscience. I'd raised the finger of suspicion and leveled it smack-dab at his midsection. But if Pete was innocent, why lie to his wife about his whereabouts the night of the murder? The time to start eliminating possible suspects was long past due. And Pete's name ranked high on my persons-of-interest list. I thought again about the footprints we'd found at the crime scene. *Hmm,* I mused, *I wonder what size shoe Pete wears.* The situation called for a consultation with my BFF. I needed to drop by the Klassy Kut for a little brainstorming, but first I decided to swing by Proctor's Cleaners and pick up my trench coat, which I'd dropped off last week.

Bitsy Johnson-Jones glanced up from the paperback novel she was reading when the overhead buzzer announced my arrival. "Hey, Piper."

"Hey yourself, Bitsy," I returned. Bitsy, bless her heart, was as sweet as could be, but there was nothing even remotely "bitsy" about her. The woman loved to eat and it showed with every jiggle of her plus-size figure. "I'm here for my raincoat," I said, handing her the crumpled ticket I'd excavated from my purse.

"Oh, yeah, I know the one. Mr. Proctor said to make sure you sign a waiver when you came to get it."

"A waiver?" That sounded ominous. "What kind of waiver?"

"It acknowledges your coat was torn when you dropped it off." Bitsy pressed a button on a remote control device and a ceiling-mounted track began revolving. Clothes sheathed in plastic whooshed past, leaving a trail of noxious fumes in their wake. I felt my headache increase in intensity. Finally the whirring and whooshing stopped. Bitsy separated my trench from dozens of look-alike bags.

"Here it is." With a flourish, she ripped off a pink sheet of paper that had been stapled to the plastic and handed it to me along with a pen. "Sign at the bottom."

I quickly scanned the document. By signing it, I agreed not to hold Proctor's Cleaners responsible for any damages.

"I didn't realize the coat was torn when I brought it in," I said in self-defense as I scrawled my signature on the waiver.

"Mr. Proctor said the garment looked as though it'd been through hell and back. Wanted me to tell you he did his best. He could see from the label that the coat was expensive so he spent a lot of time trying to remove the stains. That's why there's an extra charge."

"Be sure to thank him for me."

Great, I thought, I'd just paid a ridiculous sum for dry-cleaning a coat that in all likelihood would wind up at Goodwill. Draping the plastic-encased garment over my arm, I bid Bitsy good-bye and headed for the

Klassy Kut.

"Hey, girlfriend." Reba Mae stopped mixing a vile-smelling potion and gave me a distracted smile as I entered. "Don't suppose you brought a starving hairdresser some lunch?"

I could see at a glance she was busy. One client sat with strands of hair wrapped in aluminum foil. Another, her head covered with perm rods and encased in a plastic bag, leafed through the pages of a gossip magazine. I motioned Reba Mae aside and lowered my voice. "Sorry for the interruption, but we need to talk."

She stopped stirring and looked at me quizzically. "Looks like someone's got her panties in a twist."

"We need to come up with a way to find out Pete Barker's shoe size."

"Well, honeybun," Reba Mae drawled, "Pete's feet are gonna have to stand in line behind highlights and a perm."

"Fine," I agreed. "I'll talk to you later, but promise to give it some thought before those fumes start destroying brain cells."

When I returned to Spice It Up!, Melly smiled as she came out of the storeroom. "Did you enjoy your little outing, dear?"

I hung my coat in the cupboard. I'd take it upstairs later. "Fine," I said. "I hope you

362

weren't bored while I was out."

"Not at all," Melly said. "While you were away, I took the liberty of alphabetizing your spices. Your customers will be able to find things much easier now that everything is in alphabetical order instead of scattered helter-skelter."

I couldn't believe my ears. All my clever groupings? My eye-catching displays? Gone, all of them? "You didn't . . ."

"You don't have to thank me. I was happy to help."

I looked around to find my precious spices lined up with more precision than cadets at a military academy. Baking spices mingled with those used for barbecue. Sweet cohabitated with nutty. Warm and earthy with bitter. Middle Eastern bordered Southwest. The entire place was a disaster of gigantic proportions.

Melly's hand flew upward to fondle her pearls. "You don't look pleased. I hope you're not angry with me, Piper."

Shaking free from the initial shock, I stared at my ex-mother-in-law, seeing her clearly for the first time in ages. A network of fine lines fanned out from eyes the same silver-blue as my daughter's. Somehow she seemed a smaller, frailer version of the steel magnolia I always envisioned. Lastly, I noticed the slight quiver in her lower lip, as if she might burst into tears any moment, and my irritation faded. "I'm just amazed you managed to rearrange everything so . . . quickly."

Melly's expression cleared. "I've been planning this for weeks as a surprise," she confided. "It's how I'd keep things if I owned a shop like yours. I love working here, dear. Anytime you need to run errands, all you have to do is call. I'll drop everything and run right over."

I summoned a weak smile as I escorted her to the door. Once she was on her way, I took a box from the storeroom and went about setting things back to their prealphabetized state. Another time, another day, I'd explain my "helter skelter" system to Melly.

I'd just placed the last jar of cinnamon alongside the cloves in the Hoosier cabinet when the phone rang. It was Precious Blessing at the Brandywine Creek Police Department, calling to inform me McBride wanted to see me down at the police station.

"ASAP," she said, then lowered her voice to a whisper. "Just between you, me, and the fencepost, it might be wise to bring a lawyer."

"Lawyer?" I squeaked.

"Yes, ma'am," she assured me in a more

364

normal tone. "That would be a right good idea."

She hung up without saying another word, but she'd said enough. My headache ratcheted up a notch; a sick feeling churned in the pit of my stomach. I never would have thought to bring an attorney. Why should I? I had nothing to hide. Since I divorced the jerk I'd married, I didn't even have an attorney. But . . .

My hands shook as I punched in the number of CJ's office. His secretary informed me he'd already left for the day, but could be reached on his cell phone. *Imagine the headlines,* he'd said only yesterday. *"PROMINENT ATTORNEY DEFENDS EX-WIFE ON HOMICIDE CHARGE."* Was the man clairvoyant?

"CJ?" I didn't give him a chance to say more than hello when he answered. "I need a lawyer. You won by default."

"Hey, Scooter. What's up?"

I could hear the clink of ice cubes. "Put down your bourbon and meet me at the police station. McBride wants to question me again, and I think I should have a lawyer along for the ride."

"Whoo-eee!" he chortled. "Wouldn't pass up a chance to meet that sumbitch on his home turf. Wait up, baby. I'm on my way."

"And CJ," I added, "*don't* call me 'baby.' "

I wasn't about to enter the fray without full battle regalia. This in mind, I raced upstairs and threw open the closet. I decided on a silky turquoise shirt with a bateau neckline and tailored slacks. For an extra pop, I added a necklace fashioned from thin strands of silver interspersed with colorful Swarovski crystals. All I needed now were shoes. Nothing like a drop-dead pair of shoes to give a girl confidence. And this girl needed all the confidence she could get. As the pièce de résistance, I slid my feet into a killer pair of leopard-print pumps with four-inch heels. A swipe of blush, a dab of lip gloss, a squirt of perfume, and I felt armed and dangerous. As an added precaution, I downed two Tylenol. I was good to go.

CJ let out a wolf whistle when he saw me. "Between you and me, baby, we'll bring McBride to his knees."

We didn't speak on the short ride over. CJ parked in one of the slots reserved for visitors. My feet had already hit the asphalt before he had time to come around to open the door. "Remember," he said, taking my elbow and escorting me toward the entrance. "you have the right to remain silent."

"Silence has never been my strong suit," I

reminded him, lengthening my stride to match his.

"Anything you say can be used against you in a court of law."

Precious Blessing looked up from her post at the front desk as we entered. I made a mental note to thank her later for the heads-up, but right now I had more urgent things on my mind. Precious gave me the once-over and a thumbs-up. "Lookin' hot, Miz Prescott. Lookin' hot. Interrogation room's first door on the left. Chief said for y'all to go right on in."

Dead man walking was the phrase that popped into my head. "Beau said your prints were on the murder weapon. That true?" CJ asked, his voice low.

"Yes, but that was before I knew it was a murder weapon. I'd never have picked it up otherwise."

"Right," he nodded. "What about the bloodstains the police found the day they searched your place?"

"Canine."

"Good, good," he muttered. "You made a fine mess of things without me around to look after you." He paused just outside the hated interrogation room. "McBride's a cagey bastard. He'll try to trip you up. Don't say a word unless I tell you it's okay."

Nerves twisted my stomach into a knot at the sight of McBride already seated behind the table, a tape recorder in front of him, ready to record every swallow and stammer. A not-too-subtle reminder that anything — and everything — could be used against me in a court of law. Lordy, what was I in for?

"Have a seat," McBride said without preamble.

CJ set his briefcase on the table, and took a seat in one of the faux-leather and chrome chairs. "So, McBride, what's this all about?"

McBride's gaze lingered on me a moment or two, then traveled to CJ. "Nice to see you, too, CJ," McBride replied, his expression neutral. "Are you here in an official capacity as Mrs. Prescott's attorney? Or did you want to see if I'd spent the city's money on redecorating my office?"

"Hell, no." CJ crossed one leg over the other, careful not to ruin the crease in his trousers. "You won't be in town long enough to worry about paint swatches."

"That so? Well, we'll see."

"I tried to convince the mayor and city council you were the wrong man for the job, but they wouldn't listen to reason. Guess some folks still remember back in the day when a piece of trailer trash came up with the game-winnin' play during regionals."

McBride shrugged. "Ever stop to think I might be the best qualified for the job?"

I cleared my throat. "Um, gentlemen, can we please get on with the business at hand?"

McBride opened a folder and scanned a report inside. "This just came back from GBI. According to forensics, the bloodstains on an item of clothing found in your shop, Mrs. Prescott, match those of Mario Barrone's."

I stared at him uncomprehendingly. "We talked about this before. I thought we agreed its presence could be easily explained. Why . . . ?"

"Have to follow protocol in these matters," he explained tersely. "I need your statement as part of a public record."

"I object." CJ started to rise.

McBride motioned him to sit. "Save your breath, CJ. This is an interview, not a courtroom. There's no jury here to impress."

CJ swung around to face me, his face red, whether from indignation or indigestion, I couldn't say. "What item of clothin' is he talkin' about, Scooter?" he demanded. "You told me the bloodstains were canine."

McBride addressed his next remark to me. "Care to bring your husband up to speed?"

"Ex-husband," we said in unison.

"Okay, darlin'," CJ drawled, "do as the

man says and bring me up to speed."

I cringed, aware of how flimsy my explanation might sound, but told him the abridged version of how a second bloody T-shirt had been found following a break-in at Spice It Up!

"Preposterous!" CJ declared self-righteously after hearing the story. "No judge or jury in their right minds would believe my ex-wife planted evidence in plain sight, then called you to come find it."

"Nevertheless," McBride said, "I have to go where the evidence leads."

"You always were too big for your britches, McBride," CJ snarled.

"And you were always a pompous ass." McBride kept his tone even. "I'd be remiss in my duties, however, if I didn't officially request Mrs. Prescott to come in for further questioning."

I felt I was watching a Ping-Pong match. "Enough! Let's get on with this, shall we?"

Clicking on the confounded recorder, McBride stated the perfunctory info, then turned his icy blues on me. "For the record, Mrs. Prescott, does the purple T-shirt found in the storeroom of your shop" — he rattled off the specific date and time — "belong to you?"

I opened my mouth, but before I could

speak, CJ leaned over. "Keep your answers to a simple yes or no."

That sounded like good advice, so I took it. "No."

CJ leaned back and nodded his approval, probably wishing I'd always taken direction this well.

McBride jotted my answer in a small spiral notebook. "Had you ever seen the garment before the night in question?"

From the corner of my eye, I saw CJ give a slight nod indicating I should answer. "No."

"Do you have an idea how the shirt might have gotten there?" McBride asked.

"You're darn right I do, and so do you," I fired back, foresaking my vow of monosyllables. "Whoever killed Mario planted it there."

CJ leaped to his feet. "Leading the witness."

I stifled the urge to roll my eyes. Amber needed to wean him off *Perry Mason* reruns on late-night cable.

"Sit down, Prescott, and stop showboating," McBride told him.

CJ sneered. "This wouldn't be the first time a dirty cop planted evidence to incriminate an innocent victim."

"Are you calling me a 'dirty' cop?"

Except for the muted whirr of the tape recorder, the room went still. McBride's eyes looked like shards of ice. I could see a muscle in his jaw twitch as he fought for control. In the old days, whenever CJ made an insensitive remark, I'd give him a discreet jab in the ribs. But this time, however, my elbow stayed glued to my side.

CJ stubbornly refused to back off. "Everyone knows you need to make an arrest if you want to keep your job. Who better to accuse than the person who found the body and innocently handled the *alleged* murder weapon?"

"I'm not accusing anyone until I know all the facts." McBride avoided my eyes as he said this.

CJ picked up his briefcase. "My client has already informed you the shirt doesn't belong to her. That she'd never seen it before you happened across it. Up until now, she has cooperated fully with law enforcement, but unless you plan to charge her, we're out of here."

I held my breath.

McBride drummed his fingers on the folder. "Mrs. Prescott is free to go — for the moment."

CJ held open the door of the interrogation room, and I breezed through. A free woman. For the moment.

On the way out of the station, CJ paused to hand Precious Blessing one of his business cards. "Call me if you're ever of a mind to sue the sumbitch you work for," he told her.

She stared back at him, puzzled. "Why would I wanna sue 'im? Chief treats me real good."

CJ gave her the smile hundreds recognized from billboards along the Interstate. "Sexual harassment, discrimination, whatever, I'm your man."

"Sexual harassment?" Precious chortled. "Whoo-ee. I should be so lucky."

CHAPTER 31

"Comfort food, honeybun." Reba Mae took a plate heaped with leftover mac and cheese out of the microwave and placed it in front of me. "Take Doc Reba's advice and eat up. Mac and cheese is one of the basic food groups here in the South. It'll have you feelin' better lickety-split."

I wasn't hungry but dug in anyway. "I have to confess, Reba Mae, McBride had me shaking in my shoes. I felt the noose tighten around my neck, waiting to hear if he was going to charge me or not. How *does* the state of Georgia execute people?"

Reba poured wine for each of us before taking the seat across from me. "Gee, hon, I think they found a new, improved method of killin' folks. Lethal injection would be my guess."

"Much more civilized." I forced myself to take another bite of mac and cheese, then pushed the plate aside and reached for my wine. "I'd much rather drift off to meet my Maker in a drug-induced haze than to dangle from the end of a rope."

"McBride can't really think for one doggone minute you murdered Barrone."

"It's hard to tell what's going on behind his cop mask. I swear he can look straight through me." I shivered at the memory of his cold, detached stare. "He's the big old tomcat and, me, the country mouse he wants to eat for lunch."

"Don't suppose CJ bein' there helped much?"

I barked out a laugh. "As if things weren't bad enough, CJ made a snarky comment about 'dirty cops.' "

Reba Mae's pendant earrings swayed as she shook her head in disbelief. "How did McBride react to that?"

"Not well." I kicked off my shoes. I'd come to Reba Mae's straight from the police station. I needed my BFF to talk me down off the ledge. "McBride kept his cool, but I could see it wasn't easy with CJ pushing his buttons."

"CJ and McBride's feud dates back to high school."

"Unless it was to brag about his grades or being a shortstop, CJ never talked much about his high school days," I admitted.

"Tell me about the 'feud.' "

Reba Mae leaned back and folded her arms across her chest. "Butch told me all about it when we were dating. Seems like CJ got miffed when the coach picked McBride over him as quarterback; CJ quit the team right on the spot. The rest of the season, he bad-mouthed McBride from the sidelines. Called him names like 'white trash' and 'trailer park trash' — never to his face, of course. CJ may be dumb, but he's not stupid."

I was interested in spite of myself. "What was McBride's family like?"

"His dad was a mean drunk. Died of lung cancer a few years back."

"What about his mother?"

Reba Mae tipped her head to one side, lips pursed in disapproval. "I heard his ma took off for parts unknown when he was still a kid. Left him and his sister to fend for themselves."

"He has a sister?"

"Claudia's a couple years younger, but she doesn't live around here. California maybe."

I played with the stem of my wineglass and tried to keep my tone casual. "What else do you know about him?"

She gave me a shrewd look. "Why so interested?"

I took a sip of wine and pretended noncha-lance. "Curious, that's all."

"Um-hum." She smirked. "Accordin' to Butch, McBride had a couple brushes with the law in his youth, nothin' serious, then took off and joined the army. Didn't hear any more about him until Uncle Joe men-tioned he'd be replacin' him as chief of police. After gettin' a gander at his person-nel file from Miami-Dade, Uncle Joe de-scribed him as one tough cookie."

"Just peachy keen," I said morosely. "One tough cookie is exactly what I don't need to complicate my life."

Reba Mae topped off our glasses. "What you need, sugar, is to ditch CJ and get yourself a real lawyer."

"CJ *is* a real lawyer," I reminded her.

She leaned forward, elbows on the table. "I mean one who does more than sue companies because someone stubbed their big toe and doesn't want to work anymore."

"The problem is, Reba Mae, I don't know any lawyers except CJ and his partner Matt Wainwright. Maybe I should check the Yel-low Pages."

"Before you do that, let me ask around the Klassy Kut — discreetly," she added, seeing objections starting to form. "One of my clients might know a good criminal

377

defense attorney."

I rubbed my temples, which had started to throb again. Too much wine? Or too much Wyatt McBride. "Let's change the subject, shall we?"

"And I have the perfect change of subject," Reba Mae announced, turning to open the refrigerator. "Ta-da!"

My mouth watered at the sight of the picture-perfect, suitable-for-framing chocolate pie she held. "Maybelle Humphries?"

"Who else?" Reba Mae grinned, cutting us each a generous wedge. "It was her way of thanking me for a favor. I had to hide it from the boys, or there wouldn't be a crumb left."

I waited while Reba Mae worked her way through her slice — and half of mine — before tackling the subject of discovering Pete's shoe size. "So," I concluded, "I'm fresh out of brilliant ideas and need some input."

Reba Mae pointed her fork at me. "You're forgettin', hon, we're both moms. Footprints, handprints, we're experts in the 'prints' department. Just think how many times we mopped muddy footprints off nice clean floors or wiped sticky fingerprints off nice clean windows."

I dragged the tines of my fork through

what was left of my pie. "Nothing like Georgia red clay to make a mess on shiny linoleum."

"So all we gotta do is get us some dirt and make sure Pete steps in it."

"And how do you propose we do that? Pete spends his days in a butcher shop, not on a playground."

"How about plaster of paris?" Reba Mae suggested. "Remember those handprints the kids made in kindergarten for Mother's Day?"

I smiled, thinking how proud first Chad, then Lindsey, had been of their art projects. "I still have mine."

"Me, too," Reba Mae confessed with a sappy grin.

"What about wet cement?" I asked.

"Nah." Reba Mae shook her head. "The city council would have a conniption if we took it upon ourselves to redo the sidewalks."

I mulled over the problem. "We don't need a permanent foot impression. All I want is one good footprint so I can measure it for size and look at the tread."

Reba Mae snatched another bite of my pie. "Maybelle makes the best chocolate pie ever. She said it was Buzz Oliver's favorite."

"Here," I said, "help yourself. I'm not

hungry." I was about to shove my unfinished piece toward her when I noticed the tracks her fork had made. The dark chocolate contrasted nicely against her white dinnerware. Duh! I wanted to smack my forehead. The solution to our problem was literally under our noses.

"What, what?" Reba Mae frowned. "Did I miss somethin'?"

"What if we make up a cover story of some sort. For example, knowing Buzz's fondness for chocolate pie and being neighborly, you're about to deliver a big fat slice when you accidentally trip in front of Meat on Main and drop it just as Pete comes out? Poor guy. He'd have to step in it and get it all over his shoes on the way to his car."

"Hmm." Reba Mae gave me a sly smile. "Let's discuss this further over another teensy sliver of pie."

"Let's," I agreed. Suddenly my appetite returned and along with it a craving for chocolate.

The colorful bundle of polyester and teased hair entering Spice It Up! late the following afternoon morphed into Dottie Hemmings who was accompanied by Maybelle Humphries. The woman's rail-thin figure belied her reputation as a fine cook. Her salt-and-pepper bob framed a face more plain than pretty. I placed her age somewhere from early to mid fifties.

"Hey there, Piper," Dottie sang out. "I brought you a customer."

Maybelle smiled. "I heard business has been slow for you, but things should pick up soon."

"I certainly hope you're right, Maybelle. How can I help you?"

"The posters just arrived at the chamber of commerce office for the Barbecue Festival next month. I thought I'd swing by and pick up some spices for the sauce I'm plannin' to enter."

"Maybelle's determined to win the blue ribbon this year," Dottie confided. "Y'all know she's the best cook hereabouts."

Embarrassed, Maybelle rested her hand on Dottie's shoulder. "Stop it, Dottie. All that flattery's goin' to make me blush."

A little blush, I thought, might not be a bad idea in Maybelle's case. Add a swipe of eye shadow and a dab of lipstick and Buzz Oliver might forego Becca and her creamed soup.

"You'll find a good selection of spices in the special barbecue display I set up." A display I'd reassembled after Melly's well-intentioned effort to rectify my deplorable lack of organization.

"If you don't mind, I'll take a look around." Maybelle headed off in the direction I'd indicated.

Dottie glanced over her shoulder to make sure her friend was out of earshot. "Maybelle's determined to win Buzz's affection from Becca if it's the last thing she does."

"That sounds ominous," I said.

"Maybelle's a gentle soul. She won't even step on a spider." Dottie laughed merrily, then turned serious. "Speaking of killing, Brenda Nash's nephew Billy Wade got into a bar fight a few years back and the other guy ended up dying. His lawyer got him off on voluntary homicide. Judge sentenced him to twenty years."

Now that *was* ominous. "Why are you telling me this?"

"Never hurts to know these things. Billy Wade didn't mean to kill nobody when the fight broke out. Things just got out of hand is all." Dottie reached into her purse and slipped me a scrap of paper. "Here, take this."

I stared at the small square of paper she'd pressed into my palm. "What is it?"

"The name and number of Billy Wade's lawyer." She hazarded another look in Maybelle's direction to make sure her friend was otherwise occupied. "I heard you might be in the market for a criminal lawyer — and this one works cheap."

I thanked her and tucked the information into my apron pocket. Apparently word had spread faster than kudzu that I needed a good, but cheap, defense lawyer. I didn't know whether to laugh or cry.

"This ought to get me started." Maybelle dumped an armload of bottles and jars down on the counter. "I'm in the process of replacing my grocery-store spices with newer, fresher ones from Spice It Up! How can you tell if a spice is still good or not?"

"When in doubt, smell it," I instructed. "If it smells spicy and strong, use it. If not, throw it out and buy new. I like to replace mine before the flavor components dissipate."

"Good to know," Maybelle said, sounding pleased at the information.

The minute the pair left, I ran to the front window. From there I could see across the square to Meat on Main. I shifted my weight from foot to foot, eager to put the chocolate pie caper into action. Fortunately, most of the stores and businesses were already closed for the day, leaving the stage to us. At precisely six P.M., Pete, a creature of habit, came out of his shop and turned

383

to lock the door.

I pressed SPEED DIAL. "Showtime," I said the instant Reba Mae answered.

I couldn't resist a grin at the sight of my friend sashaying around the corner in a pair of strappy gladiator sandals with four-inch heels while balancing a plate in one hand. She wore a snug-fitting scooped-neck top — I'd lay odds on a push-up bra underneath — that made the most of "the girls," as she referred to her DDs. I saw Pete turn at hearing her approach. From that point on, our plan took wing.

Pete's feet moved forward, but his eyes stayed fixed on Reba Mae's natural assets as he walked smack-dab into her. The pie flew out of her hand and gooey dark chocolate splattered all over the sidewalk. Luckily, Reba Mae managed to jump back to avoid the worst of the spatters.

Grabbing a roll of paper towels, I sprinted over to assist in the cleanup.

"S-so sorry, Reba Mae," Pete stammered, his face beet red. "Don't know what came over me. Shoulda been watching where I was going. Instead, I walked straight into you."

"No harm done, hon." Reba Mae patted his arm, consolingly. "Accidents happen."

I took up a post on one side of Pete, Reba

Mae the other, thus effectively boxing him. Unless he shoved us aside, he'd have to step through the goo to reach his Buick parked at the curb. "Best you get home quick as you can, Pete. Your wife will want to pre-treat those pants before stains set in. And don't you worry none. We'll have this mess cleaned up in no time."

Uncertain, Pete glanced from me to Reba Mae, then down at the blotches on his light-colored khakis.

"Go on, Pete." I waved the paper towels. "We've got it covered."

The moment Pete's car was out of sight, I looked around to make sure no one was watching, then bending down, pulled out a tape measure and quickly placed it over a perfect chocolate-pie shoe print.

"Well . . . ?" Reba Mae peeked over my shoulder. "What do you think?"

"I think we can scratch Pete off our list. No way he's a size ten."

Though the sidewalk cleanup was finished hours ago, I still had work to do. I sat in my shop poring over numbers generated by my accounting program. The results were dismal. If business didn't pick up soon, I'd be forced to make some hard decisions. The notion of closing Spice It Up! for good and admitting defeat was a depressing one.

My gloomy thoughts were interrupted by a knock on the door. I hurried to answer and found Wyatt McBride on my doorstep.

"Saw your light was on so thought I'd stop by rather than call in the morning," he said by way of an explanation as he stepped inside. "My dispatcher said you phoned earlier, but I was in meetings all day."

I had debated with myself all morning if I should call him or not. My nerves had gotten the better of me yesterday when I was called in for questioning. I'd forgotten to mention seeing Diane Cloune drive off in a car similar to the one that had nearly run me down. Forgotten to mention that the vehicle in question bore a clown logo on its trunk.

"Dorinda told me you needed to speak with me and it was important," McBride said.

"I did, and it is," I replied slowly.

He arched a brow and regarded me quizzically. "Well . . . ?"

I took a deep breath, then let it out in a rush. In for a penny; in for a pound. "The night you brought Lindsey home you told me small details can come back when you least expect them."

"True."

"You also said memory is a funny thing."

He waited quietly for me to continue.

I proceeded to fill him in on the history of my coat leading up to my claiming it at the dry cleaners. Finally, I paused to draw a breath. "TMI?"

"Excuse me . . . ?"

"Too much information," I explained. "It's one of Lindsey's expressions."

"I'll file away the info about Dillard's for later," he said. "Let me get this clear, you called to tell me you remembered that your trench coat, an expensive coat that you found on sale, was at the dry cleaners?"

"No!" I cried. "That's only the reason I happened to be outside Yesteryear Antiques to see Diane Cloune drive away in a Lincoln. A big black Lincoln," I added for good measure.

"So Diane drives a Lincoln. A lot of people do."

"Are you being deliberately obtuse?" I was prattling on like the village idiot. No wonder the poor man seemed confused. I needed to calm myself. I took a deep, yoga breath, inhaling and letting air fill my abdomen, then my chest. Then I exhaled, chest, then abdomen — smooth and effortless, slow and easy just like I'd been taught.

McBride was looking at me worriedly.

"You're not hyperventilating, are you?"

I rolled my eyes. "No, I never hyperventilate. That's a yoga exercise. It decreases toxicity in the body by increasing the exchange of carbon dioxide and oxygen. Yoga happens to have a calming effect."

"Do I make you nervous?"

"Is that a cop question, or a personal question?"

His expression softened and for a fleeting moment he looked almost human before the professional mask slid back in place. "Let's start over. You were outside the antique store when you saw Diane drive off in a Lincoln. Why is that important?"

I tucked a stray curl behind my ear. "That was when I saw the clown logo on the trunk. The same logo Cloune Motors uses. You know, DON'T CLOWN AROUND. VISIT CLOUNE MOTORS. The car that narrowly missed sending me to a viewing room at The Eternal Rest was big, dark, and" — I paused for effect — "had a clown logo on its trunk."

"Are you saying you think Diane Cloune tried to kill you?"

"Yes . . . no . . . I don't know." My gaze swept over the shop not really registering the shelves of spices, the bare brick walls, the heart pine floor. "I realize it's not much to go on," I admitted reluctantly.

"Think about it, Piper. Half the cars in town sport that same stupid smiley-faced clown."

I felt so frustrated I wanted to stomp my foot like a two-year-old. I didn't want a reminder of how many cars were sold by Cloune Motors. I wanted an "atta girl." A pat on the back. Or, at the very least, a "this narrows it down."

"You're right." I sighed. "It's not like I remembered the make and model, or caught a glimpse of the license plate."

"Don't be so discouraged. Something will break in the case."

I desperately hoped he was right — and break sooner rather than later. This whole thing was taking a toll on my nerves. "Have you checked out alibis of the people I told you about?"

"Working on it, but you can scratch Pete Barker's name off the list."

"Why?" My eyes widened in surprise at hearing this. How could the man possibly know the results of our privately conducted chocolate-pie test?

"Seems as though Pete's been taking dance lessons on Friday nights. He wants to surprise Gerilee when they go on a Caribbean cruise for their anniversary."

"What about Danny Boyd?"

"He's in the clear, too. A half dozen doctors and nurses can testify he was in the emergency room with his girlfriend the night Mario was killed. That was the same night he found out he was going to be a daddy."

I kept a stiff upper lip. My persons-of-interest list was vanishing before my eyes. "Tony?" I asked.

"That's where I'm off to next."

After McBride left, I sank onto the stool behind the counter and put my head in my hands. Suspects were dropping like flies. What if all of them had alibis? Soon I'd be the only person of interest on a very short list. Who'd ever think Mario Barrone would be more trouble dead than alive?

Chapter 32

Lindsey Nicole had been the one bright spot in an otherwise miserable day. Minutes ago, I'd watched her snap the leash on Casey and race out the door, heading for the park. Lindsey had been hard at work on a book report all afternoon. Mrs. Walker, her language arts teacher, had offered her students the opportunity to bring up their grade point averages by doing extra assignments. I'd set up a workstation for my daughter at Spice It Up!, where I could keep an eye on her. Make sure she kept her nose to the grindstone — and not on her cell phone. Once the last *i* was dotted and *t* was crossed, she was out the door like a shot. You'd think she'd just drawn the get-out-of-jail free card.

Jail? Hanging? Lethal injection?

These days, my thoughts seemed to be running around and around the same morbid track.

"Yoo-hoo," a sugar-coated voice called out.

I looked up from my perch behind the counter to see Amber Leigh Ames stroll into my shop. All mile-long legs, sparkling choppers, and a perky Southern charm that flicked on and off like a bug zapper in July.

I plastered on a smile as superficial as Amber herself. "Hey, Amber. You looking to spice things up a bit?"

Amber refused to take the bait. "Where's Lindsey?" she asked, frowning.

"You just missed her, but she ought to be back soon."

"I told CJ I'd swing by and pick her up on my way home. Diane Cloune had a dentist appointment so our meetin' ended early."

I restacked an already neat stack of catalogs. "What meeting was that?"

"Diane and I are cochairing the garden club's silent auction to raise money for a gazebo in the town square." Amber rummaged through a squishy leather satchel. "Where is the girl, anyway?"

"Lindsey finished her report and took the dog to the park."

Amber fished out a compact and flipped it open. "I don't understand why that witch of a teacher came down so hard on the poor child when everyone knows school's nearly over for the year. Book reports and essays are so . . . passé."

I gritted my teeth. "That's precisely the point. The school year's almost over, and I, for one, am grateful Lindsey has a chance to bring up her grade."

"Whatever." Amber examined her already flawless makeup in the tiny mirror. "What book did she get stuck readin'?"

"*To Kill a Mockingbird*."

Amber snapped the compact shut and dropped it in her bag. "That old thing? I read that way back when I was in high school."

" 'Way back when' isn't all that long ago," I reminded her.

"True." She smiled sweetly. "At least not if you compare it to when you were in high school."

I returned the smile — minus the sweet.

"I, for one," Amber continued, unfazed, "will be overjoyed when CJ returns Lindsey's car keys. Her not being able to drive is a major inconvenience. I tried to convince him it was more punishment for me than it was for her. But my opinion didn't matter much after Miss Melly gave him a talkin' to. Seems she heard rumors while gettin' her hair done."

I added "thank Melly" to my to-do list. "Sorry it's inconvenient, Amber, but we're trying to get the point across that actions have consequences."

Amber darted a quick look at the door. Still no sign of Lindsey, but she dropped her voice anyway. "Can we talk, Piper? Woman to woman?"

I shrugged. "I'm all ears."

"I understand you're upset on account of CJ leavin' you for a . . . younger . . . woman. That being the case an' all, I hope you won't try to influence Lindsey against me. It's not my fault her daddy doesn't want her hangin' around all the time."

I all but fluttered my lashes in feigned innocence. "Why, Amber, the thought never crossed my mind. I'm certain you'd love nothing better than having a teenager underfoot all summer. Being as you're so close in age, I'm sure the two of you must have a lot in common."

Amber looked at me as if to say "are you being sarcastic?" but didn't know me well enough to decide. "I'm fond of Lindsey, I truly am, and I don't want to be the wicked stepmother. As long as we're on the subject of your children . . ." After casting another quick glance at the door, she plunged ahead, "I'd like to speak to you about your son."

"What about Chad?" I asked. "You've never even met him. When he was home on spring break, you were in Aspen skiing."

"Yes, well, I'm sure I'll meet him when he comes for his daddy's weddin'. But in the meantime, I've been thinkin' . . ."

I folded my hands primly to keep from reaching out and choking her. "Thinkin' " obviously didn't come with any regularity to Amber. It was more of an event than a happening.

"I was thinkin'," Amber continued, "it might be best if your son accepts the summer job he's been offered in Chapel Hill. Bein' a lifeguard at a wellness center sounds perfect for a young man. Keeps him out in all that fresh air and sunshine. Lets him do lots of swimmin'. Get a nice tan."

I cocked my head to one side. "And gives you and CJ even more privacy."

Did the ditz really think I was going to fall for the "fresh air and sunshine" routine? Having not one, but two, young people hanging around would certainly put a crimp in CJ's love life. Amber refused to meet my gaze.

I slipped off the stool and stood tall, maximizing every centimeter of my five-foot-two-inch frame. "I'd dearly love to have my boy home for the summer, but the final decision rests with Chad. I'm not about to interfere with my son's plans for a summer job."

Thanks to Lindsey's timely return, we were spared more verbal sparring.

Spying Amber, Casey broke free of the leash and bounded over to greet her. A prime example of puppy exuberance. Amber quickly sidestepped. "Can't you control that animal?" she snapped.

"Don't like dogs?" I asked, recovering the leash. Casey, sensing he was persona non grata, allowed me to corral him behind the baby gate I'd installed between the shop and the storeroom.

"I had a poodle once," she retaliated, sounding defensive.

"What happened to him?" Lindsey instantly wanted to know.

Amber waved a dismissive hand. "We had to get rid of him. I'm allergic."

Maybe CJ and Amber were soul mates after all. Neither was overly fond of animals — or children. A match made in heaven.

"Lindsey, I was just telling your mother about the committee I'm cochairing with Mrs. Cloune," Amber said

"Cool," Lindsey replied. "My friend Taylor said Mrs. Cloune and the dude who got killed had the hots for each other. That true?"

"Lindsey!" I scolded.

"Oh, that's quite all right," Amber interrupted, before I could launch into a lecture on the perils of gossip. "Lindsey and I are pals. No secrets, right, honey?"

She winked at Lindsey; I wanted to vomit. No secrets, my foot! I wouldn't trust the woman as far as I could throw her.

"Actually" — Amber inspected her French manicure for flaws — "Diane is still quite distraught over Mario's death."

"Distraught?" This time it was me, not Lindsey, who was the victim of rabid curiosity. Shame, shame. I'd lecture myself — later. "Why?" I asked. "From everything I heard, I thought their . . . friendship . . . ended ages ago."

"That's what they wanted folks to think," she explained, looking smug. "After Mario's . . . dalliance . . . with Vicki ended, Diane and Mario resumed their affair. They'd meet sometime in Atlanta, sometime at the motel on the outskirts of town. I recognized their cars on more than one occasion. . . ."

I fought the urge to clamp my hands over my daughter's ears. Block out the tawdry image. "I think we get the gist."

Amber frowned down at the slim gold watch circling her wrist. "Time to get a move on, Lindsey. I want to stop by North of the Border on the way home to pick up an order I phoned in."

Lindsey stuffed notebooks as well as a variety of pens and high-lighters into a shocking pink-and-gray backpack. "Takeout again?"

Amber fluttered her fingers good-bye at me. "Honey, I thought you loved takeout," I heard her say as the two of them headed for the door.

"I do, but . . ." Lindsey's voice trailed off.

Maybe it was time to for a little home cooking. Lindsey always loved my lasagna.

Spice It Up! seemed unnaturally quiet after they'd left. I gazed at the regulator clock that I'd purchased at Yesteryear Antiques along with my old-fashioned cash register. It was only four forty-five. Too early to lock up for the night. Too late to manufacture busywork. I settled back on my stool and clicked on Solitaire, content to drop and drag for fifteen minutes.

Red queen of hearts on black king of spades. A king who, minus the mustache, bore a vague resemblance to Wyatt Mc-

Bride. Next, I tried placing a red six on a red seven. A message sprang up. INVALID. Common sense warned me that even thinking about Wyatt McBride was an invalid move.

My head popped up as Diane Cloune entered the shop. Guiltily, I pointed the mouse at EXIT. Wouldn't do for customers to think I had nothing better to do than wile away the time playing a silly card game.

"Hello, Piper," Diane said. "Glad I caught you before you closed for the day."

Rising, I smoothed my sunny yellow apron. "Hello, Diane. How can I help you?"

"Since the garden club meeting finished early, Dwayne and I were able to finalize the menu for a dinner party we're hosting for potential campaign backers. After some arm twisting, Tony Deltorro agreed to cater it — with one caveat, which brings us to why we're here."

"We . . . ?"

"Oh," Diane said with a laugh. "Dwayne had to take an important call. He'll be along shortly."

I glanced over my shoulder and saw Dwayne out on the sidewalk, talking on his cell.

"Tony's busy readying his new restaurant for its grand opening, but we made him an offer he couldn't refuse." Diane smoothed a stray wisp of hair into the clip holding her low ponytail. And that was when I noticed something different about her. She wasn't wearing her signature diamond studs. I racked my brain but with no success, trying to remember the last time I'd seen her wearing them. Before Mario was killed? What about after?

I smiled and tried to sound casual. "It's rare that I see you without your diamond earrings."

"I'm having them appraised," she said, her tone frosty. Reaching into her shoulder bag, she pulled out a sheet of paper and handed it to me. "Here. Tony insisted Dwayne and I handle some of the details. He demands only the freshest ingredients."

"I'll be happy to help any way I can," I murmured, scanning the list.

"Naturally, we thought of your little store. It's our practice to patronize the local merchants whenever we can."

And *patronize* was present in every syllable.

"How thoughtful." I smiled tightly. "As it happens, I stock all the spices Tony needs. And, I can give you the name of a local grower for the herbs."

I soon had one of the small wicker baskets

I kept handy for customers' use filled with the items on Diane's list. Coriander, cardamom, caraway seeds, along with dried vanilla beans. In the meantime, I couldn't help but wonder. Were her earrings really at a jeweler's being appraised? Or had one of them been lost and not yet replaced?

I had just returned Diane's Visa Gold card when Dwayne, his phone conversation over, entered the shop. He gifted me with his patented politician's smile, then smoothed his slicked-back hair and rested a hand on Diane's waist. "Shopping completed, sweetheart?" he asked his wife.

His elbow inadvertently knocked my neatly stacked catalogs to the floor. The sound startled Casey, who had been snoozing on the other side of the baby gate, from canine dreamland. A growl started deep in the little dog's throat. I watched in stunned amazement as my overly friendly pet crouched low and bared his teeth.

"Is something wrong with that animal?" Diane asked in alarm.

"No, no, he's fine." I started toward him, intent on soothing. "Casey isn't usually like this. Must be something he ate."

Not about to be placated, Casey hurled himself at the gate, barking ferociously.

"C'mon, Diane," Dwayne urged. "It's almost closing time. We don't want to make Piper work overtime."

But Diane wasn't about to let it rest. "You're going to have to restrain that mutt before it bites someone. You don't need a lawsuit in addition to your other problems," she added snidely.

"My wife makes a good point, Piper." Dwayne picked up the bag of spices. "The Board of Health would frown on the idea of an animal in a place where food is sold."

"Spices are hardly in the same category as food." My words were lost on them. They were already out the door.

I unfastened the baby gate, picked Casey up, and petted him. Beneath my hand, I felt the dog's small body quiver with tension as I stroked his fur. "What was that all about, fella?" I murmured. Strange behavior, I thought, coming from a mutt who loves most everyone. Or was it? I thought about the missing earring, the two sets of shoe prints. Could Diane have stabbed her former lover then called her husband to help cover up the crime? I had difficulty envisioning a woman committing such a violent act, but who knows what we're really capable of until the moment arises. Wish I

knew if Diane had an alibi for the night in
question.

CHAPTER 33

After the Clounes' departure, I was in the process of turning the sign on the front door from OPEN to CLOSED when the phone rang. I stared at it, hoping the incessant ringing would stop. I'd had all the social interaction I could handle for one day.

Whoever was on the other end was as persistent as I was hesitant. Eventually persistence won. Trudging over to the counter, I picked up the blasted phone. Much to my delight, I heard Doug Winters's voice, and not Precious Blessing's.

"Hey, Piper," Doug greeted me, sounding chipper. "Just wanted to call and tell you I've been thinking about you. How're things going?"

"I'm adopting a new policy around here: don't ask, and I won't tell."

Doug chuckled. "That bad, eh?"

I smiled in spite of myself. "Worse."

"You sound as though you could use a

diversion. How about a burger and a movie on Saturday night? I'll even sit through a chick flick if that's what you want."

"Um, I don't know, Doug," I prevaricated, reluctant to inflict my ill humor on such a sweet guy. "I don't think I'd be very good company."

"Consider it doctor's orders. So how about it?"

Who was I to question doctor's orders? A night in Doug's company would act as an antianxiety, antidepressant, and mood elevator all rolled into one. "All right," I said with a sigh. "It's a deal."

"Great. I'll pick you up around six."

My spirits felt lighter when I put down the phone. Switching off lights as I went, I made my way toward the rear of the shop. I'd already started up the stairs when I remembered the trench coat still hanging in the cupboard. I'd yet to examine the damages done when I vaulted over my Beetle. Retracing my steps, I plucked it off the hook and slung it over my shoulder. Casey scampered along behind me.

Once inside my apartment, I peeled off the protective plastic covering. The grass and mud stains on the front panels were barely visible. Mr. Proctor was to be commended for the splendid job he'd done. I

flipped the coat over. At first glance everything seemed intact. Maybe the tear wasn't
as bad as Bitsy made it out to be. Maybe
the waiver releasing Proctor's Cleaners from
responsibility was merely a formality. I was
about to heave a breath of relief when I saw
it. A small piece of cloth torn from the hem
of the back vent.

I spread the coat on the kitchen table for
a better look. A triangular bit of fabric had
been ripped away, leaving a ragged edge. I
sank down on a chair — the very one Wyatt
McBride had occupied when he'd lapsed
from foe into almost friendly — and closed
my eyes. I replayed the events leading up to
the tear.

Memories unwound like the spool of one
of those old-fashioned eight-track tapes my
father used to own. It had been raining that
night. Doug insisted on giving me leftovers:
tandoori chicken and cucumber salad. I
half-turned, container in hand, when I'd
been blinded by the glare of headlights and
deafened by the roar of an engine. Out of
nowhere, a sleek black car raced toward me.
I could still smell its exhaust fumes. Feel
the heat from its engine.

I idly fingered the frayed tear. The bumper
must have grazed the hem of my coat and
torn off a small fragment. That was the only

logical explanation I could come up with. I broke into a cold sweat, knowing how close I'd come to nearly being squashed like a bug.

Mario Barrone's killer clearly didn't like me snooping around. Asking questions. Poking into alibis. In fact, he disliked it so much that he sought to silence me — permanently. Then, another thought occurred to me. My eyes popped open. I sat up straighter. What if the scrap of fabric was still wedged in the car's bumper? All I had to do was find the car. Piece of cake, right?

Find the car. Find the killer.

I reached for my cell and did what any sane woman would do in the similar circumstances. I dialed my BFF.

"Takeout again," Lindsey had whined earlier when leaving with Amber. Takeout versus home-cooked. Her complaint had seemed valid. Yet here I was at the Pizza Palace once again. My daughter's words conjured up visions of the home-cooked meals I'd served my family on a regular basis: savory stews, mouthwatering meat loaves, tender roast chicken, spicy lasagna. CJ confided once he preferred my pot roast to his mother's. His compliment made me feel I'd been crowned Queen of the Kitchen. Somehow, though, home-cooked meals weren't as tasty when eaten alone. I confess these days I often resorted to take-out menus and frozen dinners. But pizza, when devoured in a restaurant, really wasn't the same as takeout, I rationalized, as I waited for Reba Mae to join me.

I'd just taken a sip of wine when my friend pushed through the door. Reba Mae looked as tall and formidable as an Amazon as she strode toward me in her espadrilles with three-inch wedge heels. She'd taken the time to change from work clothes into form-fitting black crop pants and a bold-striped shirt. Chandelier-style earrings dangled nearly to her shoulders. By comparison, I could pass for a wallflower in my denim capris and yellow knit V-neck.

Gina Deltorro approached our table, an order pad in her pocket instead of in her hand. "The usual?"

I nodded, and she left the two of us alone.

Reba Mae settled her straw tote on the seat of an empty chair. "Okay," she said. "Let's see if I got this straight. You think you tore your coat when you dove head over teacups over the hood of your car?"

"That's the only explanation I can come up with. No way I would've entirely forgotten tearing a designer trench coat I bought at half price."

"So, sugar, what do you propose we do? Track down every big black car with a clown decal?"

Now that Reba Mae voiced my brainchild out loud, I was beset with doubt. I fiddled with the stem of my wineglass. I was grasping at straws, but desperation makes people do strange things. "I admit, it does sound sort of lame," I confessed, then brightened. "How about we start our search with all the big black cars at Cloune Motors?"

"Guess that might work." Reba Mae sounded skeptical. "Here's another glitch in your plan. Caleb says the Clounes own multiple vehicles. They switch off drivin' 'em. Sometimes Dwayne drives the Lincoln, and Diane the SUV or snazzy convertible. Dwayne even rotates 'em through the lot, periodically hopin' someone will make an offer. He shuffles cars slicker than a card shark in Vegas."

The usually talkative Gina delivered our pizza without a single word, then disappeared in the direction of the kitchen. Strange, I thought, but chalked it up to the stress of opening a new restaurant soon.

"Let me tell you the clincher." I glanced around to make certain our conversation wouldn't be overheard. The only other patrons at the moment were a young family seated along the opposite wall. A tow-haired toddler intent on throwing everything within arm's reach on the floor kept them occupied.

Reba Mae slid steamy slices onto two plates. "I'm all ears."

Between bites of pizza, I described Casey's strange behavior during the Clounes' visit. Reba Mae shook her head, amazed by all the snarling, growling, and teeth baring.

"Whoo-ee," she whistled when I finished. "The mutt's more apt to lick a person to death than to attack 'im."

"Exactly," I agreed, wiping greasy fingers on a paper napkin. "And what's more, Diane wasn't wearing her diamond earrings. When I mentioned them, she claimed they were being appraised."

Reba Mae's eyes widened in surprise. "You don't say."

Encouraged by her response, I launched into an idea that had been marinating. "A missing earring and a barking dog won't be enough to link Diane with the murder. We need something more concrete before we approach McBride with our newest theory. It can't hurt if we mosey over to Cloune Motors for a look around? Scout out the used cars. See if we turn up anything big, black, and suspicious."

Reba Mae helped herself to another gooey slice. "Not 'used,' honeybun. Pre-owned," she corrected.

"Right," I muttered. "I keep forgetting."

"We need to cook up a cover story."

"Cover story?"

"Like they do in the movies." Reba Mae plucked a mushroom off her plate and popped it into her mouth. "We need to convince Dwayne we're serious shoppers."

"How do we do that?" I shoved my plate away. "My Beetle's only a year old. I can't very well tell Dwayne I'm in the market for a new car — used or pre-owned."

Reba Mae leaned both elbows on the checkered tablecloth and gave the matter some thought. "I have it!" she said, snapping her fingers. "We can pretend we're lookin' for a car for Chad. Say the one he has now is givin' him grief, breakin' down all the time. Since he's too busy to do it himself, CJ asked you to scout around. See what you can find."

I clinked my wineglass against hers. "That oughta do it."

Pleased with herself, Reba Mae grinned back at me. "How about tomorrow afternoon? Strike while the griddle's hot."

"Deal."

"Uh-oh." Reba Mae pointed her index finger over my shoulder. "Here comes trouble."

I turned to see who she was pointing at, half-expecting to find McBride. This time, however, trouble was personified in the form of Tony Deltorro. "Uh-oh," I repeated, noting the scowl on his face.

"You . . . !" His swarthy face an unhealthy shade of red, Tony jabbed a finger at me. "Who the hell do you think you are? Who gave you the right to butt into my business?"

Gina hovered close by, wringing her hands and looking worried. The family with the toddler snatched their child from the booster seat and left hurriedly.

"Me?" I said, taken aback by the vehemence of Tony's attack.

Reba Mae tried to intervene. "Look, Tony, Piper and I . . ."

"Stay out of this, Reba Mae," Tony snapped. "This doesn't concern you."

I tried to diffuse the situation with humor. "Sorry I upset you. Next time I'll order a calzone instead of pizza."

"Cut the crap." I started to rise but he blocked the move. "I know you're the one who sicced that damn chief of police on me. The way the guy tore into me, you'd think I

412

was the one who murdered Barrone. Not you."

That did it. My chair scraped the floor as I shoved away from the table. "For your information, mister, *I* didn't kill Barrone. McBride's only doing what any good cop should do and checking out anyone who might've wanted Mario dead."

Tony and I stood almost toe to toe. Reba Mae and Gina watched the interplay as avidly as fans at a championship baseball game with two outs and the bases loaded in the ninth inning. Tony's dark eyes blazed. My face burned pink to the roots of my hair.

" 'Where were you the night Barrone was killed?' " he mimicked. " 'Do you have any witnesses who can verify your alibi?' "

"Honey, calm down. Remember what the doctor said about your blood pressure." Gina placed a tentative hand on her husband's arm, but he shook it off.

"It's no one's damn business where I was that night. Or who I was with," he shouted at me. "I've nothing to hide. For your information, I was meeting with Brig Abernathy at his big old house in the historic district, trying to convince the skinflint to accept my offer for Trattoria Milano when Mario hightailed it for the big city."

Brigance Abernathy, recluse and richest

man in town? I'd last seen Brig at Mario's funeral. Big house in the historic district? Could that be the same big old house where Reba Mae and I once followed him to? "Brig Abernathy owns the Tratory?" I asked, the thought mind-boggling.

"Damn right." He waved his arm wildly. "The old codger holds the mortgage. Planned to use proceeds from the sale to finance a new project."

Tony looked literally ready to explode. Before that could happen, I grabbed a couple of bills from my purse and slapped them on the table. Reba Mae, in need of fortification, gulped down the last of her wine, tossed down her napkin, and scrambled after me.

"McBride has some nerve," Tony ranted as we beat an undignified retreat. "Asked me about finances. Any feuds we might've had. You so frickin' desperate to get out of the limelight, you'd drop a dime on a guy trying to earn an honest buck?"

I glimpsed the anxious expression on Gina's face before the door slammed behind us. It had just dawned on the woman that she, not me, was responsible for her husband's interrogation. She'd told stories out of school, and it was coming back to bite her. Silently, she entreated me not to spill

the beans. I didn't have the heart to rat her
out.

CHAPTER 34

Zeroing in on my sense of urgency, Reba Mae rescheduled Wanda Buckner's perm for later that day to allow us ample time to shop for a replacement for Chad's hypothetical grief-causing automobile. As luck would have it — bad luck, that is, which seemed the only kind I had these days — finding someone to mind Spice It Up! wasn't quite as easy.

After the fiasco with Melly, Marcy Magruder topped my list of possible shop-sitters. She'd answered the phone on the fifth ring. I was friendly to a fault, employer-of-the-year material. When all my questions and comments met abrupt answers, I got straight to the point and asked if she was free for an hour or so that afternoon.

She barked out a laugh. "You gotta be kidding!"

So much for pleasantries. "Actually," I said trying to regroup. "I'm quite serious. I could use your help —"

"You've got some nerve asking me for favors," she said, cutting me off mid-sentence.

"Favors?" I blinked. This was hardly the response I'd expected. "I'm not asking you to watch the shop as a 'favor.' I intend to compensate you for your time. I thought you'd jump at the chance to earn a little 'pin' money as my grandma used to say."

"You ought to be ashamed to even call me after what you done to Danny."

I gripped the phone tighter, trying to decipher this strange conversation.

"Marcy, what *are* you talking about? I haven't even seen Danny recently, much less done anything to him."

"Chief McBride cornered him the other day for a long talk. Kept asking him all kinds of questions."

"What kind of questions?" But I had a good inkling after my confrontation with Tony Deltorro.

"Like where he was the night Mr. Barrone was murdered. He wanted to know if the man owed Danny money and, if so, how much. He asked Danny if that made him angry enough to want Mr. Barrone dead."

"Marcy, I'm sorry if the chief's questions upset you —"

"Upset? I'm beyond upset. I'm furious."

"Chief McBride's only doing his job," I said. Inwardly, I marveled at the fact that I'd come to McBride's defense. Surely the man didn't need my vote in a popularity poll, but if the election were held this minute, he had it guaranteed.

"Well, it's a darn good thing," Marcy continued her tirade, "that Danny was so worried 'bout me throwin' up he'd taken me to the emergency room the night Mr. Barrone got stabbed. A lot of doctors and nurses will swear on a stack of Bibles we were in the ER until two in the morning."

"I'm sorry if I caused any problems."

"Hmph!" I heard Marcy's sniff of disdain. "All this time, I thought you were so nice. Goes to show how wrong first impressions can be."

The line went dead.

I stared at the phone in dismay. Not only had I just received a dressing-down, but I was still without an able-bodied assistant to man the shop. I suppose, as a last resort, I could close for the afternoon. But what if a new customer waltzed in and placed a humongous order? I stared at the ceiling and prayed for inspiration. God must have been busy elsewhere, however, because none came.

I'll drop whatever I'm doing and run right over. Melly's words came back to me. Not exactly the inspiration I'd hoped for, but left with little choice, I punched in her number. My bad karma persisted. Melly was not only available, she was thrilled at the chance to help.

Melly arrived ten minutes early in her signature pearls and reached for the extra SPICE IT UP! apron I kept under the counter, which she was beginning to think of as hers. "I'm so glad you called, dear. The dentist's office wasn't happy I canceled my root canal at the last minute, but I explained it was a family emergency."

I stifled a groan. Melly's enthusiasm worried me. On second thought, erase "worried" and pencil in "terrified." Maybe it would have been better to close the shop and not worry about a big spender dropping by.

"Even though this might be difficult," I said, launching into my prepared spiel, "I need you to promise me that you'll leave the spices exactly as you found them. Under no circumstances are you to rearrange them. Even though it might not seem that way to you, I do have a system."

Melly nodded, but looked downcast.

"Whatever you say, dear."

"If you feel an uncontrollable urge to alphabetize, you're to simply step away from the spice. Understood?"

Melly twisted her pearls around an index finger. "They just looked so terribly . . . disorganized . . . your way."

"They're arranged according to usage. My way encourages customers to browse. Tempts them to experiment, to try something different in the kitchen." I picked up my purse and reapplied lipstick. "It's called marketing."

"Marketing . . . ?"

She repeated it as though learning a word in a foreign language. I suppressed a smile. "Do I have your promise you'll leave things as they are?"

"Absolutely, dear," she agreed, her lined face solemn. "I won't touch a single bottle or jar, unless of course, I'm ringing up a sale. So clever of you to display your products in such a fashion as to tempt folks into trying something new and different. Who would have thought you'd turn into such a savvy businesswoman? I'm proud of you."

Both shocked and pleased by the compliment, I dropped the tube of lipstick back into my purse. "Why, Melly, I do believe that's the nicest thing you've ever said to me."

Melly waved away my thanks. "Well, dear, I knew that eventually you'd be good at something. It certainly wasn't tennis or bridge."

"Right," I muttered as I headed out. Best leave well enough alone.

As planned, I swung by the Klassy Kut, where I found Reba Mae on the phone with a client. When she looked up and saw me, she held up a hand and signaled me to wait.

"I can squeeze you in around four, Mary Lou. Mm-hmm." Reba shook her head at me and rolled her eyes. "Yes, I know, darlin'. You really do need to read the directions on those do-it-yourself kits. I'm sure orange is quite strikin', but I think I can tone it down a shade or two." Or three, she mouthed. "Uh-huh," she continued, "now stop your bawlin' and leave it to Reba Mae. Just slap on a baseball cap and a pair of dark glasses. If it makes you feel better, use the back entrance."

"I guess orange isn't everyone's color," I said with a chuckle when Reba Mae ended her call. "Sounds like you just talked a potential suicide out of jumping."

"Goes with the territory. Bartenders and hairdressers oughta have a degree in psy-

421

chology. Joannie . . ." Reba Mae hollered to the young woman sweeping up hair clippings, "I won't be long, forty-five minutes max. Keep an eye on Mrs. Phillips for me. See if she'd like some sweet tea."

Reba Mae hoisted her bag onto her shoulder, and we struck out for Cloune Motors on foot.

"How's Joannie working out?" I asked as I skirted a woman pushing an infant in a stroller.

"Good." Reba Mae waved to Pete Barker, who stood outside Meat on Main enjoying the sunny afternoon. "She's willing to learn, follows directions well. Soon as she passes her GED she wants to become a nail technician. Once she gets her certificate, I'm thinking of hirin' her. Havin' a manicurist on staff would be good for business."

"Gee, there's goes my big chance." I heaved an exaggerated sigh. "If traffic at Spice It Up! doesn't pick up soon, I thought maybe I'd apply for the manicurist position."

"Don't be such a pessimist," Reba Mae scolded. "We'll get this figured out."

"I hope so, but pressure's being put on McBride to make an arrest, and circumstantial evidence puts me on his persons-of-interest list."

"Is McBride your 'person of interest,' too?" She winked. "Or is it that cute vet who keeps bringing doggy treats?"

Mention of Doug made me smile. "Doug kind of reminds me of Taylor Hicks with his premature gray."

"Taylor who?"

"You know. He's the guy who won *American Idol* a few seasons back."

"Oh yeah, him. Funny, Dr. Doug puts me in mind more of George Clooney."

"Clooney?" I regarded my BFF in amazement, but Reba Mae just smirked.

"Anyway," I continued, "Doug's a friend, and McBride's just a . . . cop." I hitched my purse higher on my shoulder. "Don't need you teasing me, Reba Mae. It's time to get serious. Are you ready to play Nancy Drew, girl detective, and Bess Marvin, her trusty BFF?"

"What happened to Lucy and Ethel?"

"Time to ramp up our game. Nancy always got her man. I can't say the same about Lucy."

We turned a corner. Even from a distance, I could see the garishly painted clown face atop Cloune Motors proclaiming Dwayne didn't clown around. Strings of red, white, and blue pennants fluttered and snapped in the breeze. I felt a tingle of anticipation as we approached.

The double doors leading into the service bay were raised. Caleb Johnson, a smudge of grease across one cheek, looked up from an engine of an older model Buick and smiled. "Hey, Mama," he said. "Hey, Miz Piper. What are you two fine-lookin' ladies doin' here? Playin' hooky?"

"We've got business with that boss of yours." Reba Mae gave her son a playful swat on the behind. "Boy, you need a haircut. Don't tell anyone your mama owns a beauty parlor, or you'll scare away customers."

Caleb grinned good-naturedly and went back to his tinkering. We strolled toward the used cars. I meant pre-owned.

"If that child of mine doesn't get that mop of his cut soon, it'll be long enough for a ponytail," Reba Mae grumbled.

"It could be worse," I counseled. "Instead of long hair, it could be tattoos and piercings."

"Nevertheless, sugar, I can't picture your son ever growin' his hair long enough to touch his shoulders."

I ran my hand along the hood of a shiny red Honda. "No," I said. "Chad's always gone in for the clean-cut, preppy look. He even likes his jeans pressed."

"Uh-oh." Reba Mae nudged me. "Put on your game face, honeybun. Curtain time. Here comes the biggest clown in town."

Dwayne Cloune adjusted his tie as he hustled out of the office, which boasted a picture window with an unobstructed view of the car lot. "What can I do for you two lovelies this beautiful afternoon?"

I bestowed my best fake smile on him. "We're looking for a replacement for my son's car. The one Chad has up at school has been giving him nothing but trouble."

"CJ's so busy with all the new cases his billboards have brought in that he wanted us to have a look-see," Reba Mae chimed, right on cue.

"In the market for a pre-owned car, are you?" Dwayne rubbed his hands together in anticipation of a sale. "I've got some beauties here on my lot. Low miles on the odometers, easy on fuel. Do you have anything particular in mind?"

Reba Mae linked her arm through his. "Why don't you just show us everythin' you've got?" she drawled.

I shot my friend a look. Did she have any idea how that sounded? I hoped Dwayne wouldn't take her literally.

Dwayne's chest puffed with pride. "Sure thing. Be happy to accommodate."

We strolled up and down the rows of cars while Dwayne extolled the merits of Car A versus Car B. I hoped I didn't look as bored as I felt. Quite frankly, cars pretty much looked the same to me. Steering wheel, tires, hood in the front, trunk in the rear. Same basic equipment. Good thing auto manufacturers distinguish their products with readily identifiable emblems so even car-challenged folks like myself can tell them apart.

"Does every car you sell have one of those cute clown decals?"

"Yep," he nodded. "Have to credit my wife for coming up with the idea. Diane said it was good advertising. She's the one who came up with the I-don't-clown-around logo. I'm thinking of putting her in charge of my election campaign when I make a run for senate."

I lingered near a late model sedan. It was big; it was dark. But was it the one? I caught Reba Mae's attention and wordlessly signaled I wanted to check it out. As BFFs often do, she took the hint.

"So it's true," Reba Mae purred, leading Dwayne down another row. "I'm dyin' to hear how a small-town boy plans to make it all the way to the Georgia General Assembly."

"I don't want to bore you . . ."

"Oh, you wouldn't bore me. I'm fascinated. Simply fascinated."

Amazed, I listened to Reba Mae transform into Scarlett O'Hara. The girl was good enough to audition for a role in Brandywine Creek's newly remodeled opera house. In no time, she had Dwayne Cloune eating from the palm of her hand. The crossover V-neck top she wore that displayed her abundant cleavage didn't hurt, either.

"Don't mind me," I said, waving them off. "I'll just browse."

Our preliminary reconnaissance had revealed several vehicles that fit my vague recollection from the night in question. Now that Dwayne was no longer hovering, I was free to examine their bumpers for a scrap of beige fabric. I ran my hand along the front bumper of a Toyota. I honed my technique on a Ford, followed by a Chevy and a Buick. The only thing I came away with was dirty fingers.

Reba Mae managed to keep Dwayne occupied as he talked about his pending political career until I rejoined them. I thanked him for his time and said I'd have CJ get back to him.

"Any luck?" Reba Mae asked once we were out of earshot.

" 'Fraid not," I admitted. "And to make matters worse, I'm more confused than ever. I'm no longer sure if the car I saw was black, gray, blue, or green. McBride was right after all. Memory is a funny thing."

We walked back to our respective businesses in silence. Before disappearing into the Klassy Kut, Reba Mae gave me a hard, fast hug. "Chin up, girlfriend. Things always look darkest before the dawn."

"Dawn couldn't arrive quickly enough," I muttered under my breath as I hurried along. Just then something shiny caught my attention in the pawnshop window. I stepped to the glass for a closer look and my eyes fastened on a velvet-covered tray holding several items of jewelry. Among them was an engagement ring in a gorgeous old-fashioned setting. A ring I'd seen many times before.

Dale Simons glanced up from a fancy silver tea set he was polishing to greet me. The man was a good hundred pounds overweight with a full beard and a raspy smoker's voice. He'd operated Dale's Swap and Shop for more years than I cared to count. "Hey, Piper. You lookin' to buy or sell? Give you a fair price."

"Hey, Dale," I returned. "The ring in the window caught my eye."

"Pretty piece, ain't it? One of a kind." He ambled over, pulled out a ring of keys that must've added another five pounds to his weight, and unlocked the display window. "Let me show you."

"I've always admired Vicki Lamont's engagement ring. She told me it was a family heirloom."

Dale rubbed a hand over his shaggy beard. "I don't normally disclose the name of my customers, but since the cat is out of the bag, so to speak, I have to admit it's a damn shame her havin' to sell such a fine piece."

I held the ring up and watched the diamond refract the light before returning it to the pawnbroker. "Let's hope Vicki can get her finances in order and buy it back."

Dale replaced the ring in the velvet tray. "Said she's tryin' to make things right with her hubby. Until then, things are tight money-wise. Folks gotta do what folks gotta do."

Dale's homespun philosophy ringing in my ears, I left the Swap and Shop. Vicki's diamond accounted for, I eliminated her as a possible suspect. I even wished Vicki well in her attempt to reconcile with Kenny — even though those efforts didn't start until after Mario's untimely demise. It was with some trepidation that I entered Spice It Up!

a few minutes later. A hasty look around re-assured me my spices were just as I'd left them.

Melly, her hands folded in her lap, sat behind the counter. "You'll be happy to note, I didn't go near your shelves. Everything is just as you left it."

"Thank you, Melly. I appreciate you canceling your dentist appointment to watch the shop for me."

"Happy to do it, dear." She picked up her pocketbook — for some reason she insisted on referring to the large purse she carried by the old-fashioned term — and was almost at the door before she hesitated. "You know, don't you, that idle hands are a devil's workshop?"

"Yes, I've heard the phrase," I answered cautiously.

"Well, I have a confession to make. Instead of sitting around twiddling my thumbs, I made a few changes on your computer program. I'm certain you'll find the new way much more user-friendly. Much more organized. Bye, dear."

My jaw dropped. Changes? On my computer? Why couldn't I just let her rearrange spices?

CHAPTER 35

Casey transformed from dog into a furry brown bouncing ball once he recognized the visitor. Laughing, Doug ruffled the pup's ears. "He's a smart little bugger. Knows which side his doggy snacks are buttered on."

I couldn't help but smile at their antics. "In doggy parlance, they must be the equivalent of flowers and candy."

"Speaking of flowers and candy" — Doug straightened and held out a neatly wrapped package — "I brought you something, too."

"You shouldn't have." I resorted to a time-honored cliché but, secretly, I was pleased as Punch.

"Go ahead," he urged. "Open it."

Inside was a cookbook. Not just any cookbook, but one devoted specifically to Indian cuisine. Delighted with my unexpected gift, I flipped through the pages. Recipe after recipe featured a smorgasbord of spices. Turmeric, coriander, ginger, cumin. I couldn't wait to experiment.

"I love it. Thank you." I hugged him. To those who live in the South, hugging comes more naturally than a handshake. Doug hugged back, and I had to admit I liked being held in his embrace. Liked the citrusy smell of his aftershave. Liked the solid feel of his body against mine. Before I got to liking things overly much, I gently disengaged myself. I hoped the heightened color in my cheeks wouldn't betray my thoughts. After securing Casey in my upstairs apartment, I grabbed a light sweater. Doug was patiently waiting when I returned. "Let's go," I said. "Don't want to be late."

We drove to a neighboring town close to the freeway, which boasted a Walmart, a Lowe's, and a cineplex, along with a plethora of chain restaurants. Doug chose a popular casual dining spot known for its burgers and pulled pork. The place was crowded and noisy, and I was grateful I didn't see anyone I knew. I didn't want to be the subject of more gossip. My private life was already the small-town equivalent of the Kardashians.

After the burgers and fries, I compromised. Instead of a chick flick, I chose one that offered a little of everything — action, adventure, humor, and romance. Even so, I had difficulty concentrating on the screen. My mind wandered hither, thither, and yon. I looked forward to the day I'd be able to enjoy a simple burger and a movie without all the distractions.

On the drive home, Doug valiantly tried to regale me with anecdotes from his practice. I proved a terrible audience. Eventually he, too, lapsed into silence for the remainder of the trip.

Someone had set me up to take the fall for a crime I didn't commit. Whoever it was didn't like me nosing around. Wanted me neutralized. They'd even planted the incriminating evidence so I'd take the rap.

I brought myself up short. *Listen to yourself!*

I sounded like a screenwriter for a B movie. Perhaps that wasn't such a bad thing, I rationalized. I'd have lots of time to pen screenplays from a prison cell. Only instead of a box number I'd have a serial number. Did Hollywood accept mail from prisoners? I supposed I could use an alias and have Reba Mae forward my masterpieces. If my screenwriting gig failed to materialize, I could try my hand at a reality series. I already had the title: *Incarcerated Innocents.* I had to stop obsessing over this.

It was driving me cuckoo.

"Planet Earth to Planet Piper," Doug interrupted my reverie. "You're home."

With a jerk, I brought myself back to the present. I looked around, surprised to find us parked outside Spice It Up! "I'm sorry," I apologized. "I've been lousy company tonight."

"I rather doubt you could ever be 'lousy' at anything."

"Thanks for the vote of confidence," I said with a wry smile. "But I can't help worrying that if McBride doesn't find the Barrone killer soon, I'm going to jail."

"Don't forget me: Mr. Alibi."

"A prosecutor could argue that I had enough time to kill Mario, then drive to the animal clinic."

"Circumstantial."

"Not only are my fingerprints on the murder weapon, but the killer planted a bloody T-shirt in a cupboard in my storeroom where the police were sure to find it. The DNA matches Mario's. Would a jury consider that 'circumstantial'?"

Doug let out a low whistle. "You need a good defense attorney."

I almost smiled — almost. I'd heard that advice so many times, I could put the words to music.

"Let me ask around," Doug offered. "See if I can come up with any names."

I reached for the door handle, but Doug was out of the SUV and around my side in a flash. "Call me old-fashioned," he said, "but a gentleman always sees a lady to the door."

I turned to thank him for a pleasant evening when he caught me off guard and pressed his lips to mine. A zing of pleasure surged through me. Much to my surprise, I found myself kissing him back — and with enthusiasm. It had been a long time since I'd been kissed by a man who wasn't my husband, but kissing, I discovered, was like riding a bike. Once you learned how, you didn't forget. And Doug happened to be an excellent kisser.

Headlight beams swept over us, then moved on. We broke apart like guilty teenagers caught necking in Lovers' Lane. The headlights belonged to a police cruiser, and while I couldn't be certain, the driver looked a lot like Wyatt McBride. Paranoia at its finest. Was the man checking up on me? Making sure his prime suspect didn't flee for parts unknown under the guise of night?

"Ah . . . um," I stammered. "I'd ask you up for coffee, but it's been a long day.

Another time?"

"Sure thing." Doug, the perennial gentleman, didn't pressure me for more. "I'll let you know if I get any leads on a criminal defense lawyer."

"Preferably one who works cheap," I added. Unlocking the front door, I slipped inside and watched Doug's taillights disappear from sight.

The streetlamps in the square provided sufficient illumination so I didn't bother switching on the track lighting. I roamed the aisles, running my hand over smoothly sanded shelves, tracing various containers with my fingertips. Here and there, I opened a bottle or jar and inhaled the earthy scent of nutmeg, the peppery scent of cloves, or the pungent smell of ginger. Spice It Up! had been my dream. My hope. But, my future? I wish I knew. My life seemed to be spiraling out of control.

Without conscious intent, I unscrewed the lid on a jar of juniper berries. Their characteristic ginlike aroma acted like a whiff of smelling salts. I was transported back to the morning I'd found Mario, lying in a pool of blood, on the Tratory's floor. Unless his killer was found soon, I wouldn't be around to see my children graduate, start a career, marry, or have children of their own. My imaginary grandkids would call Amber their grandma.

I stiffened my spine. *Not if I can help it, they won't!*

I screwed the lid back on the juniper berries. Enough with the self-pity! Time to be proactive. Memory *was* a funny thing. Frowning, I tried to recall Reba Mae's comment from the other day. She'd mentioned something about the Clounes owning multiple vehicles. That sometimes Dwayne parked them in the car lot in the hope of enticing a buyer. What if the car we'd searched for was absent the afternoon Reba Mae and I perused the pre-owned autos? Wouldn't it be mind-boggling if it was there now, right this very minute?

I stuffed my keys in my pocket and was out the door before logic had a chance to spoil my half-baked plan.

I jogged the short distance to Cloune Motors. It was after eleven, late by Brandywine Creek's standards. The streets were virtually deserted. Storefront windows stared back at me like sightless eyes. Both the Pizza Palace and North of the Border had closed hours ago. A light drizzle started to fall as Cloune Motors came into view.

Glancing upward, I saw dark clouds scud across an even darker sky. I hadn't taken the weather into account. The stupidity of my rash decision struck me. I was on a fool's errand and would likely get drenched in the process. No self-respecting Girl Scout would have rushed off without an umbrella, a flashlight, or a BFF. Too late — and too stubborn — to turn back, I hugged my sweater more tightly around my shoulders and slowed my pace. With any luck, I'd be home before the drizzle turned into a downpour.

I swept my gaze over the car lot. I had the place to myself. Vehicles were arranged in neat rows, newer models in front, older ones behind. The wind kicked up just then, making the red, white, and blue pennants overhead snap, crackle, and pop like a bowl of breakfast cereal. Lightning flickered. Thunder rumbled in the near-distance. If I intended to carry out my inspection, I had best do it quickly.

Systematically, I wove through an assortment of cars and SUVs. I didn't waste time on the light-colored ones, but concentrated instead on those in deeper hues. I ran my hand along the edges of each bumper, hoping to feel a small scrap of cloth that matched my trench coat.

A sudden, loud crack of thunder made me jump. Laughing nervously, I caught my reflection in the rearview mirror of Jeep. Pale face, wide eyes. I'd be a shoo-in for a victim in one of those Friday the 13th films. *Don't be such a wuss, Piper,* I chastised myself. *Toughen up.*

Ready to give up the fool's errand and strike out for home before the storm broke in earnest, I started down the last row of cars. My pulse quickened at the sight of a Lincoln Town Car that hadn't been there before. It was big, black, and near as I could tell, similar to the mystery car I hunted. What's more, it looked like the one I'd seen Diane drive. I approached cautiously, then crouched down to examine the bumper.

Nothing. Nada. Zip.

I swallowed a lump of disappointment the size of a baseball. The grille of the Lincoln seemed to mock me with its chrome gap-toothed grin. I gave the car one final glance — and that's when I spotted it. A bit of beige cloth wedged near the bottom of the grille's wide-spaced chrome teeth.

I sucked in a breath. Stunned, my mind leaped to the obvious. *Diane killed Mario.* Leaning forward to examine the scrap closer, I was nearly nose to metal when I felt something cold and hard jab me between the shoulder blades. The barrel of a gun? I froze.

"Couldn't leave well enough alone, could you?" Dwayne Cloune sneered. "You're one nosy broad, Piper Prescott. Now what do you suppose I do with you?"

"I know how this must look, Dwayne, but, honest, I'm not here to steal anything," I said, trying to bluff my way out. "Couldn't sleep so thought I'd take another look around. Inventory in a used-car lot changes all the time, right?"

"Pre-owned, you idiot, not used."

I inched away. "Maybe CJ should just bite the bullet and buy Chad a new car."

"Shut up with your nonsense," Dwayne snapped. "I saw CJ at a fund-raiser and mentioned you'd stopped by. He had no idea what I was talking about. Said this was the first he'd heard about Chad needing a car."

"Look, Dwayne, I'm really sorry to be prowling around after business hours."

"I've half a mind to call the police and report a burglar," he mused aloud.

I didn't need him phoning the police. If anyone called the police it should be me, me, me. I'd love to hear Councilman Cloune's explanation of how a piece from my raincoat was embedded in the grille of his wife's Lincoln Town Car.

"On second thought, get to your feet.

Keep your hands in the air where I can see them."

I sensed Dwayne would go to any length to protect Diane. I made a last-ditch attempt to worm my way out of a sticky situation. "I promise if you let me go, I won't say a word about any of this. As a matter of fact, I'll even return her diamond."

"What the hell are you talking about?" Dwayne snarled. "What diamond?"

"The one I found at the Tratory. I believe it belongs to your wife." I was shaking all over, but I forged ahead with a scenario that was playing through my mind like the reel of a movie. "Diane went to the Tratory to look for the diamond that had fallen out of an earring. You followed. A fight broke out. Mario was killed. Self-defense, right? Now," I said, clearing my throat, "I really need to hurry home and let my dog out before the storm breaks."

"You're crazier than a bedbug if you think Diane had anything to do with Mario's death." He gave me an angry shove toward the street. "If it wasn't for that damn dog, this wouldn't be happening. Stupid mutt wouldn't stop yapping at me when I ran out of the Tratory that night."

I pivoted slowly. Surprise and dismay warred inside me. After discovering the torn

441

cloth in a car Diane Cloune frequently drove, I'd assumed she was responsible for Mario's death.

But I was mistaken.

Dwayne, not Diane, had killed Mario.

My mouth felt bone dry. Rain, which was now falling steadily, ran down my face and dripped off my chin. My clothes felt damp. I shivered as much with fear as with cold.

"The damn dog wouldn't stop barking," Dwayne said, his tone matter-of-fact. "I realized I still had the knife in my hand so I tried to silence it once and for all. Thought I'd killed it, so I wiped off my prints. That was when the dumb animal let out a howl that could be heard clear to the next county. I dropped the knife and ran."

I moistened my lips with the tip of my tongue. "So you stabbed Mario," I said needlessly.

He laughed, but there was no humor in the sound. "I've heard the first time, killing's the hardest. This time should be a walk in the park."

CHAPTER 36

"Are you going to shoot me?"

"Get in." Dwayne ignored my question
and motioned with the gun toward the Lincoln. "Not there," he corrected, as I started
toward the passenger door. "The other side.
You're driving."

I tried to recall all the do's and don'ts I'd
ever heard about stranger danger. Only
Dwayne wasn't a stranger. Strange, yes, but
a stranger, no. My odds of survival, I dimly
recalled, were greater if I didn't get in the
car. Once inside, they decreased dramati-
cally. Still, Dwayne had a gun. A big, nasty-
looking gun. Did that even the odds?

Out of the corner of my eye, I thought I
saw his gun hand waver. That was the only
encouragement I needed. I decided to take
my chances. Ducking down, I crouched low
and ran. I heard Dwayne swear and take off
in pursuit. The Brandywine Police Department was only a couple blocks away. If

only . . .

I kept low and, moving in a zigzag pattern, wove through the rows of parked vehicles. I hoped I was doing the right thing. I didn't know the proper protocol to follow when being chased by a madman with a gun. Maybe zigzagging only applied to avoiding alligators.

My heart was thumping so hard I was afraid Dwayne might hear it. I paused to catch my breath alongside a minivan. It was there that I came to the realization I'd committed an even bigger blunder than leaving without an umbrella. I'd left my cell in my purse at Spice It Up!

From not far away, I heard the crunch of Dwayne's footsteps. I darted between more pre-owned cars. I felt as though I was working my way through a corn maze at Halloween. I'd never been very astute at finding my way out of those things, usually relying on my kids rather than gut instinct.

"Come out, come out, wherever you are," Dwayne called out in singsong, as if we were playing a game of hide-and-seek.

I could tell from his voice he was close — too close. I didn't move, barely breathed, terrified I'd telegraph my whereabouts. After what seemed hours, I heard him move on. I crept forward. Finally, I came to the end of a row. Beyond that was the street — the street and possible escape. All I needed to do was to break free and run as if my life depended on it. I said a quick prayer that Dwayne spent more time on the golf course than at the gun range. Preparing to sprint, I started to rise from my crouched position . . .

. . . and Dwayne stepped in front of me.

"Game's over," he said. "Now get in the car before I shoot you right here."

From this range, even if Dwayne wasn't a crack shot, there was no way he could miss a target my size. I straightened and walked toward the Lincoln, my feet lagging every step of the way.

"Quit stalling," he snarled, nudging me between the shoulder blades with the gun barrel.

I shoved a handful of sopping wet hair out of my face and climbed into the driver's seat. "What are you waiting for? Just shoot me and get it over with."

"Tempting," he grunted. "I'll admit I thought about shooting you and dragging your body into the office. I'd claim I saw someone robbing my safe, but didn't know who it was when I fired. Self-defense. It wouldn't be a hard sell — everyone knows you're short of funds. Not only is your piddly little business failing, but you need money to hire a good lawyer. In spite of what you may have heard, they don't come cheap."

I started the engine. "Where to?"

"Your place." I must've looked surprised because he added, "Pull around to the street behind and park."

My hands clenched the steering wheel so hard the knuckles ached. "What made you change your mind," I asked. "About shooting me, that is."

"Too much unfavorable publicity. Besides" — he smiled — "I came up with a better idea."

"You'll never get away with this." Lame, lame, lame! I'd heard this line a million times in a million different movies.

"We'll see," he said, chuckling mirthlessly.

"Can you at least tell me why you killed Mario? Was it because of his affair with Diane?"

"Affair . . . ?" He snorted. "Why would I be jealous? That ended ages ago."

Apparently Dwayne wasn't privy to the Klassy Kut gossip, and I wasn't in a sharing mood. I turned off Main and down a side street. "So, if it wasn't Diane and Mario's affair, why kill him?"

"Pull up to the curb and cut the engine."

"This is the spot where you waited to run me down. Why?"

"Because you're a nosy broad who refuses to mind her own business, that's why," he snapped. "I couldn't risk you stumbling across something that would point suspicion in my direction. Even a hint of scandal would ruin my chances for the senate. I've worked too long and too hard to let you interfere."

"But how did you know . . . ?"

"You sorely underestimated my powers of deduction." Dwayne barked out a laugh. "At first, I thought I'd be safe having you arrested for murder. Case closed, end of story. I even went as far as planting a shirt in your shop with Mario's blood on it. I intended to alert the police with an anonymous call. But my plan didn't work. Then over dinner one night, Diane mentioned a conversation in which you quite convincingly vowed to find the killer. One of my poker buddies is on the police force. After one too many beers, he regaled us with a story about McBride busting you for searching for clues at the Tratory. I realized you wouldn't give up unless I silenced you."

The matter-of-fact tone he used to describe my demise chilled me to the core. "It was raining that night, too," I said, in a voice scarcely above a whisper.

"If you weren't such an accomplished gymnast, I might've succeeded. Now get out of the car slowly. Remember, I'm right behind you. Did you know I won the skeet shooting championship at the Rod and Gun Club three years running?"

I got the message. Loud and clear. I crossed the vacant lot, nearly tripping over a soggy cardboard box someone had thoughtlessly discarded. Dwayne caught my arm and jabbed the gun between my ribs. "Keep moving. Don't try anything clever."

Clever seemed to have deserted me for the moment. I hoped it would return shortly. In the meantime, I needed to keep stalling until it did.

"Unlock the damn door and head upstairs," he directed.

I fished my keys out of my pocket. My fingers shook so much that it took several tries before I managed to open the door. Dwayne kept darting jittery glances over his shoulder to reassure himself no one was around.

"What are you going to do?" I didn't even attempt to keep the quaver out of my voice.

"After you write a note confessing you stabbed Mario, you're going to commit suicide by hanging."

I climbed the stairs on legs that felt like overcooked noodles. "Do you think people will buy that piece of fiction?"

"Why not? You were overcome with guilt. About to be arrested. The thought of leaving prison in a box pushed you over the edge. Now," he said, as we reached the upper landing, "once inside, turn on a light, but don't try any funny stuff."

Actually, I could use a little funny stuff about now, I thought, stifling a hysterical giggle. Turning the knob, I stepped inside my apartment and flipped a light switch. Casey flew out of nowhere in full attack mode, teeth bared. Fifteen pounds of furry torpedo launched into the air and fastened onto Dwayne's wrist.

Dwayne howled with pain and fury. The gun clattered to the floor and spun away. I dove for it. Dwayne did, too. Just as my hand closed around the grip, Dwayne wrestled it away. The gun fired, the explosion deafening. A shower of plaster rained down from the ceiling.

Dwayne cursed, his face distorted with rage, and scrambled to his feet.

Growling ferociously, Casey rejoined the fray, attaching himself to Dwayne's pant leg. Dwayne kicked viciously, sending the little dog flying through the air to land with a sickening thud against the wall, where he lay motionless.

"No!" I cried, and started toward him.

"I'm sick and tired of you and that stupid mutt!" Dwayne roughly grabbed me by the arm, dragged me to the kitchen table, and shoved me into a chair. "Time to pen your swan song."

It would be hard to convince him I had neither pen nor paper when they were both right there in front of me. Another glance at Casey, still a crumpled heap, didn't bode well for my knight in shining fur to ride to my rescue. I thought I heard the creak of a stair, but then silence. Nothing more than the shifting bones of an old building.

"Write!"

"Okay, okay." I picked up a ballpoint. Ironically, it was the same one he'd once given me as a promotional gimmick. Keep him talking, I thought. Keep stalling. "I'll write whatever you want, but if it wasn't because of Diane's affair with Mario, why did you kill him?"

"Mario was stealing my inheritance." Agitated, Dwayne's head bobbed up and down. I could see he'd started to sweat. Nervously, he ran his finger around the collar of his shirt. Not just any shirt, I observed for the first time, but a purple T-shirt identical to the bloodstained one McBride found in my cupboard. Identical except for one glaring difference. This shirt bore the slogan: VOTE FOR CLOUNE. HE WON'T CLOWN AROUND.

I paused, pen in air. "Your inheritance?"

"Yeah, you heard me. I went to the Tratory to confront the bastard, not to kill him. Mario and I are — were — third cousins once removed. Our uncle, Brigance Abernathy, is a rich old bugger. Uncle Brig decided to bankroll Mario's fancy new restaurant in Atlanta. Yet when I approached him, practically begged him, he flat-out refused to give me a red cent. He had the nerve to laugh in my face. Said he wouldn't support my run for dogcatcher, much less the senate. The old coot told me he didn't like my politics. That he might even help fund my opponent. Can you imagine how that made me feel?"

I nodded. "Angry enough to kill."

"You're damn right. Should've killed the old buzzard, too. He had it coming." A thin sheen of perspiration dotted his upper lip. "Even as kids, Mario and I never got along. He always knew what buttons to push. This time he went too far. The more he talked — gloated, actually — the madder I got. I reached my boiling point and let him have

451

it. Then, like the answer to a prayer, you stumbled onto the scene of the crime. I thanked my lucky stars. But you couldn't simply let matters rest. You had to keep poking a hornet's nest. Stir things up. Fill McBride's ear with all sorts of far-fetched theories. It would only be a matter of time till he found out Mario and I were related and demand to know where I was the night my cousin died."

All the while, I kept scribbling away, hoping Dwayne would keep talking. Give me time to form some sort of plan. I was multitasking like crazy. I wasn't about to go down without a fight. If only I had a weapon . . .

"With your confession and suicide, everything should be clear sailing from here on out."

"I'm finished," I said.

"Good. Now sign it." Dwayne seemed to be growing more and more anxious now that the dastardly deed was at hand. "Now I want to you to gather all your scarves and belts, then knot them together."

"They're in the bedroom," I told him. An idea was slowly beginning to take shape. While I didn't have a knife, a gun, or pepper spray handy, I did have the next best thing. A large container of hairspray. If I could

452

latch onto it, aim for the face, maybe I'd have a fighting chance.

I rose to my feet. Just then the door behind me crashed open, and Wyatt Mc-Bride burst through, his service weapon drawn. "Drop the gun, Cloune."

Stunned, Dwayne hesitated, the pistol loosely in his hand. *Aim for the face.* In the far recesses of my brain, I heard the advice of my instructor at a self-defense course I'd taken many years ago at the Y. Detroit was a tough town, my father had warned, and a girl needed to know how to protect herself. Graceful as a ballerina, I pivoted and jabbed the ballpoint pen into Dwayne's cheek. Blood trickling down his face, he screamed and dropped the gun.

McBride spun Dwayne around fast enough to give him whiplash and slapped on handcuffs. He turned to me once his prisoner was secured. "You all right?"

I didn't answer. Running across the room, I knelt next to my sweet little dog. Tears streamed from my eyes and dripped onto his muzzle. I gathered him up and sat cross-legged on the floor and rocked. "C'mon, baby," I pleaded. "Please, please don't die."

It was déjà vu all over again. I recalled the night I found him near death in the lot behind my shop. I couldn't bear the thought

453

of losing him then.

Couldn't bear it now.

To my immense relief, Casey's chocolate-brown eyes opened a slit. His rough pink tongue reached out and licked my arm. Sniffing back tears of gratitude, I looked up and caught McBride watching.

"What took you so long to get here?" I asked him.

CHAPTER 37

Full of sound and fury.

A nearly forgotten quote popped into mind. Shakespeare? *Macbeth*? Tenth grade, maybe? Whichever the case, it pretty much summed up the storm that had overtaken my life and nearly swept away everything I held dear. I let out a sigh that seemed to start at my toes and work its way out my fingertips. I was more than ready for some peace and quiet.

Before the night ended, though, I had to stop by the police department to give my statement. McBride insisted this needed to be done while details were still fresh. I was grateful he'd allowed me to take Casey to Pets 'R People first. After examining him, Doug had assured me my heroic little pup would be right as rain the next day.

Tucking a damp strand of hair behind one ear, I pushed through the door of Brandy-wine Creek Police Department.

Precious Blessing peered at me over a mound of paperwork. "Girl, you look like you been dragged through a gopher hole."

"Feels like it, too," I replied, conscious my face was free of makeup, my hair a halo of frizz. I was beyond caring. I spied the coffeemaker on a corner table behind her desk, the carafe three-quarters full. "Don't suppose I could bum a cup of coffee."

"Comin' right up." Precious hoisted her bulk out of the chair and hustled to pour me some. Dozens of colorful beads woven into her tiny braids formed a miniature percussion section with each step she took. "The chief likes it good and strong, but I can round up some milk if you want."

I gratefully accepted the Styrofoam cup from her. "Good and strong suits me perfectly. Thanks."

"Gettin' in a nice piece of overtime 'cause of you." Precious, her usually jovial expression serious, eyed me top to bottom. "Glad to see you're not hurt. Chief said you had yourself quite a night."

"And then some," I said, taking a sip of coffee and finding it as advertised. "What about Dwayne Cloune? Is the chief finished with him?"

"Mr. Cloune's in a holdin' cell, waitin' on his lawyer. The chief told 'im it was a right good idea. He said when you got here, you were to head straight for his office."

I started toward what had now become familiar territory, then paused. "Precious . . . thanks for the heads-up the other day. I owe you big time."

Precious chuckled. "Glad to be of service. Us girls gotta stick together."

I took another bracing swallow of "good and strong," then opened the office door. McBride stood as I entered. "You okay?"

"As well as can be expected after narrowly escaping my own suicide." I ran a hand over my hair in a vain attempt to smooth the tangled mess. "I must look a wreck."

"Considering all you've been through, you look terrific."

"Um . . . thanks." I summoned a weak smile. The compliment threw me off balance. The guy must be partial to dark circles, freckles, and frizz.

"Take a seat," he said. "How's the mutt?"

"Casey's going to be all right," I explained, sinking into the visitor's chair. "Doug suspects he sustained a mild concussion when he hit the wall. He wanted to keep him overnight for observation."

"Sorry for insisting you come in tonight, but it's standard operating procedure. I overheard pretty much all of Cloune's

457

confession, but still need to hear your version."

I wanted to ask how he happened to be in the neighborhood in time to rescue a damsel in distress. But my question could wait until later. Right now I was beyond tired. I was exhausted. All I wanted to do was go home, crawl into bed, and sink into oblivion.

He clicked on a recorder. I took another sip of coffee, drew a deep breath, then went through the events that led me here. When I was done, McBride offered to have Precious drive me home.

"I'll be fine. I have my car, and it's only a couple blocks." I rose and walked to the door where I hesitated, one hand on the knob. "McBride . . ." He stopped reading my statement and looked up. "Thanks for saving my life."

He smiled then, a genuine smile that made that cute dimple in his cheek wink in and out. "My pleasure."

Weighted down with fatigue, I plodded down the hallway and nearly plowed into my ex. "CJ," I gasped. "I didn't expect to see you here."

CJ grinned broadly, making his professionally whitened choppers gleam in the overhead fluorescents. "Dwayne called and asked me to represent him."

I couldn't believe my ears. "And you agreed, knowing he tried to kill me — the mother of your children?"

"Now, Scooter, no need to get riled. It's business, pure and simple."

"What happened to chasing ambulances?" I asked. "You have no experience as a criminal attorney."

"I'll take in a seminar or two to bring me up to speed." Setting his briefcase aside, he sketched that framing gesture I'd seen him make before. It made me want to slap him. "Picture this, darlin': PROMINENT ATTOR-NEY CHANDLER JAMESON PRESCOTT III DEFENDS SENATORIAL CANDIDATE. Just imagine all the cases this will bring in."

Imagine. I shook my head and left. I'd heard enough.

I racked up record sales the following Monday. A steady stream of customers poured into my shop the entire day. Seems I'd gone from being the prime suspect in a murder case to the local heroine. Everyone who entered professed to have never doubted my innocence. Not for a split second did anyone think me capable of murder. I smiled to myself each time I rang up a sale.

Reba Mae ducked in, but when she saw

how busy I was, left after giving me a thumbs-up. I'd filled her in on all the juicy details yesterday over brunch and celebratory Mimosas.

Bob Sawyer, reporter and photographer for *The Statesman,* had dropped in, too. My interview and picture would run in the next edition. He'd also interviewed McBride, who graciously credited my tenacity for bringing Mario's killer to light. I, in turn, generously praised McBride's timely arrival for saving my life. I refused to dwell on how differently things might've turned out if he hadn't burst in like Eliot Ness hell-bent on capturing Al Capone. Bob left, but not before promising to feature Spice It Up! in an upcoming article about the Brandywine Creek Barbecue Festival.

Best of all, Doug had personally delivered Casey who, in spite of his harrowing experience, seemed his frisky self. Presently, however, he was content to lie under the counter and gnaw a chunk of rawhide nearly as big as he was.

"Hey, Mama." Beaming, Lindsey charged through the front door, brandishing a sheet of notebook paper.

I paused in tallying the day's receipts to smile back at her. "What's that you're holding, sweetie?"

"An A-plus, that's what I'm holding." With a flourish, Lindsey placed the paper down in front of me. "Mrs. Walker had us write an essay on the career of our dreams."

"Sounds like a great topic," I said, reaching for the paper. "What did you write about?"

Lindsey studied the floor as if embarrassed. For a long moment, I thought she was going to keep her dreams to herself, but then she met my gaze, her steel-blue eyes shining with excitement. "I plan to be a doctor. Not like Chad," she hastened to explain, seeing my surprise. "I want to be a veterinarian like Dr. Winters."

"I hardly know what to say," I murmured.

"You know that I've always loved animals," she rushed on. "I want to learn how to keep them healthy. How to treat them when they're sick or hurt. Do you suppose Dr. Winters would let me help at Pets 'R People once school's out? That is, when you don't need me to wait on customers and all."

"We can ask Doug — Dr. Winters — if he could use an assistant. Melly volunteered to help here whenever I need her. I'm sure something can be arranged . . . provided you don't neglect summer school."

Lindsey nodded her vigorous assent. "Since I'm going to college, I'll need math.

Is it okay if I take Casey to the park?"

At the mention of "park," Casey stopped chewing and thumped his tail to signal his willingness.

Humming to myself, I watched my girl and my pup race off. I realized Lindsey was young, impressionable, and would probably change career choices at least a half dozen times before settling on one. Yet, I couldn't help but rejoice that she had a goal. Particularly one that required an education — not a tiara. CJ might not feel overjoyed at the prospect of two children in medical school, but the prospect gave me added incentive to make Spice It Up! an unqualified success.

I was almost finished restocking shelves when McBride strolled in. My pulse did a funny little samba at the sight of him. Now that I no longer feared imminent arrest, I reacted the same way Reba Mae swore every woman with a drop of estrogen did at the sight of him. Doing my utmost to ignore my hormonal surge, I continued shelving stock and waited for him to state his business.

McBride tucked his thumbs in his belt, a gesture I now recognized as characteristic. "Thought you might like to know that Dwayne Cloune's been arraigned. Judge denied him bond."

"Good!" I plunked a jar of spice on a shelf with more force than necessary.

"Ambition got the better of him, that's for sure," McBride said agreeably.

I made room on the shelf for the last of the jars. "So it *was* a crime of passion."

"A jury might be lenient except for his plans to kill you. You were too much of a wild card. Cloune wouldn't let anything — or anyone — interfere with his chance for election. To his way of thinking, once you were arrested — or dead — things would settle down. Case closed. He'd be home free."

"Has he confessed?"

"On the advice of his attorney — none other than your ex — he pled innocent, but the evidence works against him."

"Evidence?" I brushed a lock of hair away from my face with the back of my hand. "What evidence?"

"I'd be willing to bet a month's salary that the mystery print we found on the blade of the murder weapon will match Cloune's. We ran it through AFIS, but it wasn't in the system — until now. Should be the clincher."

"Mystery print . . . ?"

He shrugged off my question. "It's not

unusual to withhold a piece of key information during the initial stage of a murder investigation."

"One other thing, McBride." I cocked my head to one side and studied him. "How *did* you happen to rescue me in just the nick of time?"

"I've been keeping an eye on you," he confessed. "After years on the job, a cop learns to rely on his instincts. Part of our credo is to protect — and I admit that I was worried about you. Figured whoever tried to kill you once might try again. When I saw a big black car with a clown logo on the trunk parked behind your shop, I became suspicious. Decided to check it out. That's when I found your back door ajar. Instinct — and the sound of a gunshot — told me you were in trouble. I went inside and waited long enough to hear Cloune admit he killed Cousin Mario."

"And to think — that he nearly got away with it," I said.

"Diane Cloune seems more upset about losing the rock from her earring than the fact her husband is facing twenty to life behind bars. Don't suppose you know anything about a lost diamond?"

A guilty flush stained my cheeks. "I'll see that it's returned."

"Clever of Cloune to have you first write a suicide note along with an admission of guilt."

I looked at him sharply. I knew him well enough by now to know when he was holding back. "Out with it, McBride."

The corners of his mouth twitched to hide a smile. "Unfortunately for Cloune, he wasn't nearly as clever as he thought. Your 'suicide' note gave my men a good laugh."

I had to grin at hearing this. "If Dwayne had taken the time to read it, he'd have been furious. But on the bright side, he'd have had a terrific recipe for roast lamb with rosemary and juniper."

McBride unhooked his thumbs from his belt and, reaching out, rearranged the spices on the shelf behind me. I turned to inspect his changes. Ceylon, China, and Indonesia? I stared at him, alarmed. He'd just arranged the cinnamon in alphabetical order of the countries they originated from.

"What?" he asked, finding me staring.

"Please, tell me you're not obsessive-compulsive."

"Ex-military." He grinned sheepishly, showing off that danged dimple.

"One last thing, McBride." I folded my arms across my chest. "Did you honestly believe I killed Mario?"

He shrugged. "Didn't take me long to figure out you weren't the perp."

"But how?"

"Your mutt, for starters. No animal that'd been mistreated would leap into the arms of its abuser. Besides, I've been in law enforcement long enough to know a setup when I see one. And the bloody T-shirt in your cupboard was a plant if there ever was one."

I nodded slowly, digesting everything he'd told me. "That's it?"

He frowned, looking a little annoyed by my persistence, but then his brow cleared. "Any good defense attorney would have latched onto the fact that the angle of entry of the stab wound indicated it came from someone much taller than you. When I asked him, Doug Winters was quite specific about the type of shoes you wore the night of the murder. Tennis shoes. I checked yours out myself, but they bore no traces of blood. Add that to the fact, you're a terrible liar. Your skin tone gives you away every time you come close to telling a lie."

"The curse of being a redhead." I laughed. "Guess that about wraps things up."

"Guess so."

I watched him leave with mixed emotions. While greatly relieved to have the ordeal behind me, I felt oddly sad to see him walk out of my life. His presence in it had added a bit of spice, a little sizzle, some zing.

"Thanks again, McBride," I called out.

He paused and shot me a killer smile over his shoulder. "See you around. And, Piper, just for the record, I do have a first name. It's Wyatt. Feel free to use it."

Hmmm . . .

ABOUT THE AUTHOR

The author of the Bunco Babes mystery series, **Gail Oust** is often accused of flunking retirement. Hearing the words "maybe it's a dead body" while golfing fired her imagination for writing a cozy. Ever since then, she has spent more time on a computer than at a golf course. She lives with her husband in McCormick, South Carolina.